Praise for *No One Saw A Thing*

'One of the most tense thrillers of the year so far.'
JOHN MARRS

'Action-packed from the get-go, the pace never lets up in this
premium slice of domestic suspense.'
CATHERINE RYAN HOWARD

'A pleasingly cynical and cunningly constructed
story of old grudges and buried secrets.'
DAILY MAIL

'From the first chapter of this Andrea Mara novel,
I had shivers. Twisty, clever, impossible to put down.'
LOUISE O'NEILL

'I dare, nay defy, you to try and put this thriller down!'
RED MAGAZINE

'I read this in two sittings. As twisty as a corkscrew,
as taut as a garotte, this is a total masterclass in thriller writing.'
NEIL LANCASTER

'You will look hard to find a more searing
opening 15 pages of a thriller this year.'
IRISH INDEPENDENT

'The pace never flags, the tension racks up
and the pages turn themselves.'
LIZ NUGENT

'I was hooked by the end of chapter one.'
JANE CASEY

www.penguin.co.uk

Andrea Mara is a *Sunday Times* and *Irish Times* top ten bestselling author, and has been shortlisted for a number of awards, including Irish Crime Novel of the Year. She lives in Dublin, Ireland, with her husband and three young children, and also runs multi-award-winning parent and lifestyle blog, OfficeMum.ie. *No One Saw A Thing*, her most recent novel, sold more than 100,000 copies in thirteen weeks and became an instant No.1 Kindle and Irish bestseller.

Also by Andrea Mara

The Other Side of the Wall
One Click
The Sleeper Lies
All Her Fault
Hide and Seek

NO ONE SAW A THING
A THING

Andrea Mara

PENGUIN BOOKS

TRANSWORLD PUBLISHERS
Penguin Random House, One Embassy Gardens,
8 Viaduct Gardens, London SW11 7BW
www.penguin.co.uk

Transworld is part of the Penguin Random House group of companies
whose addresses can be found at global.penguinrandomhouse.com

First published in Great Britain in 2023 by Bantam
an imprint of Transworld Publishers
Penguin paperback edition published 2024

A CIP catalogue record for this book
is available from the British Library.

ISBN
9781804990780

Typeset in 10.23/13.8pt ITC Giovanni by Jouve (UK), Milton Keynes.
Printed and bound in Great Britain by Clays Ltd, Elcograf S.p.A.

The authorized representative in the EEA is Penguin Random House Ireland,
Morrison Chambers, 32 Nassau Street, Dublin D02 YH68.

Penguin Random House is committed to a sustainable
future for our business, our readers and our planet. This book
is made from Forest Stewardship Council® certified paper.

For warrior queen Alice Hayes, with love

1

IF ONLY SIVE HADN'T told the girls to run ahead.

If only her editor hadn't picked that moment to phone.

If only she hadn't slowed to look at her screen.

If only she'd used the baby carrier instead of the expensive but cumbersome pram – fine for suburban Dublin but completely unsuitable for the London Underground on a humid August Monday morning.

If only.

As with most disasters, it isn't one single event or decision or misalignment of stars that causes it but a myriad of tiny twists and turns over the course of the morning.

If they hadn't picked that day to go for brunch.

If they hadn't picked that week to go to London.

If Aaron's friends hadn't needed a twenty-year reunion to see who was winning at life.

If, if, if.

But here she is, pushing the pram with one hand, manoeuvring it out of the lift and on to the hot, crowded rush-hour platform, trying to see who is phoning her at 8.30 a.m. when she's supposed to be off work.

'Keep going, Faye – jump on with Bea!' she calls after her six-year-old daughter as the two girls, hand in hand, approach the open Tube doors. 'I'm right behind you!'

ANDREA MARA

Her phone continues to buzz, and she squints at the screen. Her reading glasses – a new and unwelcome necessity – are back in the hotel room, but she can just about make out the caller's name. Caroline. Her editor. Her editor who knows she's away but has conveniently forgotten. Still pushing the pram with one hand, she swipes awkwardly to decline the call, but it has already ended of its own accord. Phone signal lost, perhaps, now that they're underground. She glances up to see where her daughters are. Two pink denim jackets, one small, one smaller, visible just ahead. The platform is heaving with rushing commuters, pushing forward to get on to the train. Sive tries to squeeze through the crowd, murmuring 'excuse me' and 'sorry' while at the same time aware that this tourist-level politeness is not what's called for here. And now, she's pulled forward in the surge towards the doors, a few feet behind her children. Through a narrow gap in the sea of passengers, Sive sees Faye climb on to the Tube, holding Bea's hand as the two-year-old clambers on too.

And then, just like that, the doors slide shut.

Her children inside looking out.

Sive outside looking in.

Heart in mouth, she rushes forward. The pram, so awkward just moments earlier, makes an efficient battering ram as she barges through commuters, shouting her children's names. But it's no good. The train begins to slide away from the platform and Faye's eyes widen, understanding now what's happening.

Sive roars, 'Get off at the next stop! Faye, next stop!' She points forwards and down, in some approximation of a signal for 'next stop', knowing there's no way Faye can hear her or understand, but hoping another passenger will read it correctly and get the children off the train.

And so, the Tube pulls away with six-year-old Faye and

2

two-year-old Bea on board, leaving Sive on the platform, help-less and terrified.

Whatever adrenaline or presence of mind had pushed her to shout after Faye deserts her now. Her limbs are somehow loose and frozen all at once as she stares blindly at the rear lights of the departing Tube. *Jesus Christ.* Her children are on a train, in a city of eight million people, on a rush-hour Monday morn-ing. Without her. Without any adult. What the hell is she supposed to do – try to get to the next station? Run there? With the pram? Hail a taxi? Call the police? Leaving the station feels counterintuitive. What if they come back here and she's gone? But how would they get back here? Would someone on the Tube have seen what happened and return them? Did people do that kind of thing? Someone is talking to her. A woman beside her on the platform. With huge effort, Sive makes her-self tune in.

'. . . so you stay here, I'll find someone to help,' the woman says. 'OK?'

Sive nods dumbly.

'The man beside your little one on the Tube heard you. You saw that, yes?'

Sive hadn't.

'He gave a thumbs-up. He'll get your child off at the next stop. So we just need to get you there and find someone to radio ahead.'

Again, Sive nods, confused and grateful and terrified.

'The next train is due in four minutes. I'm going to get some-one. You stay here.'

Sive does as she's told, rocking the pram on autopilot, staring down the track as though her children might magically reappear if she wishes hard enough. She glances up at the train information.

3

Three minutes until the next one. She can do this. Where is the woman? She looks around. Where are the staff? All about, commuters swarm to the platform, jostling and rushing. The heat is stifling and, in the pram, the baby starts to whimper. Sive rubs his cheek and continues to rock. *Dear God, dear God, dear God.* Let them be OK. Let them not be lost in this huge city. Suddenly, staying here seems wrong. How can she stand on the platform when her children are whizzing down the track towards another place entirely? She turns the pram, just as a man in a bright orange jacket arrives beside her.

'Your child is on the Central Line train that just left for Oxford Circus, madam? Can you give me the child's name and age?' Matter-of-fact. No-nonsense. Exactly what's needed.

'Two children.' Breathless. 'Faye is six and Bea is two.'

He lifts his radio. 'Can you describe them – what they're wearing?'

Christ, what are they wearing? Her mind is blank. *Breathe. Focus.* This is not the time to fall apart. She slows her mind and pictures her children as she saw them, just minutes earlier. 'They're both wearing pink denim jackets. Matching.' The man nods for her to keep going. 'Faye has bright blonde hair. Bea has light brown hair like mine.' She stops. How else can she describe them? Fun and funny and cute and irritating and adorable and infuriating. And gone. 'They're both wearing dresses. Faye's is light grey. Bea's is purple. And they're wearing tan sandals. Faye has a *Frozen II* backpack. Bea has a *PAW Patrol* backpack.'

The man isn't listening any more. He has a radio to his mouth and he's telling someone else everything Sive just said. Two children, six and two. All alone in Oxford Circus. Or not. *Fuck.*

*

4

One minute to go until the next Tube arrives. Sive is rocking the pram harder now.

'Would you like me to do that?' the woman asks. Sive takes her in for the first time. She's a little older than Sive, in her mid-forties, maybe, with curly brown hair and kind brown eyes.

'Oh, I don't want to keep you – you're probably on your way to work?' Sive says, taking in the lanyard hanging around the woman's neck.

'I'm early – it's fine. And your train will be here any second now. Would you like me to come with you?'

'Oh God, I can't ask you to do that,' Sive says emphatically, desperately wishing the woman would do exactly that.

The man with the radio has his back to them but turns now. A train is pulling into the platform and the woman begins pushing the pram towards the opening door, queuing behind a scramble of passengers. The man smiles at Sive and gives her a thumbs-up. 'They got them,' he says. 'Go straight to the next stop. Oxford Circus. My colleagues there will help you, madam.'

Sive's legs almost give way, but the woman is calling her, urging her on to the train.

And the doors are closing and the woman is waving and the man is smiling. Everything is going to be OK.

The journey is the longest of her life, though it can't be more than a minute. It's OK. They're fine. They got them. They'll stay with them. They're not going to leave two little girls alone on the platform to wait for their mother. Their *imbecile* of a mother. Jesus Christ, how is she going to explain this to Aaron? It doesn't matter. All that matters is getting there and seeing them again. It's hot and sticky and hard to breathe, and Sive feels dizzy. Sick. More and more nauseous with every shallow breath. All around her, commuters hold on to bars and read phones, oblivious to her plight. Oblivious to her desperate need for the train to hurry the fuck up and get her to Oxford Circus. And then, suddenly, she's there. The doors slide open. She pushes the pram on to the platform, into throngs of commuters. Where are they? Shit, she should have asked the man where to go once she got here. Maybe the staff will find her? Is there some kind of meeting point for missing children? And then she sees it. Down towards the end of the platform. A flash of pale pink denim and light brown curls. She starts to run.

'Bea!' She grabs her two-year-old and whisks her into her arms, burying her head in toddler curls. 'I'm so sorry, lovey. Did you get a terrible fright? Did Faye mind you?'

A woman in an orange jacket smiles at the reunion.

'Hi, love. I'm Rita,' she says, clearly delighted to be part of the happy ending. Gently, she pats Bea's shoulder, and Sive smiles back.

Will Rita or the other security people need proof that Sive is the girls' mother? Bea's hug is visible proof. And at six, Faye is old enough to confirm who Sive is.

Faye.

Sive looks around.

'Where's Faye?'

Rita looks confused. 'Who?'

'My other child?'

'There was no other child.'

Sive hears the words but doesn't take them in. The woman can't have said what she just said. Through the roar of descending panic, she tries again.

'My six-year-old. Faye. She was with Bea?'

Now Rita looks alarmed. 'I was told to look out for a little girl in a pink denim jacket.'

'*Two* little girls in pink denim jackets. *Two*.' Sive can feel her voice getting louder. Panicky. 'They were together. Faye. Faye is six. She was with Bea.' She turns to Bea, who's still in her arms. 'Where is your sister, lovey? Bea, where is Faye?'

'Gone,' Bea says. 'Faye gone.'

2

ALL HELL BREAKS LOOSE. In Sive's head, at least, all hell breaks loose. Rita does not have her daughter. None of the staff at the station have her daughter. And while Sive's been travelling here on the Tube, her daughter has been disappearing somewhere else entirely. Still on the train? Somewhere on the platform? Right out of the station? She wouldn't, though. Surely she wouldn't leave the station. Unless she thought that was the best way to find her mother?

'What about the man on the train?' she asks, panic making her breathless.

Rita looks confused. 'The man?'

'The other woman said there was a man on the train who saw me on the platform and gave a thumbs-up.' It sounds garbled.

'The other woman?'

Sive shuts her eyes briefly and forces herself to slow down. *Stay calm.*

'A woman in Bond Street saw a man on the train. He gestured to show he understood, when I shouted at Faye to get off at the next stop. I thought he must have got them off, and that's why we got the message they were here and that that's how Bea is here. Oh, Jesus.'

Rita speaks into her radio. More orange-jacketed staff arrive. An announcement comes out over the PA system, but Sive can't concentrate on any of it. She's flailing. Sick. Panicked. Bea on her hip. Pram by her side. Scanning crowds of commuters. The rush on. The rush off. Another train. Another crowd. Another surge. No sign. No clue. No Faye.

Someone calls the police. Rita, maybe, or one of her colleagues. More announcements. More orange jackets. More worried frowns. But still no Faye. A police officer. A request for a photo, one from today if possible. Questions asked. Descriptions given. Notes taken. Photos sent. Blurred faces through terrified tears. *Is there anyone you can call?* someone asks her. Aaron. She needs to call Aaron.

In the end, she hands her phone to Rita, and it's Rita who makes the terrible call to her husband. *We're doing our best. I'm sure we'll find her in no time. Everyone on the lookout. Any minute now. Pink jacket. Grey dress. Tan sandals. Blonde hair. Do you know where she might go if she's lost? Of course you can speak to your wife.*

Aaron is shouting. Sive needs to stay calm. She tries to explain. She says all the things she doesn't believe herself right now – Faye will turn up, any minute. Any. Minute. Now.

Except she doesn't.

3

Tɪᴍ ɪs ʜɪs ɴᴀᴍᴇ, the man who got Bea off the train. He's standing in front of Sive now, explaining something, but it's not going in. Rita is speaking into her radio again, and a police officer who introduced herself as PC Denham of the British Transport Police is asking Tim questions. Sive pulls Bea closer and forces herself to tune in to what Tim is saying.

'My girlfriend got off at Bond Street and I was waving goodbye to her when I saw the lady shouting,' he says to the police officer. 'Then I realized there was a little girl, right in front of me.' He points at Bea. 'I guessed what had happened and that she was telling her to get off at the next stop.'

'And what about the other child?' PC Denham asks.

Tim shakes his head. 'I'm sorry. I didn't see any other child.'

Sive is going to throw up.

'But she was right there, too,' she manages to say. 'She got on just ahead of Bea. How did you not see her?'

Tim shrugs and then catches himself. 'Sorry . . . It did take a few seconds to work out what you were shouting, and the carriage was packed.' He lifts his hands apologetically. 'Then I noticed your little girl all on her own, and I asked around if anyone was with her and no one was. And I guessed then what had happened. So I took her off at the next stop.'

'And you were on your way to work, sir?' PC Denham asks.

Sive shuts her eyes briefly. How is this relevant? How will this help find Faye?

'That's right.'

'And where is that, sir?'

'Six years as Head of Fund Accounting at Anderson Pruitt,' Tim says, even though PC Denham hasn't asked what his position is or how long he's been there. Beneath the fog of panic, it strikes Sive as odd.

'And where is that located, sir – somewhere near here?' Denham asks.

Sive sucks in a breath. Seriously, how is this going to help?

'No, Liverpool Street.'

'But you got off here?'

Tim's face flushes red. 'To make sure the little girl was safe. I wasn't going to leave her on the platform on her own.'

'So, you handed her to who, sir?'

'One of the security staff. He knew about it. He'd had a message from Bond Street.'

'And then?'

'I was walking towards the exit for the stairs and spotted this lady with the little girl, so came back to . . . you know . . .' He shrugs.

To be part of the happy reunion, Sive thinks. To enjoy some Good Samaritan energy.

'Thank you,' she says now. 'For what you did. But are you sure you didn't see another child? She's six' – she indicates with her hand to show him how tall Faye is – 'and wearing a jacket just like Bea's. Bright blonde hair. Didn't you see her?'

'I'm sorry,' Tim says helplessly. 'I only saw the little one.'

'All right, sir, I'll just need your contact details in case we need to speak to you again,' PC Denham says, and Tim calls out a phone number.

Sive pulls Bea away from her shoulder so she can look at her.

'Where is your sister? Where is Faye?'

'Chase,' Bea says solemnly, looking at Tim and then back to Sive. 'Chase on train.'

4

AARON IS RUSHING TOWARDS her, pushing through crowds, ignoring disgruntled expressions as he barges past. All six foot three of him, here to help, and Sive instantly feels a lift. Between them, they'll fix this.

'Faye?' he says helplessly.

She shakes her head. 'Not yet.' It comes out in a whisper.

'My God.' He looks around the bustling platform, and she feels every inch of it. The crowds. The sheer volume of numbers. The size of the city. The endless entrances and exits. The dark tunnels. The oncoming trains.

'What happened?'

In short, breathless, staccato bursts, she explains.

'But how were you not right there with them, getting on the train?' he asks.

'I was just behind them, pushing the pram out of the lift. Telling them to hurry. And then—'

She closes her eyes.

'And then what?'

'My phone rang. I was trying to see who it was. Trying to decline the call.'

Aaron shakes his head.

'It didn't take more than a second, but . . .'

13

'Long enough for the doors to close. I know.' He rubs her arm, and the kindness brings tears to her eyes.

PC Denham clears her throat and addresses Sive. 'Your younger daughter said Faye was chasing someone or something? Does that make any sense to you – can you think of anything that she might run after?'

Sive shakes her head. 'I have no idea.'

Tim is still standing nearby, watching, and Denham turns to him now. 'Did you see anything like that – a child running?'

'No, but the Tube was packed. I don't think anyone could have run anywhere.'

Aaron looks confused. 'And you are?' he says to Tim.

'This gentleman took care of your younger daughter, took her off the train and handed her to security staff,' PC Denham explains.

Aaron frowns. 'And you claim you didn't see Faye?'

Claim. Sive bites her lip.

Tim stands a little taller, cheeks flushed. 'I didn't see your other daughter, no.'

PC Denham interrupts. 'We've covered this, and we have contact details, should we need further information.' Her tone says, *I'll ask the questions here.* 'If we could get back to what your younger daughter said. Sometimes kids chase after things without thinking and lose their way. Like running after a ball or a butterfly?'

'A butterfly on a Tube?' Aaron sounds incredulous, and Sive wants to tell him to rein it in – they need all the help they can get, to keep everyone on side.

'Can you think of anything your daughter might chase?' Denham says evenly.

Sive looks at Bea, thinking back on her words. *What if that's not it? What if Faye didn't chase a ball or a butterfly? What if someone chased her?*

'Bea, sweetheart. Did someone run after Faye?'

Bea looks blankly at her. A man dashing for a Tube pushes between them, separating Sive from PC Denham momentarily. Sive tries again. 'Darling, can you point – where is your sister?'

Bea's lower lip wobbles. 'Baw-baw.'

'What was that?' Denham asks, cupping her ear against the clamour of rush hour.

Sive shakes her head. 'She just wants her milk.'

'Do you think she might tell us more eventually?' the police officer asks. 'Maybe she's tired or hungry?'

'She's just turned two,' Aaron says tersely. 'She can't tell us anything.'

Aaron. Sive pleads with him silently. Playing the big man isn't going to help here; this police officer isn't one of his witnesses on the stand.

'She doesn't have many words yet,' Sive clarifies for PC Denham. 'I don't know how much she'll be able to tell us beyond what she's already said. But what if it means someone chased Faye – someone frightened her and made her run off? Maybe she's still on the train, or hiding in a station?'

'We have officers on the train now, and they're checking each stop – London Underground staff are checking too. We'll find her. There's a finite number of stations on this line and we'll get to all of them.'

'What if she's left one of the stations,' Sive whispers.

An announcement booms over the tannoy, and Aaron waits before asking his next question.

'Would there have been time?'

'There was maybe six or seven minutes—' Sive's voice disappears, swallowed by panic. She clears her throat. 'Between waiting for the next Tube and getting here. The security people were already looking for her, but they couldn't have ... they couldn't have covered every station immediately.'

'Oh my God.' Aaron runs his hand through his hair, turning in a slow circle. He looks back at Sive. 'We're in a city of eight million people, and Faye could be anywhere.'

She nods, unable to speak. Her child has disappeared on a moving train, and no one saw a thing.

5

Three days earlier | Friday
The Meridian Hotel

'ARE WE READY TO go? It's five to three.' Aaron tapped his watch. The newly purchased, eye-wateringly expensive Tag Heuer he'd treated himself to, coincidentally, just in time for the reunion. He'd been pacing up and down the hotel bedroom for five minutes now, waiting for Sive to finish feeding the baby. She could almost see the indentations in the blue-and-gold carpet. In the sitting room next door, Faye and Bea were watching cartoons. Sive wasn't quite sure why Aaron had booked a suite – why they needed a sitting room, when their bedroom already had its very own sitting room: a pale blue sofa with matching armchairs surrounding an elegant mahogany coffee table in front of a huge, yet somehow discreet TV – all in keeping with the not at all understated luxury of the Meridian Hotel. Then again, it was nice to be able to shut the door on the sounds of *PAW Patrol* and *Peppa* sometimes, too.

'I think he's almost done feeding,' she said to Aaron. 'Will you get the girls to put on their shoes?'

That might be a better use of his time than wearing out the hotel carpet. Aaron was a pacer. When she first met him, she thought it was a sign of nerves. Over time, watching him prepare for court cases, she realized it indicated something more

17

like pumped-up energy. A raring-to-go-ness. Right now, he looked like he was about to bounce off the carpet out into the hotel corridor. Only this was no court case – this was a twenty-year reunion with his old London housemates. Meaning for Aaron, she thought, hiding a smile, the stakes were *far* higher.

'It's supposed to be fun!' she'd said as she packed Bea and Faye's shared suitcase at home in Dublin. 'You're acting like it's some kind of contest. And why are you stalking your friends' work updates – why don't you just wait till we get to London and let them tell you in person?'

Aaron was on LinkedIn, reading his old housemates' profiles, and updating his own.

'You don't think for a second they're not going to look me up, too? You don't think, right now, Burner and Trigger aren't scrolling through my profile, looking for holes?'

Burner was Scott Burns, Aaron's long-time BFF, frenemy and rival. Trigger was Dave Taylor, someone whose career didn't threaten Aaron in the slightest. Once upon a time, Dave had been called Trigger to his face – an affectionate nickname inspired by a sit-com character not famed for his intellect. Nowadays, Aaron still occasionally called him Trigger, but only behind his back.

'You're genuinely asking me if Scott and Dave are on LinkedIn stalking you right now – do you want my honest answer?' She smiled at him, shook her head and began inspecting the contents of Faye's carry-on backpack. A teddy bear with a toy passport, a hairbrush, a packet of crayons, a tiny notebook. All the essentials, and no rogue liquids or sharp objects. She moved on to packing her own bag. 'Anyway, you always say Scott doesn't care what anyone thinks of him.'

'He doesn't, but he loves needling me, competing for the sake of annoying me.'

'Then perhaps become less easy to annoy?' she said lightly.

'And look, you saw Dave last summer, and you met up with Scott in June – it's not like you haven't seen them every other year since you all lived together.'

'Yeah, but this is the first time we'll all get together in one place since . . . well, since the funeral.'

'Ah.'

A pause. 'It's not just twenty years since we met, it's also fifteen years since Yasmin died. Her anniversary is on Monday.'

Sive stopped what she was doing. 'You might have told me.'

'Sorry. I don't like talking about it, you know that.'

Sive did indeed know that, and she'd learned not to ask about Aaron's deceased fiancée. Her husband was a non-stop talker and yet somehow, too, a closed book.

'Will it be weird? Maybe I shouldn't be there – I didn't know Yasmin.'

He kissed her cheek. 'Don't worry. We'll raise a glass to her but, other than that, nobody will talk about what happened. Nita doesn't like it, and we all tend to follow her lead.'

Sive nodded. Nita, Yasmin's sister, liked mostly talking about herself, so that seemed a reasonable prediction.

'Right, that's Faye and Bea done, and I'll put the baby's clothes in with mine.' She paused. 'Unless, of course, you've already packed his stuff with yours?'

Aaron shook his head absently, still staring at his phone. Sarcasm was wasted on him.

And now, a day later in this London hotel suite, despite knowing everything there was to know about his former housemates; despite his quiet certainty that he'd measure up, that he'd outdo them, he was like a cat on a hot tin roof. And their daughters were still shoeless and watching cartoons.

'Aaron. Please. Just get the girls organized and I'll be done feeding by the time you're all ready.'

He nodded, went next door to Faye and Bea, and Sive let out a quiet breath.

On the bed beside her, on the tightly tucked pristine-white cover, her phone pinged with an email. She angled her head to see who it was from, without dislodging the baby. The newspaper's picture editor, looking for a more recent photograph of an actor she'd interviewed. Damn. She glanced at the door to the adjoining room. She'd promised Aaron she wouldn't have to work during the trip to London, but this wouldn't take a second. One-handed, she typed a reply. She would ask the publicist for another photo and revert asap.

Aaron came back into the room, shaking his head in exasperation.

'Are they ready?' she asked

'Faye's insisting on changing out of her shorts and into a dress, but I've told her she can't.'

This was also very Aaron – he'd missed the choose-your-battles chapter of the parenting manual.

'It's fine, let her change.'

'Ah, Sive, I can't backtrack now! If you undermine me, they're *never* going to listen. I'm just going to be "silly daddy" for ever.' He rolled his eyes, but he was grinning. He loved being 'silly daddy', and she knew it.

'It's not undermining you if there's a valid reason. She wants to wear a dress so the stitches in her leg won't be as visible, I'll bet. That's all.'

He looked confused for a moment, as though he'd already forgotten the stitches. Then again, he hadn't been the one to pick her up when she fell off the fence. He hadn't had to hide a shudder on seeing the gash the nail had made in her leg. He hadn't had to drive her to the Swiftcare clinic for stitches and a tetanus shot, while looking after Bea and Toby too. He'd arrived home from work yesterday evening to hear all about it after the fact. And that was just the way it was. He worked full-time, she worked part-time, and it wasn't his fault he couldn't be there to help. He could, however, help now.

'Here – take Toby,' she said, standing up. 'I'll get the girls.'

Aaron took Toby and immediately nuzzled the baby's cheek. Sive stopped to watch for a moment. Aaron drove her mad sometimes, but he was a giant lump of putty when it came to the kids.

She continued through to the girls' bedroom, on the far side of the sitting room. 'Right, let's go,' she said, clapping her hands Mary Poppins style. 'Time for Daddy's big reunion.'

The Library Bar of the Meridian Hotel was humming buzzily. Its high-backed wing chairs were almost all occupied, though it was three o'clock on a Friday afternoon and most people in Sive's world were still at work. Heavy curtains in olive green and contrasting fawn draped and looped halfway across the floor-to-ceiling windows, letting in light but giving a sense of warmth and privacy too. Built into the walls were shelves of leather-bound books, creating the eponymous library, while gilt-edged mirrors and tall standing lamps completed the effect. The bar was the epitome of tasteful luxury, and not quite where Sive would normally bring her children.

Now, Faye and Bea skipped ahead, skirting between the green-and-brown velvet chairs, almost knocking a vase of pink chrysanthemums from a high polished table in the centre of the room. Sive hid a sigh. It was going to be a long afternoon, and they hadn't even sat down yet.

When they did, the mismatch was immediately clear. Sitting around a low mahogany table by the window were Scott, Nita, Maggie and Dave. On silver coasters in front of them sat a bottle of beer, a tonic water, a glass of rosé and a pint of Guinness. Sive's three children were about to immeasurably cramp everyone's style. She groaned inwardly as Faye began running towards the bar shouting about fizzy orange, followed by Bea, who tripped and fell en route.

'Ah, here they are! In your honour, mate!' Dave said, holding up his pint of Guinness and standing to clap Aaron on the back. *'Benvenuti! Salute!'*

Sive had no earthly idea why Dave – normally the least pretentious of the gang – was speaking Italian, but she kept her smile firmly in place as the others stood too and greetings and hugs and air kisses ensued. Sive had met each of them at various times over the years, but they were very much her spouse's friends. And none of them had spouses. Or children. At least none currently in their care, here in this opulent Central London hotel. Sive bit her lip.

'Sorry we're late getting down,' she said as they all took their seats again. 'The only ones staying here in the hotel, yet last to arrive.' She rolled her eyes apologetically.

'Don't worry,' Maggie reassured her in her soft Edinburgh burr. 'We're all absolutely delighted with an excuse to take an afternoon off work. I've been enjoying sitting here with my rosé, watching the world go by.'

'That's because you were forty minutes early,' Nita said, then turned to Sive. 'Maggie is the most extraordinarily punctual woman in Britain. She only has one setting, and that's "early".'

'Which of course makes us normal humans feel desperately late, even when we're not,' Scott agreed. 'And she'll be even worse now, with her fancy new watch.' He nodded towards an open gift box at the centre of the table and Sive felt a sudden unease that there would be presents exchanged; that she'd missed the memo. Why would there be gifts at a reunion, though?

Scott turned towards Maggie. 'Come on then, let's see it.'

Maggie stretched out her arm to show Scott a dove-grey smartwatch with a copper-coloured strap. 'Isn't it gorgeous?' Then to Nita: 'Are you sure you don't want it yourself?'

Nita smiled benevolently. 'Gosh, no. Brands keep sending me stuff. I have, like, eight or nine watches now. So you're more than welcome to it. You know it has GPS?'

'Amazing! Not that I know how to use it, but it sounds *very* cool.'

Dave tilted his head, scrutinizing the watch. 'Hmm, that model only works if you have your phone with you too. What you need is one that functions even without your phone. You know they can be used to help find missing people? I was reading about it at work the other day—'

'*No!* Dave's going to tell us one of his work sagas!' Scott said in mock horror. 'This is even worse than Maggie's hyper-punctuality.'

Maggie reached across to swipe at Scott, but she was smiling. 'Hey, I saw you outside, puffing away on your e-cigarette thing. You were in no rush.'

He grinned back. 'Oh, come on, leave me to my few remaining pleasures. I've given up the real things, that's something.'

'About time,' Maggie said. 'Only fifteen years too late for those poor neighbours whose shed—'

'Yeah, yeah, don't get into that. We can't all be as perfect as you, Maggie,' Scott said, cutting her off. He was still smiling, but there was an edge to his tone now. 'Anyway, we're here, it's Friday, nobody's working, and we have drinks.' He raised his glass, and the others followed suit.

Nita clapped her hands. 'Let's grab a pic, now everyone's here!' She stood, holding her phone, to take a group selfie. Sive hovered near the edge of the frame, not sure if she should be in or out.

'Here, why don't I take one?' she said, pulling out her own

phone and getting up from her seat. She stepped back from the table to take it, nudging her chair out of the way.

There they were, Dave, Scott, Nita, Maggie and Aaron, smiling at Sive's camera. Dave with his balding head and customary sheepish expression. Scott, his blond hair faded and his pallor blotchy, a pair of aviator sunglasses high on his head. Nita, the princess, whitened teeth gleaming. Maggie – sensible, understated Maggie – tucking a long red curl behind her ear. And Aaron. Just as handsome, in Sive's admittedly biased opinion, as when she first set eyes on him.

She took three photos and sat back down, promising to send them to the WhatsApp group, though she wasn't actually in the WhatsApp group.

Scott turned towards Aaron. 'So, how's everything in the criminal world? Some big cases on the go?'

Straight in, then, Sive thought, no 'How was the journey?' small talk. But this was what Aaron loved. Holding court. Talking shop. Centre of attention.

'Good. Busy. You know yourself, it's non-stop.'

'I read about this Brosnan guy you're defending. That's something else.' Scott shook his head with what looked like envy disguised as admiration. 'Sure you haven't bitten off more than you can chew?' He laughed to show he was joking, his ruddy cheeks glowing.

'I can handle it.'

'From what I've read,' Scott said carefully, 'this Callan crime gang you've got over there in Dublin are pinning everything on Pete Brosnan getting convicted so their guy isn't in the frame.'

'You are well informed, my friend.' Aaron raised the pint that had just been placed in front of him.

Scott shook his head, faux ruefully. 'They're a nasty bunch. A penchant for bagging people up and throwing them in the river, if I remember correctly.'

'How do you know so much about them?' Aaron asked over the top of his pint.

'We had a case that involved one of the Callans back in my old firm. Intimidating lot.' He exhaled audibly through pursed lips. 'You must be a little worried about what they'll do if you get your guy off?'

Sive winced. This was starting to sound as though Scott had spent the last three days reading up on Aaron's cases, ready to pounce with some carefully planned passive-aggressive digs. Scott had worked very long hours for almost twenty years, until redundancy two years ago had left him extremely wealthy but thoroughly bored.

'I couldn't do my job if I was afraid of everyone with a vested interest. You know that, Burner,' Aaron said evenly. 'Or you used to.'

'Ha. There's vested interests and there's bloody murderous crime gangs.' Scott laughed. 'What about you, Sive, aren't you worried they'll come gunning for your husband?'

Nita and Maggie shook their heads in despair. 'Scott, stop! And not in front of the kids,' Maggie admonished.

Sive smiled. 'Aaron's dealt with some unsavoury types before. He can handle it.' She clinked her gin against her husband's pint. In truth, she hated these kinds of cases. Hated thinking about them. Usually kept her head in the sand and avoided reading about them. But for every crime-gang case, there was another involving some perfectly normal person who'd slipped up and found themselves in court. The kinds of people who deserved a second chance, or at least the best defence they could get. This thought was quickly accompanied, just as it always was, with one word. *Hypocrite.*

'Anyway, enough about me,' Aaron said. 'How's piloting going, Burner? Any regrets?'

Scott used to be a criminal lawyer too. He and Aaron had worked together when they were starting out and had further bonded over their membership of the same rowing club. They'd lived together in a house in Stratford in East London, with Maggie, Dave and Nita, and both had gone on to marry and have three children each. Scott, however, on being made redundant, had left the law completely to retrain as a pilot, around the same time as Caron, his wife, left him for a millionaire music producer. Go figure, as Aaron said when he heard.

'No regrets,' Scott said, leaning back on his chair and clasping his hands behind his head. 'Seeing the world, seeing the sky . . . seeing the air hostesses,' he added with a wink.

Beside him, Nita groaned, putting one beautifully manicured hand to her forehead. Sive was caught, as always, by how like her sister Nita was. Or at least how Yasmin might have looked had she lived another fifteen years. Yasmin, the ghost hovering over every get-together. And sometimes over Sive's marriage.

'You just do take-off and landing, right?' Aaron was saying now. 'The autopilot does the rest?'

Oh, Aaron. Sive took a sip of her gin.

Scott sat forward again. 'It's not quite as simple as that. But let's just say the pros far outweigh any cons. Actually, there *are* no cons.'

'Unlike in the legal profession,' Maggie quipped, lightening the mood.

Sive smiled across at her. Maggie was forty-two, the same age as the rest of the housemates, but always seemed older. It had nothing to do with her appearance – her unlined skin and beautiful long red curls made it hard to guess her age – she just had that quiet maturity that some people have. The sensible one, back in the day, according to Aaron. The one who remembered to pay the electricity bill and put out the bins. The boring one, he said, a bit of a prig at times, a bit judgemental. Sive's impression was that Aaron felt inherently criticized because Maggie didn't drink as much as the rest of them, though as far as Sive knew Maggie had never said a word to suggest she was judging anyone at all. She'd been working in law back then too, in a fortieth-floor office on Canary Wharf. Like Scott, she'd had a career change. Unlike Scott, she'd opted for a somewhat less glamorous career managing a suburban GP clinic.

'I don't get it,' Dave said now, popping a mint in his mouth.

Maggie let out a tiny sigh.

'*Cons*. As in, *convicts*?' Scott explained. 'Dave, you are literally a pretend-policeman. How did you not get that?'

The others laughed, and Dave grinned.

'Do *not* start with the pretend-police stuff, Burner,' he said, offering around the packet of Polo mints. 'Surely there's a statute of limitations on that joke?'

'Never!' Aaron said, raising his glass, and they all clinked, even Dave, who was blushing.

Sive felt for him. While the others were flying high in their skyscraper careers, Dave had been starting a job as a civilian investigator or, as he and his colleagues called it, a 'civvie' for the Metropolitan Police. And twenty years on, that's still pretty much what he was doing. He'd changed roles now and then but, as far as the others were concerned, while they were saving the world one court case at a time, Dave's job mostly involved data searches and data entry.

To the best of Sive's knowledge, it was critical work in any police force, but the others, with their seven-figure salaries, tended to quietly look down on Dave. The running joke was that he really wanted to be, as they put it, a 'proper' police officer, and over the years his former housemates had gifted him magnifying glasses, handcuffs and an endless supply of little black notebooks whenever they all met up. His current job was in vetting applicants for police roles, and about as far from the *Line of Duty* version of police work as you could get, but, from what Sive could see, Dave was happy and well able to brush off the teasing.

'Speaking of which,' Scott said now, reaching for a gift bag at his feet, 'we have, as always, a present for you, Dave.'

Aaron drum-rolled the table. Dave groaned, but he was grinning. Nita shook her head, but she too was smiling. Maggie's face was impassive. Scott pulled out a navy baseball cap with a cartoon police badge on the front and stretched across the table to put it on Dave's head. Everyone cheered, Dave took a small bow and said it was perfect for covering his expanding baldness. How quickly they all fell back into their old roles, Sive thought, looking around the table. All except Nita, perhaps, who had just recently undergone the biggest change of all.

'So when are you due?' Sive asked her now.

'Not until February,' Nita said. 'Plenty of time still.' She took a sip of her drink. 'It's just tonic water, no gin, by the way.'

Sive smiled. 'First-time pregnancy is an eye-opener.'

'Only if you're not prepared,' Nita countered. 'I did a lot of research beforehand. I can't understand people who plunge in without reading up on it first.'

Sive nodded politely. She'd known precisely nothing about pregnancy when the line appeared on the test that first time. And had remained in a state of bewilderment, feeling her way as she went, through most of her pregnancy. Then again, the circumstances were hardly the same. Nita had planned the pregnancy meticulously, opting to go it alone with IUI instead of, as she put it, 'settling for some loser from Tinder'. Sive, on the other hand, had most definitely not planned her first pregnancy.

She glanced over to where Faye was sitting on the soft green carpet, taking off her shoes. She had taken Sive's phone and moved a little bit away from Bea, keen, no doubt, for a brief breather from her greatest fan and constant provocateur.

Nita followed her gaze. 'Two little girls – so sweet. They're probably best friends.'

Sive shook her head. 'Ha, no, they *kill* each other.'

Nita looked surprised. 'Really? How awful.'

'Oh, I just mean normal sibling stuff. Bea wants to do everything Faye does. Faye gets tired of having her follow everywhere and tries to escape. Bea, in turn, does whatever she can to keep Faye's attention. It might be a hug or it might be a kick.'

On cue, Bea sidled over to Faye and sat so close she was almost on top of her. Personal space was not Bea's thing.

'Goodness. That's dreadful that they don't get on.'

'Ah no, Faye is driven mad by Bea at times, but she's very patient with her. And woe betide anyone who dares to cross her little sister. She'll fly to Bea's defence. She overheard me telling Aaron about a kid in crèche who was pinching Bea and—'

'Pinching! That's horrendous. Was disciplinary action taken?'

Oh, good God. Nita was going to get a rude awakening when her child started nursery.

Sive smiled. 'That's just something that happens with small kids. It's no big deal. But Faye overheard us talking about it and at pick-up the following evening she stalked over to the other kid and told him if he ever pinched her sister again she'd come back and pinch him twice as hard. So yeah, Faye might be irritated by her little shadow, but she'd go to the ends of the earth for Bea if someone else hurt her.'

Nita picked up her phone and typed something. She glanced at Sive. 'Making a note to find some books on nurseries and violence. I do a lot of research,' she explained. 'Obviously, since I'm

ANDREA MARA

doing it on my own, I can't just hope for the best. I need to be organized.'

Sive had never met anyone more organized than Nita and didn't doubt her for a second. Where Maggie was the house mother – the one they relied on to quietly get things done – Nita was the house manager, a not always welcome or necessary role. According to Aaron, she'd had spreadsheets for the cleaning rota, Excel formulae for weighted calculations of split bills, and a strict set of house rules pinned to the fridge. Her unselfconscious thoroughness served her well at work – like Aaron, she worked in law, and thrived on the attention to detail required for her current role as Head of Legal in a multinational bank. This same skillset had not won her any popularity contests back when they all shared a house, but Nita had never cared for popularity contests.

'Of course. And you'll be a brilliant mother,' Sive said, glancing at her daughters as they bickered over her phone.

Nita looked over too.

'The littler one, Bea, she's so pretty. She looks nothing like you, Sive – her daddy's girl!'

'Um, thanks, I think . . .'

Nita carried on, unfazed. 'And Faye's quite pretty too, with that lovely blonde hair. You and Aaron are both much darker – where did she get the gorgeous hair?' A tinkly laugh. 'I bet people ask if she's adopted. I considered adoption, but thought IUI might suit me better. More twenty-first century.'

Sive nodded, unsure what to say to that, and peeked, instead, into the pram at her sleeping baby.

'How old is' – Nita paused, unsure, it seemed, of the name – 'the little one, now?'

'Toby's four months old,' Sive said, 'so he still sleeps a lot in the afternoon, thank goodness. The other two are enough of a handful.'

They both looked over again to where Faye and Bea were sitting together, glued to something on Sive's phone. As they watched, Bea's foot knocked against Faye's glass, sending the last dregs of her orange cordial splashing on to the strap of Faye's beloved *Frozen* backpack. Sive held her breath. It was only a small splash. If Faye didn't notice, she wasn't going to say anything. The Meridian Library Bar didn't seem like a great place for a she-ruined-my-bag meltdown. But Faye was still transfixed by Sive's phone (thank you, YouTube) and Sive dodged a bullet.

'I won't be going down the technology route with mine,' Nita mused. 'Storybooks and nursery rhymes are so important for the developing brain.'

'Well, if you'd like to practise, I could dig out a storybook and you can read it to my girls?' Sive said with a bright smile. 'I could do with taking my phone back, though I suppose it *will* mean they'll be clambering all over us . . . Then again, it'll get you used to what's ahead . . .'

A worried frown crossed Nita's pretty features. 'Oh, they seem perfectly happy there. Best to leave them while little . . .' She looked at the pram.

'Toby,' Sive supplied.

'While little Toby is sleeping.'

'Indeed,' Sive said, picking up her gin. It was going to be a long four days in London.

6

'Do you HAVE A plan in place, for if she gets lost?'

It's a different police officer. A woman called DC Hawthorn, who told the Sullivans she was their assigned liaison officer. They've moved to the Central Line platform westbound in Oxford Circus now, after Hawthorn explained that if someone finds Faye and brings her back, this is where she'll arrive. And Sive is afraid to move – glued to the spot on the cramped, airless platform, still hoping as each Tube pulls in that Faye's small figure will alight.

She stares at DC Hawthorn now, as Bea, heavy in her arms, nuzzles into her neck.

'A plan?'

'A meeting place, or a rule that she should find someone in uniform?'

Sive shakes her head. 'At home, yes. I mean, if we're in the playground, we say "go to the big slide if you're lost". But in London . . . we don't know anywhere in London.' *God, they should have had a plan.*

'Does she know the name of the station you were at when you became separated? Did you mention it?'

Sive thinks back. The rush from the hotel because they were running late to meet Maggie. The fumble for her Oyster card when they arrived in the station. The dozen times she'd cursed herself for ever agreeing to this – why didn't they just stay in the hotel while Aaron did his race? She wasn't equipped to get three small kids around an unfamiliar city. *And now look what's happened.*

'No,' she says eventually. 'I was on my own with the kids. If Aaron had been there, we might have talked to each other about where we were going. But I think all I'd have said to the kids was, "Hurry up."'

'Indeed. Which end of the platform were you on?'

'Uh, I'm not sure?'

'It's so we can narrow down which carriage she was on.'

'Oh – we got off a lift, so it was a platform entrance near a lift.'

Hawthorn makes a note. 'And does Faye know your phone number?'

'I taught her last year, but I haven't tested her in a while. Shit. Sorry. This is awful. My God, she's alone in London with no idea how to contact us.'

Aaron is rocking the pram as, all around them, passengers stream on to a waiting Tube. 'But as soon as someone finds her, she'll say who she is,' he says. 'She knows her full name, she knows our names.'

Hawthorn nods her agreement.

'People will spot a six-year-old on her own and alert the authorities. Her description and photo have gone out on social media so it won't be long now. And as her parents, you're best placed to spot her if she turns up back here.' She gestures at the platform, the departing Tube, the crowds. 'Don't worry, Mrs Sullivan, we'll have her back to you before you know it. Kids wander off all the time.'

'But what if she didn't wander off?' Sive says quietly, hoarsely, hardly believing she's saying these words. 'What if someone took her?'

Aaron shakes his head. 'People don't just take children. We'll find her, I promise.'

'OK.' She swallows. 'OK. We need to stay calm and keep searching. What about Bea and Toby?'

'Do you want to take them back to the hotel?' Aaron asks.

The response in her body is visceral. 'No. No way can I leave until we find Faye.'

'Me neither,' Aaron says quietly. 'I'll try Nita and Maggie. See if one of them can come and take the kids.'

'Try Maggie first. God, she's probably waiting for me in the Rooftop Bar.' Sive hesitates. 'Nita had a fall last night when we were out and might be a bit shaken still this morning.'

'Oh, shit. Is the baby OK?'

'Well—'

Sive is interrupted by DC Hawthorn. 'Mrs Sullivan, I have all your details now, and the photo of Faye. Anything else you can tell me – any defining features? Something a member of the public would notice?'

'Her backpack might stand out – it's a *Frozen* one.'

'We've got that, yes. No birthmarks?'

'No. Actually, she has stitches in her leg at the moment. I don't know if anyone would notice if she just walked past, though . . .'

'OK, that might be useful as something to keep to ourselves for now, to help weed out any crank calls,' Hawthorn says. She nods down at the pram. 'Do you need to feed the little one?' She gestures to a bench.

'We're going to get friends to mind them,' Sive says as Aaron moves towards the escalator, trying for a phone signal.

'Good. We have officers checking each station and we're accessing CCTV footage too. So it won't be long—'

'Oh my God, I forgot about CCTV – so can you see what happened on the train? Why she walked off, where she went?'

But Hawthorn is shaking her head. 'Unfortunately, there's no CCTV on the Central Line trains. Planned for some point in the next few years, but not in place yet.'

Sive sags, and Bea shifts in her arms.

'But there are cameras in all the stations,' Hawthorn says. 'Without knowing which one she got off at, it'll take a while to go through all the footage, but we'll get there.'

'Can't you get loads of people looking at the same time?'

'We have all available officers working on this,' Hawthorn says, which doesn't really tell Sive anything.

Aaron steps back into the conversation. 'No answer on Maggie's phone, and Dave's on his way into work but he'll see what he can do from the police side.' He turns to Hawthorn. 'My friend's a civilian investigator with the Metropolitan Police.'

Hawthorn looks like she's trying to hide a dubious expression. No doubt, Sive imagines, there's little someone like Dave can do to help.

'I got Scott,' Aaron continues. 'He was near enough to here, so he's on his way now to take the kids – he'll meet us upstairs in the ticket hall.' He swipes a hand across his glistening brow. 'He's off work today because of the race, thank God.'

Again he turns to explain to Hawthorn. 'We had a virtual rowing race early this morning. That's why I wasn't here when it happened.'

It's not meant as an accusation. But Sive can hear it. If Aaron had been there, he wouldn't have let their daughter disappear.

*

As they step off the top of the escalator, Aaron pushing the pram, Sive holding Bea's hand, she turns to her husband. 'I'm so sorry. I can't believe I let this happen.'

'It could have just as easily happened to me,' Aaron says, squeezing her arm. 'Who was calling, though? Why didn't you just ignore it?'

On cue, her phone rings again, and Sive grabs it from her back pocket. *Maybe it's news on Faye.* It's not, though. No cheery London accent greets her. Instead it's the lilting Kerry cadence of her editor back home.

'Sive! I'm so sorry. I saw it on the news. Is there anything I can do?'

It's the familiar voice that does it – the tears that have been threatening for an hour come now, smothering her voice. Sive waves her hand in front of her face, trying to steady herself.

'Sive?'

Deep breath. Calm. 'Thanks. I don't know . . .' Bea clambers at her leg, and Sive scoops her up, one-handed. Aaron is on his phone again, still rocking the pram. 'Maybe you can get the paper's social media to retweet?'

'Of course. Wait. I have an idea. Jude Barr's based in London now and I think she's covering a court case this week. She might be able to help. Yes!' Caroline warms to her theme. 'I'll speak to her editor and see if we can get Jude to you. She can be by your side, helping with the search, put updates online, live-tweeting it, that kind of thing.'

'I don't know . . .'

'It's your call, but, Sive, it's an extra set of eyes, a familiar face, and more coverage. Get Faye's photo out there, get people talking and looking. Right?'

Sive nods into the phone.

'So I'll sort that out? Where are you?'

Sive gives her the details and says goodbye, then turns to explain what's happening to Aaron.

He looks unconvinced. 'How can updates in an Irish newspaper help over here?'

'It'll be the online version, and I'm sure the *Daily Byte* has UK readers too. It can't hurt, anyway.'

'Fine. Was it Caroline who was ringing when Faye and Bea got on the train?'

She nods. He shakes his head.

'You're supposed to be on holidays. She shouldn't have been calling.'

'Which is why I was declining the call. Anyway, this isn't helping.' It rears up again. The realization. The overwhelming panic. 'Christ. Where is she? *What are we going to do?*'

'We're going to find her, that's what we're going to do. How about, once Scott takes the kids, you go back to Bond Street, in case she knows that's where she left you and gets someone to take her there? And I'll go to all the other stations on the line, one by one.'

She nods, just as Scott arrives and, with unexpected expertise, takes Bea from her aching arms. Bea who saw it all but can't tell them anything. The frustration is so sharp it hurts Sive's stomach.

'I've got this,' Scott says, putting a hand on the pram. 'Now give me your hotel key, and you go find Faye.'

7

Three days earlier | Friday
The Meridian Hotel

Scott signalled to a waiter in the hotel bar, making a circular motion that meant 'Same again.' Scott was always first to order the next round, which made him the best fun once upon a time but harder work now that there were kids in the mix and hangovers were tougher.

Sive watched as Dave quickly drained his pint, ready for a fresh one. He was always first to finish his drink, but less keen to order a round. She put her hand over her glass. 'I'd better switch to sparkling water,' she said to Scott. 'No craic looking after three kids when you're half cut.'

'Oh, come on. You've only had one!'

She smiled. 'Maybe later, but I'd love a sparkling water.'

Scott shrugged and called the waiter over to alter the order. His cheeks were redder than usual, flushed from afternoon beers perhaps. His broad nose was threaded with new veins and his eyes looked small, sunken in a face that was fleshier than Sive remembered. Back when Aaron lived with him, he was, by all accounts, the blond-haired, blue-eyed Oxford-native who got all the girls. Or at least the nice girls who wanted a 'good catch' – a man with looks, a career with prospects and in-laws with a country pile. Old money, of course. Now, he seemed to be prematurely going to seed.

'Speaking of later,' Dave said, 'I've booked a table for six at Giumbini tonight. Eight o'clock OK with everyone?'

Sive glanced at Aaron, but he was busy looking at his phone.

'I think the kids and I will have to opt out of dinner,' she said to Dave apologetically.

'Oh! Sorry, I didn't even think to book space for the kids. Would they go to a restaurant? Or how would that work . . .' He looked confused. Dave didn't have kids. He'd been madly in love just once, according to Aaron, with a girl he met online. This was back in the noughties, when online dating was still relatively new and not something everyone was comfortable discussing. Dave didn't mind, though. He'd talked about her non-stop, apparently. When the others had asked to meet her, however, he always found excuses. She was working late. She was working early. She had a cold. She had to visit her parents. Eventually, Aaron and Scott had concluded that Dave's mystery girlfriend was, as they put it, 'no Kate Moss'. *Don't be so mean*, Sive had said, when Aaron first told her the story. But Aaron had been adamant. Dave was no supermodel himself, Aaron said, so it stood to reason. That was *definitely* mean. Dave wasn't a stereotypical pin-up by any definition, but he had a jovial, soft look about him that Sive liked. He was shorter than his peers and stocky, and with the expanding bald patch on the top of his head he reminded Sive of a monk. A somewhat dull monk who talked too much, but sweet nonetheless.

When Aaron told her about the no-Kate-Moss ex who never had time to meet them, Sive had wondered if perhaps Dave had invented the mystery girlfriend, trying to keep up with Aaron and Scott. But Aaron said Dave met up with her regularly – four or five nights a week. It was just the rest of them who never got to meet her. And then she left him and broke his heart. He had never, as far as Sive knew, been in love since, though he had been dating someone for a while last year. That, too, had come to an end, and Dave was, he said, resigned to bachelor life.

'Don't worry about the restaurant,' she told him now. 'Eight would be late for the kids and, to be honest, it would just be really annoying for everyone.' Sive nodded towards where Bea and Faye were now fighting over her phone. 'Everyone including me,' she added with a grimace.

Aaron tuned in now. 'We could get a babysitter? The hotel will have them.'

'It's fine, I don't mind staying in.'

'Come on.' He stuck out his lower lip, looking both boyish and ridiculous. 'I don't want to go without you! The hotel is bound to have people they use all the time.'

She shook her head. 'Faye would be OK with a babysitter, but Bea wouldn't. And I don't know if Toby'd take a bottle. Better if I stay with them. But you go!'

'My lovely wife is a martyr to our children.' He sighed outwardly, and she sighed inwardly. She wasn't being a martyr. Bea really didn't like strangers. And Sive really was happy to leave her husband and his old housemates to their shared stories of times before she met them. The one about the traffic cone ('hilarious') and the one about the microwave (also 'hilarious') and, of course, the one about Yasmin. She didn't need to be there for that, a voyeur to their shared tragedy, especially on the anniversary.

She glanced across the table at Nita. Was it hard for her to be around these people who knew her sister? Or good, because she got to talk about her? Not that she did. Not in Sive's company, anyway. Anything Sive knew about Yasmin was from little snippets Aaron had told her over the years and a photo of Aaron and Yasmin she'd found in a box. A strip of four passport photos from one of those automatic booths everyone used before smartphones and selfies, with 'Stratford 2008' scrawled on the back. Aaron with his dark, long-on-top hair and his crinkly eyes and his wide mouth, looking very much like he did today. Yasmin with her henna-red hair and big brown eyes and pretty smile. So like Nita, but forever twenty-six.

Faye came bounding over, still clutching Sive's phone. 'I have an idea!' she announced. 'I'll mind Bea in our room, because she's really annoying. I can show her cartoons on the TV and give her biscuits, and then you don't have to mind her. I just need you to bring us to work the TV and give me the treats and then you can be back here and I'll be in charge.'

'Eh, no.'

'Why?' Eyes wide with genuine bafflement.

Sive counted out the reasons on her fingers. 'Because you've had enough TV already today, because this is really a ploy to find out where I'm hiding the treats, and because you're six and not allowed to be on your own in a hotel room. Now scoot.' She shooed Faye away, ignoring her protestations.

'So, how do you like being a stay-at-home mummy?' Nita asked, watching Faye's departure. 'It must be lovely not to have to work.'

'Oh! I do work. I'm freelance now, but still writing for the same paper I used to work for before the kids were born.'

'But who takes care of the children?' Dave chimed in, looking puzzled.

'They're in school and crèche in the mornings, so I work then.'

'Even the baby?'

'No, not yet. I work while he naps, and at night when they're all in bed.'

'Aren't you on maternity leave?' Nita asked, tapping a long crimson nail against the side of her mouth.

'Well, I cut back on work for the first two months after he was born, but it's hard to turn anything down when you're free-lance. You worry your editor will forget you.'

'I think it's lovely you have a little job to keep you going,' Nita said. 'Obviously, you don't *have* to, with Aaron raking it in.' She winked at Aaron. 'It's different for me. I need to work since I'm on my own.'

'It's not just about *having* to, though, it's also something I want to do.' Sive strove to keep the bristle out of her tone.

Aaron grinned. 'Even on holidays.' He wagged a finger in mock exasperation at Sive. 'I saw that sneaky reply when I was getting the girls ready.'

She bit back a sigh. 'If I had an assistant to field my calls while I was away, life would certainly be easier,' she said lightly.

'Touché. Anyway, for what it's worth, Sive is very good at her job, and her editor is lucky to have her.'

Sive's cheeks flushed at Aaron's compliment.

'What kind of stuff do you write?' Scott asked.

'Lifestyle stuff.' A wry smile. 'The kind of features that prompt people to comment, "Slow news day?"'

'I love those articles,' Maggie said. 'Much more enjoyable than all the bad news.'

Sive wanted to hug her. This happened every time she met Maggie, though. Maggie was nice. Not boring nice, as Aaron thought, but warm and kind and empathetic and nice. Every time they had met over the years, Sive had found herself wishing they could be proper friends. That they lived in the same country. That they knew each other better. When they were together on these brief trips to London, it almost felt like they *were* proper friends – BFFs, on the same wavelength, bonding while the others bickered. But as soon as Sive was home, it tapered off to nothing. A message from Sive to say how good the trip was. A kind reply from Maggie, but no open-ended questions, nothing to encourage further chat. And why would there be anything else? Sive was Maggie's former flatmate's wife, someone she saw once a year at most. Hardly best-friend material. But still.

'Do you get to travel a lot?' Scott asked.

'Oh God, I wish. It's not possible with the kids. I'm always envious of the younger journalists who can go anywhere at the drop of a hat.'

'They probably get all the good stories,' Nita said, somewhat unhelpfully.

Sive smiled. 'They're certainly freer to take on whatever they're asked, that's true. I have to say no if it involves travel. Ironically, there's a court case on here this week with an Irish slant to the story, and here I am in London anyway, but it's not me covering it – it's a younger, child-free journalist who has all the time in the world to do whatever she's asked.'

Did she sound bitter? She didn't mean to sound bitter. She wouldn't trade her kids for anything, though a bit of childcare in the afternoons would be extremely handy. Jude Barr, the journalist covering the court case, would probably never want kids. She'd be too cool and too efficient for kids. Sive smiled to herself. She was being ridiculous. Jude, who she'd met a few times at industry events, was probably very nice beneath the cool, efficient ice-blonde exterior and the Irish-living-in-London Sharon Horgan accent. Jude was about five years younger than her, with the kind of blunt fringe Sive could never carry off, and a spiderweb tattoo on the back of her neck. She was also very good at her job, and Sive found herself at times intimidated and at times irritated by Jude's always-on energy and unshakable confidence.

'I imagine you can do all the stories you write pretty easily from home,' Maggie said, 'and in a few years the kids will be older, and you'll be jetting around the world interviewing celebrities.'

'Here's hoping.' Sive raised her glass.

'Celebrities!' Nita was interested now. 'Tell me more! Obviously, as you know, I'm an influencer, so there's a big crossover with celebrities.'

Oh sweet mother of God. 'Well, at the moment, I'm doing an interview series with adult children of celebrities.'

Nita's eyes flashed. 'Oh, wow! Beckhams, Kardashians – that kind of thing?'

Aaron laughed. Sive flushed.

'Irish celebrities. They're mostly sports stars and chefs. *Lotta* chefs.'

'Ah.' Nita had lost interest. 'Speaking of chefs, did you see my pic from the restaurant opening last week? The one with Nigella?' She picked up her phone and clicked into Instagram. 'My followers go nuts for that kind of content. It took *hours* to go through the comments.' She rolled her eyes, but Sive wasn't fooled. Nita *lived* for her followers' comments. Now, she held up her phone to show the photo, and everyone nodded good-naturedly, humouring her.

'Does your work mind all the influencer stuff?' Scott asked. 'It doesn't quite go with the serious in-house legal look, I'd have thought.' Scott was someone who said 'I'd have thought' at the end of many of his sentences, usually when he was trying to get a dig in.

Nita wrinkled her nose. 'God, you're so old-fashioned. Of course they don't mind. Sometimes people recognize me at meetings, and it's a rather good talking point. Sometimes people don't believe I'm a lawyer, of course. You know. Saying things like, "But you're too pretty" – ridiculous stuff like that. God, I hate it.' Her cheeks flushed at the fib. Sive knew there was nothing Nita loved more than being told she was too pretty to be a lawyer then slaying them with her razor-sharp intelligence.

Now Nita's eyes lit up again and she leaned across the table towards Sive. 'Oh, I *love* your pendant. It's stunning! Which designer? I'm thinking of treating myself.'

'Aaron got it for me for Christmas. The brand is something like . . . *Miss Victoria*. Or *Miss Victoria London*? Aaron, where did you get this again?'

Aaron frowned and shook his head. 'Can't remember now.' His eyes flicked away and Sive had the sudden sense he was being deliberately cagey about where he'd bought the pendant. Why, she had no idea.

It was a moot point – Nita was already on her phone, keying it into Google. Seconds later, she held up an image similar to Sive's pendant – a woven-gold disc but without the inset stones.

'Mine is customized with the kids' birthstones,' Sive explained. 'Faye's and Bea's. Toby wasn't born yet.'

'I love it. Let me see if I can get it anywhere nearby . . . No, seems to be just available from one shop over in East London. Too far.' A pause. 'Oh! I can buy online. Excellent.' She glanced around the table. 'Apols. Instant gratification is my middle name.'

And no more than fifteen seconds later Nita had purchased herself a woven-gold disc just like Sive's.

'I'll put it on my Insta and tag the designer. I'll tag you too, of course. You're practically an influencer now, Sive!'

Indeed. A message pinged on Sive's mobile and she squinted to read it without picking up her phone. It was from the publicist she'd emailed earlier. *Damn*, she'd need to take a look, whatever Aaron might think. She palmed her phone.

'This little guy is starting to fuss,' she said. 'I'll wheel him around the corridor for a minute to get him back to sleep. Keep an eye on the girls, Aaron, won't you?'

He nodded absent-mindedly, busy showing Dave and Scott his new watch. Sive wheeled the pram out of the bar and checked her phone. The email came with an attachment, and relief swept over her. One less thing to worry about. While she was there, she clicked into Google and tapped the search bar. She didn't need to type the words. Google already knew whose name she searched on an almost daily basis. Nothing new. Nevertheless, when his face appeared on-screen, a sick feeling swelled in her stomach.

8

SIVE IS BACK IN Bond Street Tube station, standing on the platform, exactly where she'd stood an hour earlier, watching the doors slide shut. She'd been so sure Faye would be here, waiting patiently behind the yellow line. That, somehow, Faye or the universe or a kind stranger would know how to retrace those steps and find the starting spot. But she's not here. Sive moves down the platform as far as she can go, threading her way between waiting commuters, then back to the other end. But there's no little girl in a pink jacket. No little girl with a *Frozen* backpack. Panic threatens to take hold again, to paralyse her, and she works to suppress it, forcing herself to breathe slowly in the oppressive heat. Panic won't help. She needs to search.

'Excuse me. Have you seen this girl?' she asks a woman, holding out her phone to show a photograph of Faye.

'No, sorry,' says the woman, stepping forward to board a train.

She tries a nearby man. 'Have you seen this girl? She's my daughter. She's missing.'

The man looks only briefly at the photo. 'Nah, sorry, haven't seen her. Good luck, though.'

She tries the next person. The woman doesn't look at the

photo for very long either. Sive cuts in before she speaks. 'No, please look, it's my daughter. She's only six.'

'I've seen it already, love,' the woman says. 'Saw it online. I'm very sorry. I've been watching out for her, though, yeah? I'll keep doing that.' She touches Sive's arm. 'Good luck, love.'

Sive walks up and down the narrow, claustrophobic platform again, though it feels pointless. Faye is not here. Should she go back to Oxford Circus? But Faye isn't there either. *Christ. It's impossible.* She could be anywhere. There are too many stations and too many lines and too many tracks and too many tunnels. Her stomach churns. She doesn't want to think about tracks and tunnels. Why are there no police here? Why is she the only one searching this platform? Faye's been gone over an hour now; they have to take it seriously, surely? She sags against the wall, then shakes herself. There's no time for this. She'll check up at the entrance again and the westbound platform. At least it's a concrete plan.

Her mind numbs as she takes the escalator. Posters slide slowly past, hideous in their mundanity. A smiling face in a vitamin ad. A smiling face in a movie ad. Disney Paris, autumn deals. She'd promised Faye a trip to Disney when she's older. *God.* A Crimestoppers poster. A concert in Stratford next week – Jasmina Langford, opera singer. A conference in Royal Victoria Dock today – Joe White, motivational speaker. *FIND THE NEW YOU!* the poster commands in giant yellow text. *I just need to find my child!* Sive screams inside her head.

Her phone rings as she half stumbles off the top of the escalator.

'Sive,' says the caller. Snappy. Businesslike. 'It's Jude Barr. I've just heard what's happened. Where are you now?'

'Bond Street Tube station. But Faye's not here.' Her voice cracks.

'OK, I'm on my way. I'll get something up online while I'm in the cab. I already have a photo and description, but I need to add a bit of colour. I'll say that I'm part of the search. Live-tweeting. That'll get eyes on it. Sounds click-baity, but whatever works.'

It's not a question, and Sive is glad she's not expected to give her opinion. Jude Barr is nothing if not efficient.

'So, you've got British Transport Police searching, Underground staff too, and you're asking members of the public to look out for her . . . let's see, it's you and your husband, Aaron, searching?'

'Yes.'

A woman mutters something as she tries to push past. Sive moves to the side, huddling against the tiled wall to keep out of the way.

'OK. And you're here for . . .?'

'A get-together with Aaron's old housemates from when he used to live in London.'

'Great. Adding that for colour. It all helps. Your husband is a barrister, representing Pete Brosnan in his murder trial, yes?'

'Yes, but—'

'Good. I have some background on that already, and I can get a quote from your husband. How soon can we see Aaron?'

Sive shakes her head into the phone. Is Jude here to help or to get what she can for her own byline?

'I don't think—'

'Hang on, just need to get in a cab.' For a moment, there are muffled street sounds, then Jude is back. 'And you have two other kids. Names and ages?' Jude sounds like she has a pen in her mouth.

'Bea is two and Toby is four months.'

'Anyone else? Do you have family here?'

'No, no family here. I phoned home to tell them.' Her stomach turns at the memory of the call, her mother's terrified voice, her father's bewildered silence.

'Right, that's enough for me to get on with. I'm in a cab now. Where in the station are you?'

Sive tells her she'll be on the Central Line platform westbound.

'See you asap,' Jude says, before disconnecting the call.

Jude's questions ring in her ears, and one in particular niggles – the one about Aaron's case. Did Jude bring it up because it 'adds colour', or because she wants a bigger scoop? Or – a sudden thought stops her cold – does Jude think there's a link between Aaron's work and Faye's disappearance? *Could* there be? *No*. She shuts down the thought before it starts, clicks into her photo of Faye, and walks over to another commuter to ask if he's seen her missing child.

9

9.41 a.m.

'Mr Sullivan!'

Aaron turns to see DC Hawthorn wading towards him through the packed Central Line platform.

'Did you find her?'

'No, I'm sorry, sir. But our officers are searching every station. I wanted to ask—'

'Hold on, if your officers are searching every station, why don't I see any here, apart from you? This is starting to feel like it's just my wife and me taking it seriously.'

'I assure you, we are taking it very seriously. We have every available off—'

'Yes, I know what that means,' Aaron says sharply. 'The officers you can spare. How many is that?'

'Sir, I think we should focus on—'

'Please don't tell me what we should focus on. My six-year-old daughter is missing. That's all I'm focused on.'

She nods, lips closed. Browbeaten into silence like a witness on the stand. Only she's not a witness on the stand and, if Sive was here, she'd remind him that shouting at police isn't going to help find Faye.

'Shit. I'm sorry. I'm not normally like this.' There's an

51

unfamiliar tremble in his voice. He clears his throat. 'I'm just bloody terrified.'

'I understand, and I promise, we're doing everything we can. I know you're leaving now to search the next stations on the line, but I wanted to ask if you have some more photos we can use and, specifically, a picture of the backpack and the denim jacket, as they're the two elements that will stand out.'

Aaron feels his shoulders sag. 'Sure.' He pulls out his phone to scroll for pictures. 'My wife might have one of the backpack. I don't, it seems,' he says after a moment.

'Or even a screenshot of an image online? From wherever you bought it?' DC Hawthorn suggests.

Aaron shakes his head. 'I wouldn't have a clue. I don't remember what it looks like.'

A pause. 'That's fine, sir. My colleague in Bond Street will ask your wife or, if you're speaking to her, perhaps you could ask her to send one on.' She walks away, leaving Aaron standing on the platform as passengers surge around him. Is she judging him? For not knowing what his child's backpack looks like? He tries ringing Sive to ask about it, but there's no signal. Frustrated, he takes the escalator to ground level, but before he can try her again his phone begins to ring, the name Trigger flashing up on-screen.

Dave.

Christ, the last thing he needs is a call from Dave. He ducks to the side to answer, avoiding a fresh stream of commuters.

'Dave, now isn't a good time – Faye's still—'

'Aaron, look, mate, I'm sorry for what I said.'

'What?'

'The other night.'

'The other— Oh, that. Jesus, Dave, forget it.'

'No, really. I mean it. I over-reacted. I'm sorry. And now, with what's happened, it's put everything in perspective and—'

'OK, fine, but I have to go. I need to keep the line free in case there's news.' Hot and bothered, Aaron clamps the phone against his ear with his shoulder as he tries to take off his hoodie.

'I know, mate. I'm sorry I'm not there to help. I'm stuck at work for now, but my brother's on his way. Is he there already?'

'Jerry? No, not yet.' Aaron manages to get the hoodie over his head and tied around his waist. His T-shirt is stuck to his back.

'Scott's there, though, right?'

'He came and took Bea and Toby back to the hotel.'

'Ah, of course. And Maggie?'

'I couldn't reach her. Dave, I've got to go,' Aaron tries. This is starting to sound like a case of FOMO and Aaron doesn't have time for it.

But Dave's still talking.

'Ah – Maggie's probably waiting for Sive in the Rooftop Bar.'

'Yeah, I'll keep trying her. The more people searching, the better.' He glances around him. 'There aren't quite as many officers as we'd like here, so every pair of eyes helps.'

'Really? Normally for a misper as young as Faye there'd be at least—'

Oh Jesus, here comes the jargon. 'Dave, I'm hanging up. I'll look out for Jerry.'

As soon as he disconnects, his phone begins to ring again. Pete Brosnan's wife's number flashes up on-screen. Aaron declines the call. Surely even a dose like Carmen Brosnan would know not to call now? Jesus Christ, his child is missing. Aaron closes his eyes briefly, takes a steadying breath and readies himself to begin to search again.

Back in Dublin, Carmen Brosnan lays her phone on the arm of the couch and puts her face in her hands.

10

JUDE BARR. JOURNALIST. COFFEE-DRINKER. Kick-boxer. Go-getter (copyright: Jude's mother, from her kitchen chair in Longford, religiously reading Jude's every byline). Fan of *Ozark*, sushi, sci-fi and tattoos. Not, however, a fan of Mondays.

Now, on this particular Monday morning in London, she types on her phone as city streets slide by in a blur of sticky heat.

Irish Child Missing in London

Irish girl Faye Sullivan, six-year-old daughter of Daily Byte *journalist Sive Quinn and well-known barrister Aaron Sullivan, is missing in central London, since 8.30 this morning.*

She drops her phone on her lap and sighs. The child is probably sitting on a bench somewhere, waiting for her mother. This is a non-story, yet for some reason her editor has seen fit to pull her off the huge financial fraud court case she was covering to report on this instead. A colleague – male, of course – will take over the court case, while she moves to the 'human interest' story.

'It's because I'm a woman, isn't it?' she'd said to her editor, even though Jude knows well she isn't that kind of editor. 'You think I'll bond with the mammy and get a better story.'

'Your fatal flaw is your cynicism,' her editor had said, refusing to bite.

'My superpower is my cynicism,' was Jude's retort.

'I'm not sending you for your bonding skills, believe me. No offence, Jude, but you have the bonding skills of a piece of used Sellotape. I'm sending you because you're good. And this is a big story. And because Sive is one of ours and could do with a familiar face.'

So she'd agreed to meet with Sive, promising herself she'd be back in the courtroom by lunchtime. She picks up her phone again and re-reads her first line, gnawing at a hangnail. Aaron Sullivan is a well-known barrister, representing a former gang member on a murder charge. Should she include that? It's not relevant to the missing-child story, but it *will* be of interest. Jude had covered the first court appearance. She'd seen the crowds outside and the media furore. People who wanted Pete Brosnan strung up for what he (allegedly) did. People who claimed he was being set up by the Callans, the criminal gang who were (allegedly) actually behind the murder. People who had no opinions either way on the outcome but wanted to light a candle for a dead man. A father of three, murdered in a case of mistaken identity. Not the first time it had happened in Dublin, but something about this particular story had really caught and held the public's attention. Maybe because the victim's children were so young (and so photogenic, Jude had said to her editor, earning her a wry headshake), or maybe because the victim's wife was so young and photogenic. The murdered man had been a care assistant in a nursing home and was doing a night-course in physiotherapy. People liked that, too – a man in a caring profession trying to better himself. Not all victims are created equal. Jude shakes her head. Even she can admit that sometimes the cynicism goes too far. But on reflection: Brosnan story in. She begins to type again.

In Bond Street Tube station, as she makes her way on to the Central Line platform, Jude spots Sive a little way down, holding her phone screen towards a commuter. Jude has met Sive a handful of times at industry events but mostly they know one another from Twitter. Sive writes the kind of light lifestyley stuff Jude associates with aprons and cookies and toddlers, though that's probably unfair as she doesn't actually read it so can't say for sure. The last time they saw one another was at the 2019 Women in Media dinner, when they'd been seated at the same table. Sive can't be more than five years older than Jude – forty, if even – but she'd seemed like such a grown-up. That night, she'd chatted effortlessly with other guests in a way Jude never could and seemed to know people at every table. Jude knew them too, but only in a work capacity. She could never quite figure out how to cross into friendship territory and, after a while, she gave up trying. She'd leave that to the Sives of this world. Sive had looked stunning that night, in a bottle-green fishtail dress that set off her highlighted chestnut hair and dark blue eyes. Her make-up had been impeccable. Jude remembers examining it, wondering at what age she'd successfully manage impeccable make-up. She had turned up at the dinner in a long pink tulle skirt and a dash of hastily applied lipstick, spent half the dinner outside smoking, then left before dessert to go clubbing with a girl from the paper's sales department.

Now, this Monday morning in London, Sive looks very different. Her hair scraped back in a ponytail, her face deathly pale. In a pair of turned-up jeans with a light blue sweatshirt and flat tan sandals, she looks haunted and lost among the Monday-morning crowds. Jude lifts her phone to take a photo, then walks towards her.

Sive glances up as she approaches and her face crumples.

'Sorry. I'm not normally like this,' Sive says, swiping at her eyes. 'I think it's just seeing a familiar face.'

Jude nods. 'No worries. I'm here now, and I'll do whatever I can to amplify the story and get you coverage.' *And get back to Court 5 by lunchtime.*

'Can I use this pic I just took of you?'

Jude holds it up to show her. She's taken it from halfway down the platform, focusing in on Sive. Around her, slightly blurred, are dozens of anonymous Londoners. In the background, the Tube station walls look grim and austere.

'Yes. Please do,' Sive says. 'Use anything that helps. You don't need to ask.'

'Great.' Jude types on her phone. 'As soon as it reaches the news editor, it'll be up online and shared on social media. What's next?'

'I was about to start searching the other platforms here in Bond Street again. It feels pointless, but I have to do something.'

Jude appraises her for a moment. 'Maybe we should be trying to use our heads?'

'How do you mean?'

'Let's brainstorm. Work out where your kid might go?'

Sive bites her lip. 'You might be over-estimating how much thought a six-year-old puts into anything . . .'

Jude shrugs. 'True. I don't have kids. But look, the police are doing the legwork. You're the person who knows your daughter best, yes?'

Sive nods.

'Then let's take three minutes to talk through some ideas?'

'OK.'

'Good. So, if she got lost, would she stay put and wait for you, or try to make her way back to where she'd last seen you?'

'I don't know.' Sive shakes her head helplessly.

'Think back to a time she got lost. I presume she has before? My nieces are always getting lost.'

A Tube pulls into the station just then, and Sive turns, frantically scanning the exiting commuters. Jude watches too, but there's no small girl in a pink denim jacket. The crowd thins to nothing, and Sive turns back to Jude.

'A time she got lost?' Jude prompts. 'What did she do?'

'Um . . . there was one time at the school. Faye was playing with some other kids and ended up around the side of a prefab building and couldn't find her way back to me. I had to gather a search party of school-gate mums to go look for her.'

Jude nods sympathetically. She read an article once about school-gate mums, and the politics didn't sound appealing.

'What did Faye do when she realized she was lost?'

'She waited where she was, hoping I'd find her.'

'Great, so she's sensible?'

'Oh God, I don't know. And lost in London – that's a whole different thing. This is . . .' She shakes her head. 'I think I need to sit.'

She points to an empty bench and together they walk to it. The heat on the platform is unbearable and Jude slips off her jacket before she sits down. Sive, in her long-sleeved sweatshirt, seems oblivious, but she's probably numb.

'What about strangers?' Jude continues once they're seated. 'Would she go off with a stranger?'

Sive blanches visibly.

Jude works to soften her voice. They're not going to get

anywhere fast if Sive freaks out at every question she asks. 'It's very, very unlikely some stranger has her, but it's worth considering. So, would she go off with someone?'

'I . . . I don't know. We role-played it a few times. I remember Aaron and me laughing. Jesus.'

'Oh?'

'I pretended to be a stranger in the park, asking her if she wanted to see a puppy in my car.' Sive shakes her head. 'It sounds silly.'

It does sound silly, but if Jude's sisters-in-law are anything to go by, much of what parents do sounds quite silly. One sister-in-law sucks her baby's soother to clean it when it drops on the ground and another plays music to her bump, and Jude has seen all three of them sniff their babies to check if they need to be changed. All standard, they tell her. She'll have to take their word for it. 'Go on.'

'I asked her if she'd come with me – a stranger – to the car, if I said I had a puppy to show her. She said it depended on whether it was a real puppy or not. If it was real, she'd go, but no way if it was a fake puppy.'

Jude smiles, and Sive manages a watery smile back, which quickly turns to tears. 'We just laughed and left it at that. I never really imagined . . .'

Jude nods. 'Nobody does. I did a profile of missing children last year and . . . anyway, that's not what you want to hear. Would you be up for doing a short piece to camera?'

'What, now?' Sive rubs tears off her cheek.

'Yep, now. We'll go up to ground level for a phone signal. The drama of a live report will get attention. Sounds grubby, but if it helps get more clicks and shares . . .'

'I'll do it.' Sive wipes her eyes with the heel of her hand. 'Whatever it takes.'

*

Ten minutes later, Jude is attempting to upload a short but surprisingly coherent video as Sive watches over her shoulder. Jude senses rather than hears a fresh dissolution into silent sobs. *Dear God.* She bites back her impatience and swivels to look at Sive, eyebrows raised.

'Sorry.' Sive puts her face in her hands. 'It's just that the video makes it feel more serious. Less like Faye's momentarily lost and more like she's a missing person. *Fuck.* I need to get it together.'

'Listen.' Jude puts her hand out to touch Sive's elbow but stops short of making contact. Sive looks up, her face streaked with mascara. 'I mentioned that I did a profile on missing children last year. Abductions by strangers are incredibly rare. Almost all abductions are domestic – the parent who doesn't have custody taking the child from the parent who does.'

A look crosses Sive's face then. For a moment, she's forgotten her tears and is considering something. Jude waits, but Sive doesn't speak.

'So unless you and Aaron are secretly in the middle of a divorce,' Jude continues, 'and he's orchestrated some kind of elaborate kidnap of one of his children, I doubt we're looking at abduction.'

Sive nods. 'OK. OK.'

Reassured, Jude thinks, but not quite one hundred per cent.

'Is there anything you want to tell me?'

'No. Aaron and I are not in the middle of a secret divorce.' A hiccuppy half-sob follows. 'I should check in with him.' Sive taps the screen of her phone and puts it to her ear.

Jude waits, listening in case there's any kind of update, and because she's curious about this relationship – the bolshy, showy barrister and the modest, unpretentious journalist. As far as she knows, they met in court – Sive had been there watching a case Aaron had defended. A case Aaron had lost, Jude remembers, a rarity that stood out amid his trophy cabinet of wins. Some guy who'd got into a fight at his office Christmas party. The employer was a Dutch bank with a small office in Dublin's IFSC and a big, faceless HQ in The Hague, and they'd worked hard to dampen down publicity. So, in the end, nobody was all that interested in the story. Nobody except Sive, apparently, who, pre-kids, used to cover court cases. And look where that particular encounter got her – a handsome if (in Jude's opinion) arrogant husband, a very large house on Ailesbury Road and three beautiful kids. Only, one of them is now missing. Jude tunes back in to Sive's side of the phonecall, but Sive is already disconnecting.

'Nothing.' She shakes her head. 'Aaron's going station to station, searching, and DC Hawthorn wants to meet us at eleven back in Oxford Circus, to regroup. That's our liaison officer.'

'OK.' Jude looks at her watch. 'I'll finish getting the video up and we'll go. Will your husband come too?'

'Yes. Why?'

'It would be good to interview him. I know he's usually quite private about his personal life and his family, so this will be a good opportunity.'

Sive frowns, looking suddenly suspicious, and Jude has to remind herself to work on her sensitivity.

'A good opportunity to get more coverage of your daughter's disappearance, I mean.'

Sive nods and moves towards another commuter, phone outstretched, but the man hurries past, picking up speed to skirt around her.

The video posts successfully and Jude's phone continues to light up with notifications – over four hundred retweets of her earlier photo of Sive already. A dozen DMs telling her she's doing a good job. Another six to say she's capitalizing on another woman's trauma. Jude sighs. This is not how she thought she'd be spending her day. She types a message to her editor.

Video with Sive uploaded, lots of social media done, you have my copy from earlier. Aiming to be back in court for afternoon. Can you get someone to take over from me here? Sive is ... a lot. Bursting into tears etc. Understandable, of course, but send someone ... patient?

She begins moving towards the escalator, still looking at her phone, and turns to check Sive is following. But Sive is standing stock still as crowds surge past, phone pressed to her ear. Jude watches, curious, as Sive's face contorts in response to whoever is on the other end, slipping from hope to shock to wide-eyed terror.

11

10.16 a.m.

SIVE IS TRYING TO process what DC Hawthorn is saying. Words have filtered through the fog. Frozen *backpack. CCTV. St Paul's. A man.* A man holding a child's hand, exiting St Paul's Tube station. A child who looks like Faye and a backpack that looks like Faye's. A man who hasn't phoned the police or turned up at a police station or responded in any way to the calls for help from the public. Jesus Christ. *Why?*

Officers are on their way there now, Hawthorn is saying, and she'll be back in touch as soon as there's news.

'I'm coming too,' Sive says.

'There's no need, we have it in hand,' Hawthorn reassures her. But Sive is not reassured. She doesn't argue, she just disconnects the call and clicks into Google Maps.

'What is it?' Jude asks.

Sive fills her in, her words coming in staccato bursts.

'I'll come with you. It's on the Central Line.' Jude steers her towards the platform and Sive tries to steady her breathing. What does it mean? Who is the man? And . . . is this a positive lead or an even worse nightmare?

*

Without speaking, Sive and Jude take the Tube to St Paul's and emerge from the station blinking in the mid-morning glare. *Now what?* Frantically, Sive scans her surroundings. People everywhere with coffees and phones and laptop bags, but nobody with a small girl. Nobody with a *Frozen* backpack.

She turns to Jude helplessly. 'I . . . I don't know where to go. What do we do?'

'OK, first of all, remember the police are already on it. We're here as extra eyes only. So don't panic. Right?'

Sive nods, though it's not helping. How can she not panic? Across the street, she spots a police officer canvassing passers-by. Two more a little further up the road. And there's a police car at the traffic lights with another a few cars back. She allows herself a small breath.

Jude suggests they comb the streets near the station, fanning outwards. Sive has no better suggestions, so in sticky city heat, that's what they do.

Half an hour passes. A police officer passes, and asks Sive about her own missing child. She hasn't the energy to explain. Jude tells the surprised PC who Sive is and what they're doing, and they carry on their way. Peering into shops, checking inside cafés, rushing around corners. Outwards from the station, road by road, painstaking searching. Painstaking, frantic, futile searching. The streets are full of coffee-wielding workers; bankers and recruiters and marketeers. But there are very few children, and none of them are Faye. Jude pauses at a street corner to light a cigarette. The act feels incongruous to Sive, at odds with the seriousness of the situation.

Jude exhales and turns to Sive.

'There's a park through here.' She jerks her thumb. 'Let's have a quick look.'

In lieu of any other ideas, Sive follows her in.

Inside the park, they stop to take a breath. Weeping willows hang low, blocking midday sun. Bright yellow tulips sway in neatly planted beds. A path meanders through a manicured lawn towards a small, gated playground. But it's empty. Even from here, Sive can see that it's empty. They move towards it anyway, to look in through the black railings. It's tiny. One swing set with two swaying swings. A small slide, rusted on one side. No children playing here. Nobody here at all.

The path continues towards a cluster of trees and on to a pond and, with no better idea of what to do next, Sive starts down the path.

And now she sees it.

Sitting on its own, nestled in the long grass that borders the water, Faye's backpack.

Sive begins to run.

12

SIVE SNATCHES THE BACKPACK from the grass, shouting Faye's name, scanning frantically left and right. Blood pounds in her ears as her eyes go to the pond. Stagnant water glitters quietly under the sun. No ripples. No movement. But shadows. A dark shadow just a few feet in, something under the brown-gold surface of the water. Sive steps forward, her mouth dry. Unable now to call out Faye's name. She's about to step into the water when Jude grabs her arm.

'It's just the tree,' Jude says, pointing. 'The reflection of the tree. It's OK. There's nobody in the water.'

Sive slumps, exhaling, her ears still pounding.

'Is it definitely your daughter's bag?' Jude is asking. 'Couldn't it be someone else's?'

Sive looks down at the backpack in her hands. The picture's the same. Elsa in a white dress. The blue zip, the pink strap, the orange splash. She nods. 'It's . . . it's the same one.'

'Are you sure? There must be hundreds of kids with similar bags?'

As if answering her question, they hear a cough from behind.

'Uh, excuse me? Sorry, that's mine?'

A man emerges from a path a little to Sive's right. Trailing behind him is a girl about Faye's age.

The man steps closer, reaching to take the bag.

'I shouldn't have left it down like that. Sorry.' He smiles and nods towards a small plastic bucket in the little girl's hand. 'We were looking for blackberries.'

Sive doesn't hand over the backpack. The man looks mildly uncomfortable, as though he wants to insist she passes him the bag but can't find a polite way to do so.

'Sive,' Jude says, 'if it's not Faye's, we need to contact the police as quickly as possible to let them know it's a false lead.' She addresses the man. 'The police will want to speak to you, to check if you're the person they saw on CCTV.'

'I'm sorry, what?'

Jude explains briefly, then asks Sive for Hawthorn's phone number. She turns back to the man. 'You'll need to wait here until the police arrive.'

The man nods. 'I . . . Of course.'

The backpack is still in Sive's hand, and the little girl – the little Faye-sized girl – steps forward now to reach for it, wrapping her hand around one of the straps. But Sive holds on. It goes against every grain of common politeness, but there's something nagging at her. Something about the bag. The girl looks puzzled, and now she's speaking, turning to her dad, saying something about the bag, her hand still on the strap, but Sive's not listening. Her eyes roam the surface – the familiar animated characters, the small handle at the top, the blue zip, the pink strap, the orange splash. And suddenly she knows.

13

THE PINK STRAP WITH the orange splash, that's what's niggling. The orange cordial Bea spilled in the hotel. Sive tugs the bag from the little girl's hand and examines the strap more closely. She's not mistaken. It's Faye's bag.

'Where did you get this?' Sive's voice is raised. 'Why do you have my daughter's bag?'

'I don't know,' the man says helplessly. 'I didn't notice it wasn't ours. Eva's just said so now. I . . . I don't understand.'

Jude steps in. 'OK, let's take a minute. This isn't your bag?' She addresses the child, who shakes her head.

'Mine has Elsa in the blue dress,' the little girl explains. 'That one is the white dress. The rest looks the same . . .'

Sive is unzipping the bag, spilling the contents on to the grass. A teddy bear with a toy passport. A hairbrush. A packet of crayons. A tiny notebook. Faye's. All Faye's. She can't speak.

'Where did you get it?' Jude is asking the man. 'Quickly, this is urgent.'

'I . . . I don't know. We left home with Eva's bag. I had snacks packed and a bottle of water. We hadn't opened it yet, though. We were on our way back to have our picnic.'

'You took the Tube here? You got off at St Paul's?'

'Yes.'

'And did you put the bag down at any stage?'

'I don't think so.' The man sounds unsure.

His daughter speaks up. 'I took it off on the train, Daddy. The strap was too tight on me and I put it on the floor. Remember?'

The man clearly doesn't, but he nods. 'Maybe . . .'

'I did. And then I put it back on when we got off the train. I think I took the wrong one.' She looks anxious now, as though aware this is a problem but not entirely sure how. In any other situation, Sive would have reassured her, but she doesn't have it in her.

'Someone switched the bags?' she says to Jude, in a strangled whisper. 'Someone took Faye and switched the bags to confuse things?'

'Or Faye picked up the wrong bag. It doesn't mean someone took her.' But even Jude sounds unconvinced. 'OK, I'm phoning the police.'

14

Three days earlier | Friday
The Meridian Hotel

'I'm phoning a cab!' Aaron called from the living room of the hotel suite.

'Just use an app. Nobody phones any more,' Sive called back from the kids' bedroom, smiling and rolling her eyes at the babysitter.

The babysitter – the one Sive had flatly refused to book – was amazing. She'd arrived in the hotel room at exactly 7.30 p.m. Not late, but also, crucially, not early. She was called Willow, a suitably millennial name, Sive thought, taking in her long, wavy hair and flawless golden skin. Ten minutes in, and she had Faye and Bea eating out of her hand. She'd brought books. Somehow this stranger, this twenty-six-year-old referred by the hotel, had known exactly what kind of books they'd like and exactly how to connect with Sive's two little girls. Even Toby was transfixed, his eyes following Willow as she got Bea a glass of water.

'You'll need to dress Bea for bed, if that's OK,' Sive said to Willow. 'Faye is normally fine on her own, but she fell yesterday and cut her leg on a nail, so she has stitches. She might need help with her pyjama bottoms.' She lowered her voice. 'She's a little self-conscious about it.'

'No problem. I have four younger sisters. I'm very used to dealing with cuts and grazes.' Of course she was. Could they bring her home? Sive wondered. They'd get a *lot* more date nights if they had someone like Willow on call.

Faye tugged at Sive's sleeve. 'Should I look after the treats in case the babysitter wants some?'

'Thanks *so* much for offering, but I'll just let Willow know where they are and she can get them herself.'

Faye bit her lip and whispered in Sive's ear. 'OK, but does she know that I'm allowed to stay up later than Bea, and that I'm actually four years older than her?'

Faye's greatest horror was being treated the same as her baby sister.

'Willow knows everything she needs to know,' Sive reassured her. 'Don't worry.'

'All set?' Aaron asked, sticking his head around the door. He was getting ready in the enviable quiet of their bedroom, while Sive, not yet ready, was heating a bottle in a bowl of hot water.

'Just going to see if Toby will take a bottle,' she said.

'Course he will. If he's hungry, he'll take it.'

'Hmm.' Sive wasn't convinced. Then again, she thought, watching Willow read a story to Bea while simultaneously plaiting Faye's hair, maybe she'd succeed where everyone else had failed. Maybe Sive would get a night out and Aaron would be delighted and they'd both be OK with him being right about booking a babysitter. And sure enough, two minutes later, Toby was in Willow's arms, gazing up at her, sucking contentedly on a bottle.

'Told you so,' Aaron said with a grin as their cab inched through London traffic.

'Yeah, well, I still feel weird leaving the kids with someone we don't know.'

'The hotel vets them.'

'Do they really, though? Aren't they just people they use regularly? It's not like they run police background checks on them.'

'We could ask Dave to do a background check,' quipped Aaron. 'Seriously, though, how is it any different to using a babysitter at home? The hotel knows Willow just as well as you know whatsername. The sister of the girl from Bea's crèche. Now, relax and enjoy the night.'

The cab continued winding its way through busy streets of post-work pint-drinkers relishing evening sun, and Sive continued worrying, her mind flitting from one thing to the next.

The taxi stopped at a red light and Aaron took her hand. 'They'll be absolutely fine for a few hours.'

'I know . . . I just hope Faye's leg isn't sore. I forgot to tell Willow to give her Calpol.'

'Oh yeah,' Aaron said, as if he'd forgotten again that their daughter had stitches. 'Actually, do you have the receipt from Swiftcare and I'll get Garvin to put it through?'

Sive pulled the clinic receipt from her wallet and handed it to Aaron, who photographed it and began typing something on his phone.

'Aaron, you're not sending it now, surely? At eight o'clock on a Friday night? Garvin will have finished work.'

'Garvin never finishes work. And it's only one receipt. If I don't send it now, I'll forget.'

Aaron could, of course, just download the health insurance app himself and submit his own medical claims, Sive thought, as she looked out the cab window. But he consistently claimed his technical expertise was limited to email and text and stubbornly clung to that. It was part of Aaron's brand: floppy-haired super-smart lawyer who can barely send a WhatsApp. An inverse snobbery: too high-brow for tech. In truth, it was sheer laziness. And perhaps if Sive had an assistant like Garvin, she'd never do anything for herself again either.

'He's a saint,' Sive said as Aaron finished sending the receipt. 'I hope you're paying him the big bucks.'

'He asked for a raise, actually. Said he's had to find a nursing home for his mother and it's going to cost a fortune.'

'Well, I'm sorry to hear about his mother, but I'm glad he's getting a raise – he deserves it.'

Aaron shook his head. 'I didn't give it to him.'

Sive's eyebrows shot up.

Aaron lifted his hands. '*What?* You don't just give someone a salary increase because their mother's in a nursing home. What's that got to do with his job?'

'He's been a loyal, hard-working assistant for the last ten years – maybe that's what?'

Aaron picked up her hand and squeezed it. 'You're a big softie and I adore you.'

'So you'll give him the increase?'

A grin. 'Maybe. But don't tell him I said that.'

The others were already in the restaurant when Aaron and Sive arrived. Dave, proudly sporting his new baseball cap, was in the middle of one of his long work stories, punctuating the telling with gulps of whiskey. Scott was necking a bottle of beer, looking flushed and glassy-eyed. Nita was cradling her (completely invisible) bump, and Maggie was cradling a glass of rosé. They'd been seated at a round table and Sive gave silent thanks: everyone could talk to everyone. The polished tabletop gleamed under flickering candles and shining glassware, and in a silver ice bucket at the centre a bottle of champagne sat sweating, waiting patiently for the last arrivals. The two empty chairs were between Maggie and Dave and, feeling only slightly guilty, Sive discreetly nabbed the seat beside Maggie.

Maggie smiled hello and, from across the table, Nita clapped her hands like an excited child.

'Sive! You look fab. I *adore* the pared-back vibe. It takes balls to turn up somewhere like this in a simple black dress. Kudos.'

'Oh. Thank you. Good to see you again. How are you feeling?' Sive asked politely, as she slipped off her blazer.

'*Amazing*,' Nita said, beaming. 'I was so nauseous this morning – did I mention that earlier? Maybe not. I don't like to go on and on about myself. You know how some people are when they're pregnant. All "me, me, me".' She rolled her eyes. 'But I'm feeling *so* good tonight.'

Sive nodded, picking up a menu, conscious the others may be ready to order. 'Sorry to hear you felt ill this morning – nothing worse! Glad you're better tonight, though. My nausea used to last all day. I remember my friends and I used to wonder why they called it morning sickness.'

'Really? How odd.' Nita tilted her head, frowning, sounding as though she thought Sive must have been doing pregnancy wrong.

'It faded around the fourteen-week mark, and you're not far off that now.' Sive glanced at the menu then back at Nita. 'Have you had a twelve-week scan?'

'Oh yes. Last week. It was *amazing*. The most incredible experience. I'm blessed.'

Sive smiled. *Good God*, how was everything so amazing for Nita? She just remembered feeling sick and exhausted.

'That's lovely, Nita,' Maggie said in her gentle way. 'Do you have a scan photo?'

'Of course! This is the one I put up on Insta last week. I'm sure you guys saw it already.' Nita swiped on her phone, then proudly pulled up an ultrasound image and showed it around the table. They oohed and ahed and congratulated her again, and Sive had a chance to read the menu and Scott poured champagne and the night took off in earnest. A waiter took more drink orders, bottles of wine arrived, and they all fell into their roles. Nita basked in her pregnancy glow, proudly placing her hand over her wine glass when the sommelier tried to top it up. Dave began to tell them about a case at work; full of 'I shouldn't really say' and 'I'd be fired if they heard but wait till you hear.' Aaron would moan about it later, Sive knew that. He had a low tolerance for Dave and his long-winded stories, but he was in good form tonight and managed to listen without looking bored. Scott, on the other hand, was getting under Aaron's skin, and Sive couldn't tell if it was intentional. He kept talking about the freedom of his new career in flying and how little he missed his days tied to the office. He was glad, really, that the takeover had happened, he said, even though it was devastating at the time. 'You'll see sense one day,' he said, raising a glass towards Aaron. 'You'll get fed up defending the bad guys.'

'Nah, I'd miss the money,' Aaron said, rubbing his thumb and fingers together.

Sive winced.

Scott raised an eyebrow. 'Lot more money in flying than in law.' He drained his champagne and checked the bottle. Empty. He signalled to order another.

Aaron shook his head. 'For you, maybe. Don't forget I'm a senior counsel. Different league.'

Scott's face reddened as Sive gently nudged Aaron's knee with hers, but he either didn't notice or ignored her.

Aaron smiled. 'I'm *joking*. Relax, Burner. It's a bit of banter.'

Maggie intervened then, her voice a balm. 'How are the kids, Scott?'

'They're OK.' His jaw tightened. 'Actually, they're in Florida. Caron moved there at the start of the summer. It's for a contract with work and she keeps saying it's not permanent ... but bloody hell, how am I supposed to see them?' His colour and his voice rose. 'It's not like I can pop over there every other weekend. She never thinks about anyone except herself.'

Silence as they all took in this piece of news.

'That can't be easy,' Maggie said then, putting her hand on Scott's. 'How are you finding it?'

He pulled his hand away. 'How do you think?'

More silence.

'Sorry, Maggie. I didn't mean to snap. I'm just furious with Caron. And I miss the kids.'

Aaron picked up the bottle of red and tipped the last of its contents into Scott's glass. 'Here, drink that and don't be so maudlin. You were always moaning about the kids when they were here.'

Sive flinched. But to her surprise, Scott just shook his head and threw Aaron a rueful – almost grateful – smile. And for the oddest moment, she envied them – their ability to tear strips off one another but still stay friends. Sive didn't think she had a single person in her life who'd tick that unconditional box.

Aaron held up the empty bottle to ask for another as the waiter began to take their food orders.

'Aren't you going to order in Italian for us, Dave?' Nita asked. She turned to Sive. 'Dave's been learning Italian on Duolingo. He started during lockdown. German, too.' She reached over and patted him on the head. 'Our little scholar.'

Dave grinned. 'I think we'll stick to English, or we might end up with pasta for dessert.'

Everyone laughed, even though it wasn't particularly funny;

glad, Sive thought, to steer the conversation away from Scott's divorce.

'Maggie, darling, I've got something of yours,' Nita said, arriving back from the restaurant bathroom, holding a watch aloft. 'You left it on the side of the basin.'

'Oh, thanks, Nita. I was afraid I'd get it wet when I was washing my hands.' Maggie took the watch and fastened it on her wrist.

Nita shook her head in exasperation as she sat back down. 'It was your phone the last time, and you didn't notice for hours! I know the watch is new, but how does anyone not notice their phone is missing?'

Maggie shrugged.

'Because she doesn't check it fifteen times a minute, like *some* people do,' Scott said. 'Not looking at anyone in particular.' He raised his eyebrows at Nita, who was, at that moment, scrolling through her phone.

'I have my public to think of,' Nita said archly, and they all laughed, Nita too. Sive smiled. She was part of Nita's 'public' – one of her 46,000 Instagram followers. She knew all about Nita's busy job, expensive handbags, glorious holidays and marble floors, through @NitaGsWorld. She also knew all about Nita's IUI journey, and it was on Instagram Live that she'd heard about Nita's pregnancy. Aaron thought the whole thing was preposterous – who used social media to tell their friends about a pregnancy? But Aaron didn't use social media for anything at all, so his reaction wasn't surprising. He was sniffy about it, categorizing it in the same space he put soap operas and women's magazines, though he wasn't averse to peeking over Sive's shoulder every now and then when she was looking at Facebook. He was baffled by Nita's account, of course. Why did 46,000 people want to know what a very normal non-celebrity person like Nita was doing? She was a lawyer, for God's sake, not a pop star. You didn't have to be a pop star to be famous on social media, Sive had patiently explained, that was the beauty of it – anyone could build a following if their content was interesting or beautiful. Nita's IUI journey was the icing on her Instagram cake – people who couldn't imagine going it alone lapped up her story in droves and clicks and likes. And Nita thrived on it.

Now, with a self-effacing smile, she put her phone face-down beside her water glass.

'See? Even I can take a night off.'

And for a while, the conversation surfed through safe topics – travel, books, films and careers. Dave told another work story, this time about an identity theft, and went as far as taking out a notebook to check some details. This led to uproarious laughter from everyone else and affectionate jibes about Sherlock Holmes and Jessica Fletcher. Scott and Aaron reminisced about their early days working as interns, groaning about a boss they hated, their earlier sniping all now forgotten. The food arrived, and conversation lulled momentarily until Scott noticed Nita's order.

'You're eating *prawns*?' he said, doing a double-take at the sizzling dish that was set down in front of her. Sive had wondered about it too, when Nita put in her order, but didn't like to comment. And maybe the exhausting non-exhaustive list of what you could and couldn't eat in pregnancy was different in the UK. It had changed between Faye and Bea, and again between Bea and Toby, and by the end, she could never remember which shellfish or blue cheese was in or out of favour.

'It's not *me* who doesn't like prawns,' Nita said simply. 'You're mixing me up.'

'No, I mean because—' Scott started to say, but Dave stepped in.

'Scott, it was Yasmin who hated prawns,' he said softly.

A hush fell across the table. The only sound was the clink of Nita's fork against her dish.

'It's OK, you know,' she said eventually. 'We can talk about her.'

Maggie nodded but didn't say anything. Dave was looking down at his plate, and Sive couldn't be sure, but she thought he might have welled up. Aaron cleared his throat and looked around but, like Maggie, he didn't seem to know what to say. Scott busied himself with his drink.

'It's the anniversary on Monday, and we *should* talk about her,' Nita continued. 'She'd want that. She'd have hated this silence every time her name is mentioned. You know Yasmin. Always the centre of attention.'

'Well, that's true . . .' Scott said tentatively, with a raised-eyebrow glance at the others. And then he grinned. 'Remember her "signature tune", as she called it – belting out "Killing Me Softly" every time she saw a karaoke machine?'

Nita laughed. 'And she was a dreadful singer. Absolutely appalling.' And now they all laughed as the tension lifted.

'Remember that godawful sheepskin jacket she used to wear – the one she got in the charity shop in Covent Garden?' Scott said, warming to his role as ice-breaker.

'Or "thrift store", as she called it, because that sounded so much better.' That was Aaron. Sive turned to look at him, curious now. She had almost never heard him speak about Yasmin. It wasn't a subject she ever broached either, having realized very early in their relationship that he didn't like talking about it.

'That's right, I'd forgotten!' Maggie said, her fingers running lightly over a tattoo of two suns on her inner wrist. The tattoos fascinated Sive – Maggie didn't seem like a tattoo person. 'She loved her vintage,' she went on, and turned to Nita. 'Unlike you with your designer dresses. People could never get over the difference between you two, remember? You looked so alike and yet you were polar opposites.'

'Oh, really?' Sive said, for something to say; a benign way to take part in a tricky conversation in which she was the clear outsider – though she was interested, too, in this girl her husband had wanted to marry.

'Oh, yes,' Nita said. 'I was exactly like I am now – I loved my Moschino shirts and Marc Jacobs bags and—'

'Oh God, don't mention Moschino-shirt-gate,' Scott said, making a face at Dave.

Nita carried on as though he hadn't spoken. '—and my heels and my make-up, even back then. And Yasmin . . . well, Yasmin thought it was all a big con.'

'It *is* a big con,' Scott quipped, 'and you're still falling for it.'

'Says the man whose wife had a bi-weekly spa day,' Nita shot back, though not unkindly.

'Ex-wife,' Aaron corrected, and Scott threw him a look.

'I'd love to hear more,' Sive said, steering the conversation back on track. 'What was she like?'

'She bought her clothes second-hand when she could – she liked vintage style. Big into boho chic, like a brunette Sienna Miller,' Nita explained.

'Stuff *you* wouldn't be caught dead in,' Scott said with a braying laugh. Nita's eyes fell and, again, the group grew silent at Scott's ill-chosen words.

'Shit, sorry, I shouldn't have said that.'

'It's fine.' Nita looked up again. 'It's actually fine. We need to be able to talk about it, the bad bits as well as the good bits. Otherwise everyone is too afraid of saying the wrong thing and we never mention her at all. She was my sister, my opposite in every way, my only family in the world, I loved her, she died.' Nita straightened the knife on the tablecloth. 'I take that last bit back. It wasn't a passive event. Someone killed her.' She looked around at the group. 'And someday, I'll work out who did.'

15

'HELLO? NITA? YES, IT's Sive. Yes. I know, it's . . . Thanks for calling, but I'd better keep the line free. My mum was just on, too, and I need to . . . I know. Yes, but things have taken a turn for the worse and I'd really better go . . .'

Jude can only hear Sive's side of the conversation, but she looks anxious and distracted. Or rather, even more anxious and distracted. They've just arrived back in Oxford Circus station, having waited in the park with the man and his daughter until officers arrived to interview them. Sive had wanted to keep Faye's backpack, but the police had taken it. It was evidence now, of course, though they weren't sure that any crime had been committed. Everyone – the police, Jude, the man in the park – had been at great pains to reassure Sive on this front: the discovery of the backpack doesn't mean Faye's been kidnapped, it just means the little girl, Eva, picked up the wrong bag.

Now, Jude lingers while Sive tries to get this Nita person off the phone, far more politely than Jude would, under the circumstances. She looks around while she waits, and a little way along towards the ticket barriers she recognizes Aaron Sullivan, talking to a police officer. He towers over her, leaning in, gesticulating. She has her back to a pillar, and with nowhere to go and Aaron all over her personal space, it must be intimidating, Jude thinks. But the officer seems to be holding her ground.

Sive is still trying to wind up the call. 'Oh, OK. If you're sure. Oxford Circus. Which entrance? Um . . . I'll send you a pin. OK, thanks, Nita. Bye.' She closes her eyes briefly and slips the phone back into her pocket. A group of teens rush past, jostling Sive, but she doesn't seem to register it.

'Someone coming to help?' Jude asks.

'Aaron's friend Nita. She's a few minutes away in a cab. People are so kind.' A pause. 'Shit, I should probably have asked her to mind the kids instead . . .'

'Do you need someone to take over babysitting?' *Please don't ask me to do it*, Jude adds, but only to herself. It's not just because she has no idea what to do with children, but also because she's of much better use here on the search. And as long as this isn't actually a kidnap, she's still hoping to get back to Court 5.

'No, Scott can stay. I'm just not sure if Nita will be much help. She's not the most— Well, anyway, she's on her way. She tried Aaron's phone but got no answer.'

'He's there,' Jude says, pointing ahead through the crowds.

Sive frowns. 'You know Aaron?'

'I covered the first hearing in the Brosnan case. I met him then. But I remember him from lots of cases over the years, even when I was just starting out. You met him on the Dunner Bank employee case, right – that guy who killed another guy at the office party – Aaron was his barrister?'

Sive's cheeks pinken. Jude smiles inwardly. She's not above mixing business and pleasure herself, though she's never gone as far as marrying anyone.

'What was his name again, the guy who got done for manslaughter?' she asks now, steering the conversation away from the seemingly awkward mixing-business-with-pleasure part. *See, Mam, I can be sensitive*, she says in her head.

'Joost De Witte.' Sive pronounces it 'Yoost de Vitta'.

'That's right, I remember now. He got eight years, didn't he? One of Aaron's rare losses.' Sive's face is inscrutable and Jude realizes belatedly that talking about her husband's career-fails probably isn't appropriate or useful right now. *Well, that bout of sensitivity didn't last long*, says her mother's voice. *Touché*.

'Anyway' – Jude nods towards Aaron – 'I think half the popu- lation of Ireland knows your husband.'

'Well, maybe just in law and media circles.' Sive shakes herself then, as though for just the tiniest moment she's forgotten why they're here. 'Jesus Christ.' She looks around at the milling crowds. 'Where *is* she? How has nobody noticed a six-year-old child on her own?'

And this is precisely what Aaron is saying to the police officer when they join them moments later at a broad pillar beside the ticket barriers.

'With all the resources you have to hand, how has nobody found our daughter?' His tone is brusque. Angry. Jude supposes she would be brusque and angry too, if her child was missing.

'Mr Sullivan, we are doing everything we can. This new infor- mation about the backpack is helpful – we're rechecking CCTV now for a bag matching the other child's, on the assumption Faye took it by accident.'

Sive speaks then, so quietly Jude can barely hear her. 'DC Hawthorn, I can't imagine her taking the wrong bag. She loves that backpack . . . I'm terrified it means someone took her. That they switched the bag on purpose to send the police in the wrong direction.'

The detective nods. 'I appreciate the point, and it's something we do need to take into consideration. Which is why' – she pauses to take in a breath – 'we need to talk about what to do if there's contact.'

Sive's brow creases in confusion. 'Contact?'

'I realize this is difficult, but if someone gets in touch with you to say they have Faye, you *must* let us know immediately. No matter what they say about not telling the police, regardless of any threats.'

Sive nods, her face wan under the overhead lights.

Hawthorn continues. 'And I need you to stay above ground, in case someone tries to call you, or at least come up regularly if you're searching the platforms. Phone coverage is almost non-existent down there. We'd also like to do a press conference and get the message out to an even wider public. Would you be open to that?'

'Of course,' Aaron says. 'Some journalists approached me already this morning – I'm happy to talk to anyone to get the word out.'

'Good, we'll use a small function room at a hotel a minute or so down the street. I thought you might prefer that to the police station, as it's nearer.'

The Sullivans nod in agreement.

'OK. It's provisionally booked for one o'clock. I also need you to sit down with two of our detectives to answer some questions, in light of the backpack situation.'

'Questions?' Aaron looks puzzled, but Jude can't help thinking he's being deliberately obtuse. He must know they'll have questions if there's even the smallest chance of foul play.

'In the unlikely event of an abduction, we need to know if anyone has a reason to target you. If any relatives would be likely to take your child, any family disagreements, work-related disputes, and so on.' Hawthorn sees Aaron shaking his head and she holds up a placatory hand. 'Of course, I realize it's all very improbable, but it's our job to ask these questions. I've arranged to use a supervisor's office here in the station.' She looks at her watch. 'That'll be in about twenty minutes?'

Sive nods, mute. Aaron turns to pull her closer. Noticing Jude for the first time, he looks quizzically at Sive.

'Oh. This is Jude, a colleague from the paper. She's living here now, but she's from Longford originally. She's helping with the search.'

Aaron looks Jude up and down. 'Good to meet you,' he says mechanically, turning back to the police officer.

'We met at the Brosnan hearing,' Jude says.

Aaron turns back to her now, a guarded expression on his face. 'Did we.'

'Can I ask, have Brosnan or any of his old comrades-turned-enemies been in touch while you've been here?'

'Christ, this is hardly the time to be fishing for stories. Are you serious?'

Even Sive looks shocked, and Jude backpedals.

'No, I'm not fishing for stories. But I'm wondering if there's any—' She stops. 'Forget I said anything. I'm just here to help in any way I can.'

'Great.' The police officer intervenes, stepping forward. 'I'm DC Hawthorn. I missed your name?'

'Jude Barr, from the *Daily Byte* newspaper.'

DC Hawthorn looks as cynical as Aaron. 'You're welcome to help with the search and to join the press conference at one o'clock.' *No special treatment* is the unspoken message.

'Thanks. I was wondering, the guy who brought Bea to staff here – Tim, right?'

DC Hawthorn nods.

'Would you have a surname for him?' Jude asks, but DC Hawthorn is on her radio now and hasn't heard. Aaron has, though.

'Hang on a sec. Are you trying to scoop an interview with him?'

'No,' Jude says. 'I'm curious about something in his story that didn't make sense. It's probably nothing.'

'Tim Brassil,' Sive says quietly. 'That's his name. What was it that didn't make sense?'

'Just a tiny detail, probably nothing . . .' Jude is typing the name into her Notes app when suddenly a petite woman with long brown hair and sky-high heels pushes through a group of Italian tourists and flings herself on Sive.

'Oh my *God*, Sive. Aaron. I'm so sorry. What can I do?'

'Thanks, Nita. There's a press conference at one, and until then we'll keep searching.' Sive extracts herself gently from Nita's hug. 'I still can't believe this is happening.'

'I'm sorry I'm so late. I slept in. Missed the race.' Nita's eyes dart to Aaron and then to his wife, and Jude is almost certain she sees a look pass between Nita and Sive. An unspoken question from Nita, and a tiny headshake from Sive. *What's that about?* Jude wonders.

Nita is still talking. 'I'd have been here much sooner if I'd known. I picked up my phone and almost *died* when I saw.' She turns from Sive now and grasps Aaron's hand in hers.

Jude appraises the new arrival. She's remarkably pretty, with beautifully groomed hair and beautifully set make-up, but there are dark circles beneath her eyes and she looks like she's been crying. Something to do with Faye, or something else altogether? Jude's attention is pulled away from the new arrival by a text from her editor: she's got someone who can step in now, so Jude can go back to the court case. She types a reply.

I'm fine to stay here actually, no need. Not clear yet but small chance it's an abduction. Big story if it is. And no other journalists with Sullivans right now.

A reply comes through immediately:

You told me you wanted back on the court case and I've gone out of my way to get cover. He's literally on the way there.

Jude bites her lip and types again.

I'm best placed to get the most out of the Sullivans. Sive trusts me.

Another reply.

Your replacement is also very good at what he does and I've called in a favour to get him there. Not cool, Jude. Back to the courtroom now, please.

Fuck. Jude looks over at the Sullivans. If it's an abduction, this will be huge. Career-making. And she's right here. She really, really needs to stay on this.

Sive has promised me an exclusive interview.

It's not *quite* accurate, but Sive did say she could use whatever she wants without having to ask. *About a photo, which is not the same as an exclusive interview,* says a little voice in her head. Jude ignores it.

After? That could be days away. She could change her mind. The story could be over. A non-story if the kid's just sitting in some station waiting for her mum.

No, not after. Now. For the piece I'm writing today. Sive said I can quote her on anything she's said to me while we search, so effectively an interview.

Jude squirms at the half-truth.

OK then. This better be good. File copy by 5 p.m., OK? I need it
online by teatime.

Will do. She checks her watch. Just gone half eleven. That gives
her plenty of time. And Sive is so caught up in finding Faye she's
hardly going to know or care that she's inadvertently given Jude
an interview of sorts. And all of it helps with spreading the
word, which is basically what she's here for. She goes back to
searching online for Bea's white knight, one Tim Brassil and his
not-quite-right story.

16

AARON ACCEPTS NITA'S HUG, watching over her shoulder as Jude types something into her phone, all cool and important in her high ponytail and her high-heeled boots. What is she doing? Trying to interview this guy Tim, who found Bea? Journalists are all the same, he thinks, forgetting, momentarily, that he's married to one. He looks at Sive now, and her expression breaks his heart. Suddenly, it's terrifyingly clear that Sive won't survive if they don't find Faye. He extracts himself from Nita and takes Sive's hand.

'The entire city is looking out for her,' he promises. 'We'll find her.'

'Yes,' agrees Nita. 'Her picture is *everywhere*. Her little pink denim jacket and her lovely blonde hair. I put it on my Insta, obvi, and everyone said they'll look out for her. Now, what can I do?'

Aaron has no idea. And he knows Nita is doing her best, but they need people who'll tell them what they're going to do, not people who wait to be told.

Over the PA system, a voice announces a delay and, beside them, a man slaps a newspaper against his leg, muttering about an incident on the tracks.

Aaron and Sive look at each other and Aaron knows they're both thinking the same thing.

'What if—' Sive starts.

He cuts her off and pulls her into a hug. 'Don't go there.'

Nita clears her throat. 'So . . . shall I call Maggie? Bring you a cup of tea?' She looks around, as though not quite sure where one might source a cup of tea. Nita does not travel by Tube.

'I haven't been able to reach Maggie at all,' Sive says.

'I don't suppose she's still waiting for you at the Rooftop Bar?' Aaron asks.

'No, she'd have seen my calls. And surely she'd have seen the alerts on social media.'

Aaron's phone vibrates and he glances down.

'Anything?' Sive's voice is hoarse with hope.

'No. It's just Carmen Brosnan again, Pete's wife. She knows I'm away. And surely by now she's seen that Faye is missing.' He declines the call with an angry swipe of his thumb. Jude looks up.

'Did you say that was Pete Brosnan's wife?' she asks.

'I was having a conversation with my wife.'

'Aaron,' Sive says softly. 'Jude's trying to help.'

'That's fine, but Faye's disappearance has nothing to do with my court case.' And more quietly, just to Sive: 'I don't trust her.'

'Stop.' She pulls him a little bit away from Nita and Jude, moving towards a bank of ticket machines. A man rushes past, accidentally elbowing Aaron as he barrels towards the machines, but Aaron scarcely notices.

'Come on, Sive. You know as well as I do, you have to watch everything you say around someone like her. Before you know it, she'll be concocting some tabloid headline suggesting my job is linked to what's happened, just to get clicks.'

'It couldn't be, could it? Linked to your Brosnan case?' Her voice is so low Aaron can hardly make out what she's saying. He leans closer. Jude is just a few steps away, pretending she's not trying to listen. Nita is recording herself on her phone. 'Those people Brosnan used to work for,' Sive continues. 'The Callans. They're ruthless.'

'Yes, but—'

'What if they're trying to frighten you off?'

Aaron shakes his head. Sive's been watching too much TV. Brosnan's former bosses aren't afraid to target one of their own, but they're not going to come after a high-profile lawyer.

'They wouldn't, I promise.' He brushes hair from her brow, her skin sticky in the stifling Underground heat. 'That's not how it works.'

She swipes his hand away. 'Just because something hasn't happened before doesn't make it impossible. Aaron, they kill people for a living! You think you're bulletproof, but you're not.'

Aaron steps back. 'Fine. Let's follow that train of thought for a moment. Even if they did try to scare me off, someone else would take the case.'

'Maybe they're not trying to get you to drop it. Just to lose. Deliberately.'

Aaron bristles. 'Do you honestly think I'd do that?'

'Not normally, obviously, but if Faye was taken ... Well, you'd do anything to get her back.' She reaches for his hand. Despite the heat, her fingers are cold as they wrap around his.

'OK, but nobody could have known you'd be in Bond Street at exactly that moment this morning, or that Faye and Bea would get the Tube ahead of you. Right?'

Nodding now, she sags against him. He's right. He knows he's right. Nevertheless, when Sive moves away to point Nita in the direction of the promised tea, Aaron steps out of earshot to call his PA. If anyone can do some digging, Garvin can. He's a bloodhound. A genius with tech and brilliant at research. If the Callans have any history of abducting or harming children, Garvin will find it.

17

12.01 p.m.

THEY'RE IN SOME KIND of office. A train station office, full of papers and files. They're sitting at a broad desk with a thin crack running from one side to the other. Opposite them are two police officers. The usual occupant of this office is nowhere to be seen. It's all a blur; this place, this windowless room, this interview. Sive is outside her own body, watching the couple at the desk as they sit, hands clenched, waiting for questions they hope will make sense of everything. Clinging on for dear life.

One of the two BTP officers clears his throat. 'Now, Mr and Mrs Sullivan, I understand you've already given my colleague DC Hawthorn much of this information, but I need to go through it again. Anything you can tell me, no matter how minor, could help find your daughter.' He's a man in his fifties with bushy eyebrows and serious eyes. Sive can't remember his name. 'I'll start by asking you about your job, Mr Sullivan. I understand you're—'

'Wait,' Sive says. 'Shouldn't we be talking about what Bea said, now that we' – she stops to gather herself, exhaling slowly – 'now that we think there's even a small chance someone has Faye?'

The police officer looks confused. 'What *who* said?'

'Bea, our two-year-old. When we asked her where Faye was,

she said, "Chase on train." It didn't make a lot of sense and we couldn't get anything else from her. But now that we know the backpacks may have been switched . . . well, maybe it means someone frightened her and chased her and caught up with her?' She takes a shuddery breath.

The police officer is scribbling notes.

'Hold on, didn't you know about this?' Aaron asks, pulling himself up straight in the chair.

The officer's expression is composed. 'It's all in the notes, sir, don't worry. And now that things have taken a new direction, we'll focus on relevant details.' He turns to Sive. 'Can you shed any further light on your younger daughter's comment? Has she elaborated?'

Elaborated! She's two! Sive wants to scream. But that won't help. 'No, she doesn't have many words yet.'

The younger police officer speaks now, her voice sounding older than her appearance suggests. 'Mrs Sullivan, I have a two-year-old daughter. And sometimes she says things that are very factual. And sometimes she means something else entirely. And sometimes she makes things up. With that in mind, what do you think Bea meant? Could it have been anything other than literal?'

'Well, yes. If Faye was running, just for fun, Bea might use the word "chase" – she wouldn't necessarily mean that someone was literally chasing Faye.' Sive can't decide if this is good or bad. If Bea's words are literal, it's useful. But also, terrifying.

'Good, that helps. We don't want to focus too much on it if it may not be a true description of events. Would Faye run for fun, as you say, in that kind of situation? Having lost sight of you?'

'She might,' Sive concedes. 'She goes off exploring. She has no fear. She wouldn't have been particularly worried about being on her own. Whereas Bea would be anxious if she lost sight of me.'

'Which is why the young man on the Tube found Bea when he looked around, but not Faye – she had already run off, I expect.' The officer chews her pen for a moment. 'OK. We'll keep Bea's comment in mind but won't assume anyone was chasing Faye for now.' She looks at her watch and nods for her male colleague to resume.

'Right. Back to you, Mr Sullivan.' He has an air of someone who has been interrupted unnecessarily. 'I understand you're a barrister? And you're currently representing a client with links to organized crime?'

'Yes. But, as I've said, that has nothing to do with this.'

'If you wouldn't mind, sir, giving me the details anyway.'

And so Aaron does, stressing again that even if someone wanted him off the case, they couldn't have known that Sive and the kids would be in Bond Street Tube station at that precise moment. Or that Faye and Bea would be on the Tube unattended.

Unattended. Sive shudders. Like lost luggage. Only not lost luggage. Human children. Her *daughters*. And one is missing, and it's down to her. If only she hadn't told them to run ahead. If only she hadn't looked at her phone. If only she'd brought the sling instead of the pram.

'Mrs Sullivan?'

Sive realizes it's not the first time the officer has called her name.

'Sorry. Yes.'

'Can you tell me about everyone you've encountered over the course of your trip to London? Let's work back from this morning. Can you talk me through what you did?'

'Aaron left early to take part in a race and I brought the kids down to breakfast and left for the station just after eight. We didn't speak to anyone other than hotel staff. I was supposed to meet one of Aaron's friends while he was at the race.'

'Tell me about the friends you're here with – a reunion, you said?' This question is directed at Aaron, who tells them exactly what he told Hawthorn earlier. He tells them too about Willow the babysitter – someone Sive has forgotten until now – and they write down her details.

'Right. Any financial problems? Debts? Do you own your own house?'

Aaron's reply is terse. 'No financial problems. We own our house. Well, we have a mortgage, obviously, but no money problems.'

'Any disputes within your respective families? Estranged grandparents, family feuds, that kind of thing? Sometimes we see grandparents who aren't allowed access to kids taking things into their own hands.'

'No. Our parents adore the kids.' Clipped. Indignant. 'There are no estranged family members.'

Sive touches his arm. 'Aaron.'

He looks at her. She nods a silent instruction. *You need to tell them everything.*

'That's not relevant, Sive, for obvious reasons.'

'It's better if they know. Just tell them,' she says softly. Wearily.

And so he tells them the secret they've never told anyone, at least not until last night. The 'origin story', as Aaron calls it at home, in case little ears hear. How odd that the first people to know this are not family but a London friend and two strangers in a train station. Will everyone know soon? It doesn't matter. Right now, Sive just feels relieved. None of it helps, not really. But it's better to be sitting here speaking to these police officers, pretending to themselves they're providing useful information, than to be back out there, standing uselessly in the ticket hall. She looks at her watch. Twelve thirty-two in the afternoon. Faye's been gone for four hours. Sive closes her eyes and silently begs to wake up, to find it's all a dream; that she's still in their nice hotel in London at a reunion with Aaron's old friends.

18

Giumbini

AARON'S FRIENDS SAT IN silence, their eyes dipped to their plates, as Nita's words reverberated in Sive's ears.

She was killed.

As far as Sive knew, Nita's sister Yasmin had died in a house fire. A terrible tragedy that was nobody's fault. Aaron didn't like to talk about it, and she'd never pushed him for details – never known if it was faulty wiring in the old terraced house or an overheated charger or fairy lights left on too long.

Eventually, Scott spoke up. 'I know it's hard, Nita, especially with the anniversary, and we all need someone to blame when bad things happen. But Yasmin's death was an accident.'

Nita shook her head. 'He killed her.'

Now Sive was truly confused. She busied herself with her rib-eye, carefully cutting it into tiny pieces. Who did Nita think had killed Yasmin? But nobody asked the question. Meaning, she realized, they already knew the answer.

'The police never found any evidence of a stalker, or any evidence that the fire was set deliberately,' Scott said.

A stalker? Sive put down her knife and fork. Good God, how had Aaron never mentioned this? She glanced sideways at her husband, without moving her head. His eyes were on Nita. His expression unreadable.

'Aaron knows.' Nita pointed across the table with her fork. 'Maybe we're the only two who really believed in him, but that doesn't mean he didn't exist.'

Sive looked directly at her husband now, as he sat quietly for a moment, as though carefully choosing his words.

'I don't know if it had anything to do with the fire,' he said slowly, 'but I do know she thought someone was following her. And I know she was terrified.'

Sive shifted in her seat, baffled and intrigued, noting his carefully chosen words: 'she thought someone was following her'. Did he really think there had been a stalker or was he placating Nita?

Nita shook her head impatiently. 'It's too much of a coincidence. That she had a stalker and someone set fire to her house, but it turns out it wasn't the stalker? *Come on.*'

Dave, who had said nothing until now, put his hand on Nita's. He looked like he was about to cry.

'Don't say that, Nita. It's too awful.'

'It's awful, but that doesn't mean it didn't happen. The world isn't the rosy place you like to think it is.' She looked around at her friends. 'I'm right, I know I am. The fire wasn't an accident. And don't forget the neighbour who spotted that thug Michael Rosco in the area that night – he was well known for using arson as a means of intimidation.'

Sive felt her eyes widen. *Arson and intimidation?*

'Which is it, though?' Scott asked, tapping his vape on the table, like a judge calling order. 'A moment ago you were adamant it was a stalker; now you're saying it might have been some gangster who had absolutely no links to Yasmin.' He looked over at Sive. 'Michael Rosco was a well-known career criminal. Still is, actually. But' – he turned back to Nita – 'Yasmin was an art teacher. Why would anyone go after her?'

Before Nita could answer, Aaron began to speak, his tone patient. 'Nita, that neighbour who claimed she saw Rosco was full of it. She just wanted in on the action. How would she even know what Michael Rosco looked like? She was gagging for attention, that's all. And she'd seen something in the paper about Rosco and a fire he set in an industrial estate and she put two and two together and came up with ten.'

'Exactly what I said just now,' Scott chimed in. 'Why would Rosco want anything with Yasmin?'

Nita folded her arms and glared at the two men. 'I don't know. But Yasmin definitely had a stalker and the neighbour was adamant she saw this Rosco man, and it all seems too much to be a coincidence.'

'Isn't it time to let go, Nita?' Scott said now, and although Sive was sure he hadn't meant to sound patronizing, he did. 'With new life coming into the world?'

Nita frowned. 'What?'

'Fresh starts and all that. Lines in the sand to go with the lines on the pregnancy test.' Scott looked delighted with this play on words.

Silence fell again and Sive had the impression the old friends were waiting for Nita to give the green light for the night to continue. For conversation to revert to gentrification and crypto and food. Nita stared around at them, saying nothing, and in the end it was Sive's phone, ringing loudly and abruptly, that saved the day.

'Oh, sorry.' She looked at the screen. 'It's the babysitter. I'll have to answer.'

The others waved her apologies away. They'd all answer a call from a babysitter was the unspoken message, especially a stranger-in-a-hotel babysitter.

Sive tilted her body away from the table and put her hand up to her ear to hear better, asking Willow if everything was OK.

Everything was fine, Willow said, Faye just wanted to say goodnight. Sive spoke to her daughter then turned back to the table to find that the phonecall had done the trick – broken the tension and allowed the conversation to move on to safer topics.

'How is your babysitter?' Nita asked.

'All fine. I can relax now.' Sive picked up her glass of wine and took a sip.

'I can't imagine leaving mine with a babysitter. And certainly not someone I hardly know at all. You're so *brave*, Sive.'

'Ah look, I used to know a whole heap of things I wasn't going to do as a parent. TV. Soothers. McDonald's. Sugar. Bribes.' Sive took an even bigger swallow of wine and shrugged at Nita. 'And then I had kids.'

19

FOUR AND A HALF hours. That's how long it's been, and Sive can't bear it. She can't speak. She can't think. She can't breathe. She'd give anything. Anything for someone to say, *I've got her! She's here! She was hiding under a bench*. This isn't helping, and she knows it's not helping, but she can't think straight and she can't be strong and she can't do anything. And they want her to do a press conference. They've asked her to leave the Tube station and walk to this hotel and speak words about her daughter. Her chest is too tight. Her words are gone.

Jude is at her elbow, propelling her forward towards a long table behind which DC Hawthorn stands. Aaron is at her other side, pale and sombre. Reporters turn their way. Cameras click. She stares straight ahead, as the table and DC Hawthorn blur and dissolve.

'Now,' Jude says, curt and businesslike, 'it's OK to cry during the press conference. In fact, it's a good idea, it's what people expect, and if you don't cry or seem sufficiently worried, the public can turn on you like *that*.' She snaps her fingers. 'But make sure you get a few coherent words out, too. Connect with the viewers. There's something about mothers, you know? Even more than fathers. It'll get people's attention.'

It might, but will it help find Faye? How many times has Sive seen a 'missing' post on social media and retweeted it but then forgotten all about it? Has she ever actually looked out for the missing person? People will hear her speak and shake their heads and maybe even well up a bit, but then they'll switch off to get on with their lives.

Now they're behind the table, sitting on cushioned chairs. At the back of the room, the doors swing open and shut as more reporters arrive. Curious faces peer through the gaps in the opaque glass walls – hotel guests wondering about the small gathering of press and the two devastated parents. Hawthorn is speaking. Aaron grips Sive's hand. They've agreed that she'll talk, but if she can't manage, he'll take over. Hawthorn gestures. It's her turn. She faces the cameras. Jesus Christ, how is she going to do this? She closes her eyes, summoning up Faye. Her beautiful, energetic, cheery, chatty first-born child. Lost and alone and afraid. She opens her eyes.

'Faye is six and has shoulder-length blonde hair and blue eyes. She's wearing a pink denim jacket. She has a *Frozen* backpack. She loves *Frozen*. But not the original movie; she's very firm in her preference for the sequel.' A small laugh from the gathered press. 'She loves Maltesers and hot chocolate and books. She desperately wants a puppy and to try bubblegum ice-cream. I promised her she could while we were here.' Her voice cracks, but she keeps going. 'She's not from here, so she doesn't know the city and she won't know how to find her way back to me.' She swallows. Just a few more seconds. *Hold it together*. 'So if you're watching this, please, please, look out for her. Please keep us in your head when you're out today. Please look around. Look down. She's small. You might not see her. But please look out, because I need her back.'

That's all she can do. Her face is in her hands and Aaron's arm is on her shoulders and Hawthorn is standing up saying something about questions. Sive can't hear the questions. It's as though the effort to speak has used up everything she had left. None of her senses are working. But nobody asks her anything. Hawthorn is the only one speaking. Some words filter through. Eight thirty. Six minutes. Two girls. Every stop. No sign.

No sign.

20

JUDE WATCHES SIVE PUT her head in her hands and Aaron's arm go around her. The questions the press ask are fairly standard – details around times and locations. Then the inevitable 'Is foul play suspected?' from a short man near the front. Sive buries her head deeper, and Aaron pulls her closer. It's a valid question, and if Jude didn't already know all the details, she would have asked it herself. Hawthorn gives a standard, formal response about lines of inquiry and no reason to suspect and open minds and critical points. But it's been almost five hours now and it's hard to imagine any child going unnoticed for so long.

Jude steps out to the hotel corridor to make some notes for the piece she's writing and finds Aaron's friend Nita standing there, craning her neck to see in. In one hand she's holding her phone and in the other a cardboard tray with three takeaway teas that have somehow taken her over an hour to source. On second glance, Jude realizes that Nita's filming the press conference through the glass. *Classy*, Jude thinks, and prepares to tweet her own press conference photo, with no sense of irony at all.

Nita looks at her now, her face lighting up in recognition, and again Jude notices the redness around her eyes and the shadows beneath which even expertly applied concealer fails to hide.

'Oh, hello!' Nita stops filming. 'I was told they were here and I came all this way to bring the teas and then I was informed by some press officer person I can't go in!' Her words reek of indignation. 'And now these miserable cups of dishwater will be cold. Anyway, not my fault. So, you're Sive's journalist friend?'

Jude nods.

'From Ireland too?'

'Yep, but I live here now.'

'Do you! How nice. My neighbour's Irish. Working here forty years and still sounds like he's from deepest Limerick. Spends all his spare time in the Blarney Stone pub. Do you know it?'

'No . . . but I don't go to Irish pubs.'

'Oh, really! You don't like them?'

Jude feels an uncharacteristic need to elaborate.

'Well, I didn't want to move over here and just hang out with other expats. I want to focus on my career, meet new people . . .'

'Hmm, not easy to move country and meet new people at your age, I'd imagine,' Nita says, as though Jude is geriatric. She smiles, flashing dazzling teeth. 'Don't mind me. No doubt you've made plenty of friends.'

'I . . . yes.' Jude flushes. If the woman who cuts her hair counts as a friend.

'And your colleagues, in your newspaper office, of course. A ready-made social life.'

'Yeah . . . I work from my flat.'

Nita tilts her head and, for a second, Jude glimpses what looks like pity, as though this vacuous woman can somehow tell that Jude spends every night and every weekend home alone, hunched over her laptop.

'I'm out a lot, covering stories, interviewing people,' she adds quickly, irritated now, perhaps more at her own defensiveness than anything Nita has said. 'Like here, today.'

'Well, if you're looking for people to interview, I'd be more than happy to make time for you.' Nita tucks a long, glossy strand behind her ear. 'I've known Aaron twenty years. We used to live together. He was engaged to my sister. We were all very close. *Very.*'

Jude nods noncommittally. What is it with humans and their desire to get in on the action? As soon as anything happens, there's a rush from the public to profess how close they were to the victim. *My cousin's neighbour's sister went to school with that man who died.* WhatsApp groups up and down the country awash with virtual rubbernecking.

'We still are. Close, that is,' Nita continues when Jude doesn't reply. 'He's here to see me and our other friends.' She shakes her head sadly. 'Hard to believe it's ending like this. But yes, if you need someone to go on the record, I can pop you in the diary.'

Jude nods without saying anything.

Nita glances into the function room, where the press conference is wrapping up.

'What paper did you say it was?' Nita asks.

'I didn't.'

A pause. 'Right. Well, I should get these teas to poor Aaron and Sive.' She cranes her neck. 'I think they're on their way out.' Holding the tray of drinks in one hand, she dips into her expensive-looking bag and pulls out a card for Jude. 'Call or DM, any time. I'd do anything to help.' And with that, she swishes off.

The press conference is over and Jude glances back towards the hotel reception, wondering if there's somewhere she can sit to type up the interview. That's when she spots a familiar face. A tall man in a suit, with curly hair and a flushed complexion, hovering at the end of the corridor. Just like Nita, he's peering through the glass at the press conference. Or, at the Sullivans. Where has she seen him before? Jude stares, trying to remember. She prides herself on her excellent attention to detail, but she can't quite place him. Curious, she begins moving towards him, but the man is turning and walking away, his long legs carrying him through reception and out of the hotel in quick strides. Did he see her coming? Perhaps he was just an interested bystander, she thinks, as he disappears from view. But she's sure she's seen him before.

Back in the function room, the reporters are dissipating, and Nita is filming, and the Sullivans are whispering as hotel staff deftly stack chairs. Just like that, it's over. Reporters will file their pieces at speed, scrollers will shake their heads in shock, and everyone will get back to whatever they were doing before. Everyone except Sive and Aaron, who look desperately lonely.

Jude approaches them. 'You did good,' she says to Sive. 'Did Hawthorn say what's next? Where we should search?'

Sive looks up at her, shaking her head, and Jude feels the futility of it.

'I guess we go back to Oxford Circus station,' Aaron says, sounding lost, and with no better ideas, that is what they do.

They're in the ticket hall, at the same pillar by the barriers, when a man Jude doesn't know rushes towards them. A journalist? It won't be long, she supposes, before reporters from other papers realize the Sullivans are here and Jude's exclusive positioning will be eroded. She watches the man's approach. Tall and broad, he hunches his shoulders as if conscious of the space he takes up. He's wearing a baseball cap and takes it off now, exposing a completely bald head.

'Aaron, I'm so sorry, mate. Dave asked me to come help,' the man says.

Aaron shakes his hand and introduces him to Sive. 'This is Dave's brother, Jerry. I think you met before.'

Sive nods.

'Dave's had to go into work, but he asked me to help out so I came straight here after the race.'

Aaron frowns. 'But you didn't do the race. Your name wasn't on the leaderboard.'

For a moment, Jerry looks flustered. 'Sorry, yeah, I couldn't . . . But anyway, I'm free. And I've gathered a gang from the rowing club, anyone not working today. They're all ready to search. Anywhere in particular we should go?'

Aaron lifts his hands in a helpless gesture. 'Best bet is the stations on the Central Line? We've done it already, but . . .'

Jude can hear the hollowness in his voice. It would be easier if they had a concrete lead of some kind, a plan that was more specific than 'search all of London'. Or if the other kid, Bea, could somehow give them a clue. That she had actually seen what happened but couldn't tell them was beyond frustrating, and Jude can't help thinking it's worth another shot. A fresh deluge of notifications come through on her phone and she steps away to check them. More retweets, more DMs, but nothing of material use. Still thinking about the man in the suit, she googles 'Pete Brosnan known associates' then clicks on the Images tab. A barrel-chested man in a muscle T-shirt and a red beanie. A slight man with sun-and-cigarette-shrunken skin. A blond man with flushed cheeks, eyes hidden behind aviator sunglasses. None of them is her young guy in a suit. And he really didn't look like a thug. He looked like a junior analyst in a glossy City bank. And suddenly, with cold clarity, she remembers where she saw him.

21

Two days earlier | Saturday
The Meridian Hotel

'Aaron?'

Sive was perched on the side of the hotel bed, feeding Toby, while Faye and Bea watched Saturday-morning cartoons in the living room next door.

Aaron looked up from his phone. 'Mmm?'

'You know at dinner last night, that stuff Nita was saying about a stalker? Was that true?'

His eyes were back on his phone. 'Nita's always been a bit hysterical.'

'Ah, Aaron, don't write her off as hysterical. And I hate that word.'

He looked up again, grinning. 'Sorry. Nita was always a bit dramatic.'

'Do you mean it's not true? You said yourself you knew that' – she paused, unused to saying the name – 'that Yasmin was terrified of someone following her.'

God, why was this so awkward?

He sighed, then sat on the bed beside her, leaning in to kiss her forehead.

111

'That part is true. She was certain someone was following her and watching the house.'

'And you didn't think so?'

He held up his hands. 'I honestly don't know. I think she was definitely followed home one night, and it gave her a scare. She became hypervigilant. And then the more she was looking out for danger, the more she saw it, you know?'

Sive nodded.

'So, she'd look out the window at night and see a shadow across the street from our house. She'd call me and I might see the shadow of a tree swaying in the wind where she was seeing the shadow of a man. Or maybe there *had* been a man and he'd gone by then. It's hard to know.'

'God, that must have been horrible for her.'

'It was. It really started to affect her. She was anxious about going out, anxious about walking home at night – I used to meet her as often as I could so we could go home together, though I usually worked longer hours. It started to affect our relationship, too.'

'Oh?' This was weird territory, but she didn't want to stop him now.

'Yeah. She changed.' Aaron picked his phone up off the bed then put it back down. 'It was like all the fun went out of her.'

'Well, that's not surprising. I don't think I'd be much fun if I was being stalked.'

'Fair. We did go to the police, but they never found anything concrete.'

'And then there was the fire,' Sive said softly.

'Then there was the fire.'

In her arms, Toby settled in for a snooze, milk-drunk and content. It felt odd and wrong to talk about fire and death, but it had taken so long to get to this point she couldn't stop now.

'What about this Michael Rosco person that Nita mentioned? You don't think the neighbour was right about seeing him? Or were you just saying that to soothe Nita?'

He shook his head vehemently. 'I'm not soothing anyone. The neighbour was wrong.' His voice was suddenly hard. Impatient. 'A gossip, trying to get in on the drama.'

'Right.' She changed tack. 'So what did the police think happened?'

'A candle.' Quiet now. Sive squeezed his hand. 'She loved those scented candles and used to light them most nights. Even more so after she got scared that someone was following her. I think she got comfort from lighting up the house.' He coughed. 'Bad choice of words. Because that's exactly what happened. She fell asleep on our bed after a shower one night. A curtain caught fire, and the house went up in minutes.'

'Oh, good God.' Sive's hair fell across her eyes, but with Toby on one arm and Aaron's hand in hers, she couldn't sweep it out of the way. 'I'm so sorry.'

'It's weird talking about it.' He shook his head. His eyes glistened and she squeezed his hand again.

'I'm just glad you weren't in the house. Wait – you weren't, were you?'

'No, I was at work.' A defensive expression crossed his face then, one she'd seen often when watching him in court. It was a look he got when he was crossing slightly thin ice, daring anyone to challenge him. She didn't push.

'Anyway,' he said, with forced brightness. 'We'd better get the kids ready for this brunch with the gang.' Gently, he brushed her hair out of her eyes and kissed her forehead.

'Couldn't we do our own thing this morning and meet your friends later? It's going to be so boring for the kids.'

'Ah, but I only get to hang out with these guys once in a blue moon.' Aaron put his arm around her shoulder and nuzzled into her neck. 'For me? Please?'

It was hard to say no. He really didn't get to see this particular group of friends very often. Back home in Dublin, his social life consisted of work functions; he didn't have a gang of his own. He'd gone to boarding school in Meath because his parents had travelled a lot, and his secondary-school alumni had, in turn, settled far and wide with their illustrious, LinkedIn-shiny careers. So yes, it was hard to say no.

'I guess . . . although how much do you really enjoy it? Sitting there sparring with Scott, you putting him down, him putting you down?'

A grin. 'I'm a lot more skilled at it than he is.'

'You actually enjoy it, don't you?' she said, marvelling.

'Ah, we both do. It's just banter.'

Sive wasn't so sure Scott felt the same way.

'Bear in mind his wife's left him. He may not be in a solid place for your so-called "banter".'

'He'll bounce back,' he said, with, as was always the case for Aaron, complete conviction.

'Right, well, if I'm going to sit through another day of Nita's judgey comments about my parenting, you owe me. Jesus. That woman thinks she knows it all and she's literally just had her twelve-week scan.'

'She's always been like that. It's her way of making herself feel good. She compares herself constantly with other people and needs to come out on top to know she's doing OK at life. Jobs, homes, money, shoes.'

'Erm. Pot, kettle? I know someone else who compares constantly . . . ?'

'Who?' Aaron said, eyes wide, feigning innocence. 'Anyway, that's why Nita's having the baby. Another box to tick.'

Sive looked down at sleepy Toby in her arms. 'Ah, come on, nobody has a baby just to tick a box.'

Aaron raised an eyebrow. 'You've met Nita, right? Does she seem the motherly type?'

'Just because a woman wears expensive shoes doesn't make her incapable of being maternal. Do you think all mothers come in Laura Ashley dresses and neat little aprons?'

'Laura who?'

Sive rolled her eyes. Her phone beeped on the nightstand and she glanced at it. An email from a photographer about another of her interviewees.

'Work?'

She nodded. 'I don't have to read it.' Even though she really did.

He kissed her cheek. 'Ah, you're fine, don't let me stop you. But put on an out-of-office then, will you? This is supposed to be your holiday too. Family time.'

An out-of-office. She didn't have the luxury of turning down work. But Aaron, with his support staff and Garvin, his extraordinarily competent assistant, didn't get it.

'Right, if you burp Toby, I'll send a quick reply, and then we can get going.'

She passed the baby to Aaron and watched as he lifted Toby to hold him cheek to cheek. She smiled to herself, giving silent thanks to the universe. One imperfect, lovely husband and three imperfect, lovely kids. Sive Quinn was one lucky woman.

For two more days, at least.

22

FIVE HOURS MISSING. SIVE wipes her eyes and stands up straighter. They're in the Oxford Circus ticket hall, standing around doing nothing, and they need to get back to searching. Tears aren't going to help Faye. Aaron squeezes her hand. His face is pale and his eyes red-rimmed. This is just as hard for him, she reminds herself. *Is it, though?* asks a little voice in her head. She pushes it away.

Dave's brother, Jerry, hovers nearby, unsure about how exactly to take his leave, perhaps. In the end, he does an awkward little bow and says he'll get the lads from the rowing club to meet him at Tottenham Court Road and take it from there. He'd suggested Nita might join them, but she'd declined, deciding instead to trawl nearby streets in an Uber. It didn't sound to Sive like the most efficient way to search, but then, was any of it any use really? Her thoughts turn for one tiny moment to what she had discovered about Nita in Maggie's house late last night. How odd that it had seemed like such a big deal. Something she'd considered addressing directly with Nita. Now, it didn't matter at all. Her mind flits to Toby and Bea. Are they OK with Scott? What if Toby won't take a bottle? She crosses her arms tightly across her chest, feeling her milk let down; her body nudging her. Maybe they should go back to the hotel? She can't, though. Not when Faye is still out there.

Jude walks over, staring at something on her phone.

'Sive, what was the story with that guy Tim again? The one who found your other ki— eh, Bea – he was on his way to work?'

'Yeah, his girlfriend got out at Bond Street and he saw me shouting through the closed door.'

'And that's when he noticed Bea?'

'Yes.' She swallows against the tightness in her throat. 'He took her off at Oxford Circus and found staff.' She stops for a quick breath. 'They'd just heard from Bond Street, except nobody realized Faye should have been there too.' How did she let this happen? She sags against Aaron.

'Right,' Jude says, pushing on as though there is no time for comforting, and she's right: there isn't. 'And where did he say he worked?'

'I don't know. An office on Liverpool Street, I think.'

'And you met him?'

'Yes, he was walking towards the exit, and he looked back and saw me so came over.'

'Ah ha,' Jude says. 'That's the bit I was curious about.'

'What do you mean?'

'If he was working in Liverpool Street, why didn't he get back on the next Tube? Why was he leaving at Oxford Circus?'

'Oh. Yes, I'm not sure.' Even as Sive says it, she remembers thinking there was something odd about Tim. Not odd about him, actually, but about something he said. She tries to remember now, but she can't. Jude is still talking.

'Mm. It doesn't quite add up . . . And I saw him in the hotel just now.'

'What?'

'He was hovering outside the press conference. Looking just like any office worker on a lunch break. Only he's a long way from his office.'

'That's weird.'

'Yep.' She holds up her phone. 'According to LinkedIn, he works at a place called Anderson Pruitt on Liverpool Street. So why was he exiting here?'

Before Sive has a chance to answer, Aaron cuts in. 'How is this relevant? He clearly didn't take Faye. Where was she? In his briefcase?'

Sive puts her hand on his arm. 'Aaron.'

Jude is unfazed by the outburst. 'Absolutely, I agree. He clearly didn't have Faye with him. But why did he lie about where he was going?' It's a rhetorical question, but she pauses and looks from Sive to Aaron before continuing. 'When someone lies, no matter how small that lie is, it's always worth probing. Why lie?' She says it so simply, so matter-of-factly, even Aaron has no retort this time.

'You're right,' Sive says. 'There's probably a perfectly logical explanation, but it's worth checking. We'll tell DC Hawthorn.'

A shout from a few feet away grabs her attention. Maggie, with her long red curls flying behind her, is running towards them, dodging through a cluster of surprised tourists.

'Oh my God. Guys, I'm so sorry.' Her face is distraught, her eyes wide with shock. 'I didn't know. I'd have been here hours ago. Is there any news?'

Sive and Aaron shake their heads.

'Sive, I forgot my phone at home this morning and when you didn't show I had no way to contact you.' Maggie takes a breathless gulp. 'Then none of the others showed. After the race. At the Rooftop Bar. And I figured our brunch was cancelled. So I went home.' Another gulp of air. 'It still took me ages to find my phone, or I'd have been here much sooner. I'm such an idiot.' She looks like she's about to cry. 'It was down between the couch cushions. I only realized when I sat down and this stupid thing' – she points at the smartwatch on her wrist – 'came back in range and all the notifications came through. And then there were all these missed calls and I didn't know what was going on and then I saw it on the TV news.' The tears spill over now. 'Oh my God, I nearly died. I'm so, so sorry.'

She pulls Sive into a hug but, for Sive, there's no comfort in it.

'How did you find us here?' Jude asks with what sounds to Sive like a touch of scepticism.

Maggie looks at her quizzically.

'This is Jude,' Sive explains. 'She and I work for the same paper.'

'Ah. Good to meet you.' Maggie turns back to Sive. 'Once I saw the press conference on TV, I got a cab straight here. I tried phoning the others but couldn't get anyone, then I texted Jerry and he told me where you were.' She looks around then addresses Aaron. 'Are the others here? Scott and Dave and Nita?'

'Scott's minding the kids. Dave has to work until later. And Nita's just gone. She's taking an Uber to search the streets from inside a car.' Aaron rolls his eyes. 'And don't worry, you're not the only one who didn't realize until now. Nita slept in and only turned up at half eleven.'

Maggie nods. 'Yes. She stayed at mine and I didn't want to wake her this morning after—' She stops herself and glances at Sive. 'Anyway, I'm here now. Tell me what to do.'

But that's the problem, Sive thinks. She doesn't know what to do or where to look or how to help. She just needs someone to fix this. To respond to the press conference. To turn up with her daughter.

That's when DC Hawthorn comes running towards them. Sive is vaguely conscious of two or three people running behind her; journalists, she thinks. But all her focus is on Hawthorn.

'We have a witness.' The officer tries to catch her breath. 'Someone who saw Faye.' She stops, eyes running from Sive to Aaron as though assessing how they might take whatever she's about to say. 'Maybe you should sit down.'

23

BRUNCH HAD BEEN BOOKED for eleven in a hipster café in Hackney called Besk. It was full of couples and groups of twenty- and thirty-somethings eating smashed avocados with their Saturday morning Bloody Marys. Tables just inches apart, with mismatched schoolroom-style chairs backing on to each other, child-friendly it was not. Sive grimaced as she tried to manoeuvre the pram through the café. Aaron had gone ahead with the girls and was searching for additional chairs when she reached the table.

'Oh, sorry, mate,' Dave said. 'Forgot the kids would be with you.' He took a swig from his bottle of beer. Sive's stomach churned at the thought of beer before breakfast, holiday or not.

Scott raised his glass. 'Mimosa. Hair of the dog. Fancy one?'

'Not my style, Burner,' Aaron said. 'Bit . . . feminine, isn't it?'

'Only if you're not comfortable in your own skin, I'd have thought,' Scott replied with a smile, thwacking Aaron on the arm with a rolled-up newspaper.

Sive let out a quiet sigh.

Twenty minutes later, Sive had set Faye and Bea up with colouring pencils and paper and was trying to eat her eggs Benedict while holding Toby on her lap. Every time she lifted her fork, her elbow nudged against Maggie, who was sitting at her side. She longed for the space of the hotel bar yesterday afternoon, especially when Faye, bored, got up to take a wander around the café.

'Is she OK?' Nita asked, frowning.

'She's exploring,' Sive said. 'The staff might not like it, though,' she conceded, and called Faye back. Faye appeared not to hear her, heading to the rear of the café, where the bathrooms were located.

'She'll have a little explore inside the bathrooms and come back then,' Sive said, reaching across Maggie to right Bea's sippy cup for the third time.

'It's not great for kids here,' Maggie said. 'Sorry, Sive, we should have thought of that.'

Sive waved it away.

'How about,' Maggie continued, 'when this lot are doing their virtual race on Monday morning, you and I and the kids go for brunch in the Rooftop Bar. There's tons of space there, and it'll be quiet on a Monday.'

'Oh. What a lovely idea,' Sive said, though she didn't think it was a lovely idea at all. Rooftops and kids were hardly a good mix, and she had no idea where it was or how to get there.

'Good plan,' Scott said. 'We'll be busy with the race so you may as well be having a nice slap-up meal with Maggie.'

'How long will the race take?' Sive asked.

'The race itself isn't long. But by the time everyone gets showered, and so on . . .' He lifted his hands as if to say that could take any amount of time. 'How about we join you ladies in the Rooftop Bar after? Get the beers in to celebrate my win?' He gave Aaron a dig with his elbow.

'Oh, you're going to win, are you? We'll see about that.'

'What machine are you using, Aaron?' Dave asked, popping a mint in his mouth and offering the pack around. Bea reached for one and Sive stretched across Maggie again to gently bat her daughter's hand away.

'Oh, let her have a sweet!' Dave offered the pack again. 'I've got plenty.'

'She's a bit young for Polo mints,' Sive said with a smile.

'Oh. Right,' he said, in a tone that suggested he thought she was being over the top. 'Anyway, go on, Aaron – what rowing machine you using?'

'One in Scott's gym,' Aaron said. 'You using the machine you have at home?'

'Yeah, and Jerry's got one in his place, too. He doesn't know if he can get off work yet, though.' Dave grinned. 'Hopefully not, since he'll beat all of us.' Sive had met Jerry once or twice at get-togethers. Like his brother, Jerry had that kind of soft-featured, eager-to-please look about him, and he was out and out the best rower, but he was on the B-team when it came to this group of old friends. A peripheral joiner: invited to rowing events but not so much to general socializing or hipster brunches.

'I think there's twenty-two of us now, so should be a good race,' Scott said, and Nita nodded. She was doing it too.

Sive listened, baffled again at the idea of a rowing-machine race. It had started in lockdown when they couldn't meet up to row on the water. They'd used rowing machines at home, connecting virtually. And now that it was possible to get back out on the water, they were still regularly using machines for impromptu races. It made no sense to her, but then again, it meant Aaron would be joining her far sooner tomorrow morning than if he was travelling to row on actual water. *So there's that*, she thought, glancing up to see Faye making her way straight for a waiter carrying hot plates. *Less time solo parenting.*

Sive weaved her way through the tables to bring Faye back to her seat, and when she sat down herself, Scott was pointing at something in the newspaper.

'See this – body found in Dublin. Smothered with a plastic bag.' He hunched his shoulders in an exaggerated shudder. 'Links to the Callan gang, those fellas you're up against, Aaron.'

'I'm not up against them,' Aaron said. 'I'm defending Pete Brosnan from a clear frame-up.'

'Far as I heard, a gun was found buried in his garden, though?' Scott said, and Sive could hear the challenge in his voice.

'Yes. To *frame* him.'

'But what makes you so sure Brosnan's innocent?'

'Well' – Aaron smiled magnanimously around at the interested faces – 'he wasn't in the country at the time of the murder.'

Scott looked confused. 'Then why is it going to trial? Wouldn't flight records or passport control prove that he couldn't have done it?'

'Yeah, unfortunately, he and Carmen – that's his wife – took the ferry. Drove down through England, across France, and on to Spain. He's afraid of flying.'

'So if there's no real proof that he was in Spain, how do you know he was?' Scott asked.

'That, my friend, is where technology comes into play.' Aaron smiled benevolently.

Ever the showman, Sive thought, with a mix of irritation and pride.

'How do you mean?' Scott pulled his vape from his blazer pocket. If he started his judge-with-a-gavel thing again, Sive might have to excuse herself.

'His phone, his Fitbit, his laptop,' Aaron explained. 'Everything he has shows he was in Spain.' A satisfied smile from Aaron as his audience nodded appreciatively. All except Scott.

'Hang on.'

Five heads swivelled towards Scott.

He tapped the vape on the table for emphasis, and Sive hid her grimace in her cold cappuccino. 'Couldn't his wife have gone to Spain on her own and brought his phone and Fitbit and laptop? To make it look like he was there?'

Four heads swivelled back to Aaron.

'Eh, no. She wasn't there on her own, she was there with him. Neighbours in the apartment complex would have seen them.'

'Sure, but how well do the neighbours know them? Couldn't someone else have gone with Carmen? Someone everyone will assume was her husband? Wear the Fitbit, carry the phone, make a few calls? Easy, I'd have thought.' Scott looked pleased with his deduction.

Dave tilted his head, considering this. 'Wow, would that work? That's kind of impressive, Scott. You'd make a good criminal. There was this one case at work where—'

Aaron interrupted with a *tsk*. 'You've been watching too much *Law and Order*,' he said, shaking his head and smiling to show he was just a touch sorry for Scott and his outlandish suggestions.

Scott smiled back. 'I'm right, though. It wouldn't be that hard. If, say, Brosnan had a brother. Does he have a brother?'

Aaron shrugged. Pete Brosnan did have a brother, Sive knew that, and she knew Aaron knew it.

'No idea if he has a brother or not, but I'm pretty sure, if he did, he'd hardly go all the way to Spain with Carmen Brosnan just to give his brother an alibi.'

'Why not? If it works, your guy gets away with murder.'

Aaron sighed as though explaining something to a small child. 'Look, the truth is' – he picked up a piece of bacon and popped it in his mouth, chewing while his audience waited – 'the Callans were trying to take out a drug dealer and pin it on Brosnan.

Two birds, one stone. But they got the wrong guy. And Brosnan got *me* as his lawyer.' He poked a thumb at his chest and the pleased smile was back. 'So the Callans are fucked.'

Sive felt a knot in her stomach and glanced around on instinct to see if anyone was listening. She knew it was silly. As if someone in a London café would hear Aaron and report back to criminals in Dublin. But all the same. They were infamously merciless and this kind of cavalier talk from Aaron made her uneasy.

'*Sure*.' Scott nodded to emphasize his sarcasm. 'No doubt Ireland's deadliest crime gang are quaking in their boots.'

'It's exciting, though, isn't it?' Dave said. 'To be involved in law and justice and catching the bad guys. That's how I feel about my job too. The way we—'

Aaron swiped the baseball cap off Dave's head. 'Yes, yes, we know. Where would we be without Officer Dave keeping law and order on London's streets.'

Dave grabbed the hat and put it back on his head. 'Very funny. What I do is important, you know,' he said, but he was grinning. 'If the police didn't catch anyone, there'd be nobody for you to defend. We're a team, you and me.' He punched Aaron lightly in the shoulder and Sive thought she saw a small frown cross Aaron's face.

'Anyway,' Scott said, 'here's the story about the body found in Dublin, in case you want to see it.' He passed it to Aaron, just as Bea knocked over a glass of milk, splashing the edges of the newspaper.

'Oh, shit, sorry,' Aaron said.

'Don't worry, I'm finished with it. Bin it when you're done or give it to Dave for the crossword.'

'Already did the crossword at home, mate, but let me see this story about the body.' Dave leaned in to read too.

'My goodness, enough about bodies and plastic bags!' Maggie

exclaimed. 'Let's get back to planning the rest of your trip. Sive, do I have your number – should I take it in case there's any problem Monday morning?'

Maggie *did* have her number. Sive knew this because she always texted Maggie after their visits to London, thanking her for showing them around and spending time with them. Secretly hoping for an ongoing friendship. Text messages that clearly didn't mean quite as much to Maggie as they did to Sive; she smiled inwardly at her own neediness.

'I think you should have it already, but let me know if you don't.'

'Great. Shall we meet at the Rooftop Bar at ten? I've taken the day off work so let's start it in style while this lot are sweating on their rowing machines!' Her eyes crinkled.

'Brilliant,' Sive said. 'That sounds perfect.'

'We used to love going there back in the day. It was our place. We were like the cast of *Friends*, only far less good-looking and with far more tequila,' she said, laughing. 'Guys, do you remember the time—'

But she was interrupted by Dave, who was pointing at something in the newspaper.

'Aaron! Have you seen this? "Well-known businessman Hugh Pemberton arrested." He was one of your witnesses, years ago, wasn't he?'

Aaron shook his head. 'No, not one of mine.'

'What? Hugh Pemberton – little white moustache and wire-rimmed glasses. Short. Rich. Remember?'

'Nope. Maybe he was one of your cases, at work?'

Dave looked baffled, then his face changed. 'Actually, I think you might be right there. He was.' He nodded slowly, as though remembering something, and Sive wondered if they were about to be blessed with another long story about Dave's job.

Aaron folded the newspaper and his eyes went to his phone beneath. 'Damn.' His fingers rapped the table, usually a sign of nervous energy.

'Everything OK?' Sive asked.

'Two missed calls from Garvin.' He looked up. 'My assistant,' he clarified for the others. 'What the hell does he need on a Saturday morning?' He pushed back his chair, almost hitting the seat behind. 'Sorry, guys, I'll have to phone him. Price of success,' he added in a mutter. 'Zero time off.' He made his way between the tables and out of the café, one hand cupped to his ear to shield him from Saturday morning chatter.

Sive watched her husband's retreating back, suddenly conscious that Scott was watching too, with what looked like barely suppressed resentment blotched all over his face. Scott caught her looking and, just as quickly, neutralized his expression.

'Definitely don't miss that life,' he said, and she smiled politely.

'No rest for the wicked,' Dave chirped, with a nod towards Aaron's departing back. 'Though of course my job is the same – always on. Day or night.'

'That is not one bit true,' Nita said. 'You literally clock in and out at set times. When you work at night, it's because you're on a night shift.'

Dave coloured and shrugged. 'It's important all the same.'

Sive felt bad for him. It couldn't be easy hanging out with these over-achievers.

'I think it sounds really interesting,' she said. 'What kind of cases do you see?'

Nita and Scott groaned in unison. 'Don't get him started!' Nita said, adding a half-hearted: 'Just kidding.'

Dave ignored her. 'Not allowed to say anything about specific cases, Sive. People think it's just admin work, but we have to be very ethical – access to all sorts. Actually' – he glanced around and lowered his voice – 'a colleague of mine just got reprimanded for doing background checks that weren't actually linked to any investigations. We all heard about it, but nobody knows what he was up to. Random audit picked it up. So, we have an office sweep going, betting on why he did it. What do you reckon it was?'

'Checking out someone he fancies, no doubt about it.' Scott knocked on the table for emphasis. 'That's what I'd do.'

'Nah, he has a long-term girlfriend. Any other ideas? The pot's £80.'

'Just because he has a long-term girlfriend doesn't mean he's not looking up stuff on other women,' Scott said.

Nita wrinkled her nose. 'Ugh, gross. Scott, not everyone's like you. You really do not give one jot what anyone thinks of you, do you?'

Scott's face clouded. 'You sound like Caron.'

'Jeez. Soz. Touchy,' Nita said, giving his arm an affectionate squeeze. 'Ooh, speaking of exes, maybe Dave's colleague was looking for dirt on his girlfriend's ex.' She warmed to her theme. 'Or blackmailing his girlfriend's ex. Let's go with that. He was blackmailing the ex to get him to . . . stump up child support.'

'That is weirdly specific,' Dave said, 'but thank you for your input.' He pulled out a notebook – Dave was famous for carrying a notebook at all times – and wrote something down. Sive couldn't tell if he was serious or playing up to his 'brand' for his friends' enjoyment.

Maggie joined in then. 'Maybe there's no child support – maybe your colleague was blackmailing the ex for money.'

Nita clapped her hands and declared this to be far more interesting.

Dave laughed again and said there was probably an innocent explanation, like Scott had suggested.

Nita raised a perfectly groomed eyebrow and pointed out that getting information on someone he fancied was hardly innocent. Scott took offence and sparked a heated debate that Sive half listened to while helping Bea with her food. Faye wandered off again and began chatting to a young couple at a table near the back of the café. Sive crossed her fingers the couple didn't mind having a talkative six-year-old interrupt their brunch and, although she knew she should probably intervene, she didn't have the energy. Parenting, she often thought, was eighty per cent trying to decide when to get involved and when to leave well enough alone. She took a final forkful of her eggs Benedict, at this point congealed and cold, and glanced over at the café window. Scott was out there now, with his vape, standing beside Aaron, who was still on the phone to the office. By the time she realized it wasn't actually the office, it was almost, but not quite, a moot point.

24

MAYBE YOU SHOULD SIT *down.*

Sive stares at Hawthorn, wide-eyed, but it's Aaron who answers.

'No, we don't need to sit, just tell us – someone saw Faye?'

'Yes, on the Tube.' A pause. 'Holding hands with someone, according to our caller. Holding hands with an adult.'

And though she knew this was coming, from the moment she realized the backpack in the park was Faye's, Sive feels her legs dissolve as the floor rises up to meet her.

'Are you OK?'

The voice is Hawthorn's, Sive thinks, though it's Aaron's arms she can feel pulling her up. A camera flashes from somewhere above. She can hear a journalist asking a question and a police officer asking for space.

'Sorry,' she says to Hawthorn, furious with herself now. There's no time for this. 'Just tell us. Please. Everything.'

Hawthorn turns and says something to the journalists, keeping them at bay, then faces Sive again. 'Do you need to sit down? Or go back to your hotel?' she asks, her eyes deep with concern.

131

'No!' It comes out sharply. 'I'm not leaving here. Sorry. I'm not normally like this. Please, just tell us.' *Dear God. Someone has taken Faye by the hand and walked off.*

Hawthorn looks back at the reporters and steers Sive and Aaron a little way away to the wall opposite the ticket barriers. Jude and Maggie follow.

'OK,' Hawthorn says. 'A woman called. There were numerous calls, of course – that always happens when we do a press conference. But this particular woman phoned to say she noticed a little girl matching Faye's description on the Tube this morning. It was the backpack that stood out – she said she'd been looking for something similar for her granddaughter. She remembers a pink denim jacket too. And that the little girl was holding hands with an adult.' She glances back at the hovering journalists, then lowers her voice. 'Crucially, she noticed the stitches in Faye's leg. We haven't mentioned those in any of the alerts, they're not referenced on social media and we didn't say it at the press conference. So this woman sounds like a credible witness.'

Sive's stomach plummets. The thought of this woman spotting Faye and not knowing she was missing. Doing nothing because she didn't know there was anything wrong. *Jesus.*

'That's all she remembers. The Tube was crowded, she said, and she has a strong sense that the little girl was holding someone's hand, but the lady didn't notice or pay any attention to who the adult was. She was looking at the backpack.'

'Which backpack?' Jude asks quickly. 'Which picture?'

'The one with Elsa wearing a *blue* dress. Meaning, we can assume the bag actually belonged to the other little girl, Eva, but since the witness remembers the pink jacket and the stitches too, we know it was Faye she saw, and therefore this must have been *after* the backpacks were mixed up.'

Sive tries to work out what this means. But really, since the bags may have been switched any time between Bond Street and St Paul's, it doesn't tell them much.

'Right, where was the woman when she saw Faye?' Aaron asks.

'That's a problem. When she thinks back on it, she can remember the bag and the pink jacket and the cut on her leg, but she didn't pay attention to where she was at the time.'

Oh God. So close, and still nothing.

'She herself got off at South Woodford Underground station.'

Sive has no idea where this is or what it means, but Hawthorn looks wary.

'Is that near here?' she asks.

Hawthorn takes in an audible breath. 'It's about fourteen miles away. Or fourteen stops on the Tube.'

'Fuck,' Aaron says. '*Fuck*. So whoever has Faye could have got off at any stop between Bond Street and South Woodford?'

Jude clears her throat. 'Or even beyond that? Unless the witness can remember them getting off the Tube before her?'

Hawthorn shakes her head. 'She doesn't remember seeing them get off the Tube. But she reckons when she stood up to gather her belongings at South Woodford, they weren't there. The crowd had thinned considerably, and when she thinks back to looking around, she didn't see them.'

'Right,' Aaron says. 'So you have officers in every station between here and South Woodford, and people combing CCTV?' It's a demand, more than a question.

'Of course. We were already on that.'

'And as we're now looking at a kidnap, I expect you've scaled up resources?'

Hawthorn lifts her hand in a placating gesture. 'I think it's too soon to say we're looking at a kidnap. It may be a well-meaning commuter looking after Faye, intending to reunite her with you. Someone who doesn't realize we're already searching for her.'

Aaron snorts. 'It's all over the news and social media. Nobody could miss it.'

'Our witness doesn't use social media,' Hawthorn counters. 'It was only when she saw the press conference on TV that she realized.'

'But even if someone didn't see the alerts, they'd bring her to a police station,' Sive says. 'People who find lost children don't just take them home . . . And don't we have to assume that whoever is with her deliberately switched the backpacks, in an intent to mislead? That doesn't sound like someone who just "doesn't realize"'.'

She looks at the faces surrounding her. Hawthorn is working hard to maintain an expression of calm professionalism, but there's anxiety there too, just beneath the surface. Aaron is white and angry and terrified. Maggie is still in shock, still catching up. And Jude, ever the observer, is cool and composed, but for the first time, there's a flicker of concern there too. And somehow, that unnerves Sive more than anything.

25

Tower of London

FAYE LEANED ON THE wooden fence, eyes like saucers, transfixed by actors in medieval costumes. Bea, too small to rest her arms on the top rail of the fence, peered through the middle instead. And Toby slept soundly against Sive's chest, snug in his sling.

'I love this,' Faye whispered, almost reverentially. How strange that this huge tourist attraction on the bank of the Thames was the most relaxing part of the trip so far, Sive thought, rubbing Toby's velvety head.

Beside her, Maggie was reading the brochure.

'Did you know that the ravens in the Tower are fed on biscuits soaked in blood?'

'OK, thanks, but I did *not* need to know that.'

'It's funny,' Maggie went on, 'I've lived in this city for twenty years, but I've never been to the Tower of London.'

'I suppose that's how it goes. I've never been to the Cliffs of Moher back home, or the Blarney Stone. We don't make time to be tourists in our own countries.'

'Gosh, even I've been to the Cliffs of Moher!' Maggie said. 'Yasmin and I went when we were at uni.'

'Oh, you were in college with Yasmin?' Sive asked, checking

to see if Aaron was listening. He was a few feet away, deep in conversation with Dave. Not that it mattered really, but it felt strange to talk about her husband's deceased fiancée in his hearing.

'Yes, that's how I met the others. Yasmin and I were best friends, and then Nita, who's Yasmin's sister obviously, was at uni with Scott and Aaron. We were all looking for somewhere to live at the same time and decided to get a place together.'

'And Dave?' Sive asked, as Toby began to stir in the sling.

'His mother owned the house we rented in Stratford.'

'Wait, so you all lived with Dave's mother?'

Maggie laughed. 'Gosh, no. That would have cramped our style as twenty-somethings trying to be cool and glamorous in turn-of-the-millennium London. She lived in an apartment and Dave was a kind of *in situ* landlord. I think she thought he would make sure we didn't have too many parties. "Always take matters into your own hands" – that was one of her favourite things to say. In this case, poor Dave was her proxy.' Now it was Maggie's turn to glance over to where Dave and Aaron were huddled together, still not listening. She raised an eyebrow. 'And let's just say, Dave was *not* the most efficient person to leave in charge of anyone's interests.'

'Oh?' Sive prompted.

'Ah, not that anything went wrong. But he was so keen on being best pals with everyone I don't imagine he'd have objected, no matter what we wanted to do.'

'I get you. Yeah, I can't picture Dave bossing you all about.'

Maggie sighed. 'He is not famous for taking the initiative, no,' she said, and Sive had the strong impression there was a story behind this, but Bea began pulling at her leg, asking for snacks, and that was the end of the conversation.

*

'Will we go see the Crown Jewels next?' Aaron called over as the medieval re-enactment came to an end.

Sive nodded, handing rice cakes to Bea and Faye.

'Sure. And it looks like we can get into the tower where the little princes were kept. That sound good to everyone?'

Maggie and Aaron nodded. Dave held up a hand, like a schoolchild asking for permission.

'I might go on home. I've seen all this before. It's great, don't get me wrong, but I've been here with my mum seven or eight times. Quite the fan of all things royal, my mum.'

'Oh, sure!' Sive said. 'Of course, you head on.'

'But we should make a plan for later. I know we booked that Japanese restaurant, but what about cancelling and everyone come around to mine instead? Bit more relaxing?'

Sive and Maggie nodded in unison.

'Right, I'll go, then. Aaron, mate, I was thinking you and me could meet for a pint beforehand?'

Aaron hesitated, uncharacteristically unsure.

'Just the one, in the Lion,' Dave said.

Aaron looked at Sive, perhaps appealing to her to jump in and negate the plan. But Dave didn't wait for an answer.

'Right, see you there at seven. See the rest of you at my place at eight.' He clapped Aaron on the arm, waved at Maggie and Sive, and disappeared into the throngs of tourists.

Maggie raised her eyebrows. 'Wow, Aaron, a whole hour of Dave and nobody to rescue you. Very best of luck.' There was affection in her words, but something else too, Sive thought. Irritation, maybe? She hadn't quite got a handle on the dynamic of this group of old friends. They seemed to her a mismatched bunch, people who wouldn't be friends if they met today. Then again, that was how it went, she supposed. She could say the same of her colleagues from her first job as a journalist. Back then they had lived in each other's pockets, but they'd have little in common if they were thrown together at this stage in life. Still, they met up once a year for pints and reminiscing, bound by the ties of the past. If she was really honest, she could probably say the same about her college friends. Not out loud, because they were officially her *best* friends. But she didn't confide in them. She didn't tell them how hard she sometimes found motherhood, and how lonely, especially those early days home alone with Faye. She didn't bare her soul the way women in books and on TV did. If she was really, really honest, Sive would admit that while she had lots of friends – former colleagues, college buddies, school-gate mums, book-club pals – she'd never, ever had a *best* friend, not the kind you see in the movies. And yeah, if she met her so-called besties now for the first time, twenty years and a lifetime on from their days in UCC, they might not have so much in common.

Maybe it was the same for Aaron's old housemates. Scott with his needling and sparring. Dave with his long-drawn-out stories. Nita with her narcissistic tendencies. And Maggie – well, Maggie was lovely. Maggie was someone Sive could be friends with.

'I wish you'd said something to get me out of meeting Dave,' Aaron said to Sive now.

'Hey! You're big and bold enough to sort out your own social life,' she said, grinning. 'Although, it does mean I'm stuck getting the three kids organized and out the door to Dave's. Wherever Dave's is.'

Maggie looked up from the brochure. 'I'll show you. It's not far from your hotel.'

Aaron was shaking his head. 'No, we won't bring the kids. It's easier if it's just the adults.'

'Of *course* it's easier if it's just the adults, but we didn't bring them all the way to London to keep leaving them home alone at night.'

'They won't be alone. Book the babysitter. Willow, or whatever her name is.'

Sive let out an exasperated sigh. How was this always her responsibility?

'Why can't *you* book the babysitter?'

'I don't have her number – you do,' Aaron said with a smug grin. 'Though if you want me to start calling twenty-year-old model look-alikes, I'd be happy to . . .'

Sive groaned. 'I don't know. I feel bad leaving the kids with a stranger two nights in a row.'

Aaron shook his head. 'Dave will have heart failure if you turn up with the kids. No offence, kids!' He picked up Bea, swinging her high and burying his face in her tummy. She squealed with laughter. 'His apartment is all glass and chrome and sharp corners, and I'm certain his invitation didn't extend to these guys.' He tickled Bea again as Faye pulled at his arm, asking for a turn.

'Fine. I'll call Willow.'

'And once you do that,' Maggie said, 'how about you and I go get some takeaway coffees, if Aaron's OK to stay with the kids?'

Sive could have hugged her. Yes, she and Maggie could definitely have been friends.

'I don't know how you do it,' Maggie said as they took their places in the queue for coffee. 'Three kids and a job. Wait, do mothers hate when people say that?'

Sive grinned. 'I don't mind one bit. I honestly don't know how anyone does it. As soon as I've figured it out, I'll let everyone know.' She hesitated. 'Speaking of things you're probably not supposed to say, did *you* ever want to settle down? Do the whole marriage-and-kids thing?'

Maggie shook her head. 'There was one guy. But I realized I was settling. You know that episode of *Friends* where they make marriage pacts in case they never meet anyone?'

Sive nodded as they shuffled forward in the queue.

'Yeah. Luckily, I realized in time that it wasn't a good reason to settle down with someone. I'm happy on my own. I have my four sisters, who are my best pals in the whole world, and I have good friends.' She stage-whispered: '*Other* friends, not just that lot.' She grinned, pointing back at where Aaron was swinging Faye around by the arms while Bea clapped and Toby snuggled in the sling.

'Yes, you're quite . . . an eclectic bunch?' Sive said. 'I guess everyone had more in common twenty years ago?'

Maggie nodded. 'We had glossy new careers, plenty of money and a party lifestyle in common, yes. And we had Yasmin. She was the tie that binds.'

'What was she like?' As her words hit the air, Sive realized that much as she wanted to know more about Yasmin, she was also looking for a deeper connection with Maggie.

Maggie smiled. 'She was the best friend I ever had.' She held up her arm, turning it to show Sive her wrist. 'We even got matching tattoos. How utterly over the top is that.' She traced her index finger over the two suns. 'My mother went nuts. But I'm glad I did it. It's a touchstone, a quiet, constant reminder.'

Sive nodded. 'It's beautiful.'

'And apt as a symbol,' Maggie said. 'Yasmin was like the sun. We all wanted to bask in her light. If she was in bad form, we instinctively tried to make her happy, and when she was happy, we all wanted to be with her. We were drawn to her, I suppose.'

'Were she and Nita very alike?' Sive asked.

'I would say Nita paled in Yasmin's shadow. Ha, more man-gled sun analogies! And please never tell Nita what I've just said – she was super-jealous of Yasmin back then, though she'll never admit it.'

Sive nodded conspiratorially. 'Why was she jealous?'

'Yasmin was effortless where Nita always tried really hard to be the best, to win at life. It wasn't about being liked, it was about being admired and envied. That was her fuel. Well, you've met Nita, I'm sure you know.' Another conspiratorial smile as the queue limped slowly along. Ahead, a young couple moved together, hands in each other's back pockets, faces turned to one another. Sive found herself wondering if Aaron and Yasmin had been like that. She and Aaron had missed that stage, going straight to pram shopping and scans.

She looked to where Aaron stood with the kids. He was wav-ing at her, pointing at his watch, gesturing to say he'd come over. But she and Maggie were almost at the top of the coffee queue and Sive raised a hand now to say, *Nearly there, hang on*.

'Aaron doesn't talk about Yasmin,' she said to Maggie.

'I'm not surprised. It took him a long time to get over what happened. He blamed himself, of course.'

Sive turned to face Maggie.

'What? Aaron blamed himself?'

Maggie bit her lip. 'Oh, sugar. You didn't know that?'

'No. He never, ever talks about her. I've seen one photograph of them together, and he doesn't even know I've seen that. I knew she existed because he told me a brief version of the story before I met you all the first time.' She paused. 'I guess in case her name came up.'

'Right. So what exactly do you know?' Maggie asked carefully.

They were at the top of the queue now, and Maggie pulled out her purse, ready to order.

'Aaron and Yasmin had moved in together and were planning their wedding. She was at home. He was at work. A fire broke out. And she died. That's it. He surely can't blame himself?'

'Oh.' Maggie's eyes widened. 'Sive, you really don't know the rest of the story?'

26

Tower of London

BEFORE SIVE COULD ANSWER, the barista asked for Maggie's order and suddenly Aaron and the kids were there too, and that was the end of the conversation. For now, at least.

They went to see the Crown Jewels, saw one more re-enactment, then decided it was time for a cake break, this time in a tearoom Maggie recommended, a few minutes' walk from the Tower of London. The tearoom, a pretty log-cabin, was right in the middle of a small park with a playground, much to the girls' delight, and as soon as they'd finished their brownies they begged to go out to the swings. Aaron feigned reluctance as they pulled at his arms, until eventually allowing them to yank him off his chair.

'You owe me for this!' he said to Sive in mock exasperation, then turned and followed the girls out of the café.

'Hey, I've got the baby,' she called after him. 'He's the hardest work of all!'

'Hmm, I think Aaron drew the short straw,' Maggie said, nodding at a snoozing Toby.

'Well . . .' Sive began cutting the remainder of her cinnamon bun into tiny pieces, pushing them around her plate. 'I wanted to ask you more about what you said earlier, about Aaron blaming himself. It seems odd. I mean, how could he have done anything if he was at work?'

'Ah, he wasn't at work though, he was in a bar.'

'Oh.' Sive turned this over. Did it matter that he'd said he was at work, and not in a bar? 'But surely that still didn't make it his fault?'

Maggie stirred her coffee. 'Did he tell you about the stalker?'

'Yes. Well, no. The first I heard was at dinner with you guys last night, and I asked him about it this morning. It sounds like it's not clear whether or not the stalker was real?'

Maggie placed her spoon on her saucer and nodded slowly as though choosing her words carefully.

'Nita now believes there was a stalker, though at the time she didn't,' Maggie said finally. 'Yasmin certainly believed it – she was terrified. Dave was worried about her too, I remember that. He had a big soft spot for Yasmin and, though he never actually saw any stalker, he was a fairly staunch defender of anything Yasmin said.'

'And you?'

'I never knew for sure. I believe Yasmin was scared after that first time when she was followed home. Whether or not she imagined the rest, I don't know. Scott didn't believe it at all, and used to say as much to Yasmin. He could be a real fuckwit at times.'

Sive picked up a piece of her bun and put it down. 'What about Aaron?'

'I think he felt the same as me – unsure. But he did try to catch the guy.'

'Wait – what?'

Maggie glanced through the café window to where Aaron was

pushing Bea on a swing. 'I probably shouldn't be telling you this . . .'

Sive was baffled. 'Aaron tried to catch the stalker he didn't quite believe in?'

Maggie nodded. 'I think he felt if the stalker was real, it was a valid way to try to catch him, and if he was a figment of Yasmin's imagination, it would nevertheless do no harm to show her he was taking it seriously.' A light breeze rustled through the trees outside and they both turned their heads towards the window and the swings beyond. 'Two birds, one stone, as Aaron himself might say.'

'Seriously? What did he do?' Sive couldn't quite imagine Aaron trying to catch a stalker, but then again, when he put his mind to something . . .

Maggie shook her head, her red-gold hair glistening in the sunlight. 'Crikey. I can't believe he's never actually told you. I think it's best to let him do it.'

'Ah, Maggie, don't leave me hanging.'

'I promise you it wasn't anything bad,' Maggie reassured Sive, draining the last of her coffee. 'But it was the night Yasmin died, so it's a . . . difficult topic.' Maggie pursed her lips. 'And not my place to say.'

A shadow crossed her face and, suddenly, her eyes looked sad.

Sive put her hand on her arm. 'I'm sorry. I shouldn't have brought it up. It must have been awful.'

'It was. Yasmin was our linchpin. The centre of everything. Aaron loved her, obviously. Dave idolized her – to him, Yasmin could do no wrong. Scott had her on a pedestal – I think he saw her as a trophy Aaron had won, a trophy he wanted too. Nita, jealousy aside, adored her, of course – she was her only family in the whole world. And me – well, she was my best friend. I've never had a friend like her since.'

'I'm so, so sorry. No wonder Aaron doesn't say much about it. It must have been horrific.' *God, how many times can one person say the words 'awful' and 'horrific' and offer the same platitudes?*

'Talk to Aaron about what he did that night,' Maggie said. 'As I say, it's not my story to tell – but if you ask him, he might be ready to share.'

27

'AARON, NOW THAT WE know there's an adult with Faye . . . that it may be a kidnap, we need to seriously consider that it could be linked to your Brosnan case.' Sive touches her husband's arm as she says it, her voice urgent but somehow gentle too. Handling him, Jude thinks.

Jude watches Aaron's jaw tighten, his head shake.

'Sive, how would they have known you'd be in Bond Street this morning? How would they have predicted you'd let the girls on the Tube ahead of you? It's nonsense.'

Jude notes the 'you'd let the girls on the Tube ahead of you' wording and sees Sive flinch. But she keeps going:

'What if someone grabbed an unexpected opportunity? Maybe they were going to do something else.' Sive's voice quivers. 'And then when Faye and Bea got on the Tube on their own, they took their chance.'

Their friend Maggie is holding Sive's hand and rubs her arm now.

'But Sive,' Maggie says gently, 'how would they have known you and I were meeting this morning? That you'd be in the Tube station at all?'

Sive straightens up suddenly. 'Wait. Maggie, you said your phone was missing.'

'It was, but I found it.'

'Could someone have taken it to find out our plans?'

Jude glances at Aaron, who is shaking his head. Hawthorn looks sceptical too.

'Oh no, sweetheart, it was in my house,' Maggie says in her soft Scottish accent. 'Down between the couch cushions. Probably from last night, when we were googling for updates about—' Maggie stops abruptly and Jude has the impression something passes between the two women. Then a small headshake from Sive and an apologetic look from Maggie. What's that about? Jude wonders.

Hawthorn interjects. 'Though it seems very unlikely that someone from this Irish crime network is targeting you, I want to reassure you that we're liaising with the Irish gardaí. Speaking of which . . .' Hawthorn holds up a finger, then steps away to answer a call, back into the maelstrom of commuters and – Jude notes – a growing cluster of reporters.

Jude's phone beeps and she steps away too, turning her back to Maggie, Aaron and Sive. A text from her editor asking if she's on target to send the interview with Sive by five o'clock, as promised. So just over three hours to go. Jude clicks into her Notes app. There's plenty there – everything Sive said about roleplaying stranger danger, losing Faye at the school, their lack of familiarity with London, and Aaron's court case. She gnaws on a knuckle, considering. She can include the sojourn to St Paul's as long as she doesn't mention the backpack, she reckons. Definitely not the backpack, or the witness on the Tube. She's here to write a good story, not jeopardize a police investigation. Or worse, a child's safety. She types a reply.

You'll have it by 5.

As she hits send, from the corner of her eye she sees Hawthorn finish her call and turn to the Sullivans, beckoning them over. Jude carries on looking at her phone screen, but now she's listening intently, trying to catch what Hawthorn is saying. Scraps of words drift across, struggling against the clamour of the Tube station.

'. . . Willow . . . checking again . . .' *Something to do with the park where they found the backpack?*

Sive replies, though her words are unintelligible, then Hawthorn seems to move on to something else. Her voice drops and some moments go by before Jude catches any fragments.

'. . . new information . . . six months . . .'

Jude risks a discreet glance. They're not paying her any attention.

More words filter over: '. . . with you stable . . . tracker . . .'

Why does it suddenly sound like they're talking financials? Mortgages?

Hawthorn seems to be asking them something, and the Sullivans both look shocked.

Hawthorn's voice carries again: '. . . Garda Síochána in Ireland . . .'

Sive is speaking now, but her voice is too low; Jude can't catch it. She keeps watching, trying to pick up on body language. Aaron is shaking his head. Emphatic denial. Sive's eyes are wide, but she too is shaking her head. Whatever Hawthorn is suggesting, the Sullivans don't agree. Jude is surprised. Surely with their daughter missing, every lead is worth following? That reminds her of something else and, a quick search on Google later, she's clicking on the phone number for Anderson Pruitt and asking to speak to Tim Brassil.

The receptionist buzzes her through to someone else. A female voice answers and Jude asks again for Tim.

'We have no one by that name working here, sorry,' the woman says, and disconnects the call.

28

Two days earlier | *Saturday*
Clarinda Gardens

'Wow, DAVE'S DOING ALL right for himself!' Sive said to Maggie as they were buzzed through the gate to the courtyard. 'Clarinda Gardens is *not* what I expected.'

The three-storey red-brick building was wide and sprawling, surrounded by gently sloping lawns, all within the confines of a high wall and a secure gate.

'Yes, it's lovely,' Maggie agreed. 'It's an old schoolhouse that was turned into apartments in the 1960s. This is where Dave's mother used to live, back when we all rented the house in Stratford from her.'

'Ha! I was picturing his poor mother in a one-bedroom flat while these twenty-somethings were living it large in her house.'

'Gosh, no.' Maggie arched her brows. 'Dave's mum knew how to look after herself. No slumming it for her.'

Sive scanned the manicured gardens and picture-book schoolhouse. It must have cost a small fortune.

Maggie read her mind. 'Dave's mother got a big life insurance payout when Dave's dad died. He fell down the stairs and cracked his head, died three days later.'

Sive clapped a hand to her mouth. 'Oh my God, poor Dave. What a horrific thing to happen.'

'Mm. Well, from what I gather, the dad was quick with his fists. The whole thing wasn't quite the tragedy you'd imagine.' Maggie grimaced. 'And the bottle of vodka he'd had before he fell certainly didn't help his balance.'

'Oh.' Sive wasn't sure what to say.

'Indeed. Anyway, Dave and his mother swapped homes about ten years ago, and that's how he ended up with this rather nice apartment.'

'But what about Dave's brother? Didn't he want in on the apartment or the house?'

'I don't think it was up to him . . . Dave was always the favourite. I suspect Jerry reminded their mother a little too much of her husband.'

Sive stopped and turned to Maggie. 'You don't mean Jerry's also . . . quick with his fists, as you put it?' She'd met Jerry. He seemed jovial, friendly, unassuming.

Maggie was swift to reassure her. 'Oh, no. He just looks a lot like the dad – tall, lumbering, same eyes. So their mother always favoured Dave and poor Jerry wasn't part of the house swap at all. I wonder sometimes if he resents that.'

'I would. It's very beautiful here,' Sive said, following Maggie towards one of a number of identical red front doors. 'Lucky Dave.'

The interior of Dave's apartment was at odds with the gentle, schoolhouse exterior. Aaron was right – it certainly *was* all sharp corners. Floor-to-ceiling windows, a marble breakfast bar with three chrome-and-leather stools, a shiny black piano by the wall, an L-shaped sofa in pristine cream and a huge glass coffee table. The kids would have loved it. Sive would have had a stroke.

Thank goodness for Willow. The babysitter had been every bit as competent this evening as the night before, taking Toby from Sive so she could get ready, chatting to the girls like they were old friends. Maggie, who'd come to help Sive with the kids while Aaron had a pint with Dave, was happily redundant. And Sive even managed to leave sufficiently early to stop off to buy a bottle of chilled rosé and a box of truffles, which she now handed to Dave.

'Aw, you shouldn't have. It's just a bunch of old mates getting a takeaway together,' he said, but he seemed pleased.

Aaron was already there, sitting in a leather chair by the window, beer in hand. Sive smiled over and Aaron raised his drink in salute, but his expression was tense, his mouth set in a tight line. Scott was on a small stool opposite him, talking animatedly. Sive couldn't hear what it was about, above the sound of Britney Spears' 'One More Time', but she hoped they weren't facing another long night of Scott and Aaron jabbing at each other.

'Taking it back to the nineties,' Dave said, nodding towards the speaker on the breakfast bar. He was smiling but looked tense too. *Good God, what had he and Aaron been discussing over their pints?* 'I'll get out the guitar later and we can have a session. I do a pretty good Oasis and Blur medley with Scott on backing vocals.' He turned to Maggie: 'Could you pass me some wine glasses?'

She rummaged in a high cupboard behind them and came back with two tiny wine glasses that looked like they'd been stolen from a pub.

'I don't drink wine myself,' he explained. 'Those are about the only glasses I've got. Shall I open this?' He picked up Sive's bottle of rosé. 'Or do you fancy a beer?'

Sive and Maggie both opted for wine and Maggie pulled a

corkscrew from a drawer. She certainly knew her way around Dave's apartment – maybe this was the new 'party house' when they all got together, however infrequently that might be.

Nita arrived just then, carrying two bottles of champagne, and air-kissed everyone in turn. Scott stood to greet her, but Aaron did not. He still had a strained expression on his face, and Sive decided it was time to break up whatever chat Scott was having with him.

Dave turned down the music and nodded towards the champagne bottles. 'Cheers, Nita. I don't have champagne glasses, though. This do?' He held up a tumbler.

'It will taste just as good, no matter what glass it's in,' Nita said. 'Remember the time at someone's wedding when they ran out of everything but pint glasses and they served me a pint of champagne?'

'Oh, yeah, Burner's wedding, wasn't it?' Aaron called from the far side of the room.

Now he speaks, Sive thought, wincing on Scott's behalf as she moved across the room towards her husband.

'Oh, yes. Sorry for bringing it up, Scott,' Nita said, popping the champagne.

Scott grimaced. 'If we didn't talk about the awkward things, there'd be little left for us, right?'

'True that,' Nita muttered, thinking, perhaps, about Yasmin and the fire and the real or imaginary stalker as she poured herself a tumbler of champagne.

Sive took a seat on one side of the L-shaped couch and Nita joined her. Nita looked beautiful in a short black smock dress and sky-high heels, the kind Sive used to wear before working from home and school runs became her norm. She felt underdressed now, in her jeans-and-nice-top combo and her flat sandals.

'God, I am *exhausted*,' Nita said, pushing her hair out of her eyes. 'I should have booked a spa day for today after the week of work I've just had, but oh no, Nita had to go shopping instead.' She took another sip of champagne.

Please don't talk about yourself in the third person all night, Sive begged, but only in her head.

'Did you pick up anything nice?' she asked politely.

'A few bits in Harvey Nicks. How was your day? Oh!' She put a manicured hand to her mouth. 'Gosh, I should have invited you to come shopping with me! I'm so sorry, Sive. How rude.'

'Not at all, don't worry. Sure, I had the kids. And we had booked tickets for the Tower of London. Maggie came too, and Dave for a while.'

'Oh, really?' Nita's eyebrows arched. 'How nice. I might have gone if I'd known . . .'

There was absolutely no way she would have gone, and Sive knew it.

'Oh, sorry . . . I think Aaron said it to everyone in an email back when we were booking the trip.' Sive looked to Aaron for help, but he was staring at his phone now, oblivious to the conversation. Maggie jumped in.

'Yes, he did say it,' she confirmed. Then: 'Nita, my love, don't worry. You'd have hated every second of it. Lots of walking and standing. Children everywhere. I enjoyed it, but you were better off in Knightsbridge, I promise.'

That seemed to placate Nita. 'Anyone for another drink?' she asked, draining her glass and standing up.

Everyone was for another drink, it seemed, including Sive, who was starting to feel extremely glad the kids hadn't been invited. They were absolutely better off in the hotel room with their books and their cartoons, and she was absolutely better off not guarding the glass-topped coffee table from her Duracell Bunny children.

'Your home is beautiful,' she said to Dave, as Nita poured rosé into Sive's tiny glass and – to Sive's surprise – another champagne into her own tumbler.

'Oh, cheers. Yeah, had to do it up after my mum moved out. It was very old-lady.'

'And now it's very middle-aged-man,' Scott said with a grin.

'Very funny. It worked out well, though. My mum wanted to be back in her childhood home and I wanted fewer rooms to keep clean.'

'You never rented out the Stratford house again?' Sive asked.

'Nah. Wouldn't have been the same. Especially after—' He stopped and took a swallow of lager.

'He means especially after Yasmin died,' Nita said quietly.

Dave took off his cap and ran his hand across his head. 'Yeah. She and Aaron had already moved out by then, but that house will always make me think of those times when it was the six of us together. It just didn't feel right to have a different gang move in.'

'It sounds like it was idyllic, when you all lived there,' Sive said, wondering if that was an odd thing to say, considering how it had ended.

'It was,' Maggie said. 'Of course, we thought we knew everything. And that we were so grown up and sophisticated. Dave, would you have the old photo albums? We could show Sive?'

'Nah. They're gone.'

'What do you mean, *gone*?'

Dave shrugged. 'Lost. Thrown out. My mum, probably.'

Maggie frowned. 'Are you sure? Aren't they—' She stopped. 'Anyway. What a shame. It would have been nice to look back. No smartphones then, of course, so mostly just terrible shots of people with badly applied make-up lit by too-bright camera flashes.'

Sive thought about the one strip of passport photos she'd seen of Aaron and Yasmin and imagined an entire album filled with loved-up pictures. Perhaps it wasn't such a bad thing that she wouldn't see them.

She glanced across at Aaron. He wasn't looking at his phone any more but didn't seem quite tuned in to the conversation either. Nita, who had kept the open bottle of champagne at her feet, reached now to pour a third glass.

'Nita, aren't you supposed to lay off the booze when you're pregnant?' Scott asked.

Nita held up the tumbler. 'Have you seen how tiny these glasses are? Three of these is the equivalent of one normal glass.'

This wasn't at all true, especially as Nita was filling each glass to the brim. Sive was surprised and, at the same time, annoyed at herself for being surprised. She prided herself on being acutely non-judgemental, especially in any debate with Aaron, who never held back when it came to expressing his opinions on other people's behaviour. She watched Nita sip the drink. It did seem strange to go to all the trouble of assisted reproduction and not follow basic health guidelines . . . Anyway, Sive wasn't going to say a word. She'd had enough uninvited commentary on her own pregnancies, especially her first. Good God, people had had a lot to say when they realized she was pregnant with Faye. *Isn't it very soon? How long have you known Aaron? Was it planned? Will you keep it? Are you sure it's his?* She pushed the memories away. Now that they were a happy, double-income, beautiful-house-in-the-best-postcode nuclear family, nobody ever asked for their origin story.

She stood and walked to the window. 'The view out over the gardens is lovely,' she said, deflecting attention from Nita and her champagne. 'It's like a secret enclave in the middle of London. Did your mother miss it at all when you swapped?'

'Not really,' Dave said. 'She always loved that old house in Stratford, even after her knees got bad and she couldn't get up the stairs any more.'

'I can't imagine your mum as a little old lady with dodgy knees!' Nita said. 'She was quite the battleaxe when we lived there. Remember we were always terrified about her letting herself in to check if we'd cleaned the kitchen properly?'

'And the bathroom, because you used to leave make-up stains all over the sink. And then blame it on Yasmin!'

'Well, she couldn't tell us apart, so I made the most of it. "Those two brown girls, I never know which is which,"' Nita said in a strong cockney accent that was presumably supposed to mimic Dave's mum.

'Nita! She never said that. She couldn't tell you apart because you were sisters. She wasn't a racist.'

'Hmph.' Nita took another drink, but she was grinning into her glass.

'I reckon the main reason for the surprise visits was to check for overnight guests,' Scott said. 'She wasn't running a house of ill repute, she used to say. Imagine if she'd known what was right under her nose – Yasmin staying over in Aaron's room every single night.' A glance at Sive. 'Oops, sorry. That was probably inappropriate.'

Sive smiled to show she wasn't one bit fazed. *Not one bit.*

'I'd love to see it again sometime,' Nita said, softly now. 'I don't suppose we could all come crashing in on your mother, though, Dave. Or could we?'

Maggie cleared her throat, and Sive glanced over. Had Nita said something wrong? Maggie was looking down now, hands clasped on her lap.

'The house is gone,' Dave said quietly. 'We had to sell it.'

'Oh.' Nita's reply was a soft breath of surprise and sadness. The last time she had lived with her sister, Sive realized, was in that house in Stratford.

'I didn't know that,' Scott said. 'Where's your mum living now, then?'

Dave's cheeks flushed. 'She's . . . she's had to go to a care home. She couldn't manage on her own any more, and I . . .' A helpless shrug.

'Couldn't she have moved in here?' Scott asked, and Sive could hear a hint of goading. 'Plenty of space, I'd have thought?'

Dave grimaced. 'I suppose, but . . .'

'Don't be an ass, Scott.' Unexpectedly, it was Nita, and not Maggie, who jumped to Dave's rescue. 'Dave's at work all day and his mum needs looking after. The care home is the best place for her. There's no shame in it, Dave,' she added, her tone gentler.

Sive glanced over at Maggie and found her staring at Dave and Nita, a perplexed look on her face.

'Are you OK, Maggie?'

'What? Yes. All fine.' A quick smile.

But something was up with her, Sive was sure of it, watching as Maggie clasped and unclasped her hands. She really didn't look OK at all.

29

AARON GRIPS SIVE'S HAND as they stand on Regent Street, forcing smiles for the video call with Bea. Scott is holding the phone for her, and he turns the camera towards Toby now, who's snoozing in his arms. Reassured, Aaron disconnects the call and, together, in silence, the Sullivans walk back inside Oxford Circus Tube station, down to the ticket hall.

The other reporters have disappeared from sight, temporarily at least, but just ahead, Aaron can see Jude, leaning against the wall opposite the ticket barriers, out of the way of the never-ending stream of passengers. Like a leech, he thinks, holding on for her scoop. Did she overhear some of Hawthorn's update earlier? Aaron couldn't help feeling she'd been trying to listen in. Not for the first time today, he wishes Sive hadn't told the police officers their secret.

He looks around as they reach Jude. 'Where's Maggie?'

'She needed to make a call and went outside to hear better.' She chews her lip for a moment. 'Meanwhile, I've been speaking to Hawthorn about Tim Brassil, the guy who found Bea.'

Aaron tries to contain his eyeroll.

'Why?' Sive asks.

160

'Because he doesn't work where he said he worked.'

'*What?* Do they think he had something to do with Faye's disappearance?'

'It's unlikely,' Jude says, 'but they're contacting him to find out why he lied. To rule it out. On another note, Aaron, I've been speaking to some colleagues at the paper about organized crime and the Callans.' She draws air through her teeth. 'It may be worth—'

Aaron cuts her off. 'This has nothing to do with them.'

'Let her talk,' Sive says. 'Jude, please go on.'

Jude looks from Sive to Aaron, then continues. 'Apparently, they're not afraid to go after wealthy, influential people when it suits their needs. Now, we know Aaron's case is that Brosnan is being framed because he wanted out and the Callans can't have people leaving. They could have shot Brosnan, but this is a two-birds-one-stone set-up. They shot the other guy and set Brosnan up to take the fall. Only he has Ireland's top criminal defence lawyer defending him. Right?'

Aaron looks Jude in the eye. Is she mocking him? But her expression is serious.

'We have a very good defence prepared. It's unlikely Brosnan will go to prison,' he says evenly.

'So, don't the Callans have a reason to target you? To get you to step back from the case or lose deliberately so Brosnan goes to jail?'

Jude's scrutinizing him now in a way he doesn't like, and Aaron feels an unfamiliar burn of unease. Maybe it's better to keep her on side.

'I'm certain that's not what this is.' Jude is about to say something else, and he holds up his hand. 'But I'll tell Hawthorn anyway.'

Jude nods, happy, no doubt, with making her point.

Sive turns to Aaron. 'Have they any history of . . . Would they hurt children?'

Aaron pulls out his phone. 'I asked Garvin to check into that.' A look that might be satisfaction crosses Jude's face. 'I'll see if he got anything.'

Garvin picks up straight away, as though he's been waiting for his boss's call. He begins to give his findings in his customary formal tone before Aaron has to ask. One of Garvin's many talents is anticipating Aaron's needs. Sive says it's because Aaron has him petrified – that he's permanently primed to respond, like a nervous dog. But she's never had any staff reporting to her and doesn't understand how boss–employee relationships work.

'In the time I've had to research thus far,' Garvin is saying, 'there is some suggestion that the Callans have been involved in three separate tiger kidnappings, two of which involved children. The children were not harmed – or, to be precise, if they were, it was not recorded.'

'So we can safely say they don't hurt children.'

'I . . . well, I suppose . . .'

'Right. Anything else?'

'Nothing for now, but can I help with the search in any way?'

Aaron runs his hand through his hair. 'How would you help with the search when you're in Dublin and we're in London?' It comes out unintentionally sharp. 'I need to keep the line free.' Aaron disconnects and glances at Sive, who is waiting expectantly.

'Garvin says they don't target children. Ever.' It's only a small lie and, if it makes Sive worry less, it's worth it.

Sive lets out a quiet exhalation of tiny relief as Aaron's phone begins to ring.

It's a withheld number. He answers.

'Aaron Sullivan.'

A woman's voice begins to speak. Slow and deliberate. Every word carefully enunciated.

'I have Faye.'

Aaron's mouth is suddenly dry. He reaches for the pillar behind to steady himself as his legs go slack.

The woman keeps talking. Unhurried. Dispassionate. 'I'm going to tell you how you can get her back.'

Any reply Aaron might have is stuck in his throat. He slumps against the pillar now, as she continues.

'You can choose to carry out my instructions, or you can lose your ch—' An announcement crackles over the PA system, momentarily drowning out the woman's voice. Aaron presses the phone to his ear, desperate to catch every word. '—won't like what I ask you to do. It might be the toughest thing you've ever faced. A dilemma. You'll see.'

And the line goes dead.

30

Two days earlier | Saturday
Clarinda Gardens

BY THE TIME THE takeaway arrived in Dave's flat on Saturday night, Maggie seemed back to herself and Sive wondered if she'd been imagining the peculiar look on her face when the friends had been talking about Dave's mother. She watched as Maggie busied herself, laying out forks and glasses of water, moving a chess set and a pile of newspapers off the coffee table – still the unofficial 'house mother' after all these years – while Dave topped up drinks.

Now they were sitting around the coffee table with plates on their knees, and the conversation turned to how Aaron and Sive met. Sive squirmed. She hated this.

'We met in court,' Aaron said with a smile, just as he always did. He liked to provoke a reaction.

'Oh, what had she done? Bit of shoplifting? Credit-card fraud?' Scott asked with a laugh. Then: 'Just kidding, Sive.'

Aaron ignored this and continued with his story. 'I was representing a guy who'd killed a co-worker. Poor fucker hadn't a hope, even with me defending him. He was convicted. Pretty sure that's the last case I lost, and I'm still morto, to be honest. But the upside was, I met my lovely wife.' He smiled over at her.

'Well, they say most people get together at work, so I guess you guys tick that box even if it wasn't quite "eyes meeting over the photocopier",' Scott said. 'I met Caron at the photocopier. Not that it did me much bloody good, now that she's taken me for half of everything I own and run off with that producer fucker.'

Maggie patted Scott's knee. 'You got three lovely kids out of it, so there's that.'

'Even if they're on another continent now,' Aaron said.

Sive shook her head at him in quiet warning, but he didn't see. Or pretended he didn't see. This obsession with beating everyone worked well for him in a courtroom but was far less appealing in social situations. Aaron never differentiated between work and personal life, though. She thought back to what Maggie had said earlier, about Aaron trying to catch Yasmin's stalker. She wasn't all that surprised. It was *very* Aaron. No sitting around: get up and *do* something was his modus operandi. He was always doing something, always trying to win or achieve or outsmart. *Lots* of outsmarting. And lots of catching people in lies. Aaron's favourite hobby was catching people in lies. Sive preferred to give people the chance to tell the truth (notably, her kids), but Aaron enjoyed the cat-and-mouse game of setting traps and watching people walk right into them. He did it in court, of course, where it was actually his job. But he did it behind the scenes, too – in his office, with his support staff.

She still cringed when she remembered hearing about the earliest days with Garvin, Aaron's perfectionist assistant, who had, in a rare and never repeated oversight, forgotten to arrange an important client lunch one busy December Friday. Aaron had discovered the mistake when he rang the restaurant with a last-minute request for a specific type of champagne, but instead of letting Garvin know, as Sive would have done, he baited Garvin, pushing him to see if he'd lie or tell the truth. He asked him if the restaurant had phoned back to confirm. Watched Garvin squirm as realization spread over his face. Let him lie about the restaurant phoning to finalize numbers. Watched him rush off to make an urgent phonecall in a desperate bid to secure a booking. Waited while Garvin tried to figure out how the booking had been made if he hadn't done it. And then brought it up at every performance review in the eight years since. *Trust is everything, Garvin. Lying about small things means a person might lie about big things. No smoke without fire.*

And so on and so on, ad nauseam. It never needed to go that far, in Sive's opinion. If Aaron hadn't led Garvin into trying to cover up, it would have been over before it started. But what would she know? She'd never had staff. And as one of Dublin's most successful barristers, Aaron presumably knew what he was doing. So yes, she could certainly imagine him trying to catch Yasmin's stalker, and she was curious now to find out more about what he'd done. But Maggie had come back to the hotel with them after the Tower of London and had stayed to help her with the kids while Aaron had gone off to meet Dave for a pint. So Sive would have to wait to ask him her questions.

The conversation moved from Scott's separation to Nita's pregnancy to Maggie's many godchildren then back to Scott's kids and their reaction to their parents' divorce.

'It's hit them hard,' Scott said, his jaw muscle twitching. 'And Jesus, the guilt. I'd literally give my right arm to save them the pain of what they've been through . . .' He looked around the room and took a swig of his beer. 'I'm deadly serious. I guess it's something you can only understand if you have kids, though.'

Maggie let out an exasperated sigh. 'Scott, please don't do the whole "you'll only understand if you're a parent" thing. Honestly. People who are not parents have empathy too, you know. And we all come from parents.' She clicked her tongue. 'This is the hill I will die on. Child-free people are not incapable of understanding what it must be like to be a parent.'

Sive sipped her rosé, nodding agreement.

But Scott wasn't for turning. 'Until you know you'd literally die for your child, you can't understand what it's like.'

'I would,' Maggie said.

'You would what?'

'If it came to it, some impossible situation, and it was my life or a child's, I think I would.'

Scott laughed. 'I hope you wouldn't die for my kids – ungrateful little whelps.'

'I suppose nobody knows until they're in that situation,' Maggie mused. 'And maybe I'd be saying something very different if it really happened, but yeah . . . A child with their whole life ahead of them, versus me, who's already been around the block for forty-two years. I think I would.'

Dave chimed in then. 'Fair play, Maggie, but count me out. Kids are cute an' all, but not *that* cute.' He shrugged and grinned.

Nita laughed. 'Count me out too. Ask me again in six months, but for now, no thank you.'

Maggie shook her head. 'But that's my *point*. You say, "Ask me again in six months," as though you'll change so profoundly. As though I'm incapable of ever understanding that love. I understand love. I have my sisters and my parents and—'

'Lucky you,' Nita said simply, and Maggie's cheeks flushed.

'Sorry, I shouldn't have said that.'

A short silence followed, and Sive jumped in. 'Listen, I have three kids and I'm not even sure I'd die for them.' Everyone laughed more loudly than it warranted, glad, she thought, to move away again from the spectre of Yasmin's ghost.

Only Aaron remained unsmiling. 'Would you not?' he asked Sive. 'I would,' he went on, without waiting for an answer. 'Give up my life for my own kids? Definitely.'

Sive shuddered involuntarily at his choice of words and quietly hoped it was never put to the test.

Maggie began to clear plates and Sive got up to help her. Nita got up too, tottering now on her heels, and fetched a fresh bottle of champagne from the fridge. Nobody else was drinking champagne. Had she really had a full bottle? Sive bit her lip. Maybe it was the resurfacing of old memories about Yasmin? The anniversary? Was Aaron's presence disturbing her? But she'd seen him plenty of times over the years, even if this was the first 'official' reunion.

Sive stood beside Maggie as they stacked the dishwasher, out of earshot of the others thanks to 5ive, whose 'If Ya Gettin' Down' played from the speaker on the breakfast bar.

'Is Nita OK?' she asked.

Maggie shook her head. 'I don't know. I'll try to grab a quiet minute with her.'

'Just . . . the baby. It can't be good. And yet, she's a grown adult. We can't forbid her to drink, can we?'

'I know. It's the kind of thing you think you'd do easily until you're actually in the situation.' Maggie reached below the sink for dishwasher tablets.

'You really know your way around!' Sive said. 'Shouldn't Dave be the one cleaning up?'

Maggie rolled her eyes. 'Yep.' She glanced over at the others sitting chatting while she switched on the dishwasher. 'Though

I think he might be . . . well, he might be going through some stuff. I'll leave him in peace for now.'

Sive opened her mouth to ask what 'stuff', but there was no way to do so without sounding nosy. She looked across the room at Aaron. Perhaps he'd know. For now, she'd add it to her ever-growing list of questions about these London friends and their complex pasts.

31

Sive's mouth opens in shock as Aaron's phone slips from his hand and clatters on to the tiles.

'Aaron, what is it? Did they find her?'

He shakes his head mutely. Sive grabs his arm.

'Aaron! Who was on the phone?'

Aaron, wide-eyed, looks at Sive, then at Jude, then, with visible effort, manages to speak.

'Jude, could you give me a minute with my wife?'

Jude nods. 'Of course.' She steps away, taking out her phone as Aaron picks his off the ground.

'Aaron, you're scaring me. Who was it?'

'I don't know.' His fingers are tight around her arm and he's steering her further away from Jude. 'They said they have Faye.'

Oh God.

'Who?' she whispers.

'I don't know.' Aaron's voice is small. Lost. 'A woman. She said she has Faye and . . . and I have to do something to get her back.'

'What do you have to do?' She's shaking his arm now.

'She didn't say. She just said that if I follow her instructions, we'll get her back. And if I don't, we . . . we won't.'

'Is it money? We have money. We can sell the house. We can get whatever they want.'

But her husband is shaking his head.

'The woman didn't say anything about money. I think . . . it's something else.'

She's crying now and shaking him hard. 'But how are we supposed to know what to do?'

'Shush, Sive. We need to keep this to ourselves.' He glances over her shoulder. 'One of the reporters from earlier is back,' he mutters. 'Come this way.' He steers her along the wall, out of the path of passing commuters and the journalist's line of sight.

'Aaron, what the hell do we do?'

'She'll call back,' Aaron says simply. And on cue, his phone begins to ring.

'Hello?' he says, putting it on speaker, and they huddle together to listen.

'I trust you've had time to digest my first call.' The voice is clear, modulated. Polite. Normal. Not the voice of someone who takes children. Not the voice of anyone Sive knows. 'Now, I'll tell you what I'm going to ask you to do. But first of all, let me be clear. No police. If you go to the police, you'll never see Faye again. I'm the only person in the world who knows where she is, so don't test me.' Sive starts to reply, to say they won't tell anyone, but the caller keeps talking. 'You won't like it, Aaron, but your task is this.'

32

Clarinda Gardens

THERE WAS A CERTAIN inevitability about it, Sive thought afterwards. The way Nita made her way slowly to her feet, wobbling in her heels. The search behind her, looking for her phone on the couch. The reach for the bag that was sitting on the floor. A black Miu Miu bag she'd bought that afternoon. The way she missed the strap, then swooped again to grab it. This time she caught one side of the open bag and managed to upend it. The contents spilled far and wide across Dave's polished concrete floor. Six people moved simultaneously to gather the scattered belongings. A Marc Jacobs wallet, splayed on the rug. Half a dozen credit cards. A £50 note. A Charlotte Tilbury lipstick. A pack of pocket-sized tissues. A box of anti-histamines. A tube of Bio Oil. A small but heavy make-up bag, mercifully zipped. A blister-pack of paraceta-mol, half full. A box of Ovidrel. A Baume de Rose lip balm. A packet of Pregnacare supplements. And a photograph of Yasmin.

It was Sive who picked up the picture of Yasmin, and she couldn't help staring at what was only the second ever photograph she'd seen of her husband's deceased fiancée. In this one, Yasmin was on her own, sitting on a sunlit bench under a palm tree. She looked younger than in the other photo – seventeen or eighteen,

Sive reckoned – and her hair was henna red here too, but darker, a less vibrant shade. Perhaps at that point she was just dipping her toe into dyeing it. She was wearing a turquoise string top and cut-off denim shorts, her legs crossed at the ankle as she sat licking an ice cream. A family holiday, maybe? Though as far as Sive knew, Nita and Yasmin's parents had died when the girls were small, and they'd been raised by their mother's cousin in North London. Sive passed the picture back to Nita, still staring at it. There was something about it that niggled, but she couldn't work out what it was. Perhaps she too had had more than enough to drink.

Nita shoved her belongings into her bag, apologizing as she did so. The spill seemed to have sobered her up. Actually, Sive wondered now, watching Nita fasten the bag and walk across the room to retrieve her jacket, she seemed perfectly fine. Was the tipsy thing all an act, to get attention? It wouldn't be beyond Nita. Attention was her fuel. Maybe she hadn't been drinking the champagne at all? Sive remembered tipping a glass of Pinot Grigio into a plant pot at a friend's house when it was too early to tell anyone she was pregnant with Bea. And the same with a cup of tea when her mother-in-law added Sullivan-levels of milk. But there was no plant here. And it really had looked like Nita – savvy, smart Nita with the carefully planned pregnancy – had downed a bottle of champagne on her own.

Her Uber was outside the main gate, she said, as she waved a cheery goodbye; sorry to leave so early but she needed to catch up on work in the morning. Aaron stood and put down his drink. He'd walk her out. The others nodded, and Nita didn't argue. The short silence that followed when Aaron closed the door was broken by Maggie.

'So, Sive, how's work going for you? I hope you won't have to do Sunday morning catch-up like Nita!'

Sive smiled. 'I hope not.'

'Sive's her own boss, isn't she?' Scott said. 'Can take all the time off she wants. That must be nice.'

Sive kept smiling. 'It's more like *never* being able to take time off. I don't mind. I like what I do.'

'I suppose you can quit any time,' Dave mused. 'Aaron's coining it in.'

Scott shook his head. 'There's not as much money in law as you might think, Dave.'

'Eh, have you seen their house? Big, huge mansion with electric gates and security cameras?' Dave smiled sheepishly at Sive. 'I googled it.'

Scott shook his head. 'Houses are cheaper in Ireland.'

'They most certainly aren't,' Maggie said. 'Believe me, I looked at buying a summer house in the west of Ireland, but it was *way* beyond my budget.'

'Maybe Aaron gets his money somewhere else, then,' Dave said with a wink.

Sive squirmed. What an odd conversation. Perhaps this was a hangover from when they were young and openly comparing notes on starter salaries in their respective jobs.

Aaron returned and, relieved to have a break in the how-much-Aaron-earns discussion, Sive asked him if Nita was OK.

'She's fine,' was all he said, before picking up his beer and joining Dave and Scott, who had moved on to admiring Dave's fifty-inch TV and discussing their respective streaming services. There was little enough Aaron and Scott agreed on, but on the topic of television sets they were united – the bigger the better. Sive watched Aaron clap an arm around Scott's shoulder and she let out a small sigh of relief. Relief tinged with envy, she realized, for friendships free of second-guessing.

She turned to Maggie. 'So that was all . . . a bit odd? Nita, I mean?'

Maggie pursed her lips. 'After seeing what spilled out of her bag, I have an inkling . . . but I'm not sure.' She paused, then said: 'How about we have a girls' night tomorrow night. You and me, glass of wine somewhere nice. I'll invite Nita too. And we can try to get to the bottom of what's going on?'

'That sounds good. I need to check with Aaron, though. Might be a bit harsh to leave him in the hotel with the kids when it's supposed to be his trip . . .'

'It's your trip too, and anyway, all the guys are staying home tomorrow evening to get a good night's sleep before the race on Monday morning. No point in you staying in too, is there?'

This was true. In fact, Aaron might be just as happy. If she was there tomorrow night, they'd both feel the need to *do* something – put on a movie, order room service, talk. If he was on his own, he could read the Sunday papers and watch sport. A dream night for Aaron, now that she thought about it.

'You're on,' she said to Maggie. 'Right, I'd better get that husband of mine home soon, or the poor babysitter will think we've abandoned our kids for good.'

She caught Aaron's eye and tapped her watch. He nodded, unsmiling. She remembered again how tense he'd been earlier. And Maggie's untold story about Yasmin's stalker. Was the reunion stirring up bad memories? She watched him from across the room. Or was his upcoming case getting to him more than he'd let on? Maybe Scott's comments in the café had hit home. Maybe his client's alibi wasn't as airtight as Aaron had first believed. Maybe . . . but Sive couldn't help thinking it was something else entirely.

33

YOU WON'T LIKE IT, Aaron, but your task is this.

Sive and Aaron hold a collective breath, waiting to hear what the caller wants in return for Faye. But there's a break. No words. No voice. All around, the sounds of the London Underground buzz and blare but, from the phone in Aaron's shaking hand, there's nothing. Sive feels panic rising – has the woman disconnected? What if she's gone and never calls back? What if something happens to this woman and they never find Faye? What if—

There's a click. And then the voice starts again.

'This won't be easy, Aaron, but remember, you have a choice. What you have to do, to see Faye again, is this. Record a video of yourself, right now, telling the public the truth. About what you've been doing all these years.'

Sive stares at the phone, then at Aaron. *What is she talking about?*

After a short pause, as though waiting for Aaron and Sive to absorb what she's saying, the woman continues. 'About how you win your cases, Aaron.'

Another pause, this time so long Sive worries again that the woman is gone. She leans closer to the phone to speak.

'Hello? Are you still there? What are you talking about?'

Aaron shakes his head, shushing Sive.

There's a click on the line, then they hear the woman's voice again. 'I think your colleagues at the Bar might like to know how you win your cases. And some judges will be very interested too. And the gardaí.'

Sive can't wait any longer. 'Just tell us where Faye is! You can have money, you can have whatever you want – I need my daughter back. Please.'

But the person on the other end of the line continues to talk to Aaron as though Sive hasn't spoken at all.

'I think the police would be interested in how you pay the mortgage for your house on Ailesbury Road and for your private-school education for Faye. Even "Ireland's top barrister" couldn't be earning quite as much as you are.'

There's something utterly soulless about the voice. It's almost robotic, like a scam caller. Though not quite.

'Wait, how do we know you're for real?' Sive says. 'Let me speak to my daughter.'

Silence. Then another faint click.

'I'm not with your daughter right now. She's sleeping in another location. It's not possible to speak with her until the drugs wear off. And by then, if you've done what you need to do, you can see her in person.'

'Where is—'

The woman keeps talking. Still calm, unhurried, unemotional.

'Once you do what you're told, I'll tell you where she is.'

Aaron opens his mouth to speak, but Sive gets there first. 'If you can't let me speak to her and you're not with her right now, how do I know she's where you say she is?'

Again silence. And again a click.

'I was with your daughter an hour ago. She misses you very much. She cried a bit, but she was mostly brave. Her leg hurts, of course. One of the stitches has come loose. But you can get it re-done once you get her back.' A pause. 'That is, of course, *if* you want her back.'

34

2.36 p.m.

'OF COURSE WE WANT her back,' Aaron hisses at the caller as Sive stands staring mutely at the phone, trying to get her head around it. At the other end of the line, the invisible line, is the one link with her daughter. *How can this be happening? Who is this cold-as-ice woman who has taken Faye?*

Aaron takes a shuddery breath. 'Just tell me what to do. Where to go. How to get her.'

Sive forces herself to focus and, almost on autopilot, pulls out her own phone and clicks on a microphone icon.

But now there's just silence.

'Hello?' Aaron says, holding his phone close to his mouth.

Then there's a click. 'It's simple. Record a video of yourself. Tell everyone the truth about what you've been doing. About pressuring witnesses to change their stories. About the blackmail that keeps your clients out of jail and your pockets lined with cash. Put the video on Twitter and tag ten accounts on a list I've just texted to you. You'll be the talk of the town. And you'll never work again. As you like to say yourself, no smoke without fire.' A pause and a click. 'But don't even think about claiming you've been forced to make a false confession. If you do, you'll never see Faye again.'

The call is disconnected.

Sive is cold and sick and dizzy, desperately trying to pull her-self together, to take action. To do whatever they have to do to get Faye back.

'Is . . . is there a text?' she asks, watching Aaron click into something on his phone.

'Yes. RTÉ. Sky. BBC. The *Irish Times*. The *Daily Byte*, and so on.' He looks up at her. 'I can't do this. I'll be struck off.'

'Aaron! Who cares? Just do it. This person has Faye!'

'We don't even know for sure, though . . .'

'Fuck's sake! She knew about the stitches on her leg. Nobody knows about them. And even if there's only a one per cent chance that this is legit, that this insane woman has her, that she'll really give her back, we have to try! Just make the video!'

'Hey,' Aaron says, making shushing motions with his hand and throwing his eyes over to where Jude is standing. 'Lower your voice.'

'Don't tell me to lower my voice. Someone has taken Faye and she wants you to make some stupid speech in a video, so make the stupid fucking speech in a video!'

'But I—'

'I can't believe we're having this conversation. Just do it!' She grabs the phone from his hand and goes to his camera. Stand-ing just six inches from him, she clicks on video and nods at him to talk.

He shakes his head. 'This is insane! I'm not making some crazy confession. You don't think I did any of that stuff, do you?'

'Of course bloody not, but who cares? Just say it! It's how we get Faye back. And as soon as we have her you can make another video telling everyone what happened, that you were forced to make a false confession.' *How does he not get this?*

'But Sive, some people will believe it. They'll reckon there's no smoke without fire, like the woman said.'

'So what! You don't care what the public thinks of you, you never have. Just do it. For Faye.'

'But there'll be investigations.'

'Let them investigate. It's a made-up bloody confession. Christ, you literally said on Saturday night in Dave's house that you'd give up your life for our kids. This isn't your life, it's just a video.'

Silence now, as Aaron stares at the phone but still says nothing. 'Aaron,' she whispers. 'This isn't . . . is this because—'

'No! It's not that. It's just hard. This could be the end of my career. No matter what I say afterwards, there will always be people who believe it. But I'll do it. Of course I will. Fuck. Start recording.'

35

2.41 p.m.

JUDE IS SUPPOSED TO be giving them space, but she can't help inching closer. Aaron looks like he's about to make some kind of speech, with Sive filming. A plea to the public? She moves another step. Neither of them is paying her any attention. Now she's within earshot. A Tube station announcement drowns out Aaron's words but, once it's over, she tunes in.

'. . . and I . . . I've been blackmailing witnesses in order to put pressure on them. To win cases. Regrettably.'

Jude stares. Did he really just say that? Sive stops filming and starts doing something on her phone. Jude abandons all pretence of giving them space.

'What was that?' she asks, stepping right beside them.

Sive and Aaron look at each other, and something unspoken passes between them. Aaron's eyes widen, as though asking permission, and Sive shakes her head. Just the tiniest motion, but Jude catches it.

'A video. You'll see it now, it's going on Twitter,' Sive says brusquely, tapping the screen of her phone at lightning speed.

'About *blackmail*?'

Aaron closes his eyes briefly. 'Yes. There's a certain irony to that word, all things considered.'

'*Aaron,*' Sive says, and there's a clear warning in her tone.

'You've been blackmailing witnesses?' Jude is incredulous. 'To retract statements against your clients – is that it?'

'No. I have not.' Clipped. Emphatic.

'Then why did you just . . . what's going on?'

Sive looks up from the phone. 'Jude, we can't say, so don't ask.' She turns to Aaron. 'It's done. I've tweeted it, tagging the list.'

Jude nods, surprised at Sive's assured, terse tone. The woman who's been falling apart all morning seems to have finally pulled herself together. Jude takes out her own phone now and clicks quickly to Sive's Twitter account. The video is there, with ten accounts tagged – TV, radio, newspapers, including her own. *What the hell?* She clicks into the video and holds her phone to her ear. It's not much longer than what she already overheard.

'You've just confessed to blackmail. Someone made you do this? Linked to Faye's disappearance?'

'Jude, please,' Sive urges. 'Don't ask us.'

Jude frowns. 'OK.' She looks down at her phone. Sive's video hasn't been picked up yet. Sive doesn't have a big following and the media accounts haven't spotted it. 'Will I retweet it?' Jude asks. 'Do you need it to get traction?'

'No,' Aaron says. 'We've done what we were asked to do. Nobody said we had to amplify it.'

Jude nods. So someone's made him do this and he's following specific instructions. *Jesus. This is huge.* It means it's definitely premeditated, and linked to Aaron's work. This is so much bigger than anything she's ever covered before.

Aaron's phone rings. He glances at Jude and Sive as he answers.

'Yes.'

Jude can only hear Aaron's side of the conversation.

'But we've done what you—'

'But—'

He looks up. 'She's gone.'

Jude blinks. *She? The kidnapper is female?*

'What did she say?' Sive asks.

'We need the tweet to get some traction. Then she'll call back. She mentioned you.' Aaron looks at Jude. 'She said she's seen your tweets and knows you've been with us all morning. To ask you to retweet it.' He looks up to the station ceiling and rubs his face. '*Fuck.*'

Jude nods, already tapping her phone. 'Of course.' She retweets Sive's video clip, with a simple 'please watch'. Within seconds, there are replies, likes and retweets. The responses vary from 'WTF?' to 'Did someone make him do this?' to some variation of 'I always knew he was dodgy'. But it has the desired result. Within minutes, the clip has been retweeted over four hundred times and the media outlets have now picked up on it too. Jude holds up the phone to show Aaron.

'Is this what the person wants?'

Aaron and Sive nod, their faces grey. There's no pretending any more. Faye Sullivan has not wandered off. Faye Sullivan is not with some well-meaning stranger. Jude feels a rush of dread, shot through with adrenaline. Sive was right. Faye Sullivan really has been kidnapped. And Jude Barr has an exclusive interview.

36

Sive locks eyes with Jude. 'OK, this is really important. You can't say a *word*. Not to anyone.'

Aaron mutters something about journalists under his breath then, out loud, says, 'What happened to not telling her? Five minutes ago, you were warning me to stay quiet.'

He's right, but Sive ignores him. Jude has already heard more than enough to guess. Better to include her and keep her on side than risk alienating her – or worse, risk her publishing something that jeopardizes Faye's safety.

'Not a word, for now anyway,' Sive continues. 'Obviously, when we have her back, we'll need your help to undo the damage, by telling the whole story. But nothing yet.' *Because it's all lies, of course it is.* She pushes away the niggling worry that there's some tiny truth in what he was forced to say. *Now is not the time.*

Jude hesitates, then nods. 'What about the police, though? Won't they see it and guess what's happened?'

Aaron swears under his breath, and Sive feels every ounce of it. They hadn't thought of that.

She bites her lip, running through options. 'We'll say it's a fake – a deep-fake video that someone is obviously posting at a time when Aaron is not in a position to respond.'

Jude looks sceptical. 'OK. So that's what we'll say if Hawthorn asks? I'm not sure how credible it is.'

'It'll have to do. I'll tell her up front, get ahead of it.' Sive types a very brief message to Hawthorn:

Deep-fake video of Aaron doing a 'confession' online. Ignore, it's a distraction, someone targeting him when too vulnerable to deal.

'OK,' Jude says. 'And I'll back you up if she asks.'

'I can't ask you to lie to the police, Jude . . . '

A shrug. 'I'm only repeating what you've told me – how was I to know it wasn't true? Anyway, what did the caller say?'

Sive glances around, but nobody is paying any attention. 'It's a woman, and she phoned Aaron to say she has Faye. That he needed to make this online confession in order to get her back. So now, we wait for another call. To find out where she is.' *Please let it be that simple. Please let Aaron's video be enough.*

'Did she say anything else?' Jude asks.

'That it was Aaron's choice – he could make the video and get Faye back, or choose not to. That he had to confess, even though it would mean judges and gardaí getting involved.'

Jude raises her eyebrows. 'She used the term "gardaí"?'

Sive nods.

'So she was possibly Irish? Did she have an Irish accent?'

'Oh. God, you're right. The accent was quite neutral; it didn't sound particularly English . . .'

'And you're sure it was legit?' Jude asks. 'The fact that it was a woman seems strange.'

'We can't be sure of anything, but we have to hope it was legit, because it's our only lead.'

Jude pulls a notebook and pen from her bag. 'Can you remember any more of what she said?'

'I recorded it. The last parts, anyway,' Sive says, pulling out her phone.

Aaron looks up, surprised. 'You did?'

'Habit,' she says briskly. 'Work.' She clicks an app on her phone and the three of them lean in to listen.

'. . . and tag ten accounts on a list I've just texted to you. You'll be the talk of the town. And you'll never work again. As you like to say yourself, no smoke without fire.'

Sive clicks the pause button, declines a call from Hawthorn, and looks at Jude. 'It's a little hard to hear over the background noise, but it's clearly a woman, if somewhat robotic-sounding, and I think you're right that she's Irish.'

'Can you send me the recording?' Jude asks, scribbling furiously in her notebook.

Aaron shakes his head. 'No way.'

'When Faye is safe, yes, but not now,' Sive says. 'It's too risky. If the person finds out we told anyone . . .'

'That's fine. Can you play it again? Does it go on further?'

Sive presses play, and Jude leans closer. After a moment, she straightens up.

'What's the weird pause-and-click thing? Like it's stopping and starting?'

Sive shakes her head. 'I don't know.'

She casts her mind back. It's blurry now, the call, the sequence of events. But something is nagging at her. She plays the recording again, holding it close to her ear. She shakes her head.

'What is it?'

'I didn't catch it on this recording, but thinking back, I feel like when we tried to talk, the woman kept speaking. Almost as though we weren't there. Or she couldn't hear us.'

'Like she was playing a recording of herself? A sound file?'

'Exactly.' Sive nods. 'But why? Because she couldn't do a live phonecall?'

'Or she was disguising her voice, speeding it up or slowing it down?'

'Maybe. Meaning,' Sive says, turning to Aaron, 'it's possibly someone you know.'

37

One day earlier | Sunday
The Meridian Hotel

SIVE'S MOUTH WAS DRY when she woke on Sunday morning, and her head ached slightly. Not a hangover, just the inevitable bleariness that seemed to follow every night out now, no matter how tame. Beside her, Aaron snored. In the cot by the window, Toby stirred but didn't wake. It must be early, Sive thought, if even he was still asleep. No sounds of cartoons yet from the living room – the girls were still in bed too. The peace would have been lovely if she hadn't been worrying about Aaron. She'd tried to talk to him when they'd got back last night, once the babysitter had left, but hadn't got much.

'Is everything OK?' she'd asked as she pulled on pyjamas. 'You seemed distracted earlier.'

'Huh?' Aaron was in bed already, looking at his phone.

'You looked kind of . . . tense? I was wondering if Dave or Scott had said something that bugged you? Something when you went for the pint in the Lion, maybe?'

He was still looking at his phone.

'Or,' she continued, 'is it about Yasmin? Bad memories?'

Now he looked up. 'Nope. Just tired.'

Just tired. Aaron's go-to response when he didn't want to talk.

189

Hers too, to be fair. Maybe that's how it was for every married couple. She searched for a way to ask him about Yasmin's stalker, but nothing felt quite right. It seemed voyeuristic somehow. Nosy. Aaron lay back in the bed and switched off his bedside lamp.

'I'm shattered. Night,' was all he said, turning to face away. Within minutes, he was snoring, just as he was now – she looked at her phone – at 6.30 a.m. She needed to go back to sleep. Toby never slept past six. What a waste to be awake before him. Just as the thought passed through her mind, Toby stirred and began to cry. And that was that – Sunday in London had begun.

'Oh God, my head,' Aaron groaned, half an hour later. 'What time is it? And why did I drink so much?'

'It's seven. You didn't. We're just getting old.' She was sitting up in bed with Toby snuggled in her arms, drowsy after a feed.

'How are you so chirpy?' He leaned up on one elbow to drop a kiss on Toby's head, then one on Sive's cheek.

'You started earlier than me – your pint with Dave. How was that, by the way?'

His face clouded. 'It was fine. You know Dave, never stops talking.'

'And Scott? You looked tense when you were talking to him.'

'Scott's just Scott,' he said, which told her precisely nothing.

'It must be hard sometimes on trips like this,' she tried, 'when people bring up Yasmin?'

'It was a long time ago. And Nita's right, we spent too long avoiding it.' He pulled himself up to a sitting position and leaned back against the headboard. 'Talking about her, I mean. Especially on her anniversary.'

'Maggie said you tried to catch Yasmin's stalker?' *Bull by the horns*.

'Yeah. The night she died.' He picked up Sive's hand, and began tracing circles on it.

'Really?' She turned her head to see him more clearly. 'I never knew. What did you do?'

A hollow laugh. 'It was dumb, really. But the first time Yasmin was followed, she was on her way home from the Rooftop Bar. And then, any time she went there, she felt like the same person followed her home. Only if she was on her own, not when I was there too.'

'She used to go to the bar on her own?' Sive immediately wondered why she'd asked that – she'd often gone to bars alone, especially on work trips. But everything she'd heard about Aaron's housemates back in the day gave the impression they had lived in each other's pockets.

'No, I mean, if she met the others there when I was working late and made her own way home. Those were the times she was followed. Or thought she was followed.'

Sive nodded. 'OK, I get you. Go on?'

'So she started to associate the stalker with the Rooftop Bar. She was certain he must be a customer, and there frequently enough that he always seemed to be around when she was. She stopped wanting to go there at all.'

'Understandably.'

'But then she started to see him outside our house. Shadows she said were human. She got really paranoid.'

Sive frowned. 'Did you think she was making it up?'

'No, *she* definitely believed he was real. And I'm sure she was followed that first night. But as I said, I could never be quite certain about the rest.'

From the living room came the sound of a door opening, then whispers, then TV. The spell would soon be broken.

Sive sat up straighter, shifting Toby in her arms. Still Aaron traced circles on her hand.

'So what did you do?'

Aaron let out a long breath. 'Right, this is going to sound silly, but I put up a photo on Facebook – Facebook was the new, shiny thing back then and we were all still figuring it out and—'

'Wait, you had Facebook?' Sive couldn't let that one go. Aaron had no social media of any kind and a particular contempt for Facebook.

A sheepish grin. 'I was young. Anyway, I put up a photo from another night we'd had in the Rooftop Bar – a terrible, grainy photo, but I whatchamacallit . . . tagged Yasmin and made it seem like she was there that night. It was her idea. Then I was to go there and see if I could spot someone looking for her.'

'It sounds . . . like a long shot?'

'It was. But who knows, it might have worked.' He began twisting her wedding ring, the antique diamond that had belonged to his grandmother. 'Given me a chance to watch the watcher, as such.'

'But, like, not dissing your plan or anything, but surely the stalker wouldn't have been Facebook friends with her?'

Aaron laughed. 'Oh Lord, we had no idea about privacy settings back then. Everything was public. So if there was someone stalking her, they could have found her on Facebook.'

'And what happened on the night?'

'Nothing,' he said. His eyes cut away as he spoke, and she couldn't help thinking there was more to the story.

'No stalker?'

'No.' He dropped her hand. 'No sign of anyone on their own, anyone watching other customers. And then' – he swallowed audibly – 'I got home to find the house on fire.'

'Oh God, Aaron.' Sive's eyes filled with tears.

'Yeah.' He went quiet and she let the silence lie as Toby snuffled into her and the sound of *PAW Patrol* drifted from next door.

After a while, in a quiet voice, she asked if he thought the stalker had set the fire.

'As Nita said the other night, it's hard to imagine the two things aren't related.' A shrug that looked slightly manufactured. Maybe he needed to believe there was a stalker, someone to blame. Although, at dinner on Friday, he'd been less convinced. What had changed since then?

'It's so sad, the whole thing.'

He slipped an arm around her waist. 'We have our chequered exes, don't we, you and me.'

'We do not come without baggage, that's for sure,' Sive said with a wry smile, blinking away the tears.

'How long now?'

'Eighteen months.'

'And not a peep from the family, right?'

'Not a peep.'

He kissed her temple. 'I told you so. You need to stop worrying. No one will ever find out.'

'Hopefully,' Sive said, passing Toby to Aaron before slipping out of bed to check on the girls. Aaron was a lot more relaxed than she was when it came to their origin story.

At the breakfast buffet, the kids were in high spirits – delighted with the 'all you can eat' element, now that they understood how it worked. Faye accidentally set the pancake machine to make fifteen pancakes, which Sive then hid on various plates on their table rather than admitting they'd wasted so much food. Bea ate her first ever bowl of Coco Pops, served to her by her kindly older sister, then demolished two mini portions of jam when Sive wasn't looking. Sive drank three cups of coffee and wondered when the holiday part of the holiday would begin. Aaron, wearing Toby in the sling, read the Sunday papers. Sive grimaced. She should have taken Toby and left Aaron to jump up and down with the girls.

'Swap?' she said after a while, and Aaron reluctantly handed over the baby, kissing his head as he did. Sive slid the paper towards her and let out a contented sigh. The rules were simple – whoever was holding the baby didn't have to move. She smiled up at Aaron. 'Any chance of another Danish?'

The paper was open at a local news page, and as Sive scanned it she spotted a name that sounded familiar. Pemberton. The man they'd been discussing at brunch yesterday. Arrested and charged with a litany of crimes, going back decades. She skimmed it as she finished her coffee, and turned the page, where another name jumped out. Rosco. Police seeking Michael Rosco, to help with their inquiries in a number of investigations.

'Aaron?'

He'd just arrived back from the buffet with a plate full of mini Danishes and Bea on his hip. Faye was still up there, busy with the juice dispenser.

'Yeah?'

'I just spotted this in the paper – a reference to Michael Rosco. Isn't that the name the neighbour mentioned? In relation to the . . .'

She trailed off. She wasn't going to refer to the fire in front of Bea, even though Bea was too young to understand.

'Yeah. He has fingers in lots of pies, though, so it's not un-usual to see his name in the paper. Right.' He grinned. 'Before we head off, is there anything to be said for another pancake?'

*

Today, they were planning a cable-car ride, then a river taxi along the Thames that would take them right up to Big Ben. Only Scott was joining them – Nita had work to do, Dave was visiting his mum, and Maggie was meeting her sister. Sive was glad to have a break from the group activities, especially because the adults tended to walk much faster than Faye and Bea. She kind of wished Scott wasn't coming either, and immediately felt bad for thinking it. She sighed as she drained her coffee. Still. Only two more days and they'd be back to the welcome mundanity of home life in Dublin. She folded the newspaper, kissed Toby's head and stood to shepherd Bea and Faye from the restaurant. As she shooed them forward between the tables she glanced back to find Aaron poring over the newspaper, his forehead furrowed in a deep frown. She couldn't be sure, not from this upside-down, faraway angle, but it looked like it was the same page she'd just shown him. The page with the Rosco story – the story he'd dismissed. His fingers rapped the table as he read. Fast, unconscious tapping, something he typically did when preparing for court; an all too familiar sign of taut, nervy energy. Over Rosco, Sive wondered, or something else altogether?

38

FIVE OF THE LONGEST minutes of Sive's life pass as she, Aaron and Jude stand in Oxford Circus ticket hall, waiting for the woman who's taken Faye to phone back. They huddle by the wall while afternoon passengers mill past, swiping through barriers, getting on with their day, oblivious to the Sullivans' panic. When the phone finally rings, Aaron puts it on speaker, and the three of them cluster to listen.

'Good, Aaron, well done,' says the woman's voice. She sounds calm and clear. Like a teacher, praising a pupil. 'Your story is everywhere, on Twitter at least. Now, I'm not stupid, I know you'll retract all of it, say you were under duress. But the thing is, Aaron, they'll look back on your cases. And they'll dig. And they'll distance themselves. And they'll talk. No smoke without fire.'

Sive can't wait any more. 'Where is she?! Where is Faye?!'

A pause and a click. 'To find your daughter, check your texts. Go there with your wife. Nobody else. If the police show up, I'll hurt Faye. Believe me.' And that's it. The call is disconnected.

'Quick! Check! Is there a text?' *Please God, let there be a text. Please let Faye be there.*

Aaron is fumbling with the phone, far too slowly, and Sive cranes her neck to read.

'It's an address.'

'Where?'

'In Leytonstone. It's just a street address, I don't know what kind of building it is—'

'It doesn't matter. We need to get there now.'

'Shouldn't you tell the police?' Jude says. Sive has almost forgotten she's there.

'No!' Aaron shouts it. 'You heard what the nutjob said. No police. She'll hurt Faye.'

'But they must have ways of arriving unseen. They're the police – that's what they do. And they could catch whoever did this?'

Aaron turns to her, eyes blazing. 'I don't care who did this! Right now, we just need to get Faye back. Sive, let's get a cab outside.' He moves towards the escalator.

But Sive is looking at the map on her phone. 'The Tube is quicker.'

'I'll come with you, as far as Leytonstone,' Jude says. 'I can drop back and stay out of sight before you get to wherever she's being held.'

Aaron shakes his head, but Sive answers before he can say anything. 'Jude, thank you, but no. We need to do this by the book. If you could wait here in case DC Hawthorn is looking for us, that would be good. She's due back in the next few minutes and I know she's trying to call me about the video, but the last thing we need right now is to explain this to her. So, whatever you can do to distract her, please do. Likewise, any other reporters.' She looks over to where Maggie is on her phone, a little way back towards the exit. 'And Maggie, too. She's still on a call to Dave, I guess, but she'll be wondering where we are. Make something up.'

Jude nods as Sive and Aaron rush towards the ticket barriers. *Thirty-three minutes to Leytonstone. Thirty-three minutes to Faye.*

39

The Grapevine

NOW THIS WAS MORE her thing, Sive thought, walking through the glossy candle-lit bar to a cluster of stools around a high table near the back. No Scott and Aaron bickering, no Dave with his long-winded stories, and (sorry, kids, no offence) no children. Just the girls and the chats. Maggie and Nita were already there. Maggie had a pint of Guinness in front of her. Nita had what might be sparkling water. Or gin and tonic? Sive couldn't tell. She knew Maggie was hoping tonight would be the chance to get to the bottom of whatever was going on with Nita. Intervention-lite. Sive hoped so too, but she'd need to play a more passive role. She'd met Nita maybe five times in total – it wasn't her place to participate in any kind of intervention, light or otherwise. The two women waved as she approached. Maggie looked sparkly, in a black shirt-dress with a trio of gold chains around her neck, shimmering in the candlelight. Nita looked beautiful too, in an olive-green strappy dress that was just the right balance of out-out and Sunday Night with the Girl from Ireland She Didn't Know Very Well, Sive reckoned. Her lips were painted bright crimson and, yet again, Sive was struck by how like Yasmin she looked. Dark circles beneath her eyes provided the only evidence of last night's excess.

'Pull up a stool. What would you like to drink?' Maggie asked, signalling to a server.

Sive decided on a glass of cava, which arrived promptly to the table. As she sipped, Maggie asked her how the cable car had been. The cable car had been good, she told them, and the whole day was almost perfect, apart from – she hesitated, wondering if it was the mouthful of cava or the irresistible lure of bonding that made her want to share confidences – apart from Aaron and Scott at it again.

Nita and Maggie leaned in, eyes sparkling, ready to trade stories.

'It's so bloody annoying!' Nita said. 'I mean, oh my God, we all know Aaron is super-successful, blah, blah, blah. And ditto Scott. Why can't they just shut the fuck up about it?'

Sive laughed. Nita's cut-glass BBC accent was the most perfect thing when she swore.

'And I guess poor old Dave was trying to keep up?' Maggie asked.

'No, he was visiting his mum today,' Sive said, 'so he wasn't there.'

'Really?' Maggie looked surprised. 'Did Dave say that?'

'Well, Aaron said it.' Sive took another swallow of cava. 'Why?'

'No reason,' Maggie said, though there very clearly was a reason. Sive did not know her well enough to push.

'And now it's just us girls, with none of those irritating boys,' Nita said, raising her glass. 'Cheers, ladies!'

They clinked and Sive wondered again what was in Nita's glass and how Maggie might go about bringing it up. She didn't have long to wait.

'I'm absolutely in awe of you, Nita,' Maggie said, 'going it alone. Obviously, I've never had children, but I imagine pregnancy isn't easy. All those rules!' A wide smile. Sive winced.

Maggie was great. One of the warmest, most diplomatic people she'd ever come across – at least based on the handful of times they'd met – but this felt very awkward already.

'I wonder if Sive has any tips for you?' Maggie went on, raising her eyebrows somewhat unnecessarily in an unspoken message to Sive.

'Oh, sure. Ask me anything!' Sive said gamely. 'Not that I'm any kind of expert.'

A wary look crossed Nita's face and somehow the shadows below her eyes deepened. 'I've read all the books, I'm pretty on top of things.'

'Well, sure, but there's nothing like lived experience,' Maggie said. 'Sive, how did you feel when you first found out you were pregnant with Faye? Overwhelmed about changing your lifestyle?'

Sive bit her lip. *Oh my God. So clunky.* But there was no going back now.

'Well, I didn't know I was pregnant for the first two months, so it took me a while longer to change my lifestyle.' Sive laughed, and took another sip. She was starting to feel light-headed.

'Oh! Wasn't it planned?' Nita asked. Nita had never not planned anything.

This was shaky territory. 'No. We weren't together very long at that point. Faye was a surprise.'

'My, oh my! A one-night stand that turned into a marriage?' Nita asked, her eyes lighting up.

'Not quite. We were together; it wasn't a one-night stand.' *God, the hypocritical defensiveness.* She drained her drink and caught a server's attention. 'Will I order another round?'

'Oh, yes,' Nita said, swivelling and making a 'same again' circular motion with her finger.

'I remember now,' Maggie said. 'Aaron told us he'd met

someone through work and he was going to be a dad, and it *did* all seem very quick at the time.' She put up her hands. 'Gosh, that sounded so judgemental! No judgement here. I've had my fair share of dating disasters.'

Nita leaned in. 'Really? Do tell, Maggie. You never let us in on anything about your love life.'

Maggie winked. 'No chance. Some things this girl will never tell.'

Nita pleaded with her, but Maggie was adamant, in turn making Nita even more determined. Why wouldn't Maggie tell? she asked. Was it someone famous? Someone they knew? The drinks arrived, interrupting Nita's flow momentarily, but then she kept going.

Was it someone married? Maggie put her hands up at that. No way would she sleep with someone who was married, she said. Nita shrugged. All's fair in love and war, she reckoned, and monogamy was overrated. *Relationships* were overrated, in fact, she said, gesturing at herself. Sive glanced at Maggie, wondering if this was another 'in' to bring up Nita's drinking, but Nita was still talking – asking now if Maggie was embarrassed about the person she'd been dating. Maggie's cheeks pinkened.

'That's it!' Nita said triumphantly. 'You're embarrassed! Is he terribly ugly? Awful in bed? Come on, Maggie! Have another drink and spill the beans!' Eyes glassy, she gestured for yet another round, though they were only a quarter-way into their fresh drinks.

Maggie sighed. 'I'm not embarrassed. It was just easier to keep it to ourselves.' Her cheeks were still pink, though, and Sive couldn't help wondering about the 'not embarrassed' claim.

'Oh, come on! Tell me so I can begin some unmerciful teasing. Do I know him?'

Maggie shook her head, but she was laughing. 'No way.'

Nita drew back. 'It's someone we know!'

Maggie shook her head, but she was faltering.

Sive studied her, remembering suddenly how she'd set the table and cleaned up last night. How she'd known where everything was – the glasses, the corkscrew, the dishwasher tablets.

'Oh, wow. It's Dave, isn't it?'

Maggie clamped her hand to her mouth. 'Shit! How did you guess?'

Nita's jaw dropped. 'Dave! Our Dave? Maggie. You wouldn't. You couldn't. Seriously? When? How long?'

Maggie put her face in her hands and spoke through her fingers. 'We were together for six months. We broke up about a year ago. That's all there is to say.' She looked up, smiling sheepishly. 'Now, no more on this!'

'I'm sorry it didn't work out,' Sive said.

Nita scoffed. 'I'm not. It's Dave!' She must have noticed Maggie's expression then. 'Oh, Maggie, I'm being horrible. You were serious about him?'

Maggie nodded.

'And what happened?'

'He was hung up on his ex.'

Nita looked baffled. 'What ex? How do I not know about all these women he's been dating?'

'I mean from years ago,' Maggie clarified. 'Not-Kate-Moss girl? The one who broke up with him before we ever met her?'

'Oh, for goodness' sake. How is he still hung up on her?'

'I know.' Maggie sighed. 'But he couldn't seem to move on. He tried to pretend, but after a while it was obvious he was pretending. So I walked away.'

'And did you . . . you didn't live together, I imagine?' Nita said, still clearly confused.

'No, but we spent a lot of time together. I stayed over in Clarinda Gardens most weekends.'

'And none of us guessed . . . you must have arrived and left separately any time we met up?'

Maggie laughed. 'Actually, we left together, but nobody noticed.'

'Goodness. And no one knew at all?'

'Only Jerry, Dave's brother, and their mother.'

'That old battleaxe?'

'Ah, she only seemed like that when she was our landlady and we were in our twenties. She was actually OK beneath the prickly exterior.' Maggie's face clouded now as though something was bothering her, but just as quickly she smiled. 'Anyway, that's my secret.' A laugh. 'Gosh, now that I've said it, I'm wondering why I didn't tell you sooner.'

'Maybe because Dave's "no Kate Moss", as he might say himself,' Nita smirked, 'and not the sharpest knife in the drawer?'

Maggie shook her head. 'Dave's as smart as anyone, believe me. The "Trigger" thing is the role we cornered him into back then and it just kind of stuck.'

'What *are* you on about? What role?' Nita wobbled slightly on her stool. 'We didn't corner him into anything.'

'But we *did*. We were the self-professed high-flyers and he was the landlady's son – the only one who didn't go to uni, the only one not on a fast-track C-suite career. And so we made assumptions about him, presumed he wasn't as smart as we were.'

'Erm, that's because he's not?'

Patiently, Maggie shook her head again. 'How many instruments do you play, Nita?'

'None. What's that got to do with—'

'Dave plays piano and guitar. How many languages do you speak?'

'One. English. I don't need—'

'Dave taught himself Italian and German and speaks both

very well. He plays chess for relaxation. He does the crossword every day. He's been promoted numerous times at work. Just because he didn't go to uni and took the "not smart one" role when we lived together doesn't actually mean he's not intelligent. We were just assholes.'

Nita still looked dubious. 'Well, we were definitely assholes. But I don't know what you mean about "roles".'

'Sure you do. Your role is the princess. The one who's too pretty and too vacuous to be a brilliant lawyer, then surprises everyone with her razor-sharp intelligence.'

Nita grinned. 'God, am I that obvious? This is starting to sound like *The Breakfast Club*. What about everyone else – do Aaron.'

'He's the alpha male who takes no prisoners but melts as soon as he sees his kids.' Maggie smiled at Sive as she said it.

'And Scott?' Nita held up a finger. 'Wait, I know – he's the Jack the Lad, the one who doesn't care what anyone thinks of him.'

'Except, of course,' Maggie said darkly, 'he very much *does* care.'

'And you, Maggie?' Sive asked.

'I'm the sensible one. Always have been.' She looked wistful. 'My older sister was flaky and constantly in trouble, so I went for sensible, and it suited me.' She smiled. 'Most of the time.' She sipped the top of her untouched Guinness. 'Gosh, I should switch to something else, I can't keep up with you two and your dainty drinks. Sorry, Sive, for abandoning your national beverage.'

'My country and I forgive you. Try the cava – it's lovely and crisp and going down extremely well.'

It certainly was. An hour later, she'd had two more, and was starting to wish she'd had a bigger dinner to soak it all up. She texted Aaron to warn him to be ready to get up with Toby during the night and to have a bottle prepared. Although – she looked at her watch – with the rowing race on in the morning, he'd probably be asleep. She couldn't wait to tell him the gossip about Maggie and Dave. What other secrets did this group have from each other, she wondered, looking from Nita to Maggie as they traded stories from the 'old days', filling her in on details and context so she wouldn't feel left out.

'Wasn't that the night Scott burned down his neighbours' shed?' Nita was saying now.

Maggie nodded. 'That was such a mess.' She turned to Sive to explain. 'Scott used to sneak out back for a cigarette at his parents' house whenever he was visiting. The man was twenty-five years old and couldn't admit to smoking. Anyway, as I'm sure you've heard, this one night, his mother came out to look for him and, in a panic, he flicked the cigarette over the wall into the neighbours' garden.'

'Scott was an idiot back then,' Nita said, shifting on her stool and teetering slightly. She grabbed the table with both hands to steady herself and turned to Maggie. 'There was cut grass or something and it caught fire? And the shed burned down. Such a plonker.'

Sive smiled, shaking her head. 'I'm adding that to just one of the many stories Aaron's never told me.'

Maggie blinked.

'But that's literally why he's nicknamed Burner,' Nita said. 'How could you not know?'

'Wait, is that not because his name's Scott Burns?'

Nita and Maggie both burst out laughing. 'His name's Scott Callanan!' Nita explained. 'Aaron started calling him Burner after the shed fire, and it stuck.'

'Oh, gosh, we shouldn't be joking about it. It could have been catastrophic if the house had caught fire too,' Maggie said, trying to rein in the laughter. 'Scott got charged with destroying and damaging property. Ended up with a conviction and had to pay a fine, I think.'

'Yep.' Nita lifted her glass to her mouth but misjudged the angle and two ice cubes clattered to the table. Was she drunk? Sive wondered. Without acknowledging the spill, Nita scooped the ice cubes into an empty glass and carried on talking. 'A criminal record for a careless cigarette, all because he was afraid of Mummy Callanan. It was a sore point for a long time.' A grin. 'I don't think he appreciated the nickname.' The last three words slurred together. *Appreesenickname*.

Maggie tilted her head and suddenly sat up straighter. Her expression was one of confusion, swiftly followed by what looked to Sive like dawning realization. The solving of a riddle.

'What is it?' Sive asked.

'Something about Scott that suddenly makes sense . . . or rather, doesn't make sense.' She shook herself. 'Don't mind me. Right, more drinks?'

Two things happened then. Nita fell off her stool, and everyone found out the truth.

40

Monday
3.06 p.m.

THE WORLD WHIZZES PAST outside, but Sive and Aaron don't see it. They don't see anything. They hold hands, looking down, not speaking, as the Tube slides from stop to stop, taking them to Leytonstone. To Faye. *Please God, to Faye.* Sive doesn't believe in God. She's a science person, through and through. Except when she's desperate. Then she begs. *Please God, let her be there. Let her be safe. She's only six. Please, please let her be OK.*

She forces herself to focus on Faye. On good things. On happy memories. Faye starting school, trying and failing to hide her fear. Faye at her gymnastics show – easily the least coordinated child in the hall but delighted with her participation medal. Faye's recent note to Sive, supposedly written by Aaron: 'To mum. by faye a pupy. frum dad.' Faye trying to escape from Bea, then seeking her out minutes later because she's bored without her. Faye's hugs. Squeezy, cheek-to-cheek hugs that fix everything. *God*, what she'd give for one of those.

The Tube pulls into Leytonstone and she clicks into Google Maps, refreshing it with fumbling fingers. The address they've been given is a six-minute walk from the Tube station, on Halford Road, just off Leytonstone High Road. Street View shows a row of small shops. Plain, unremarkable but well-maintained facades. Not the kind of place you'd associate with crime. A butcher's, a laundrette, what looks like a gift shop. She can't tell which one is number thirteen. It looks so suburban and normal and everyday.

Running to catch up with Aaron, Sive tells him about the six-minute walk and the butcher's and the laundrette and the gift shop. Side by side, they emerge on to the sunny street, as unconcerned passers-by go about their Monday afternoon.

'This way, I think,' Sive says, 'via Church Lane.' Her voice is almost at a whisper, every word a struggle as her stomach knots. They're running again, Aaron a little ahead, Sive watching the Maps app on her phone.

'Cross at the crossing,' she says. 'We need to be on the other side.'

He does so without looking back, and she follows. An elderly lady stares after them, wondering, no doubt, what they're running from. They pass chippers and small shops, a thrift store and a supermarket, then stop outside a library as Church Lane comes to an end.

'Left or right?' Aaron says, breathless.

'Right, then we cross over, and Halford Road will be on the left.'

They thread through traffic, ignoring a beeping horn, and begin running again, along Leytonstone High Road. Sive looks at her phone, then up.

'Just past the pub, turn left.'

Aaron dips out of sight as he rounds the corner on to Halford Road. She's just seconds behind him. Not far now. *Please let her be OK.*

Ahead, she sees the row of shops.

'Aaron, we're here.' Gulping to catch her breath. 'This is it. Thirteen. Look for thirteen.'

Two teens stroll past, heads in phones, and look up, surprised at Sive's panicked words.

The butcher's shop has no number. Nor does the laundrette. But the gift shop does, on a blue-and-white patterned tile, and it's thirteen.

Oh my God. They're here. This is where she is.

They stand outside, momentarily paralysed. What now? Would Faye be inside the shop? Or in some kind of flat above? That makes more sense. Maybe it has nothing to do with the gift shop. But there's no access to whatever's above from outside, so they go in.

Sive looks around. It's a typical twenty-first-century gift shop – quirky cards and abstract prints, handmade jewellery and bamboo everything. There's something familiar about it – maybe not the shop, maybe something *in* the shop – but it's so fleeting Sive can't capture what it is. A girl behind the counter looks up. She's about twenty, with purple hair and a stud in her nose and half a smile for the incoming couple.

'We're looking for our daughter,' Sive says, because how else is she supposed to start something like this.

'Oh,' the girl replies. 'There's nobody here but me.'

Aaron strides towards the counter and the girl stands up straight, slightly alarmed.

'This is 13 Halford Road?'

'Yes. Did your little girl run off?'

'We were told she was here. How do we get upstairs? What's up there?'

'That's a flat. There's an entrance out back.' She shrugs, but she's wary too.

'Who lives there?'

'Victoria. The owner.'

'We need to get up there. Now.'

'Well, I'm sorry, but Victoria's busy doing accounts.'

'I don't care how busy she is – we need to get up there, our daughter is there.'

The girl looks baffled. 'I really don't think—'

But Aaron's not listening. He's moving towards the door at the back of the shop.

'Hey! That's private!'

Aaron pulls open the door, and Sive follows, conscious that the girl has come out from behind the counter and is still calling after them. They're in a small corridor now, at the end of which is a back door and some stairs. Aaron takes the steps two at a time and tries the door at the top, but it's locked. He hammers on it, shouting Faye's name. There's no sound from inside.

Sive stands two steps down from Aaron, waiting. Praying.

Please let her be OK. Please, God, I'll do anything.

Behind her, the girl is standing at the bottom of the stairs.

'I'm calling the police.'

'Don't call the police. Please don't,' Sive begs, turning to her. 'Someone's taken our daughter. And they sent us here but told us not to call the police. Please, just let us find her first.'

The girl shakes her head but takes the phone away from her ear.

Aaron hammers again and again. 'Faye! Faye, are you in there? Shout if you can hear me!'

And then the door springs open.

41

The Grapevine

IT ALL HAPPENED IN slow motion. Sive reached to catch Nita as she toppled off the high stool, but it was too late – Nita landed flat on the floor, banging her head on the tiles.

'Oh my God!' Maggie was immediately on her knees beside her friend. 'Can you hear me? Are you OK?'

Nita seemed disoriented. Her eyes were open, but she didn't appear capable of answering Maggie, at least at first. A bartender rushed over and knelt beside them.

'Did she hit her head?' she asked. 'Shall I call an ambulance?' She was already fishing a phone from her back pocket.

'Yes. She's pregnant. I think it would be safer to have a scan.' Maggie's voice cracked. 'Please. Call an ambulance.'

Nita, still lying on the floor, began to push herself up on her elbow. She shook her head, winced, and put her hand to her temple.

'Don't.' A whisper. 'Don't call an ambulance.'

'Sweetheart, I'm sure the baby's fine, but it's safer to get you checked out.' Maggie looked at the bartender and nodded. 'Go ahead, please. My friend is notoriously pig-headed' – she smiled at Nita – 'and is not going to listen to sense.'

Nita sat up. 'Stop. Please.'

'Nita, you've hit your head and you're dr—'– Maggie glanced at Sive – 'you've had a few drinks, and you're not thinking straight.'

'I am thinking straight. I don't need an ambulance.'

'But the baby—'

'Maggie, there *is* no baby.'

Sive looked from Maggie to Nita as she processed what Nita'd just said and realized that she wasn't as surprised as she should be. She turned it over. On some level, she must have known there was no baby. There was no way Nita didn't know what was safe or not safe, no way she'd have finished a bottle of champagne on her own if she was really pregnant.

Maggie's face was inscrutable as she sat back on her heels. The bartender slipped away. Sive stood and reached down to help Nita up.

'I'll ask for an ice pack for your head.'

The bartender was ahead of her and arrived with a bag of ice wrapped in a tea towel before hastily retreating again.

'Thanks.' Nita was standing now, leaning against the high table. She put the makeshift ice pack to her head and smiled grimly. 'I guess I'll bow out of the race in the morning.'

'Nita.' Maggie spoke softly. 'I'm so sorry. When I saw the box of Ovidrel in your bag last night . . . I recognized it from doing the drug orders for the GP clinic.' She turned to Sive. 'It's a fertility drug. Nita would have had to inject it before IUI,' she explained, then turned back to Nita. 'I wondered if maybe . . . Nita, I'm so, so sorry.'

Nita's eyes widened. 'Oh God, no, Maggie. It's not that. It's . . . I was never pregnant.'

'What?'

'Oh, Christ. Let's order another round. I need gin for this,' Nita said.

Sive signalled for the round and they all took their seats. Nita turned to Maggie.

'I *thought* I was pregnant. You must believe that. I really did. I felt different. My breasts were sore. I felt sick. Every smell made me nauseous. It was textbook stuff.' She sighed. 'And I got carried away. I was just so excited. I made my announcement on Instagram and, obviously, all of you saw that too, and my work colleagues and my other friends, and then . . . when I found out I wasn't, I couldn't bring myself to tell anyone.'

'Nita.' Maggie was shaking her head, baffled. But Maggie didn't have 46,000 followers on Instagram. Maggie didn't have an Instagram account at all. Sive, a social media dabbler at best, got it. She'd watched the excitement in the comments on Nita's post. Her followers were thrilled. Dynamic, successful, beautiful Nita, orphaned daughter of immigrant parents, now going it alone with single parenthood. *Love you so much*, the commenters said. *Inspirational. You go, girl! You've got this!*

But Sive could see that Maggie was bewildered.

'How long were you planning to pretend? Although, bloody hell, with all that drinking, you weren't exactly covering it up.'

'Yes. My therapist would class that as a cry for help. Or a cry for attention.' She tapped a nail against her lip. 'I need a new therapist.'

Maggie was still perplexed. 'But what about the ultrasound you showed us?'

Nita looked sheepish. 'Just one I took from Google Images. I needed something visual for my followers on Insta.'

'OK, forget your bloody Instagram people for a second – why didn't you tell us the truth? We're your friends.'

'I know. I'm sorry. But reunions are hard when everyone's doing so well.'

'Doing so well? You're Head of Legal in a huge multinational!

You earn a million a year, as you've told us many times. What is your definition of "doing so well"?'

'Career is just one box ticked. What about relationships and children? There's Aaron with Sive and his three children, and there's me with nobody.'

Maggie's jaw dropped. 'Nita! I am literally sitting in front of you, a single woman with no kids. Do I not count?'

'But, Maggie, you *have* family. You have your sisters and your parents. You've said it yourself so often – your sisters are your best friends. Yasmin was my only family in the world. Sure, I have a beautiful house and a big salary, but I have no family. Nobody at all. I needed this to happen. I needed it to be true.'

'And what – you figured you'd try again and become pregnant before you'd have to admit you weren't?'

A small nod. Nita, usually the confident, vibrant centre of everything, looked shrunken and vulnerable. 'I'm sorry.'

The drinks arrived, providing a welcome distraction, and in the time it took to pass them around, Maggie appeared to defuse a little.

'Is your head OK?' she asked when the server departed.

'I'll be fine.'

But an hour later, when they got up to leave, she seemed wobbly still, and Maggie decided Nita should stay with her overnight, promising a nightcap to sweeten the deal. Sive couldn't tell if Nita's unstable walk was due to her fall or to the gin, but she agreed to go back to Maggie's for a nightcap too. She could go to the hotel from there, and she'd still make it to bed by midnight.

Maggie lived on Silchester Road in a brownstone terraced house with a huge bay window at the front. To Sive, it looked like the kind of house she'd seen on English TV dramas her whole life – pretty, compact, neat, urban. Very Maggie. The inside was very

Maggie too. Original floorboards in the living room were varnished to a high shine and half covered by a faded Persian rug. A modest television set sat on a nest of oak tables, and above it hung a wall tapestry depicting what looked like an Irish Celtic cross. And at the centre of everything was an ornate black fireplace inlaid with Moorish tiles. Nita, still rubbing the bump on her head, decided to forgo the drink and go straight to sleep, already halfway through the living-room door as she said it. Maggie followed to show her up to the spare room, calling back for Sive to make herself at home. Sive couldn't help having a little look around the living room while they were gone – at the books on Maggie's shelves and the prints on her walls and the photographs on her mantelpiece. She picked up a framed picture of two girls, one of whom she recognized immediately as Maggie. She looked to be about eighteen or nineteen in the photo, and had her arm slung around the other girl, both of them grinning at the camera, backpacks at their feet. They were wrapped up in sensible windbreaker jackets and posing at what Sive was almost certain were the Cliffs of Moher in the west of Ireland. She remembered now that Maggie had mentioned she'd gone there during her time at uni. The other girl – dark-haired and about a head shorter than Maggie – was someone Sive didn't know, though, as she squinted, she couldn't help thinking there was something familiar about her. She put the photo back on the mantelpiece at the sound of Maggie coming down the stairs and sat on the plump, cream-coloured sofa.

Maggie arrived a moment later, brandishing a bottle of Baileys and two tumblers of ice.

'Well! Hard to know how to unpick all of that!' She tilted her head, eyes wide in an exaggerated show of bemusement. 'Nightcap?'

Sive nodded, and Maggie poured.

'Is Nita OK?'

'She was asleep before her head hit the pillow. Bloody hell. If she wasn't an injured patient under my care, I could happily strangle her. What on earth was she thinking? We're supposed to be friends.'

'I know. But when you tell a big lie, it's very, very hard to backtrack.' *Understatement of the year*.

Maggie looked at her quizzically. 'You sound like you're speaking from experience?'

Sive's cheeks heated up. 'Ha. Maybe if we count lying about how much TV my children watch.'

Maggie said nothing for a moment and Sive had a sudden urge to fill the space. To tell her the secret, the true origin story. Faye's origin story. To tell this person she didn't really know very well at all. And maybe that was the appeal. Instead, she sipped her drink and changed the subject.

'I was admiring your photos. That's the Cliffs of Moher, if I'm not mistaken?' She pointed towards the mantelpiece.

'Yes.' Maggie's eyes welled up suddenly. 'Gosh, look at me, getting all emotional. It's the drink.'

'Oh, sorry. I didn't realize it was something upsetting . . .' Sive trailed off, unsure what to say.

Maggie rose to retrieve the photo then sat again, staring at it, smiling as a tear slipped down her cheek. 'Good God, why am I getting so teary!' she said, wiping dust from the glass. 'I still miss her.'

'Who?'

Maggie looked surprised. 'Yasmin,' she said, pointing at her friend in the photo. Sive stared, confused, as Maggie rubbed her thumb affectionately across the image of the girl. The dark hair, the unfamiliar face. This wasn't the girl from Aaron's photos. Sive had never seen this girl in her life.

42

THE WOMAN STANDING AT the door to the flat above the gift shop is tall and thin with short grey hair and huge glasses pushed to the crown of her head, and Sive is not thinking straight, not one bit, but she does think one thing, which is that this woman does not have Faye. Even before Aaron finishes shouting and the woman shakes her head in confusion, in her gut, Sive knows. Aaron's not listening. He steps forward, pushing past the woman, and strides into her flat, shouting Faye's name. The woman's cheeks are red now, and her hands are on her hips and she looks angry and defiant and just a little nervous too, as anyone would with a six-foot-three stranger raging about his missing child.

Sive follows him, but her heart's in her stomach. This is all wrong. They've been lied to. Or they're in the wrong place? As Aaron searches, shouting, going from room to room in the small flat, as the downstairs shop girl calls the police, Sive looks at her Maps app. This is the right place. Did she take the wrong address from Aaron's text? She asks him now for his phone, and he yells at her instead, tells her to help look for Faye. She's not here, Sive says. This woman isn't a kidnapper. We're in the wrong place.

But Aaron's not listening. He's pulling bedclothes off the bed and looking in closets and searching for an attic hatch.

'*Aaron!*' Sive shouts it, shocking him into listening. 'Give me your phone. Let me check I got the right address.'

He does, but keeps searching.

'The police are coming,' calls the girl downstairs as the owner stands in her living room, yelling at Aaron to get out.

The address is correct; she made no mistake. Then it's a wild goose chase. For whatever reason, the kidnapper has sent them to the wrong place. Defeated and deflated, Sive sinks to the woman's floor.

This seems to catch the woman's attention, to calm her. She comes over to Sive and hunches beside her.

'Are you going to be sick?'

Sive shakes her head. 'Our daughter's been taken. They sent us here.'

'Oh my. Well. That's not something that happens every day. Aren't the police searching for her?' A pause. Realization spinning across her face. 'Oh! You're that couple. The little Irish girl?'

Sive nods. 'We got a message with this address. Warned not to tell the police.'

'I see.' Then, softly: 'She's not here. I'm terribly sorry.'

'If the police come, it's going to make it worse,' Sive whispers. 'I don't know why we were sent here, but we were warned we'd never see her again if we tell the police.' She looks at the woman, pleading.

'Kayla!' the woman shouts. 'Could you phone back to say it was a false alarm? Put them on to me if necessary.'

Kayla peers in, checking perhaps to see if Sive is forcing her boss at knifepoint to make this retraction. Satisfied that this isn't the case, she nods and turns away, pulling her phone from her pocket.

Aaron is back in the living room now, running his hand through his hair.

'Where is she? Where the fuck is Faye?'

'Aaron, she's not here. We've been sent here for some unknown reason, but Faye's not here, and this woman—'

'Victoria,' the woman supplies.

'Victoria is not a kidnapper. We need to contact the caller and ask where Faye really is. Please. Can you call back on the number she used?'

Aaron hesitates, then pulls out his phone. He puts it on speaker, and together they listen as the call goes to a recorded announcement:

'This number is no longer in service.'

43

3.37 p.m.

JUDE IS SITTING WITH Maggie on a low stone bench on Oxford Street. She's been typing up her interview with Sive, tapping out words on her phone, while Maggie stares at her own screen, at the Retweet and Like counters on Aaron's video going up and up and up. Maggie had arrived back in the ticket hall just as the Sullivans disappeared on their dash to Leytonstone and Jude had suggested they go outside for a breather and, for Jude, a much-needed cigarette. They've been sitting here since, waiting for news, although, Jude supposes, Maggie doesn't exactly know what kind of news to expect – Jude had kept it very vague, explaining that the Sullivans were given a lead but that if she said too much, it could jeopardize Faye's safety.

Frowning, she tweaks a paragraph of her article a third time, but it's still not right. None of it is. She's going to need an extension on her deadline. She messages her editor to say it'll be six before she can send it, then closes her phone, letting the words breathe for a bit. *It'll flow better with fresh eyes. Surely.*

She lights another cigarette and turns to Maggie.

'So. I guess Aaron's video is officially viral,' Jude says.

'Gosh, I still can't believe it. I did wonder if it was doctored at first.' Maggie bites her lip. 'I know you can't say, Jude, but I assume someone's forced him to make it, and it's to do with Faye's disappearance . . . And it's all linked to wherever Aaron and Sive have gone now, this lead they're following . . .'

Jude looks straight ahead, watching a bus move slowly through traffic behind a line of black cabs.

'You're right. I can't say anything,' she agrees, though it's all quite self-evident: the video, the Sullivans' sudden departure, the secrecy. Maggie's not stupid.

Maggie nods. 'Of course. As long as they get Faye back, that's all that matters. But with that video out there' – she shakes her head – 'his career is effectively over.'

Jude wonders if there's a tiny touch of *Schadenfreude* in the way Maggie says it, but then decides she's wrong, this is just cynical-Jude reading too much into everything.

'Mm, not easy to come back from that,' she agrees.

'Then again, I imagine he can retract everything.'

Jude stretches her legs, crossing her ankles, almost tripping a passing shopper. 'He can certainly *try*.'

Maggie nods. 'I know what you mean. No smoke without fire.'

Jude sits up straighter. 'That's what the caller said.'

'Did he? I guess that's his aim. Tarnish Aaron's reputation beyond saving.'

'Just funny that you'd use the exact same saying.'

Maggie's pale features redden. 'What do you mean by "funny"? Are you trying to say . . . What *are* you trying to say?'

Jude exhales smoke, examining Maggie's face. She's clearly flustered by Jude's words but didn't seem surprised at the reference to a 'caller', even though this is the first time Jude has mentioned it. She thinks back now to the call. Standing with Aaron and Sive, listening to the woman who has Faye. Where was Maggie at that point? On the phone. To their friend Dave. Or so she said.

Jude thinks for a moment, then says, 'You said, "Did he?" when I mentioned the caller. But actually, it was a woman.'

'*What?*'

'I'm sure you guessed' – guessed or *knew*, Jude thinks – 'and don't breathe a word to anyone, but someone phoned Aaron and said they have Faye. The caller was a woman.'

'A woman. My God.' Maggie looks shocked, and Jude can't help but think it's genuine.

'You're surprised to hear it was a woman?'

'It just doesn't seem like the kind of thing a woman would do. Kidnapping a child for blackmail. Are they sure it's not just some nutcase *pretending* she has Faye?'

'The caller knew about the stitches in Faye's leg, so they figured she was legit. That information wasn't made public.'

'Right. Gosh, this is all so surreal.' Maggie turns to Jude again, eyes narrowed. 'So why were you asking me about saying "no smoke without fire"?'

Jude bites her lip and stubs out her cigarette. It's not the first time her 'trust no one' approach to life has taken her a touch too far. As she opens her mouth, still not sure what she's going to say, her phone rings. *Saved by the bell*. Sive's name flashes up on-screen.

She turns from Maggie to answer, clamping a hand to her ear as a horn beeps loudly just feet away. 'Did you get her?'

'Faye isn't here.' A short silence. Jude pictures Sive on the other end of the line, trying to compose herself. 'It wasn't true. We're back to the start. We have no idea where she is.'

'Oh, shit.'

'We're at the address in Leytonstone, but we're coming back to Oxford Circus now. Aaron still doesn't want to tell the police, but I think we have to. The person who took her played us, for whatever sick reason. I don't think there's anything to gain by not telling the police, and no doubt they've seen the video, Hawthorn's been trying to call me . . . anyway, I'd better go. I'll let you know if anything changes.'

Jude disconnects just as a reply from her editor comes through.

> Fine to extend deadline to 6, but no later. Is Sive OK? Hope you're reining in your eyerolls. What she's going through is hideous.

Jude is confused. My eyerolls?

> Your message earlier, about Sive bursting into tears all the time.

Jesus. Had she really said that? She scrolls up. She had.

> That was before . . . And . . . Yeah, sorry, no excuse. I'm a bitch. Eyerolls have been reined in, promise.

Jude tells Maggie all of it then – everything the woman on the phone said, the coerced video, the rush to Leytonstone. Maggie nods, saying little. Jude wonders if it's because she guessed most of it already or if she's still a little put out by Jude's line of questioning before the call.

'I can't help thinking it has something to do with Aaron's job,' Jude says after a moment. 'I'm going to make a few calls.' She clicks into Contacts on her phone. A woman with two straining shopping bags sits down beside them, and Maggie moves closer to Jude to make space on the bench.

She still looks upset. 'Gosh, they're back to square one, with no idea who was on that train or why Faye went with them. I just wish Bea could say what happened.'

'I know.'

'Didn't she say anything at all?'

'Just "chase", but nobody knows if she means someone chased Faye or if it's just a random word. And the guy, Tim, who was with Bea saw nothing either. Speaking of which . . . I wonder if the police found anything more about why he lied.'

'What did he lie about?' Maggie asks.

'He said he worked in a place called Anderson Pruitt, only he doesn't. I've told Hawthorn, and she said she'd look into it, but she didn't seem too interested.'

Maggie looks perplexed. 'I've got to admit I'm with Hawthorn on this – how would this man kidnap Faye if he was right there with Bea?'

'I doubt he kidnapped Faye. But it's important to know why he lied, isn't it?'

Maggie nods, her expression suddenly thoughtful.

'And I'd very much like to know why the woman on the phone lied about where Faye was,' Jude adds. 'Why do it? Why lie?'

'I have no idea,' Maggie says, 'but in my experience, everyone lies. If this weekend is anything to go by, anyway.'

Jude is immediately curious. 'Your friends, you mean? What did they lie about?'

Maggie glances at the woman beside her, then shakes her head. 'It doesn't matter. Silly stuff.'

Jude watches her a moment longer. Something on Maggie's face tells her it's not 'silly stuff' but, for once, she doesn't feel she can push for more.

Maggie leans down to rummage in her handbag and pulls out a small, olive-green notebook with the word 'Addresses' in gold letters on the front. Jude hasn't seen anyone use an address book in years and her interest is piqued, watching as Maggie licks her thumb and index finger to page through the notebook. She flattens it on her knee and begins keying a number into her mobile. The writing is tiny, but Jude can make out what looks like the first name 'Caro' – or 'Carol', maybe? The phone number looks like a landline. As Jude peers across, Maggie looks up. She closes the notebook, stands suddenly, almost elbowing the woman beside her, and picks up her bag.

'Aren't you going to wait here for Sive and Aaron?' Jude asks.

'I'll come back to meet them in a bit, but first, there's something I need to check,' Maggie says, and without explaining further, she rushes towards the entrance to the station.

44

SIVE DISCONNECTS FROM HER call to Jude and moves through the gift shop as though walking through thick glue. They need to get going, take action, do something; she knows this, but her body's not cooperating. *Faye is not here.* Why did the woman on the phone lie? Aaron pulls the heavy glass door open, and a bell chimes. Victoria moves forward to hold the door, a tiny act that feels like an attempt to help in any small way. A jewellery case inside the door catches Sive's attention. *Miss Victoria London.* Sive touches the pendant around her neck.

'Aaron, wait. My chain – did you buy it here?'

He turns. Anxious. Impatient. Broken. 'What?'

Sive points at the jewellery stand and at her own pendant. 'This chain you bought me for Christmas, with the kids' birth-stones. It's custom-made and only available from one shop, as far as I remember' – she addresses Victoria – 'I take it you're that one shop?'

'Yes, I make them myself.' Victoria steps closer, looking at Sive's pendant. 'That is indeed one of mine!' She looks delighted, then seems to remember why they're here.

Sive turns back to Aaron. 'Does that mean something?'

He frowns, shakes his head.

227

'Victoria, you're sure this is the only shop that sells these?'

Victoria nods. 'I love making them, but I haven't got the time or the energy to get other stockists interested.'

'So, Aaron, were you here in this shop before? That must mean something?'

He shakes his head.

'How did you order it, then? It's customized with the kids' birthstones so it must have been bought directly from Victoria.'

He opens his mouth to answer then closes it as a thought seems to strike him. He looks perplexed, and then something else that Sive can't quite read. A sudden realization?

Victoria coughs gently. 'Just to say, I sell them on the internet too. Selling online is a lot easier than trying to distribute to other shops – the pandemic taught me that.'

'That's right,' Aaron says. 'I bought it online. We need to go.'

He walks out and Sive follows, sure of only one thing. Her husband is not telling the truth.

Jude phones as they're heading for the Tube station.

'What about talking to your younger daughter again?' she asks, without wasting time on a greeting. 'She kept saying "chase", and it surely means something. And she's the only one who saw what happened.'

'Believe me, it's driving me insane, knowing she saw and yet can't tell. But I don't think there's anything we can do about it.'

'OK. Just a suggestion. Maggie and I were talking about it after you called. I'm going to do more digging on Brosnan and I'll keep up the social media momentum.'

'Is Maggie with you?'

'She rushed off. Said there was something she had to check. I might have upset her, though . . . I was a bit, eh, clunky with something I said . . . Anyway, it doesn't matter. She'll be back later, I'm sure.'

'Oh. OK, I'd better go – we're heading into the station.'

As they wait on the platform for the Tube, Sive tells Aaron about Jude's call.

'My God, that girl needs to let go of the Brosnan thing. She's obsessed.'

'She's a journalist who knows her stuff and she's trying to help. Do you have any better ideas?' Sive snaps. A woman a few feet away looks over. Sive lowers her voice and steps closer to Aaron. 'Sorry. I'm just feeling so useless. We can't search an entire city and I can't think of a single place to go right now. It's impossible.'

He pulls her closer, leaning against a metal pole. 'I know.' He sounds exhausted. 'I'm sorry for getting cross about Jude. But the Brosnan thing is so far-fetched, and I'm worried she's here for the story and what she can get out of it. She's had zero suggestions all day, other than chasing that one angle.'

Sive turns her face up to his. 'Actually, speaking of "chasing", she also suggested we try talking to Bea again . . .'

'We already know she can't tell us anything.'

'But in lieu of any other ideas, maybe it's worth a try? And we should check how they're doing, anyway.' She turns her face into his chest again, pressing it against his hoodie, inhaling the faint smell of sweat and fabric conditioner. The scent of normal life. 'I'm worried about Toby taking a bottle and Bea going so long without us.'

'You mean go back to the hotel? I don't know . . .'

She reaches for his hand and squeezes it. 'I feel sick at the thought of going back without Faye. But it's worth trying Bea again. She's the only one who knows what happened.'

Aaron nods, though he looks unconvinced.

'Maybe by then the police will have more witnesses and can narrow down the search area,' she says. 'And we can go back out with a more concrete plan?'

He nods, more emphatically now. Sive pulls away from him to get her phone, and puts the Meridian Hotel into Google Maps.

Bea rushes at Sive as soon as they walk into the hotel suite, and Sive does everything in her power to bite back sobs. Toby is napping in the travel cot, having taken a full bottle, according to Scott, as Aaron grips him in a half-handshake, half-hug.

'We really appreciate this, Burner. You're a good pal. I know I've been a bit shit to you this weekend, and I'm sorry. You've been a lifesaver today.'

Scott shakes his head. 'Hey, I was as bad. Jesus, I can't believe this is happening . . . No news?'

There is no news. There is nothing. DC Hawthorn called them on their way here to tell them just that – she couched it in other terms, talk of scaling up and manpower and resources and witnesses and sifting and CCTV, but it all came down to a big nothing. Faye was nowhere.

And now they're going to try to interrogate a two-year-old.

Sive leans into the travel cot to kiss Toby's sleeping head then sits Bea on the sofa and reaches inside her backpack for a packet of toddler biscuits. Bea claps her hands and squeals when she sees them, bouncing up and down with excitement.

'Now, lovey.' Sive smiles at her. 'I need you to tell me about Faye. Where is Faye?'

Bea is reaching for the biscuits, ignoring Sive's words. Sive puts the pack on the floor and slides it under the sofa.

'Wait now. You can have a bicky when you tell me where your sister is. Where is Faye?'

'Faye gone. Chase.'

OK. Nothing new there. What were they thinking? But Sive keeps trying.

'Who chased Faye? A man?'

Bea nods.

Sive's stomach plummets. 'A man chased Faye?'

'Man chase.' Bea nods emphatically.

'Oh my God.' Sive turns to Aaron.

'But can we take it seriously? She didn't say it earlier ... maybe she's just repeating what you said?'

'Maybe. But we should tell Hawthorn.' She turns back to Bea. 'What did the man look like? Was he tall, like Daddy?' She points at Aaron.

Bea shakes her head, though it's not clear if she really means 'No, he's not tall like Daddy' or 'No, you're not understanding me' or 'No, no more of this please, just give me the biscuits'.

'Chase,' she says again.

'Aaron, pull up some images of the Callans on your phone.'

'What?'

'Just do it!'

Aaron passes her his phone, muttering that it's a waste of time.

'Bea, is this the man who chased Faye?' She shows her daughter the first image.

Bea shakes her head. The same for the next, and the one after that.

'I told you,' Aaron says, and Sive thinks if she wasn't busy trying to find their missing daughter she'd murder him on the spot.

'Aaron,' she hisses.

She turns back to Bea.

'This one, lovey? Is this the man?'

Bea shakes her head. 'Bicky! Now!'

And that is that.

Sive's at a loss about what to do next. Her gut tells her to get back out there, to keep searching, no matter how futile. But where to go? she asks Aaron. He needs to make a call, he says. What kind of call could he possibly need to make in the middle of all this? But he's insistent, and goes out to the corridor to do so.

Scott shrugs. 'You know Aaron. Always doing a million things at once. Maybe he's trying to firefight that video.' A beat. 'It's gone pretty viral.'

Sive shakes her head. 'I don't care about that. I know Aaron doesn't either. We can fix it later.'

Scott nods emphatically, feeling guilty, perhaps, for rubbing salt in the wound. His phone beeps, and he checks it. 'Dave's finished work for the day so he's on his way. Another pair of hands would be good.'

'Oh God, yeah, he can help with the kids. You're so good to do this.'

He brushes it off. 'I meant an extra pair of hands to search. I'm fine here. I have three of my own, remember? Just because Caron has them living on another continent doesn't mean I've forgotten everything.'

She nods, so grateful now she thinks she might cry.

Toby stirs in the travel cot and Sive scoops him out, glad of the excuse to hold him, to feed him.

'Maggie still out searching?' Scott asks.

'She's gone somewhere to "check something", according to a journalist colleague of mine who's been helping. No idea what she's checking.'

'And Nita? Has she helped at all?'

'Nita arrived a bit before the press conference and then headed off to join the search. From inside an Uber.'

'Right.' He rolls his eyes. 'Jeez, she took her time. Getting her beauty sleep, was she? She didn't even turn up for the race – I noticed her name wasn't on the leader board.' He makes a *tsk* sound.

'Ah. Well, she took a tumble and hit her head last night, so we didn't disturb her this morning.'

Scott's face falls. 'Oh, crap. I feel bad now. Is she all right? Is the baby OK?'

'She's fine. Everything's fine,' Sive says, sidestepping the question. Nita's story is not hers to tell. Though she can't help wondering what Scott knows of all the other secrets revealed in Maggie's house last night.

45

Silchester Road

SIVE SAT IN MAGGIE'S living room, staring at the photo of the smiling girls at the Cliffs of Moher, unable to keep the confusion from her face.

'You didn't recognize Yasmin?' Maggie said. 'Oh, of course, you've probably never seen a photo of her.' She put the picture back on the mantelpiece. 'I can't see Aaron as the type for photo albums and nostalgia.'

'I . . . I *have* seen a photo of Yasmin. Just one. Well, four. A strip from a photo booth I found in a box marked "London". Aaron and Yasmin posing and kissing and pulling faces, with "Stratford 2008" marked on the back of the photos.'

'Ah, so a few years after the Cliffs of Moher. She'd probably changed a bit, though not much. God, when I think how young she was.' She shook her head, the sadness palpable.

'But in the photo I saw, her hair was completely different and' – Sive squinted at the photo on the mantelpiece again – 'honestly, her face looked different too. But I knew Aaron was going out with Yasmin in 2008 and the family resemblance was there, so I just assumed . . .' *Oh.*

Maggie frowned. 'Family resemblance?'

'To Nita . . .'. *Of course.* 'Maggie, did Yasmin dye her hair henna red?'

'Yasmin? No, never. She wasn't really into hair and make-up. Nita did, though. Deep-red hair for most of her twenties.'

Nita. Of course. Bloody hell, Aaron.

Maggie tilted her head. 'Wait, you surely don't mean it was Nita in the pictures you saw?'

Sive nodded slowly, thinking, too, of the photo that had fallen out of Nita's bag the night before. Not a snap of her sister on a sunny bench: a photo of her younger self.

'I think it must have been.'

'But you said they were kissing.'

'Yep.'

Maggie's mouth was a perfect O. 'No. Way.' She shook her head. 'No, I'd have known. We all knew everything about each other.'

'Says the woman who's just confessed to secretly dating Dave?'

'Touché. Wow. Aaron cheating on Yasmin with Nita? The absolute fucker. Sorry.'

Sive shook her head. 'No "sorry" necessary. He is a fucker.' For cheating on Yasmin, for never telling Sive, and, *bloody hell, Aaron,* for letting her spend time with Nita, blissfully unaware of their shared history. Somehow that felt embarrassing now. Should she bring it up with Nita? Tell her she knows? *And poor Yasmin.* Fucker didn't even come close. 'Kind of makes it worse that he was cheating on his now-deceased fiancée, doesn't it, even if he obviously couldn't have known she was going to die.'

Maggie's face crumpled slightly, and Sive caught herself. 'Sorry, that was insensitive.'

'It's OK. You're right, though, it does – irrationally – make it worse. I wonder if Yasmin knew? What the hell was Nita thinking!' She sounded as though she was close to tears. 'Sorry. I've never quite got over her death. And I've had far too much to drink tonight.' She circled the tattoos on her wrist. 'I can't believe Nita would do that to her own sister.'

'I can't believe *Aaron*. They're as bad as each other. Self-absorbed narcissists, the pair of them.'

Maggie raised her glass. 'I'll drink to that,' she said with forced cheer, her eyes still shining with tears. 'Do we say anything to them?'

Sive thought for a moment. 'Not now. I'll ask Aaron when we get home to Dublin. Not that it matters really at this stage, I suppose. But I'm curious. And . . . kind of horrified. He's a lot of things, but I never saw him as a cheater.'

Maggie patted her knee. 'He wouldn't cheat on you. He was besotted with you from the first moment. I remember how thrilled he was, telling us you were expecting a baby.'

Sive closed her eyes briefly. *Here we go again.* She let out a long breath and plastered on a smile. 'That's so lovely to hear.'

Maggie must have heard something mechanical in her tone. 'What is it?'

Sive knew she shouldn't do it, but the urge to finally confide in someone was so strong.

'Oh God. Maybe it's the drink talking. But that's not the whole truth.'

Maggie's eyes widened, and Sive braced herself to tell her story.

46

THE HOTEL CORRIDOR IS quiet, expensive carpet muffling sounds. At the end, near the window, Aaron is still on his call. He turns as he hears the door click and Sive freezes when she sees his face. It's clear he's furious.

Sive mimes sleep and points at the door to tell him Bea is napping and he's to come back in via the master bedroom. He nods, then turns his back to continue his call. She watches for a moment. Watches his hand go up, gesturing as if trying to make a point. Watches as he leans forward, resting his forehead against the window, shoulders slumped now. His voice is too low for her to hear. What could possibly be more important than the search for Faye? Perhaps it has something to do with the court case. Maybe Aaron's repeated protests are hiding a fear that Jude is right.

He won't want this to be his fault.

The realization is suddenly crystal clear. That's why he's so adamant that it has nothing to do with the court case. Because then it's Aaron who brought this to their door. Shaking her head, she goes back into their suite.

*

'What now?' Scott asks. He's sitting on a wing chair by the living-room window, pointing a remote control at the television to turn down the sound. BBC News is on-screen, and the ticker at the bottom is about Faye. *Six-year-old Irish girl still missing in London.* Sive turns away.

'I honestly don't know, but I think we go back out. If you're OK to stay with the kids?'

He nods, pointing with his chin to where Toby is asleep again in the travel cot. 'All that little guy does is snooze. Piece of cake. Where will you go?'

'I guess we ask DC Hawthorn where to search . . . God, this is such a nightmare.' She sits on the sofa, face in hands.

Scott says nothing.

What is there to say? It's like when someone dies and—

She cuts off the thought before it can finish. *Faye's not dead. Someone has her, and they'll give her back.*

The door opens and Aaron arrives, beckoning behind him.

'I'll go back out and wait on the corridor, mate,' says some-one in a loud whisper. 'Don't want to disturb the kiddos.' Dave, Sive thinks. She doesn't know if she has the bandwidth for Dave right now.

But Aaron tells him to come through. 'Bea's asleep in the other room and Scott's got Toby quiet as a lamb, don't worry.'

Something heavy in Aaron's voice draws Sive's attention. She glances up at him. He looks . . . cagey. Guilty? Something to do with the call just now?

Dave shuffles into the room and looks at Sive.

'I'm so sorry,' he says, and she nods. 'I saw the press confer-ence online. It's *got* to help. We see it at work all the time. People *connect*, you know? See the human behind the news story. There's actually quite a bit of science behind it—'

Mercifully, Aaron cuts him off. 'We need to plan next steps.'

'Absolutely. Strategy. So, you guys have been searching Tube stations?'

Sive looks up at Aaron. He raises his eyebrows in an un-spoken question, and she nods. There's no reason to keep their wild goose chase a secret any more. Aaron fills them in and Sive tunes out. Her mind is full of Faye, and only Faye. Her bright blue eyes. Her tiny nose. Her gap-toothed smile. Her away-with-the-fairies take on life. Her delighted reactions to the smallest things. Her woeful attempts to steal biscuits from the up-high press. The way she can't lie to save her life. Her desperate wish for a puppy. Her fear of even the smallest bugs. Her magpie love for all that sparkles. Sive touches the pendant around her neck the way Faye loves to touch it.

Miss Victoria London.

It can't be a coincidence.

'Aaron?' She pulls her hands away from her face. 'The person who took Faye sent us to that gift shop for a reason. It's literally the only place you can get the necklace.'

'Not strictly true. That one was bought online.' *Stubborn as ever.*

'I know, but from her website. Like, there must be thousands of jewellery websites in the world. And we were sent to this one. What does it mean? And why do it? Why pretend Faye is there when she's not?'

Dave clears his throat and they look at him. 'I don't know why they picked the jewellery place, but' – he takes off his cap and rubs his head – 'to answer the second question, I imagine it was to get Aaron to make his confession video.'

'Obviously,' Aaron snaps.

'But that doesn't explain why Faye wasn't there,' Sive says. 'Aaron made the video. He did what was asked. What was the purpose of dragging us out there? Was it to keep us away from something else? To distract us?'

Dave looks from one to the other, still rubbing his head.

'I assume it's because the person who made the call wanted you to record the video: to destroy your career and to embarrass you.' He stops to take a deep breath, as though readying himself for something difficult, or perhaps enjoying being the voice of authority, his moment in the spotlight.

And his next sentence turns everything upside down again.

47

5.00 p.m.

DAVE ENUNCIATES EACH WORD carefully. 'That person who forced you to make the video' – a pause – 'I'd imagine they never had Faye at all.'

Sive sits up straight. 'What do you mean, they never had Faye?'

'I mean, I'm guessing they leveraged off an opportunity,' Dave says, putting his cap on the coffee table and sitting on the other side of the sofa. There's a certain tinge of superiority in his voice. A certain enjoyment in finally holding court.

Sive stares at him. 'But why—'

Of course. To get Aaron to make the video.

'You mean someone who has nothing to do with this pretended they had Faye, in order to force Aaron to record that clip?' Sive glances at Aaron to see his reaction, but his face is unreadable.

Dave nods.

Scott looks intrigued and impressed. 'That's actually quite clever. I rather think you could be right.'

'I do work in the area of law enforcement.' Dave shrugs with faux nonchalance. 'Teaches you a thing or two.'

Sive remembers something. 'But the woman on the phone knew about the stitches in her leg, which nobody could have known if they weren't literally with Faye.'

Dave holds up his hands. 'Can't answer that bit, but yeah, seems to me like someone pulled the wool over your eyes.'

Sive doesn't know what to think. If the person never had Faye, they've wasted hours on a pointless journey and false hope. And they've lost what they believed to be a link to her whereabouts – a phone number, albeit out of service, connecting them to the person who has Faye. Sive looks over at Aaron again, needing him to tell her that Dave is wrong. That there's still hope. That they're not back to square one. But Aaron is rocking back and forth on his feet, looking at the floor.

'Aaron?'

Silence.

'Aaron?' she says again. 'You know something, don't you? This is linked to the pendant you bought me? Wait . . . and your phonecall just now?'

'I didn't buy you the pendant. Garvin did.'

'Who's Garvin?' Scott asks.

'His assistant,' Sive says, trying to make sense of it. 'Garvin bought the pendant?'

Aaron throws up his hands. 'It's part of his job! The clue is in the title. Personal assistant.' He's defensive. Defiant. Daring them to challenge him. 'He does whatever needs doing and, in this case, that included sourcing the pendant with the kids' birthstones for your Christmas present.' He looks at her now and the defiance dims. 'Sorry.'

'Jesus Christ, I don't care if Garvin bought the pendant – what the fuck does this have to do with my missing child?' She's shouting at him. If this has some bearing on Faye's disappearance, how could Aaron not have told her earlier?

A heavy sigh. 'I spoke to Garvin just now. When you spotted the connection between the gift shop and the pendant, it started to click.'

'But you said I was wrong? That the connection meant nothing?'

'Sorry. I wanted to speak to him before we jumped to any conclusions. I still didn't think he'd actually done it – just that there was some odd link that would make sense once I'd spoken to him. So I called him a few minutes ago. And he started laughing. He fucking laughed at me.'

'What?'

'Said all this stuff about years of being treated like shit, gaslighting, bullying, blah blah blah. That he's been dreaming of the day he could force me to . . . well, you know. All that stuff he made me say in the video.'

Scott whistles. Dave shakes his head. Sive is numb.

'Apparently, when I asked him to submit the medical receipt on Friday night, that tipped him over the edge. Like, it's his literal job.'

'Maybe not on a Friday night, though,' Scott says, unhelpfully. Aaron shoots him a look.

'It hardly warrants doing this! He could have just quit his job, for fuck's sake.'

'Not quite as satisfying, I'd have thought,' Scott says, under his breath.

'He said he was going to take whatever he could from the office to go to the police . . .'

Sive stares at her husband. 'What would he have been taking to the police?'

Aaron shakes his head. 'No idea. He's deluded. But then, when he saw that Faye was missing, he realized he had a way to make me, as he put it, dig my own grave instead.'

Scott's eyes widen. 'Come on, only a sociopath would do something like that.'

'Garvin *is* a sociopath. That's why I hired him. He's excellent at his job and completely unemotional. Or so I thought.'

Sive still can't quite take it in. 'He made that phonecall, pretending to have Faye, to make you post the video?'

'Apparently so. Fucking destroyed my career in a single hour on a Monday morning. Said sending me to the gift shop where he'd bought the necklace was a "nice little touch" he came up with at the last minute.'

Sive shakes her head. 'But the caller knew about the stitches – that's how we knew it was legit . . .' It dawns on her as soon as the words are out. 'Oh. He knew about them because you sent him the medical receipt.'

Aaron lowers his eyes. 'Yeah. "A perfect irony", he said.'

Sive is still not convinced. 'But the person on the phone was a woman. Are you sure he's telling the truth? Was there someone helping him?'

'He used a function on something called Scratch? Speeds up and slows down voices. It can make a woman sound like a man and a man sound like a woman. I don't know anything about it.'

'I do,' Dave chimes in. 'Very easily done. Scratch is a basic coding program, but there are plenty of voice-changer apps that do the same thing.'

'So that was the click and pause we kept hearing,' Sive says. 'He was playing pre-recorded voice files, like Jude thought.'

'Yeah.'

'Fuck.'

'Yeah.'

'I want to kill him.' Sive knows this is true. She would literally kill Garvin right now if she could. Push him off a high building or put a bullet through his head. She has never known anything so clearly.

'Not if I get there first,' Aaron says. 'But that doesn't help. Right now, we need to focus on Faye. She's still out there with some stranger.'

Some stranger, Sive wonders, looking at her husband, *or someone closer to home?*

48

Silchester Road

MAGGIE SAT FORWARD ON the couch. 'OK, Sive. You've got my full attention. What's not "the whole truth"?'

'Aaron isn't Faye's biological dad.' Sive felt better the second the words were out. Her mother didn't know. Her brother didn't know. Her BFFs from college didn't know. Nobody in the world but Aaron and Sive knew this secret, and that's the way it had to stay. They'd agreed from the start. Sive hadn't felt comfortable hiding the truth from Faye's biological father but, as Aaron kept pointing out, a convicted criminal would hardly be the best role model in Faye's life. And anyway, he was still in prison.

'Wow. Well, that's *surprising*, but not exactly earth-shattering. There are lots of blended families today. Goodness, it's all coming out tonight. Is Faye's dad in her life?'

'No . . . it's complicated.'

'You know, you guys didn't have to pretend. Did you think we'd judge you?'

'It was just easier to keep it to ourselves,' Sive said, which was only half the truth. 'Nobody knows. You're the first person I've ever told.'

Maggie's cheeks pinkened with what might have been pleasure at the shared confidence.

'Gosh. Well, I'm honoured. And here for any bean-spilling you need to do, any time.' She raised her glass to clink Sive's. 'You met Aaron through work, I think, covering a court case? So I guess Faye's dad was someone you were seeing shortly before you met Aaron? Stop me if I'm being nosy.'

'No, that's fine. Yes. Someone I was seeing . . .' *May as well be hanged for a sheep as a lamb.* 'Aaron was his lawyer. Joost – that's my ex, he's Dutch – was charged with manslaughter and Aaron was his barrister. I wasn't covering the court case for the paper; everyone just assumes that, and we let them. I was there because my partner was in the dock.'

'Oh my. Manslaughter?'

'Yes. The whole thing was horrific.'

'I'm so sorry.'

Sive waved it away. 'It's the victim's family I feel sorry for.'

'What happened?'

And Sive told her story. About the earnest, charming Dutchman she met at an industry awards dinner – he was there with the bank he worked for; she was doing a stint covering the paper's financial pages. Joost De Witte was the perfect gentleman. Funny. Clever. Different to other guys she'd dated. Direct and unambiguous at work and with friends – said exactly what was on his mind at all times and couldn't understand why Irish people used so many 'flowery' words for every small announcement or request for help. *Just say what you mean! Don't use ten words when you can use two!* he used to beg. He was direct and unambiguous with Sive, too – he didn't want marriage; he didn't want kids. He was in Ireland for the long term, though – *God,* he loved Ireland and all things Irish – and could see a future with her. She wasn't quite sure about the future thing, but she liked him. And, in hindsight, she could see that she'd been lonely – new to Dublin, missing her family and friends in Cork. And she enjoyed spending time with Joost. Well, mostly. Except when he talked about work. He was a perfectionist and often impatient with the way things were done by others. Critical, regularly, of his colleagues. And that's where it started to go wrong. He couldn't help himself. If he saw anyone cutting corners or taking time out, he had to comment on it. *We're here to work*, he used to say. *Not to look at Facebook or take five coffee breaks.* He even reported some of his colleagues to their manager, an action that did not make him popular. One colleague was given a verbal warning for consistent lateness, something his manager hadn't noticed until Joost pointed it out. Another colleague was passed over for promotion. Things escalated. Joost was ostracized and isolated. His teammates wouldn't share information or cafeteria tables with him. Sive listened to his woes on the nights she stayed over. Her approach – always – was diplomacy and collaboration. She worked on the basis that you catch more flies with honey than with vinegar. It had served her well throughout her years in journalism – she had a knack for getting interviewees to open up. Relatable warmth was her modus operandi, where Joost's was to say exactly what was on his mind at any given time, no matter who he offended. *But I'm right!* he used to say, exasperated. *That guy Diarmuid was late three days in a row!* And Sive would try again to tell him that it wasn't his business. That it was between Diarmuid and his manager. *Stay in your lane*, she used to tell him. But Joost never could.

And then the firm threw alcohol into the mix.

It was during Christmas drinks that it all came to a head. The company had cancelled the usual Christmas party some years earlier, during the downturn, but had introduced casual office-based drinks instead, and it turned out most people preferred this to stuffy five-course meals in hotels with expensive wine and sub-par food. It was also far cheaper for management, who were happy to provide crates and crates of German supermarket beer, along with a few bowls of crisps and the obligatory box of Celebrations. By Joost's first Christmas party, one life-altering Friday in early December, the casual office-based drinks had become quite the occasion. The budget for supermarket beer had been increased and extended to supermarket wine, and everyone got uproariously drunk. Late that night, after far too many beers, Joost found himself face to face with four of his colleagues in the men's bathroom. Nobody would agree on exactly what had happened. Joost said Diarmuid hit him. Diarmuid's friends said Joost lashed out first: that Diarmuid had been taunting Joost but hadn't hit him. Either way, Diarmuid was knocked backwards and hit his head on the side of the basin. He died two days later in hospital and Joost spent his first night on remand in an Irish prison. There was, in fact, CCTV footage, Sive told Maggie, because the bank had a discreet, undisclosed camera in the men's bathroom. But, of course, because it was hidden from employees, it was illegal, Sive explained, so the footage was ruled inadmissible. Even Sive never saw it, and the bank moved quickly to remove the cameras.

'The thing is,' Sive said, when Maggie asked her more questions about the video clip, 'Diarmuid Grant was still dead. Even if the judge had allowed the footage, at most it might have got Joost a lesser sentence. But he was guilty of taking a man's life, whether he hit first or not. Nothing changes that. As Aaron always says, it's the law of unintended consequences. Joost didn't mean Diarmuid Grant to die, but when he hit him, that's what happened.'

Maggie had a curious look on her face. A look with which Sive was becoming familiar – she'd seen it when Nita's bag spilled on the floor the night before, and when Dave was speaking about his mother, and when they were talking earlier in the bar about Scott burning down the neighbours' shed.

'What is it?'

Maggie shook her head. 'No, I'm just fascinated. Gosh, Sive, that must have been an awful time for you.'

'It was, but that pales in comparison to what it must have been like for Diarmuid Grant's parents, hearing their son was dead.'

'Of course. But remember, just because someone else suffers more, it doesn't mean we're not suffering too. There's always someone worse off and, by that logic, we'd never be allowed to admit to finding anything difficult at all.'

'I guess. It's all a blur now. I was numb. I mean, you read about these one-punch deaths, but it's so shocking when it happens in real life. When you know the person who did it.'

'And then you met Aaron because he was defending Joost?'

'Yeah. I know. Doesn't paint me in the best light, does it?'

Maggie put up her hands. 'I learned a long time ago not to judge. And hey, you didn't fake a pregnancy to your forty-six thousand Instagram followers.'

Sive laughed, though Maggie was just being nice. Sive was fairly sure that what she had done was far worse. Betraying Joost, then lying to everyone she'd ever known. *You're not betraying him*, Aaron had said. *He betrayed you when he hit Diarmuid Grant and brought this on both of you. It's quite sensible to walk away.* Aaron had wooed her from the first moment they'd met, and she liked to tell herself she'd resisted initially. In truth, there was a mutual attraction from very early on that she'd had to work hard to suppress. There was something mesmeric about the way Aaron took charge of everything – Joost's defence, Sive's wellbeing – like a soothing balm after weeks of anxiety. To Sive, if felt like sitting back while someone fixed your computer or massaged your back or washed your hair. Telling you to hold still and do nothing and all would be well. The confident expert who seamlessly took control. The opposite of Joost, who had bumbled his way headlong into trouble and couldn't seem to find his way out. Aaron was magnetic.

And, as Aaron liked to point out, they'd had the decency to wait until Joost was found guilty before taking the step from friendship to relationship. Or affair? *It's not an affair*, Aaron had always said. *He's in prison. That annuls your relationship.* That wasn't true, of course. Lots of people stayed together after one was convicted of a crime. Maybe it was easier if you were some-one who grew up in that world and took prison sentences as acceptable collateral damage. Maybe it was easier if it was a so-called white-collar crime – where the victim was a faceless corporation. Maybe it was easier when people didn't die. If Joost had just punched someone and that person hadn't died, it would be an embarrassing Christmas-party story and nothing more. But then, morally, what difference was there, really? The action was the same, regardless of the consequence. Of course, Joost had never meant for anyone to die, but it was the fact of that death that changed everything. She couldn't stay with Joost, knowing he'd ended a life.

Still . . . it niggled. Not every day. Just sometimes, when she looked at Faye, at her long limbs and her golden skin and her blonde hair, so like Joost, who had no idea he had a daughter. Joost who was sitting alone every day in prison, counting down the days to freedom.

49

Monday
5.59 p.m.

SIVE CAN TELL THAT DC Hawthorn is frustrated at how long it's taken them to come back to Oxford Circus and how vague they're being about where they've been, but she manages to bite it back. It's not quite appropriate to chastise a couple who are frantically worried about their missing child, Sive supposes, even if they have been AWOL for the last three hours, and cagey about what they've been doing. Aaron doesn't want to tell the police about Garvin. The video's been taken down now, and they've continued to dismiss it as a deep fake, so it's over, as far as he's concerned. Sive thinks this is a mistake. Why not tell the police everything – what is there to lose? They'd debated over and back in heated whispers in the cab on the way to meet Hawthorn: Aaron adamant that it wouldn't help find Faye. *What's the point?* he'd said. It would only be a distraction. If they reported it, the police would have to interview Garvin, wasting time following up in case there was even a tiny chance Garvin did have Faye. Whereas Aaron knew Garvin was sitting in his apartment in Dublin 8, laughing his head off. Nowhere near London. Nowhere near Faye. *OK, but as soon as this is over, we report that fucker*, Sive had said. Aaron gave a half-hearted nod. Because his mind was on Faye? Sive wondered, or because he was worried about what Garvin might say to the police? She looked at her husband as he stared out through the window of the cab. How much truth was there in what Garvin was saying? Aaron wasn't averse to cutting corners to get what he wanted. But small stuff. *Surely only small stuff.* Or was there more to what Garvin was claiming? Had Aaron really blackmailed witnesses to manipulate cases? She couldn't help thinking she should be more certain that he hadn't. That in a normal marriage with normal people, a spouse's immediate reaction to any accusation would be absolute certainty in her partner's innocence. Why wasn't she certain? Maybe because the news about his affair with Nita was still sinking in? Or was it more than that . . . an underlying fear that had always been there. And what if all of this – Aaron's grey areas, his habit of sailing close to the wind – had something to do with why Faye was missing? Not Garvin – but someone else whose path Aaron had crossed? Trampled on? She let that thought percolate for a moment. It didn't add up. How could anyone have known where she and the kids would be that morning? Unless someone had been following them . . . The cab lurched around a corner and her stomach turned. She hadn't eaten since the hotel breakfast, but the thought of food made her feel even sicker. How many hours was it now? She looked at her phone. Almost six o'clock. Faye had been missing for nearly ten hours.

And now they're back, standing on Oxford Street, in the heavy evening heat, yet again at a loss as to what to do. Hawthorn asks if they want to go to the supervisor's office in the station, warning them it won't be long before reporters realize they're back. But Aaron wants to stay here, out on the street, where they'll feel more useful. Sive is numb. Completely numb. As though her mind is shutting down to protect her from thinking the worst.

Hawthorn leaves, and Jude texts. She's in a Regent Street coffee shop, working on something, but she'll come to meet them now. To regroup, she says. And less than ten minutes later, she's here beside them, listening while Aaron gives her more details about their false lead in Leytonstone. Sive is only half tuned in as they swap questions and answers – Is Maggie here? Aaron asks. No, she never came back, Jude says. Are their other friends coming? Dave will follow once he runs home to get his car, Aaron says. Scott is staying with Bea and Toby, and Nita is sharing her participation in the search on Insta Live.

Jude is saying something else now, and Sive forces herself to listen properly.

'In light of the fact that Leytonstone was a dead end, I tried the guy Tim Brassil again – the one who found Bea – to see why he lied about his workplace.'

Aaron lets out an audible sigh. Sive ignores it. 'Go on?'

'I tracked him down on social media and I've sent him DMs on Twitter and Instagram. So we'll see.' A pause. 'I also went back to looking into the Callans.' Jude holds up her hand to stop Aaron before he objects. 'It can't do any harm. Unless you have other ideas?'

Aaron has no other ideas.

'Right. I've done some more digging, and if the Callans are setting up Brosnan to take the fall for this murder, they won't be afraid to go to extremes to make it happen.' She pauses. Around them, evening-rush-hour commuters hurry into the station, dashing for trains. 'If they wanted to put pressure on Aaron to fumble the case, they wouldn't be beyond taking a child.'

Sive thinks she might throw up.

Aaron is shaking his head. 'You don't know what you're talking about. This isn't a TV show. This isn't—'

'Aaron, for fuck's sake! Stop! Just let her help!'

'Sive, I—'

She faces him, taking his hands in hers. 'It doesn't make it your fault. Just let Jude do her stuff. Let her ask her questions, and if it comes to nothing, so be it. But if there's even the smallest chance these people have Faye' – she squeezes his hands – 'it's worth chasing. OK?'

He bows his head, the fight in him suddenly gone.

Sive looks up and spots Hawthorn making her way towards them, skirting through throngs of commuters. Looking exhausted now, the DC swipes half-heartedly at the wisps of hair that are matted to her forehead and, with a curt nod at Jude, she turns to the Sullivans.

'Two small updates. Firstly, we've spoken to your babysitter, Willow, and to the hotel – she was babysitting for another family this morning, so we have no concerns that she was involved.'

Sive is nodding before Hawthorn finishes her sentence. She never thought Willow was involved. 'And?'

'A very minor update on Faye's biological father, Mr De Witte.' As Hawthorn speaks, Sive can feel Jude buzzing to life beside her. 'As I mentioned, we discovered earlier this afternoon that, contrary to your belief that he's still in prison, he was released six months ago. We've not yet been able to track him down, but we're working on it, with assistance from the gardaí.'

Aaron is frowning furiously at Hawthorn, nodding pointedly towards Jude, but Hawthorn doesn't catch it and Sive doesn't care. What does it matter any more?

'As far as we can ascertain, and the details are still unclear, he's every bit a model citizen now, having reinvented himself as some kind of guru on, well, reinvention. But obviously, model citizen or not, since we know he's out of prison, we can't rule him out.'

'I promise you, you can,' Sive says emphatically. 'Apart from the fact that he doesn't know Faye exists, he never, ever wanted kids. There's just no way on earth he'd take her.'

She's conscious of Jude beside her, eyes wide, taking it in.

And Aaron, eyes down, squeezing her hand.

'Indeed.' Hawthorn purses her lips. 'Well, I'll be happier once we find him.'

And then Aaron's phone rings twice, and everything changes again.

50

AARON JUMPS WHEN HIS phone rings, just as he does each time it rings now, ever since Sive's panicked call this morning.

But it's only Scott.

'Aaron, everything's fine with the kids, but there's something the little one said that might have an impact on things.'

'Bea? What did she say?'

'Well, you see, I put the TV on for them. Hope that's all right.' Aaron nods into the phone. 'And there was an episode of that cartoon *PAW Patrol* – you know it?'

'Yes, but Scott, I need to keep the line free. It's fine if the kids watch TV.' He swipes at a bead of sweat that's trickling towards his eye. 'Whatever it takes.'

'Wait. Bea started pointing at the TV, saying, "Chase! Chase!" at the dog character, you know the one – well, they're all dogs, aren't they? But one character is called Chase. And maybe that's what was in her head earlier? Maybe she didn't mean someone chased Faye. Maybe she was talking about her backpack. She has one with *PAW Patrol* on it, I think?'

Aaron let out a breath. 'Jesus. She does. And she probably had it this morning.' And maybe Bea left it on the train or lost it and wanted it back. But that's all it was. A backpack. Nothing to do

257

with anyone chasing Faye. Which was good. Aaron let out a breath. A small breath. It didn't mean much in the bigger night-mare, but imagining their six-year-old daughter being chased by someone had been a whole other level of horror.

'Scott, I need to tell Sive. I gotta go.' Then: 'Thanks. You're a good pal. I don't deserve you.'

A pause. 'It's nothing. I know you'd do the same.'

Almost as soon as the call ends, Aaron's phone rings again. Carmen Brosnan. *Jesus Christ, has the woman no sense?* Aaron rejects the call and shouts for Sive, to tell her what Scott has just said about the backpack. Jude-the-journalist is straight out with her phone, typing.

'Hold on, don't post anything about that,' Aaron says. 'We need to tell Hawthorn first.'

She meets his gaze coolly, clearly not happy with being stopped in her tracks.

'I'm typing a note to myself. I know not to make anything public without police approval. I'm not a schoolgirl doing work experience, Aaron, I'm a journalist who's been in the job for fif-teen years.'

She clicks into something on her phone and reads, mouthing the words silently. Aaron holds back a retort as Sive watches and waits. Jude is a born attention-seeker, and clearly loves holding court, but of course Sive can't see that. She's completely fallen for the helpful-colleague act.

A frown creases Jude's forehead now, then just as quickly clears.

'What is it?' Sive asks.

Jude holds up her phone. 'Tim Brassil. He just replied on Twitter DM. Turns out he got let go from Anderson Pruitt a month ago and he's been job-hunting since but hasn't told his girlfriend. So he had no reason to get back on the Tube to Liverpool Street after he handed over Bea.'

'OK . . . but why did he lie to the police?' Sive asks.

'Well, he was at pains to point out that he *didn't* lie. He apparently said, "Six years as Head of Fund Accounting at Anderson Pruitt", which is not, technically, a lie. He did do six years, he just doesn't work there any more.' Jude rolls her eyes.

'So, another complete waste of time,' Aaron says, not trying to disguise his contempt.

Jude frowns. 'Not at all. It took ten minutes to do some googling and send the messages.'

'Which came to nothing.'

'Eh, yeah, but if we only chase down leads that will come to *something*, there's a fatal flaw in that plan, isn't there, Aaron?'

Aaron really wants to tell her to fuck off back to Longford now, but Sive is throwing him a warning glance.

'It's good to rule him out. Thanks, Jude,' Sive says. Peacemaker to a fault. 'I'm glad you followed up.'

'No worries. The lie niggled, and I needed an answer. No smoke without fire, as they say.'

She's answering Sive, but she's staring straight at Aaron.

51

One day earlier | Sunday
Silchester Road

'I SHOULD HEAD BACK to the hotel soon,' Sive said, looking at the clock on Maggie's mantelpiece. 'Toby will be awake during the night, and Aaron doesn't always hear him.'

Maggie's phone began to ring then, making both of them jump. Maggie looked at the screen and her cheeks turned pink.

'Is everything OK?' Sive asked.

'Yes. It's just Dave.' Maggie swiped to decline the call.

'Oh?' Sive said, eyebrows arched.

Maggie smiled and her face bloomed bright red. 'He . . . calls sometimes.'

'At eleven at night? Maggie, you dark horse! Are you back together?'

'No.' Maggie smoothed her skirt, looking down at her lap as she spoke. 'It'll never work out as a relationship, I know that.'

'Are you sure?' Sive asked softly, conscious that Nita's teasing earlier made it hard for Maggie to say how she really felt.

'I'm sure. He was kind and attentive, but needy too, and it could be cloying. He wanted my full attention, even though I didn't have his.'

'Because of no-Kate-Moss ex?'

'Because of no-Kate-Moss ex. The constant push-pull was too much. Needing me there for him, but then disappearing off into his own head, thinking about her.'

'Well, then, it sounds like you have things just right – friends with benefits, eh?' Sive nodded towards Maggie's phone.

'He might want to talk. Maybe after last night, and that whole weird thing—' She stopped. 'Anyway, yeah, he sometimes calls and, hey, we're both single and' – a shrug and a half-smile – 'both adults, so . . .'

'I love it! All the secrets coming out tonight. Well, if he's coming over, I really should go. And I've just remembered I'll be on my own with the kids when Aaron is off doing the race.' She let out a small sigh.

'I have a sneaking suspicion you're not enjoying our wonderful reunion,' Maggie said with a grin.

Sive rolled her eyes. 'It's fine. But maybe we should have got someone back home to mind the kids. Or maybe Aaron should have come on his own. It's not about your group of friends,' she added hurriedly. 'Reunions in general can be tense.'

'Agreed. And is it really friendship if there's constant pressure to compete?'

'*Self-imposed* pressure,' Sive said, thinking about Nita, Dave, Aaron and Scott, each of them working so hard to stay in the conversation, to be seen, to be relevant, and none of them paying attention to anyone else in the process. 'We might be the only sensible ones.'

Maggie laughed at that.

'And the gas thing is,' Sive went on, 'they're all doing absolutely great – there's no need for the competing. I mean, look at Scott, a pilot now!'

There was that look again.

'What is it?'

Maggie traced a circle around the rim of her glass. 'Yeah, I don't think Scott's really a pilot.'

'What?'

'It struck me earlier tonight in the bar, when we were telling you about the time he burned down his neighbours' shed. He got a criminal conviction for that. Nothing serious enough to get him turfed out of the legal profession but, as far as I'm aware, you can't be a pilot with a criminal conviction.' She felt around behind her on the couch. 'Let me grab my phone, and I'll google it.' She stood and checked under the cushion, then grimaced as she spotted her phone poking out from under the couch. 'Don't tell Nita I lost my phone in my own living room. Anyway, let's see . . .'

A few clicks later, she had it: 'Disqualifying Convictions from the Civil Aviation Authority'. She opened the PDF, scrolled and pointed at the screen. Sive leaned closer to look. ' "Destroying or Damaging Property under the Criminal Damage Act of 1981." That's the charge that was brought against Scott.'

Sive shook her head in confusion. 'So you think he made it all up – the pilot thing? Why?'

'I guess he couldn't bear to turn up at the reunion without a badge of achievement. "Divorced Dad Still Thinking About What to Do After Redundancy" doesn't have quite the same ring as "Pilot".'

'That's insane!'

'Agreed. But you know what Scott's like when it comes to measuring up to Aaron. And it doesn't help that the redundancy came about because Scott's firm was taken over by an Irish company. Salt in the wound.'

'God, that's so stupid, though.'

'Oh, I agree. But you know how competitive Scott is. And Nita's just as bad.'

'Yes, well. We know what Nita did. Jeez. Please tell me Dave's not covering up that he's been secretly fired from his beloved job?'

'Ha. No, Dave is very happy in his job. He's a lifer.' A pause. 'The job is not the problem.'

'I can hear a "but".'

'There is indeed a "but" . . .' Maggie picked at the hem of her dress, then straightened it. 'Remember he was talking about his mother when we were in his apartment last night?'

'Yeah?'

'And he said she's in a nursing home? The thing is, his mother died last year.'

'Oh no. That's awful. You mean he never told anyone?'

'Exactly. I only knew because I stayed in contact with her after Dave and I stopped seeing each other. I used to call around to have a cup of tea. Despite what you've heard from the others, she was a perfectly nice lady who was a bit lonely in that big old house in Stratford. Then one day I called in and there was no answer. A neighbour spotted me and told me she'd passed away.' She shook her head, twisting her glass in both hands. 'I remember feeling so odd about it. We're used to hearing news like that from friends and family. It's strange to call, chocolates in hand, ready to chat, only to find someone's dead.'

'That's sad.'

'Yes. I sent a card to Dave, but I don't know if he ever got it. He didn't text, anyway. We weren't really talking for a while after we split, so that didn't surprise me terribly. When we did start speaking again and, well, you know . . .' She took a sip of her drink. 'I brought up his mum's death, but he brushed it away like he didn't want to talk about it. So it was really strange that he spoke about his mother last night in the present tense and never mentioned she'd died.'

Sive nodded, remembering now Maggie's startled expression when Dave was chatting about his mum.

'I suppose he didn't want to bring on a rush of condolences or awkwardness, but still,' Maggie continued, 'it's the kind of thing you should feel comfortable sharing with friends.'

Sive shook her head. *What a group.* All of them pretending, everything for show, her own husband included – though of course she was a willing participant in his lie.

'And then there's poor Nita and her insane deception,' Maggie continued, glancing up at the ceiling, above which Nita slept.

'Will she try again for a baby, do you think?' Sive asked.

'I guess so. The fertility medication in her bag suggests she already is. And – I'm thinking again of what we discovered about her affair with Aaron – when Nita puts her mind to something, nothing can stop her.'

Sive raised her eyebrows. 'You think she chased him? Her own sister's fiancé?'

'Who knows.' Maggie shrugged. 'Maybe it was the other way around.'

'It doesn't paint either of them in a great light. Not that I'm one to talk, after how I got together with Aaron.'

'That's different, though. Sounds like you and this guy Joost were finished by then?'

Sive nodded. Only because she'd put distance between them. Pulling slowly away instead of telling him directly that it was over. This was her fatal flaw – fudging around, hoping other people would get the message.

'And how long does he have left on his prison sentence?'

From upstairs came a creak, and they both looked at the ceiling, but there was no other sound.

'Just Nita turning in bed, I'd imagine,' Maggie said. 'She'll have a sore head tomorrow. Anyway, go on, when does Joost get out?'

'He has eighteen months left but could be released sooner . . . I set up a Google Alert with his name and I check *a lot* to see if there are any mentions of him online.'

'Eh, I hate to break it to you, but prisoners aren't allowed smartphones.'

'Oh, I know. But Joost loves all things tech. Loves Twitter, used to have a blog. I know, as soon as he's out, he'll be back online.'

'And are you worried he'll make contact? Want to meet Faye?'

'He doesn't know about Faye, and we want to keep it that way.'

Maggie blinked, her mouth a surprised O.

'I know . . . but Joost never wanted kids. He wouldn't have any interest in getting to know her.'

'But . . . but surely he'll make the connection, work out the timing, Faye's age?'

'We're *very* careful. Aaron doesn't use social media at all, and I never post anything about the kids. We live in an airtight bubble of privacy.'

'Is Aaron really that worried about Joost being a bad influence?'

'Yeah. And you know Aaron – what he says, goes. Never takes no for an answer.'

Maggie gave her a funny look.

'What is it?'

'Just . . . does it ever get a bit much? He's brilliant, he's fascinating to observe, he's so good at his job. But sometimes it seems exhausting. The whole uber-alpha-male thing.'

'That's what I like about him,' Sive said lightly, not entirely sure where this was going. 'And he's not like that with me and the kids. He's a big softie at home.'

'Sure, but how someone behaves with other people counts for a lot, doesn't it?'

Sive had no idea what to say to that.

Maggie put her hand on Sive's arm. 'Don't mind me. It's the drink talking. I'm still thinking about this guy Joost and his court case and Aaron's insistence on keeping him at a distance. It sounds like a beer-fuelled row that ended horrifically, but maybe it doesn't mean Joost is the devil incarnate?'

Indeed, Joost was never the devil incarnate. But Aaron was steadfast on this point, to a level that didn't always make sense to Sive. As far as he was concerned, Joost could never under any circumstances be let back into their lives.

52

SOMEONE – ONE OF HAWTHORN'S colleagues – hands a coffee to Sive, and she drinks it on autopilot, barely registering that it's too hot and burns her mouth. Aaron is pacing, squinting in the evening sun; enlarging and reducing a map of London on his phone. *It's pointless*, she tells him silently. *We don't have a clue where to look.*

Jude is standing beside her, typing on her phone with one hand, a cigarette in the other. She hasn't mentioned Joost, but it's coming any second, Sive can tell.

'You holding up?' she asks Sive, without taking her eyes off her screen.

'No.' Sive shakes her head. 'I feel like such a fucking waste of space. First I let it happen, and now I'm here with a coffee in my hand. Like some fucking tourist.'

They're standing outside Oxford Circus station, with oblivious workers rushing past. Keen to get home to dinners and Netflix and pets and books. Eager to plug in earphones and turn on podcasts and put another day of work behind them. Safe in the knowledge that their kids are exactly where they're supposed to be.

'So,' Jude says, 'obviously I heard what Hawthorn said about Joost . . .'

'Yeah. She told us earlier he was out of prison, but I didn't want to . . . well, Aaron wanted to keep it between us.'

'Oh!' Jude's eyes widen, and Sive can almost see the lightbulb going on above her head. 'Oh wow, I should have copped. I heard Hawthorn say, "With you stable . . . tracker," earlier. I thought it was financial stuff, something about a mortgage. But she was saying, "With Joost able to track her," about Faye?'

Sive nods. 'We kept telling her he wouldn't, he doesn't know about her, he doesn't want kids . . .'

Jude opens her mouth to say something else, but her phone rings, interrupting her.

'It's one of my Dublin contacts.' She glances across at Aaron. 'I'll take it over here.' She moves in the opposite direction, out of earshot. Sive can't blame her. Aaron's resistance to the idea that this is linked to his case is getting ridiculous. Surely all that matters is finding their daughter? *She's not his daughter*, says a little voice in her head. She ignores it. Aaron is bull-headed and arrogant. Single-minded to the point of irritating everyone around him. He can be selfish. Blinkered. Judgemental. His faults are many. But he loves Faye every bit as much as he loves his biological children. He'd do anything for her. Of that, Sive has no doubt.

'Sive, Aaron!'

Sive swivels to see Jude rushing towards them. 'That call I got. The body that was found—' She stops, catching her breath.

Oh my God.

Jude shakes her head vigorously. 'No! Not here, not Faye. Jesus. No, in Dublin. I don't know if you saw it in the news – a body found on Friday? Asphyxiated with a plastic bag?'

Sive can't think straight. Aaron is nodding. 'It was in the paper.' He turns to Sive. 'Remember, Scott was looking at it on Saturday morning at brunch – asking me if I was worried about going up against gangland killers.'

'That's it,' Jude says. 'The papers reported that the murder was believed to be gang-related, but they didn't name the victim or where he was found until today.'

Aaron's phone starts to ring. He glances down.

'Carmen Brosnan again. For fu— Oh. Oh, shit.' He looks up at Jude. 'The body found in Dublin – it's Pete Brosnan, isn't it?'

'It's Pete Brosnan.'

'Fuck.'

Sive blinks at Aaron. 'You mean the Callans murdered him?'

Aaron lifts his hands. 'Maybe.'

'Probably,' Jude says, matter-of-factly. 'I guess their two-birds-one-stone plan wasn't quite as rock solid as putting a plastic bag over Pete's head.'

Jesus Christ. 'So it's not them.' Sive says it quietly. Carefully. Fearfully. Hopefully. 'If they killed Pete Brosnan on Friday, they have no reason in the world to take Faye. There won't be a court case. Aaron's not a threat. This has nothing to do with the Callans.' The relief is immense.

But short-lived. Because, again, they are back to square one.

As Jude steps away to phone Hawthorn with this latest news, Sive's phone rings and she sees Maggie's name pop up on-screen.

'Maggie.' An irrational – or rational? – surge of anger takes hold. Why hasn't Maggie been here, helping?

'Sive, apologies for running off like I did. There were a few things I needed to look into.' Maggie's voice sounds strained. 'And I'm so sorry, but I discovered something you won't like at all.'

53

Sive closes her eyes, the phone pressed to her ear.

'What is it, Maggie?'

'It's about that court case. Your ex. Joost. You said the footage from the camera was ruled inadmissible. Because the camera was in the bathroom and employees weren't aware of it?'

'Yes. What does this—'

'Employers aren't supposed to have cameras in bathrooms, that's true. But it wouldn't make the footage inadmissible. It would be different if, say, police officers procured footage through illegal means. But they didn't. So I was surprised to hear the judge hadn't allowed it.'

'OK. What are you saying?'

'Sive, I've looked up everything I can and made a few phone-calls, and, off the record, it doesn't seem to me that Aaron ever tried to have the video introduced as evidence.'

'What?'

'I'm sorry to say this, and I hope to goodness I'm wrong, but it's possible Aaron messed up. Or . . .' She trails off.

'Or?'

'Or deliberately held back the video.'

'But why?'

'I don't know. Is there a reason he'd have wanted your ex to go to prison?'

Sive is reeling. 'He . . . Joost was going to prison either way. The video could have meant a lesser sentence, but—' She doesn't even know what she's trying to say now.

'Maybe,' Maggie says heavily. 'But it could have got him off. Depending on what it shows. If the other man, the victim, hit first, and it was shaping up to be four against one, well . . . look, I don't know.' She sounds tense still, but apologetic too. 'I might be wrong. I haven't practised law in quite some time, so I'm rusty. And, obviously, he was prosecuted under Irish law, so I'm less familiar with it. And I haven't seen the video, therefore this is truly just my opinion.' Another pause. 'But it's possible Aaron deliberately withheld key evidence that might have seen Faye's father avoid prison.'

54

THIS IS TOO MUCH. Too much to take in on top of everything that's happened today. Sive is not able to process what Maggie is saying. But suddenly, her husband – pacing, squinting at his phone – her husband is a stranger.

No.

No, there has to be a reason. Aaron is a lot of things, but he wouldn't withhold evidence. Would he? She stares at him. *Would he?* To get what he wants? She's seen how he operates. Never anything that could get him in serious trouble. Just close enough to creep into a grey area. Like not sending back a new laptop when two arrived in error. Like inflating a water-damage insurance claim to pay for an over-priced rug. Like overstating his expenses on his tax return. Small things. Things Aaron claimed everyone was doing, despite Sive's protestations. But small things can lead to big things . . . And Aaron had been very persistent when he first asked her out. And now she knows he cheated on Yasmin. All this deceit. Could he really have done this to Joost? To her? Aaron is not above lying. But to Sive?

Maggie is still on the phone, silent now. Jude is close by, listening to Sive's side of the conversation.

'Maggie, I'm going to pass you to Jude. I need to speak to Aaron.'

She hands the phone to Jude, and turns towards her husband, who's leaning against a clothes shop window, hunched over his phone.

'Aaron.'

He looks up. His face is pale and drawn, his eyes red-rimmed.

'What is it?'

There are two ways to do this; lead him into a lie or give him a chance to tell the truth. She has always been an advocate of the latter, but, *God*, she needs to know now if he would actually lie to her. If he lies about this, he could lie about anything.

'When Joost was on trial, why wouldn't the judge allow the video clip of the fight?'

He frowns. 'What? Why are you asking me this?'

'I need to know.' She stops, realizing as the thought slips into her mind for the first time that what she's about to say next is true. 'I'm worried Joost has something to do with Faye's disappearance.'

He shakes his head. 'No. He doesn't even know Faye exists. We've made sure of that.'

'What about the video, though? Why didn't the judge accept it?'

'You know this. Because the bank shouldn't have had the camera in the bathroom. It was illegal.'

'But wouldn't that mean the *bank* was in trouble, and not that the clip couldn't be used? It was still evidence,' she says, to the greatest debater she's ever known.

He tilts his head and, when he speaks, his tone is that of a parent humouring an over-eager child. 'That's not how it works, I'm afraid. The evidence was gathered in an illegal manner so it was inadmissible. I did try. But the judge ruled it out.'

There it is. There's the lie. If Maggie's right, then Aaron never tried at all. Sive reaches out to touch the wall behind her. Everything is loose and dizzy. If Aaron is lying about this, what else is he lying about?

'Aaron, Maggie checked. I told her the story about Joost last night and—'

'You did what?'

'We had a few drinks and we were swapping war stories. Sharing confidences, I suppose. I . . . I told her about Joost. And Faye. And the fight in the bathroom, and how we met. She says . . . well, you know what she says.'

'What the fuck were you thinking? We agreed we'd never tell!' He's hissing his words, his face white, his cheeks blotched. 'You – what the hell?'

'Don't you dare try to make me the bad guy here. I shared a confidence with a friend. You fucking sent someone to prison!' She is not hissing. She's shouting, and heads are turning. In her peripheral vision, Sive sees Jude come closer.

'This is not the time,' Aaron says, visibly working to calm himself down. 'Our daughter is missing.'

'I know! And I've been reassuring the police that since Joost doesn't know Faye exists and never wanted kids, it couldn't be him. He has no motive. Now suddenly he bloody well does have a motive – you sent him to prison!'

'Don't you get all self-righteous on me. You ran a mile when he was arrested.'

Sive takes a breath. 'I'm not proud of deserting him. There are better people than me who could get past something like that, I know. Maybe it's because we'd only been dating a few months. Maybe it's because I was pregnant and afraid of what it would mean for my baby if she grew up with a murderer for a father. I'm not proud, believe me. But I never deliberately sent someone to prison. I never withheld crucial evidence in a court of law.'

'You don't get it,' he says dismissively. 'You're not a lawyer.'

'No. But I'm a human. And I'd never have done what you did. I'm phoning Hawthorn now, to tell her they need to prioritize tracking down Joost. If you get caught in the crossfire, so be it.'

She turns and walks away.

55

SIVE IS TRYING TO find her Oyster card and she knows it's somewhere in the bottom of her bag, but she can't find it and now
the contents of her handbag are all over the ground, just before
the ticket barriers. Impatient noises rumble up from people
behind her.

'My child is missing!' she shouts back, and belatedly wonders
if they'll think she's quite mad, searching for her child among
her belongings on the ground.

'I've got this,' a voice says.

Jude. Softer than usual. Kneeling beside her. Gathering her
things.

'Your Oyster card? Is that what you need?' Jude holds it up.

Sive nods, and Jude takes her hand to help her stand.

'I can't do this. I don't know what to do. Faye is gone
and Aaron is . . . I don't know who Aaron is any more. I
can't—'

Jude's phone rings, interrupting Sive mid-sentence. Jude
glances at the screen, then at her watch, biting her lip. She looks
back at Sive, an unfamiliar expression on her face. Something
that might be empathy? She declines the call.

'OK. Look, I heard your side of the conversation with Maggie,

I got the gist of what's going on.' Softer Jude is gone. 'You phoned Hawthorn?'

Sive nods. 'She says they'll prioritize finding Joost now.'

'Good.' Jude steers her out of the way of the ticket barriers. 'As I said earlier, the vast majority of kidnaps are domestic – the non-custodial parent taking the child.'

'But that's *not* what this is – Joost doesn't *know* Faye's his daughter. If he's taken her, it's because of what Aaron did to him. Bloody hell, Aaron should have thought of it.'

'Yes, well. It strikes me that Aaron's the kind of person who does as he pleases and spends very little time worrying about it afterwards. Perhaps what he did to Joost just wasn't at the forefront of his mind?' Jude grimaces. 'No offence.'

'I'm way beyond taking offence,' Sive says tightly.

'Good. Let's focus on working out where Joost might go after prison. Hawthorn said he's a motivational speaker now?'

'Yeah, but I've searched "Joost De Witte" a million times and there's nothing.' She exhales slowly in a bid to stay calm. 'He always hated having such a distinctively different name among all the Johns and Brians at home, especially during the court case, so he's obviously managed to stay offline.' Something comes to mind then. 'Actually, he mentioned once he might use another name when he got out of prison, so I wonder if that's what he's done . . . changed it.'

'To what?'

Sive casts her mind back. Had Joost said what he'd choose?

'Something linked to his real name, he said, I remember that, but one that would help him blend in. That's all. Nothing more specific.'

'Don't worry. The police will get the name soon enough.' Jude's phone begins to ring again. She frowns and, once more, declines the call.

'Don't you need to answer?' Sive asks.

Jude shakes her head, but her phone is ringing a third time, the name visible on-screen.

'Isn't that your editor? Just take it,' Sive says. 'It's fine. You've given up your whole day for me. Honestly, I can never thank you enough for what you've done.'

Jude shakes her head but answers the call and, although she turns slightly, Sive can hear her side of the conversation.

'I'm sorry, but Sive has withdrawn her permission . . . I know . . . I know, sorry. Yep. OK.'

Jude disconnects and meets Sive's eye.

'What was that? What permission?'

A sigh. 'I told my editor I had an exclusive interview agreed with you. I know. I'm the worst person in the world and I'd hate me too. I couldn't do it, though. Jesus. Seeing you scrambling on the ground for your Oyster card, so lost, so . . . broken. I couldn't.'

Sive, to her own surprise, and clearly to Jude's too, laughs.

'*That's* what prompted you to kill the story? Not my missing child? Not my lying fucker of a husband? My lost fucking Oyster card?'

'Yeah, I know . . . doesn't make me look great, does it?'

And Sive's still laughing, but now she's crying too. Heaving sobs, pent up for hours, bursting through the tightness in her chest and in her throat. Crying for all of it. For Faye, for Aaron, for their family. For the sheer futility of the impossible search. Tears stream down her face, uncontrolled and unstoppable. She has never been more alone in her life.

Until, suddenly, she's not. Suddenly, there are arms around her.

'Sive, Sive. It's OK. I'm here.' And Jude is pulling her into a hug. Arms tightening around her back. And the comfort of human kindness makes her feel better and cry harder all at once.

They stand like that, in the station, as commuters swerve past, until Sive's sobs begin to subside.

'Better?' Jude asks after a while, her voice soft.

Sive nods into her shoulder then pulls away, wiping her eyes. 'God, I'm such a fucking mess.'

'Stop. Your child is missing, you're out searching, doing everything you can possibly do.'

She blows out air, steadying herself. 'Let's get on with finding Faye.' A pause. 'And, Jude, do the damn story. Send it in. Every bit of coverage helps, and you're only going to piss off your editor if you don't.'

'No, honestly, it's fine. She'll get over it.'

'It's written up, ready to go?'

Jude nods.

'Then press send. It all helps. And I know what it's like, trying to make a name for yourself in journalism. You've helped me all day, let me do this one tiny thing for you.'

Jude looks surprised and touched.

'Why would you do this for me when I was about to go behind your back?'

'But you didn't go behind my back. You didn't go through with it. And after what I've just found out about Aaron, that counts for everything.'

'Right, where to next?' Jude asks, after phoning and emailing her now-mollified editor. 'Back to Bond Street?'

Sive shakes her head. 'No. You were right all along. The search is too huge. We need to think. If it's Joost, where would he take her?'

'OK. Let's work it out. Here? Back at the hotel?'

Sive nods. 'Back at the hotel. I need to check on Bea and Toby.'

'Right. And I'll ask Hawthorn for an update. What about

Aaron?' She nods back towards the street. Aaron is still there, knowing better than to follow Sive when she's this angry. 'Will I tell him the plan?'

'He knows the plan. The plan is all about finding Joost.'

Jude nods, and Sive picks up her bag, then, together, they go down to the Underground.

At the hotel, it's groundhog day. Bea runs into Sive's arms and Sive buries her face in Bea's hair. It's nearing eight now, and Bea would usually be asleep, but these are not usual times. Toby is in Scott's arms in the wing chair at the window. The TV is on, showing *Bluey*, another of Bea's favourite cartoons.

'You're good at this,' Sive says to Scott, managing a watery smile. 'Thank you.'

'It's nothing. Seriously, whatever I can do. Today's given me a lot of perspective. My kids might be in Florida, but at least they're—' He stops, sounding unexpectedly choked up.

Sive is more grateful to Scott right now than she's ever been to anyone in her life, and forgives him every jibe ever, past, present and future. That thought makes her well up yet again, and she'd hug him, only she might wake the baby.

Scott clears his throat. 'I take it there's no news?' he asks, shifting Toby gently from one arm to the other.

Sive shakes her head, wrapping her arms around herself for warmth, though it's not cold in the hotel room.

'None . . . Let me take Toby and give you a break.'

'He's fine here, and I'm fine – I've got Nita helping now,' he adds, nodding towards the door to the kids' bedroom. 'She's fixing her make-up in the bathroom.'

On cue, the door opens and Nita swishes into the hotel living room, make-up bag in hand.

Her mouth drops when she sees Sive.

'*Sive, oh my God.*' She flies into her arms. 'How are you doing? I was out *all* afternoon, searching everywhere. Miles and miles, but nothing.' She shakes her head. 'But I've got all my Insta gals on the case, everyone. That's fifty thousand pairs of eyes.'

'I thought it was forty-six thousand followers,' Scott says sardonically.

Nita throws him a sidelong glance. 'Well, you know how it is. A few more popped along today when I was live-streaming the search. Everyone just wants to help.' Nita turns to Jude. 'Hello, again! You've still got my card, yes?'

Jude nods, and Scott looks at her now, curious, no doubt, about who she is. Sive explains.

'And is Maggie coming?' he asks then.

'No, she left earlier to check into something, she said, then she rang me and—' Sive stops. She isn't going to get into it now. Scott doesn't need to know what Aaron did to Joost. 'I don't know where she is now, actually – I passed the phone to Jude when we were talking.'

Sive turns to Jude, who perches on the sofa, phone, as always, in hand.

'She was a little cryptic. Said she was still "checking some things",' Jude says. 'And she said something again about "everyone lying" – same as she said earlier.'

Sive purses her lips at Jude, to tell her to keep the news about Aaron withholding evidence to herself. Jude gives a tiny nod.

Sive turns back to Scott and Nita. 'There's a chance that the person who took Faye could be my ex-partner Joost. He's Faye's biological father. He's back after being away for a while and it's . . . it's possible he's realized he's got a daughter.' That's easier than admitting the real reason Joost might target them.

Nita's eyes grow huge, but she doesn't respond and Sive wonders now if she already suspected something. Her comments about Faye being adopted may have been a little more literal than Sive first realized.

Scott's mouth drops open and his surprise is genuine. 'Aaron's not . . . why didn't he ever say? That's . . . so who's this guy Joost?'

Sive shakes her head. 'I'll explain another time.' She spots Dave's baseball cap on the coffee table. 'Is Dave out on the search?'

Scott nods. 'Yep. I offered to swap places with him, but you know Dave. Prefers a more active role.' He gives a wry smile, nodding down at a sleeping Toby in his arms. He looks up at Sive. 'Hey, you're shivering. Shall I turn off the aircon?' He moves to stand, taking care not to disturb the baby. 'Dave was wittering on about how hot it was when he was here and I switched it on high to stop him moaning, but maybe it's gone a bit chilly?'

She shakes her head and pulls a hoodie from the back of a chair. 'This will do. It's just tiredness, I'm not really cold.'

'No, you're really shivering now,' Jude says, stepping closer. 'Sit down. I'll make you tea.' She's as no-nonsense as ever, but the kindness in her words makes Sive well up. 'Have you eaten at all?' Jude asks.

Sive shakes her head, but there's no way she can eat. 'Tea would be good.' She sits on the edge of the sofa, wrapping her arms around herself, rocking back and forth. Bea clambers up beside her, a picture book in her hands, the one the babysitter brought.

'Maybe I should call the girl, Willow, who babysat the other night,' Sive says.

Scott raises his eyebrows. 'Only if you want to, but not on my account. I can stay all night. Honestly, I'm not flying this week.'

Sive remembers what Maggie said last night, about Scott pretending to be a pilot. Who cares? Who cares about any of it? But then she thinks of what Jude said just now, repeating Maggie's words. *Everyone lies.* And if people lie about small things, they'll lie about big things. Like Aaron. *Fuck.* Her head is spinning now, trying to untangle all of it.

Jude hands her a cup of tea. She puts it to her lips, warming her hands. Beside her, Bea snuggles in. Her nose is running slightly, and Sive feels in the pocket of the hoodie for a tissue, before remembering it's not her hoodie, and Aaron has never, ever been known to carry a packet of tissues in his pocket. Instead, her fingers close around a piece of paper, and she pulls it out. It's a newspaper clipping, folded in two. She opens it, spreading it on her lap with one hand, holding the tea with the other. It's an article from Saturday's newspaper, about the arrest of Hugh Pemberton. She casts her mind back to the discussion over brunch – Dave thought Aaron knew who Hugh Pemberton was, but Aaron was adamant he didn't. Then why did Aaron cut out and keep the article?

She begins to read.

Businessman charged in operation targeting Ealing crime gang

Businessman Hugh Pemberton (73), arrested earlier this week, has been charged by Crown Prosecution Services with six counts of grand larceny and sample charges from a litany of over four hundred similar alleged crimes.

She stops reading. 'Scott, what was that thing about Hugh Pemberton – Dave thought Aaron knew him?' She holds up the clipping.

'Dave thought he was a witness for one of Aaron's cases years ago. But Aaron said he hadn't heard of him.'

Sive closes her eyes, picturing the conversation. The exchange between Dave and Aaron. Aaron turning over his phone and frowning at it. Telling them he needed to return a work call. Sive's annoyance at the double standards.

Why, if he'd never heard of Hugh Pemberton, did he have this article in the pocket of his hoodie? Had he really been returning a call during brunch on Saturday morning? Or was he *making* a call – something to do with Hugh Pemberton?

Jude, competent as ever, is on hand. 'Want me to do some digging on Pemberton?'

Sive shakes her head. 'I think we need to prioritize Joost. Figure out where he might be. What his new name might be.'

'OK . . . actually, I have an idea. You said he'd choose a name linked to his own, but simpler, to blend in. If I'm right, *witte* is the Dutch word for "white" . . . One sec—' Jude mutters to herself now, typing something into her phone.

Scott holds up his. 'Dave just texted. He and Aaron are going to meet to continue searching together. They're—'

'Found him. He's anglicized his name.' Jude interrupts. '*Witte* is Dutch for "white" and Joost is a derivative of Josef, the Dutch for Joseph. Joost De Witte is now Joe White.'

Joe White. Why does that sound familiar? Sive closes her eyes, casting her mind back. Joe White. A name. A poster. A Tube station poster. In Bond Street this morning. Joe White, motivational speaker. *FIND THE NEW YOU!* in giant yellow text.

Oh. 'Oh my God.'

'What is it?'

'Joost is in London. Right now. He's speaking at a conference at Royal Victoria Dock.'

56

SIVE IMMEDIATELY PHONES HAWTHORN, who calls back minutes later with more questions for Sive about the relationship, how it ended, if Joost is dangerous. *Is Joost dangerous?* He killed a man. But Sive's not sure he's dangerous. *Not even to the man who stole six years of his life?* The police have the name of where Joe White is staying, Hawthorn says, a hotel near Royal Victoria Dock, and officers are on their way. Should Sive go there too? she asks. But Hawthorn says no, stay put. It may be another dead end. Sive asks her for the address anyway, already getting up off the sofa, but Hawthorn firmly tells her no. She'll be in touch as soon as there's news.

Jude is still on her phone, searching, when Sive disconnects the call. Bea is snuggled into her side and the Pemberton article is on her lap. It doesn't matter now, but why would Aaron pretend he didn't know who this man was? Or maybe he really didn't know, and Sive is jumping to conclusions – doubting her husband on every front, having discovered what he did to Joost?

'Where have Aaron and Dave gone to search?' she asks Scott.

'Down by the docks.'

Her stomach churns. 'Why?'

'I imagine just somewhere to try. It must be impossible to know where to start.'

'Near Royal Victoria Dock?'

'Possibly . . . Somewhere in East London, anyway. Why?'

She shakes her head. The police know Joost is staying in a hotel near Royal Victoria Dock, but Aaron wouldn't. Unless. 'Scott, in Dave's job, can he look people up? He was talking the other day about a colleague doing unauthorized background checks. Can Dave do that? Search confidential information the public can't access?'

'Oh yeah, he can pretty much search anything – he has to, so he can vet police applicants. I mean, he's not supposed to do checks that aren't linked to work – he'd really have to stand over it if there was an audit.'

But, Sive thinks, for something like this, Dave might just break the rules.

'I'm not finding too much on Joost, even with knowing his new name. Want me to keep looking?' Jude asks, holding up her phone.

Sive touches the newspaper article. 'Maybe your colleagues at home could help find some stuff on this Pemberton guy? Specifically' – she takes a shallow breath – 'any links between Hugh Pemberton and Aaron Sullivan.' She looks at her watch. 'Or is it too late to ask them?'

'They're pals,' Jude says. 'It's never too late.' She walks into the master bedroom to make her calls.

Sive's phone rings, and Bea, who is getting sleepy by her side, jolts awake. It's Hawthorn. She fumbles for the Call Answer button in a blurred panic.

'Joost isn't here,' Hawthorn says, before Sive can ask. 'It's the right hotel and he's checked in under the name Joe White. But he's been gone since seven this morning and the room is empty. We're in touch with the conference organizers, to see if they can help. I'll be back as soon as I know. Sit tight.'

Sit tight. Sive closes her eyes, pulls Bea in close, and prays.

When Jude comes back into the living room, her face is pale.

'What is it?'

'We looked into Hugh Pemberton and any connection with Aaron. Turns out Hugh Pemberton has links to a London career criminal. Pemberton's the clean face on the cleaner side of the business, or at least he was until his arrest last week. Some of the papers are holding off reporting it; some went right in with barely disguised references.'

'OK. What does this have to do with Aaron?'

'The other guy's name – the career criminal – is Michael Rosco.'

Sive goes cold. *Of course.*

Scott lets out an audible breath.

'You know the rest, then?' Jude asks, looking from Scott to Sive. 'That Rosco was seen near your husband's house the night of a fatal house fire fifteen years ago?'

'Yes.' Sive nods, looking over at Nita. 'The night Yasmin died.'

57

Fifteen years earlier
The Three Barrels

AARON CHECKED HIS WATCH. Nita was late. Again. She was always bloody late, and he couldn't decide if it was deliberate, to keep him hanging, or if she just valued her own time more than anyone else's. Probably a bit of both. The pub was bustling that Tuesday night, despite the drizzle outside and the long wait until payday. London was always bustling, though, every night of the week. Aaron sipped his pint and opened the paper.

'So sorry!' Nita swished in twenty minutes later, kissed him on the lips and sat beside him on a small stool that was much better suited to her tiny frame than to his six-foot-three height.

He tapped his watch.

'Got caught up at work. You know how it is. Saw your Facebook post, by the way, which was mildly confusing? Since when are you on Facebook, and why are you posting a photo of you and my sister in the Rooftop Bar when you're clearly here with me?'

Aaron explained the plan to spot the stalker. Nita was unconvinced.

'You honestly think some stalker is looking at her Facebook wall?'

'There are literally police warnings going out every week, telling people not to post personal information on Facebook – that burglars are even using it to rob houses when people share holiday photos.'

'Oh, for goodness' sake, as if criminals know how to use social media. Anyway, I don't believe for a minute there's an actual stalker – that's just Yasmin's way of getting attention.'

Aaron grimaced and took a swallow of beer. Nita never shied away from bringing up and putting down Yasmin when they were together. He didn't like it at all. It was much easier to pretend he wasn't cheating when they weren't talking about his fiancée. But Nita treated it like a game – that she was secretly seeing her sister's partner added to the fun for her. As for Aaron, he was starting to wonder what he'd been thinking. He *hadn't* been thinking, that was just it. Nita was flirty, always had been, and he enjoyed that. And in the last few months, she'd reminded him more and more of fun-Yasmin, the way Yasmin used to be before she became obsessed with this stalker she thought was watching her. That was it, really – Nita was the version of Yasmin he used to love spending time with. Still loved. If they could just get past this bloody stalker. Tonight might do it. Maybe when she realized nobody had reacted to their Facebook 'trap', she'd stop worrying. Aaron stared into his pint as Nita prattled on about some television show starring housewives. Who was he fooling? The attempt to trap the stalker wasn't going to alleviate Yasmin's fear. If anything, it was feeding it. He sighed, wondering how to untangle himself from all this.

An hour and two drinks later, he checked his watch and told Nita they needed to get going to the Rooftop Bar.

'But why? It's way out of my way and I'm happy here.'

'Because that's the whole point,' he explained. 'I shared the photo and now I need to go there to see if the guy shows up.'

She laughed harshly. 'What *guy*? There is no guy. Yasmin is being a drama queen.'

He threw up his hands. 'Maybe he doesn't exist, but I've promised her I'll do this and I need to see it through.'

She folded her arms. 'And I want to stay here.'

'Don't be like this. I promised her.'

Her eyes narrowed. 'I'm staying. You can choose to stay here with me or follow my sister's ridiculous wild goose chase.' She pulled out a compact to check her reflection. 'Your choice,' she said, eyes still on the mirror.

He knew what she was really saying. He pushed back his stool and stood, then, without another word, walked out of the bar, leaving an open-mouthed Nita staring after him.

Aaron picked up his pace when he spotted how late it was. If there was even a one per cent chance this guy existed, he should really have been in the Rooftop Bar already to look around. He pictured Yasmin at home, hiding behind the curtain, anxious and alone. Guilt washed over him, tinged with irritation. When his Blackberry rang, he assumed it was her, and readied himself to fib, to say he was already there, in the bar, as promised. But it wasn't Yasmin. It was Hugh Pemberton. The call that changed everything.

58

Monday
8.28 p.m.

SIVE IS TRYING TO phone Aaron, and Scott is trying to phone Dave, but there's no answer from either of them. Sive lets out a frustrated breath. There's no point in going to Royal Victoria Dock, if that's what they're doing, now that Joost is definitely not at his hotel. But more than that, Sive wants to know what Aaron's hiding from her. Why he pretended he hadn't heard of Pemberton, yet had the newspaper clipping in the pocket of his hoodie. Whether or not he knows about the links between Pemberton and Rosco and the fire. And why, if there's even the smallest chance that any of this is linked to Faye, he's been lying to her.

Jude is still on her phone, still researching and googling and phoning and noting. As Sive watches, her face changes. She looks up.

'I just found a recording of Joost's . . . Joe White's talk. It was live-streamed earlier today. At nine this morning.' She pauses, as though waiting for Sive to understand. 'Sive, he couldn't have taken Faye. He was at the conference centre, waiting to speak, when Faye got on the train.'

291

'No.'

'Unless he's Superman, there's just no way he got from Bond Street station to the conference podium in less than thirty minutes, and definitely not with a six-year-old in tow. I'm checking on Google Maps now. Hold on . . .' She looks down and back up. 'No. Not possible.'

Sive puts her head in her hands.

'OK. We've wasted enough time,' Jude says brusquely. 'I'm going back to the Pemberton angle. Did you read this piece on Rosco?' She holds up her phone. 'On his use of arson as a means of intimidating people?'

Sive shakes her head.

Jude purses her lips. 'I imagine it's quite likely the fire fifteen years ago was started by Rosco and there was a link with Hugh Pemberton.' A pause. 'And Aaron.'

'But what about Yasmin's stalker?' Sive says, maybe because she really believes Yasmin had a stalker who set fire to her house or maybe because she needs to distance herself from the idea that this has anything to do with her husband.

'Stalker?' Jude is confused. Scott fills her in.

'Are you saying you think Yasmin's stalker has resurfaced?' Jude asks. 'And has something to do with Faye's disappearance?'

Sive throws up her hands, accidentally jostling Bea in the process. 'I don't know. But we've ruled out a link with Aaron's Brosnan case and it looks like it wasn't Joost, and with this' – she holds up the newspaper clipping – 'it's starting to feel like there must be some link to what happened to Yasmin back then.' She glances at Nita, who's gone pale. 'That someone's returned to finish what they started. Maybe Aaron was the intended target all along.'

Bea slips off the sofa, rubbing tired eyes. She walks to the coffee table and picks up her sippy cup to take a drink. She puts it back down beside Dave's baseball cap, then breaks into a wide smile. She points at the cap, at the cartoon police logo on the front.

'Chase!' she says in delight. 'Chase hat!'

59

THE ROOM STANDS STILL. Time stands still. Jude looks confused. Scott looks shell-shocked. Nita looks white as a ghost. Bea is delighted and puts Dave's cap on her head.

'I Chase.'

Sive hunkers down beside her daughter and gently removes the cap. She points at the logo on the front. 'Chase?'

Bea nods and takes it to put it back on her head.

Sive puts a hand to the floor to steady herself. 'Oh, sweet Jesus.'

'Sive! What is it?' Jude is on her feet.

'She means . . . she means it's like the cap that her favourite cartoon character wears. His name is Chase.' Sive sits on the floor now, desperately needing the small stability it brings. 'Chase is a dog in a TV show called *PAW Patrol*. He wears what looks like a police officer's cap.' She's speaking slowly. Mechanically. And yet aware that she's not explaining it very well.

Scott tries to help. 'The dog is a police officer in the show. And yeah, the cap we gave Dave looks a little like the one he wears. Shit. I thought Bea meant the backpack. Oh my God. This is my fault.'

Sive shakes her head but can't think straight.

Scott is still talking. 'She was pointing at the TV, saying "Chase!" and I realized she meant the cartoon character, and not that Faye was literally chased, and then I told Aaron, and we thought it was about Bea's *PAW Patrol* backpack. Oh God. Sive, what is . . . what does it mean?'

Sive reaches for the coffee table, fumbling and dazed. Her hand wraps around her phone and she slides it towards her. Scrolling now, back through the photos of the cable car and the river taxi and the Tower of London, she stops when she finds a photo from Friday. The one from the hotel bar. The one she took of the group, early on, before the cap was presented to Dave. She zooms in and turns the screen to Bea.

'Bea, sweetheart. That's Dave, yes?' She points at the screen. Bea nods. 'Was Dave on the train with Faye?'

Another nod.

Oh God.

60

SIVE PHONES HAWTHORN AND stays as calm as she possibly can to tell the story. Then she tries Aaron. Jude tries Maggie. Scott tries Dave, though they agree he won't say what they've just discovered. No answer from anyone.

Why would Dave take Faye? It makes no sense. Tired of years of being the butt of every joke? Tired of being the 'pretend policeman' while the others swanned around glass-box offices with seven-figure salaries? Or has he had some kind of breakdown? Sive remembers what Maggie said, about Dave's mother. Why had he pretended his mother wasn't dead? She tries Maggie herself, but it rings out. Should she go to Clarinda Gardens? Faye could be there right now in Dave's apartment. Hawthorn is sending officers to Dave's address and trying to reach Aaron by phone. Did Aaron work some of it out? Is that why he arranged to meet Dave? Is this all linked to Pemberton? She forces herself to order her thoughts as she pulls on her trainers and shoves her phone in her bag. Forces herself to think back over the day. Faye's disappearance. The call from the woman. Aaron's coerced video confession. The futile journey to Leytonstone. The admission from Aaron's PA. The news about Pete Brosnan's murder. The truth about Joost's trial. The Pemberton newspaper clipping. She

296

puts her hand in the pocket of the hoodie, as though it might yield more information. There are no more clippings, but she does find half a packet of Polo mints. She looks at the hoodie. A plain navy zip-through, like so many others.

'Scott.'

He looks up.

'Whose hoodie is this? It was on the back of the chair.'

He scratches his head. 'Dave's, I think. He was moaning about being too hot earlier and took it off.'

Dave's. So *Dave* cut out the clipping about Pemberton and kept it. And Dave took Faye. Her mind goes back over the day again. Something floats close, then out of reach. Something about the video. And Aaron. And Pemberton. And Dave.

She thinks back to the video, to Aaron's confession. What if Garvin was right? What if Aaron really did win cases by black-mailing witnesses? Dave had said Pemberton was a witness in one of Aaron's old cases, and Aaron had denied it. Could he have blackmailed Pemberton into dropping a statement or lying on the stand?

'Scott, you said earlier that Dave can look up information about people?'

'Yep.'

'Could he have helped Aaron with his cases? Run background checks for him? Checked criminal records, and so on, on pros-ecution witnesses?'

'Sure . . . it doesn't explain why Dave would take Faye, though.'

'We need to go to Dave's apartment.' Her voice quivers and she works to control it. 'The police are ahead of us but, if Faye is there, I want to be there too.' *Oh God, please let her be there.* 'Scott, Nita, are you OK to stay here?'

Scott nods. Nita has glazed over, trancelike, wondering no doubt if she'll finally uncover what happened to her sister.

'Can you keep trying Dave, but don't say anything about what we just discovered?' Sive says to Scott.

'Will do.' He still looks shell-shocked.

'And I'll keep trying Aaron. I need to make sure he knows Dave is possibly dangerous. And . . . and that Dave is the only one who knows where Faye is.'

61

Fifteen years earlier
Outside the Rooftop Bar

AARON DEBATED WHETHER OR not to answer Hugh Pemberton's phonecall. His gut had been telling him for days now that getting involved with this guy was a mistake. He'd seemed such an easy target at first. Rich. Well spoken. Well respected. One well-heeled wife and three teenage daughters who would be horrified if it got out that Hugh Pemberton was on the sex offenders register. Dave – bless him – thought that Pemberton was a witness against a client Aaron was defending. He'd been *delighted* handing over the information on Pemberton. *Take him down a peg or two*, he'd said. Dave loved nothing more than sticking it to the man. Especially the rich, well-spoken, well-respected man. Aaron enjoyed it too, but not for the same reasons – for him it was all about the money. And if these people hadn't broken the law in the first place, none of them would have found themselves handing over thousands of pounds in cash to Aaron Sullivan.

But Pemberton wasn't quite like the rest of them. When Aaron approached him at his club, he hadn't seemed worried. Most targets rolled over and paid up quickly. Especially as Aaron always solemnly promised it would be a one-off payment, and he always stuck to that. Where this kind of business went wrong, he knew, was when people made repeat requests. Nobody wanted to pay in perpetuity. And Aaron didn't want to push anyone to extreme responses. So he stuck to his word. One payment, and that was it. But Hugh Pemberton simply listened and said, 'I'll be in touch.' *He'd* be in touch? It was Aaron who'd made contact, letting him know how to pay and when. There was something a little unnerving about the whole interaction. Then nothing for five days. Now this call. Aaron debated with himself for another moment, before answering.

'Mr Pemberton. Are you ready to pay?'

'Where are you right now, Mr Sullivan?'

'Excuse me?'

'It's very simple. Where are you?'

'I'm just outside the Rooftop Bar. But tonight's not the night for your payment. We need to arrange a—'

'The Rooftop Bar. That's what I thought.'

And the call was disconnected.

Aaron stood on the street corner, staring at his phone. What was that about? Why did Pemberton want to know where he was? Aaron looked over at the entrance to the building, the top of which was home to the Rooftop Bar. Gut instinct kicked in. Suddenly, he didn't want to go there. Pemberton had been a mistake. Aaron couldn't quite put his finger on why, but he knew now that he wanted to steer clear. He turned on his heel and walked away.

Thirty minutes later, deep in thought, he rounded the corner on to Haddington Street. It was only then that he registered the sound of the sirens. It was then that he saw the flash of blue lights and the burn of orange flames. And it was then that he knew why Pemberton wanted to know where he was. To make sure he and Yasmin were really out of the house, as the Facebook photo showed. Warnings weren't meant to kill people. But Yasmin wasn't in the Rooftop Bar. Yasmin was at home. Aaron began to run.

62

Monday
9.00 p.m.

SIVE GRIPS THE SEATBELT, not because the cab is going fast but because she needs to grip something. Beside her, Jude is on her phone, scrolling and typing. Sive had struggled to pull words together when they got into the car, and Jude had taken over, explaining to the cab driver that it was urgent, that they needed to get as quickly as possible to Clarinda Gardens, but even at this time of night, there's traffic. The police are on their way. They're probably there now. They're the right people to get her. *It will be OK.* Sive says it to herself, over and over.

And Dave's not dangerous. Dave wouldn't hurt Faye. Surely Dave wouldn't hurt Faye?

She tries Aaron again, but still there's no answer. Slumping back against the seat, she lets out a shaky, exhausted breath. Jude looks at her, then reaches for Sive's hand and squeezes it. She doesn't let go.

'I can't get hold of Aaron,' Sive says. 'He's with Dave somewhere and he has no idea Dave took Faye.'

'Do you know where they are?'

'Scott said somewhere in the Docklands, and I thought it was linked to Joost, but Jesus, none of this has anything to do with Joost. I just can't . . .' She trails off. She just can't *anything*.

'I gave Maggie another try,' Jude says. 'I don't know why she's not picking up. I'm getting worried.'

Sive turns to her. 'What did Maggie say to you, when I passed you the phone that time outside Oxford Circus?'

'She said, "Everyone lies." She said it earlier today when you were in Leytonstone and again on the phone.'

'Do you think she'd worked it out about Dave?'

'Maybe . . .'

'Did she say anything else at all?'

'No, but she was phoning someone, I think. She got an address from a notebook. A name that might have been Carol?'

Sive shakes her head. 'I don't know who Carol is. Maybe we're jumping to conclusions. Maybe Maggie's just lost her phone again.'

'How far away are we now?' Jude asks.

Sive looks at Google Maps. 'Still fifteen minutes. I'm going to check back with Scott, see if he's had any luck reaching Dave.'

Scott picks up after one ring, sounding breathless.

'What is it, Scott? Are the kids OK?'

'They're fine. Don't worry.'

'Jesus— I can tell there's something wrong – what is it?'

Silence.

'Scott!'

'OK. I was bathing Toby, and Nita was in the living room with Bea, and someone tried to let themselves into the master bedroom with a key card. The chain was on the door so it just opened a bit.'

'Oh my God.'

'It's OK! We're all OK. The person – it was a man's voice – said

303

to open the door and nobody would get hurt. Nita – I can't believe she did this, fair play to her – she picked up a table lamp, unplugged it and threw it against the door. And then she started screaming.' A small, shaky laugh. 'You haven't lived till you've heard Nita's scream. I nearly died. I don't even know what she was trying to achieve with the lamp, but it worked – between that and the screaming, she managed to scare him away.' An audible exhale. 'I know this is the last thing you need to hear, and Nita thought we shouldn't tell you, but I really felt it was too big a deal not to say . . .'

'Was it Dave?'

'No, definitely not. She'd know his voice. She said the person had a "rough" accent. But you know Nita. To her, almost everyone has a rough accent.'

'Any chance it was someone from the hotel and she misunderstood?'

'No. The "open up and nobody will get hurt" bit kind of puts paid to that . . .'

Sive is reeling. 'Is someone trying to take Bea too? Oh my God, should we come back?'

'Sive, I'm not going to let anyone in here. You have my word on that. No more bathing Toby. Nita's in the kids' room with them now, and I'll join them as soon as I hang up. The four of us will stay together, and we've already called the police. You go to Faye.'

OK. She disconnects. What the hell is going on? Who has just tried to get into their hotel room, why isn't Aaron answering his phone, and where on earth is Maggie?

Before she has time to process any of it, her phone rings again. Hawthorn.

'Is she there? Do you have her?'

'I'm sorry, Sive, she's not. The flat in Clarinda Gardens is empty.'

Sive is going to be sick. She works to find words to respond to Hawthorn, but she can't.

Then a message pings through. Without disconnecting from Hawthorn, she checks it.

It's from Dave's phone.

A location pin.

And nothing else.

63

Two days earlier | *Saturday*
The Lion

AARON LIFTED A HAND to wave at Dave, who was already sitting at the bar with two pints in front of him and his new baseball cap on his head. It wasn't clear if he was being a good sport or if he genuinely liked the cap, but either way, it was very Dave to wear the joke present that anyone else would have shoved in the back of a closet.

Aaron wasn't really in the mood for this. People always thought men wanted to escape for 'pints with the lads', but he wasn't bothered. Or maybe he just wasn't bothered when it was Dave. How, he wondered sometimes, were they all friends? As a group, they could be good craic. Individually, he had realized in recent years, he didn't really like Dave, Scott or Nita all that much. Maggie was fine, if a little boring. But he was here now, and could surely suck it up for an hour. He slid on to the stool and took a swallow from his glass.

'Cheers, pal. I'll get the next one, if there's time.' The beer tasted good. Maybe this wouldn't be so bad.

'Yeah, no worries, I'll keep an eye on the clock. The others are due at the apartment at eight.'

The bar was almost empty, save for a couple at a small table by the window and a barman cleaning tables down the back. Saturday night had not yet kicked in at the Lion.

'So how's tricks? Good to catch up one on one,' Aaron said, half meaning it after two more mouthfuls of beer.

'I'm all right, but there's something I wanted to ask you.'

'Go on?' If he was asking for free legal advice, Aaron was walking out. People always thought it was OK to ask lawyers for free legal advice.

'It's about that bloke Pemberton.'

Aaron froze.

'Yeah?'

'The one in the paper this morning. The guy who got arrested.' Dave swivelled on his stool and looked Aaron straight in the eye. 'You said you'd never heard of him, but I know I'm right. He's one of the witnesses you got me to check into back in 2008. Why did you say you don't know who he is? It's been bugging me all day.'

Aaron shook his head. 'Think you're mixing me up with some other lawyer friend.'

Dave's face tightened. 'You're gaslighting me now. All those years helping you win cases, and you're going to act like it never happened?'

Aaron took another sip of his pint. Slowly. Calmly, as he scrambled for an answer that would satisfy Dave.

Dave kept talking. 'I have notes. I kept notes on every single case. Pemberton is there, in black and white, in my own handwriting. So don't make this any worse by claiming again that you've never heard of him.'

Fuck. 'Oh, for God's sake, Dave. I didn't want to get into it in the group earlier. Why were you bringing it up in front of the others? All that was between you and me.'

'But what's the big deal? We didn't do anything wrong.'

Aaron laughed. 'You don't think running background checks

and digging dirt to force witnesses to change their statements might be a tiny bit problematic?'

'I mean nothing *morally* wrong. We did it for the right reasons. "Doing something legally wrong to put something morally right": those were your words, the first time we did it. Remember? The woman who stabbed her husband in self-defence?'

Aaron remembered. The pillar-of-the-community husband. The wife who lost it. The emphatic denials from his friends and family: No *way* was he abusive. So generous and charming and kind, wouldn't hurt a fly. *She* was the one who was trouble. A terrible temper, according to the wealthy investment banker who lived next door. And now she was concocting this abuse story to stay out of jail. But Aaron knew. He could hear it in the tenor of her voice. See it in the tremble of her hands. She'd taken it and taken it and taken it until, one night, mid-fight, she'd picked up a kitchen knife. And that was the end. But the pillar of the community had pillar-of-the-community friends. Statement after statement, claiming she was trouble. She was the one with a history of violence. And, as far as Aaron could see, she was going to jail. Unless he could do something. So he began to do his homework. Witness by witness. Quietly searching. Looking for chinks. Small lies that might suggest bigger lies. Anything to break credibility. He was getting nowhere, until he remembered Dave. And Dave's access to data. It didn't take long to convince his friend. Dave was always eager to please but, more than that, he liked to see people put in their place. Powerful people taken down. Successful people reminded they were no better than anyone else. So if he could help an innocent woman avoid jail and, in the process, humiliate a wealthy investment banker, Dave was there for that.

He did some searching. It turned out the wealthy investment banker had been cautioned twice for soliciting prostitutes, Dave told Aaron with more than a touch of glee. And from then on, it was easy – tell the truth, or *we'll* tell the truth to your wife and children, Aaron advised the banker. Change your story. Perhaps you've only just remembered the fights you overheard. The times he roared at her. The bruises on her cheekbone when she came out to collect the milk, huddled and shrunken, hiding inside her dressing gown.

And so he did. The investment banker neighbour told the truth. Actually, Aaron and Dave never quite knew if it was the truth. Maybe he'd never overheard any such fight or seen any such bruises. But they knew the woman had acted in self-defence, and the end, they agreed, justified the means.

And now, two decades later, Dave was sitting at the bar, looking at Aaron in a way he didn't like very much at all.

He sighed, affecting nonchalance. '*Yes*, we did it for the right reasons. But you know damn well we'd still be in trouble, so you need to forget about Pemberton or ever discussing this again. Especially in front of other people.'

'The thing is,' Dave says, and there's a new edge to his tone, 'I kept notes on everything. Not just the witnesses you asked me to dig into. The cases, too. The people you were trying to keep out of jail. Pemberton was to be a witness for the prosecution in a case against a Patrick Kavanagh.'

Aaron swirled his beer in his glass. *Fuck.*

'I googled Patrick Kavanagh to find out more about this case Pemberton was involved in. Turns out Patrick Kavanagh is also the name of a famous Irish poet, so that's what comes up first when you google. Hard to find out much about anyone else with the same name.'

Aaron said nothing.

'So I went through my notebook and searched the other names you gave me. The other innocent defendants we were "saving". Brendan Behan. Eavan Boland. Patrick McGill.'

Aaron winced inwardly. *Dave and his bloody notebook.*

'Know what they have in common? They're all Irish poets. But then, you do know that. Because you gave me the names. Poor old Trigger, he'll never realize. That's what you thought. Right?'

'Dave, it was just . . .' But Aaron couldn't think of anything.

'Just what? Just a whole load of fictional court cases? Why were you getting me to dig dirt on these people if they weren't actually witnesses?'

Aaron stared down at the polished bar, as though it might provide an answer. He picked up a beer mat and tore off one tiny piece.

'Some of them were.' It sounded sullen to his own ears. Defensive.

'Oh, I know. Believe me. I checked through every single one of them. In the early days especially, they were real. But not later. Not by the time I looked up Pemberton and found out he was on the sex offenders register. What did you do with that information, Aaron, if it wasn't to get him to withdraw his statement in a court case?'

The beer mat was in small pieces now, and Aaron swept them into a pile on the bar, but still didn't speak.

Suddenly, Dave grabbed Aaron's wrist. The shock of the unexpected contact jolted him.

'This Tag Heuer watch you were showing off the other night – how much was that?'

Aaron said nothing.

'You think I'm so stupid. All those years feeding you information, believing it was to help people who needed it. Small people who'd go under without a helping hand. Davids versus Goliaths. Like that first woman. And maybe I was stupid to believe you back then, but not so much that I can't put two and two together now. It was blackmail, wasn't it? Just like Nita and

Scott suggested when I made up a story about a colleague running background checks for personal reasons.'

Still Aaron stayed silent.

'I trusted you, Aaron. I thought we were in it together, for the greater good.'

'The greater good,' Aaron scoffed. 'Who the fuck do you think you are, lecturing me? Are you seriously telling me you never knew what we were really doing? Did you honestly think there were that many innocent clients on trial? That it was as simple as getting witnesses to withdraw statements? That that's how good people win?' The couple at the table looked up, and Aaron lowered his voice. 'There are no good people. Only smart people, who know how to win at life. You weren't too moral to take the payments I made, were you?'

Dave looked away. 'Those were thank-you payments.'

'Ha! Try explaining that to the authorities. "I took my share of the blackmail money as a thank-you for the illegal background checks I ran."'

'I didn't . . . that money wasn't—' But for the first time since Aaron arrived, Dave was stuck for words. His pint, still half full, sat untouched now on the bar.

'Oh, but it was. And there's a paper trail for every single payment. You're part of this.'

'But I didn't know it was from blackmail. I thought—'

'More fool you,' Aaron snapped. 'Best of luck making that sound credible. And it doesn't change anything. You still broke the rules. Whether you did it for what you thought were valid reasons or not, the outcome is the outcome and you have to take responsibility.'

Like Joost, Aaron thought, pleased with the neat comparison. People needed to learn to take responsibility.

And then it was time to meet the others in Dave's apartment and, as far as Aaron was concerned, that was the end of that.

64

Clarinda Gardens

WHILE AARON AND SIVE were wrangling their children from the hotel breakfast buffet on Sunday morning, Dave was on his own in his Clarinda Gardens apartment. Outside, the sun was shining. A perfect August morning. But inside, the room felt grey and blurred and dim. Dave's head hurt after too many beers last night, and even the walk to the coffee shop and the takeaway cappuccino hadn't helped. Last night's detritus lay scattered around the living room still; beer cans and stained glasses and the smell of spilt wine making his stomach turn. He hadn't the energy to clean up. He sat on the sofa, with a coffee in his hand, the paper on his lap and Aaron's words ringing in his ears, stark now, in the sober light of day.

More fool you. Best of luck making that sound credible.

He'd been an idiot. He'd trusted Aaron. He'd genuinely thought they were doing good. That poor woman; the first woman. Aaron had shown him a video. Her shaking voice, her red-rimmed eyes; just like his own mother before his father's fall.

Dave *had* to help that woman. If she'd gone to prison, it would have been a far greater wrong than any little thing Dave

312

did. A simple search on a police computer, that's all it took to help her. To save her. Just like he'd saved his mother from his dad – a little push down the stairs, righting the wrongs of years of abuse. You have to take matters into your own hands, Dave's mother always said, though in this instance, it had been Dave's hands. Dave had saved his mother and Dave had saved the woman in Aaron's video.

Although ... maybe he shouldn't have taken the money. Looking back, if he was being really honest with himself, if what he did was truly for the greater good, he should have said no to the money. That time and every time. And being really, really honest, a small, grudging part of him had to admit that he knew everything Aaron was doing wasn't OK. But it was easier to tell himself they were doing good than to face up to Aaron and stop the money. Would he be able to stand over that if his bosses found out? If there was a formal investigation? Bloody hell, he should have known better. *Fucking idiot.*

He took a gulp of coffee and put the cup on the table. On his knee, he opened the paper, scanning headlines about a sports star caught in an affair and an actor who'd lost weight. He flipped forward to local news, and there it was – another article about Hugh Pemberton. Suddenly, he wanted to punch Aaron. Right now, if Aaron had been here in the room, Dave would have liked nothing better than to punch him in his smug face, over and over. The anger he'd felt towards himself just moments earlier changed direction, took a new course. *Aaron bloody Sullivan.* The way he'd claimed so casually at brunch that he'd never heard of Pemberton. Making out like Dave was wrong. He scanned the article. Would there be any link to Aaron? If there was, would Dave be caught too? Probably. He'd lose his job. He'd have to sell the apartment. God. Why had he done it? Then his eye fell on two words that jumped out. *Michael Rosco.*

A thinly veiled suggestion that Pemberton and Rosco were working together. Michael Rosco, who was seen outside Yasmin and Aaron's house on the night of the fire. Michael Rosco, who was known to set fires to intimidate victims. Victims and rivals and offenders of any kind. And blackmailers?

Dave sat up suddenly, knocking his knee against the coffee table, upending his cup. Hot coffee leaked all over the table and on to the floor. He saw none of it. He only saw what had been right in front of his eyes all this time. Aaron was blackmailing Pemberton, Pemberton was working with Rosco, and Rosco was seen near Yasmin's house the night of the fire. Even Dave could put that two and two together.

65

Fifteen years earlier
The Stratford house

YASMIN WAS AT THE kitchen sink, elbow deep in suds, when Dave walked into the kitchen. He picked up a tea towel and a huge, never-quite-clean roasting tin from the draining board. Yasmin turned and smiled, then pushed her bottom lip out to blow a strand of hair from her face. The strand flew upwards and right back down over her eyes. He could offer to brush it out of the way. He could . . . but, of course, he couldn't. She lifted her arm then, dripping sudsy water, and used the inner part of her elbow to swipe at her hair, laughing as she did. Her laugh was beautiful. Everything about her was beautiful.

'Thanks for the help. I don't know what I'd do without you, Dave.'

She nudged him gently in the ribs. He smiled back, just as Maggie came into the kitchen. She stopped short when she saw him.

'Dave, there's really no need. We can do the dishes ourselves.'

'It's no bother.'

'I think Carol might prefer if we weren't using our landlord for slave labour . . .'

'I'm not your landlord,' he said, 'and what Mum doesn't know won't hurt her.'

His mother wasn't particularly concerned about Dave being used for 'slave labour', but she *had* told him time and again to keep out of their way. To give them space. To remember they were paying tenants, not friends. To take the rent and maintain distance. Business was business, and Dave shouldn't get above his station.

'I'll have the rent for you this evening. I'm just waiting for Scott's,' Maggie said as Scott and Aaron ambled in through the back door, smelling of cigarette smoke.

'Who's taking my name in vain?' Scott asked.

'I need to pay the rent tonight,' Maggie said, nodding towards Dave.

'Oh yes, we wouldn't want Mummy to be cross,' Aaron said, picking up another tea towel and thwacking Dave with it. Dave laughed. It wasn't funny, but it was better than being ignored.

A loud shriek pulled everyone's attention towards the doorway to the hall. Nita. Whenever there was shrieking in the house in Stratford, it was always Nita.

'Oh, bloody hell, another spider, I'll bet,' Aaron said. 'I'll go.'

But Nita came thundering down the stairs and into the kitchen before he had a chance to see what was going on. She was holding up a light pink shirt in one hand and a red football sock in the other.

'Who left this sock in the washing machine? My shirt is ruined! It's Moschino, for fuck's sake!'

She looked around at all of them, eyes flashing, then settled on Dave.

'It was you, wasn't it? You're the one who wears these.' She held the sock higher. 'Jesus, Dave. You're so fucking dumb sometimes.'

'Nita.' Maggie's tone carried a warning message. Not a 'that's not nice' message, more of a 'don't shout at the landlord' message.

'You're in the shit now, Dave,' Aaron said, slapping him on the back and making a quick exit to the garden. Scott followed without a word, cigarette pack already open.

Maggie steered Nita out of the kitchen and into the living room as Nita ranted about the cost of the shirt.

'Shit. I feel awful. I'll buy her a new one,' Dave said to Yasmin.

'She's over-reacting, it's just a shirt. She has hundreds.' She touched his arm. 'You're one of the good ones, Dave.'

And Dave knew he'd never love anyone more.

It was getting worse. Yasmin was terrified, staying home more and more, scared she'd see her stalker. None of the rest were any use. Aaron didn't seem worried, Nita was dismissive, Scott was outright sceptical. Maggie had seen the man that first night, the one who followed Yasmin home, but even she didn't seem convinced there was still someone watching. So it was down to Dave. He hadn't actually seen the stalker. He hadn't seen anyone, but he believed Yasmin. If she said someone was following her, hanging around outside the house, Dave believed her. So he watched and waited, night after night, to make sure she was OK. Standing on Haddington Road, opposite the house Yasmin shared with (*traitorous, treacherous*) Aaron, so he'd spot if someone approached. Always on high alert. The man who followed Yasmin that first night hadn't returned, but if he did, Dave was ready. And he knew a thing or two about law and order. He'd warn him off, explain he was police. He wouldn't get physical. Not unless the stalker didn't listen. One way or another, he'd keep Yasmin safe.

He could see her at the window now, peering out, as he stood across the street, watching. A man appeared, seeming to materialize out of the darkness, making his way along the footpath.

Yasmin stepped back from the window, unwilling to be seen, and Dave's heart broke for her. The man stopped for a moment outside Yasmin and Aaron's house. Dave straightened up, hackles rising, ready to act. The man was dressed in dark clothes, a baseball cap pulled low over his face. Dave stepped out on to the road. But the man moved on to the house next door, turning into the driveway, lost from sight now behind a high hedge. Dave let out a breath and looked up. Yasmin was back at the window. Watching and checking and worrying. Dave wanted to tell her it was OK, he was on duty, she was safe. But it was awkward. She was engaged to Aaron. Aaron, who spent his nights in bars with Nita. Aaron, who didn't deserve Yasmin at all. Dave's time would come. He just needed to be patient. He'd tell her he loved her, maybe even tell her what Aaron had been doing behind her back. Explain he'd been minding her, keeping her safe. That they might have a future together. He didn't know if Yasmin loved him yet, but she liked him. She told him he was nice. And he was nice. That was Dave's superpower. He was the nice one. And Yasmin was the one person in the house who treated him as a friend. Nita was dismissive. Maggie was formal. Aaron slagged him. Scott ignored him. But Yasmin was kind. Yasmin liked him. And if he waited for the right moment, maybe Yasmin would love him.

That's when he saw the flames. And he knew then he'd left it too late.

66

IT'S DARK AND QUIET down by the river, and Aaron wonders for the hundredth time if there is any point to this. Why would Faye be here? But he keeps going. Because fruitless as the search is, *not* searching is even worse. Beside him, Dave is quiet, the gravitas of the situation having put paid to his customary chatter.

He should call Sive, Aaron thinks, see if there's any news on Joost's location. He pulls out his phone and at first can't understand why the backlight's not working. He presses the power button, but nothing happens. *Shit.* He shakes it then, as though this will somehow put power into it.

'Damn it, Sive might be trying to call me. Or Hawthorn. Can I use yours?' he asks Dave.

Dave holds up his phone and shakes it, mirroring Aaron's action.

'Same problem here, mate. Power gone. Haven't been able to charge it since the race this morning.' A sigh. 'It's been a long day.'

Aaron nods curtly. *Dave, master of stating the bleeding obvious.*

They're near Silvertown, deep in the Docklands down by the

river, a part of East London Aaron's never been in before. The skyline is punctuated with cranes, and it's dusk now, with street-lights on the riverbank casting scant glow. Aaron and Dave pick their way between two tall apex-roof warehouses, Aaron stumbling slightly over something – a plank of wood or a scrap of metal; it's getting too dark to see. A sense of utter futility washes over Aaron. And now they're out of contact with everyone too.

'Why didn't you charge your phone at work?' he asks Dave, failing to keep the irritation out of his voice.

'I was off today. Booked the day off for the race and the brunch after.'

'What? Weren't you at work all morning? That was why you couldn't help with the search.'

For a moment, Dave says nothing. Then: 'Yeah, I mean, I booked the day off but then got called in to cover someone. Just forgot to charge my phone while I was there.'

Aaron shakes his head in frustration. Dave isn't making sense. It's a moot point, though; neither of them has power in their phone and there's nothing they can do about it.

'Shit, now I don't even know what time it is.'

Dave pushes up his sleeve to look at his watch. 'Just after nine.'

Aaron notices the familiar copper-coloured strap. 'Is that Maggie's watch?'

A beat. 'Yeah. I borrowed it.'

'You saw her today? Is she out searching? I tried her earlier but couldn't get her on the phone.'

'No . . . No, I borrowed it yesterday, actually. I haven't seen her today. Did you say Sive's still at the hotel?' Dave asks.

'Yeah, with Scott and Nita and the kids. No point in everyone being out, especially this time of night. Christ, though. I still can't believe this is happening.'

'Yeah.' A pause. 'Could it be karma?'

'I'm sorry, what did you say?'

'Karma,' Dave says simply. 'Sins of the father and all that.'

'What the fuck are you on about?'

'I'm *on about* what you did.' He puts 'on about' in air quotes.

Aaron sniffs the air near Dave. 'Have you been drinking?'

Dave shrugs. 'Maybe. But anyway. Yeah. Karma's a bitch.'

'Christ, we've been over this. So you did some illegal background checks for me and pocketed some extra cash. Are you really bringing this up when my child is missing? Get over yourself.'

'It's not just that, though, is it? I saw another article in the paper.'

Aaron's skin runs just a little colder. 'What article?' he asks, though he already knows. The Sunday-paper article. Something like the one Sive saw over breakfast in the hotel yesterday morning.

'The one about Pemberton, and his links to Michael Rosco.' Dave says it conversationally. Casually. 'You were blackmailing Pemberton about being on the sex offenders' register, weren't you, and he got Rosco to set the fire to scare you off.'

Aaron keeps his expression neutral. He says nothing.

'Oh, the big man has finally gone quiet. As well you might, mate. Rosco set fire to your house that night, and Yasmin died. You may as well have lit the match yourself.'

'That's not—'

'Don't.' Dave holds up his hand, just an inch from Aaron's face. He steps closer. Dave's a head shorter than Aaron, but he's stocky and, instinctively, Aaron steps back. His foot slips on something and he stumbles slightly.

Dave laughs softly. 'Not so mouthy now, are you?'

Aaron shakes his head. 'Dave, you literally apologized to me this morning for everything you said on Saturday in the pub.'

'Ha! That sums you up. You're so bloody arrogant. I didn't owe you an apology. Anyone else would have wondered what was going on, why I was apologizing when in fact *you* were the one in the wrong, *you* were the one who duped me all those years. But you just took the apology at face value. You're the true definition of a narcissist.'

'I doubt you even know what that word means. And, Jesus, this isn't the time, Faye is missing, for fuck's sake!'

Dave holds up his index finger. 'Ah, ah. We're talking about this now, Aaron. You murdered Yasmin. Your blackmail business led directly to her death.'

'It's not that simple.'

'Oh, but it is. Jesus, how could you?' Dave's voice shakes now. He's dialled down the grandstanding, and Aaron jumps at the chance, making a split-second decision to shoot for sympathy.

'Oh, God.' He briefly puts his hands to his face in a show of what he hopes looks like contrition. 'Obviously, I'd never have left her on her own or gone near someone like Pemberton if I'd known. It's the law of unintended consequences. Sometimes bad things happen even when we don't intend it. It doesn't mean we should be held accountable, if the intent wasn't there.'

'I've heard you interpret the so-called law of unintended consequences in exactly the opposite way, so don't even try it.'

'OK. But I've lived with the guilt for fifteen years. I'd do anything to undo it.'

'Easy to say now.' Dave's voice is hard. 'But you chose to break the law, and Yasmin died. The blame is on you.'

'I *know*. And believe me, I felt awful. But I never meant it to happen – who does it serve if I spend the rest of my life wallowing? And look, now isn't the time—'

Dave moves an inch closer, and Aaron can smell the whiskey on his breath.

'So you just get on with things,' he says flatly. 'The big house, the perfect kids, the beautiful wife. The money.'

Dave steps closer again, staggering slightly.

'You arrogant fucker. Her blood is on your hands. I loved her. Did you know that? I loved Yasmin, and you killed her.'

Aaron takes a step back, confused. 'You loved her? What are you on about?'

Had Dave been having an affair with Yasmin? No fucking way.

'I loved her,' Dave repeats quietly. Simply. 'She didn't know it. I used to watch her. Mind her. After that night someone followed her home, I stayed close, to keep an eye on her. I used to stand outside your house, when she was home alone, to make sure she was safe. When you were too busy to bother. When you were with Nita.' Another step closer. 'You didn't deserve her.'

'Dave, what the fuck. You were her stalker?'

'No! I wasn't a stalker. Someone else followed her home that first night. And after that, I was her lookout. A few nights a week, whenever I wasn't working. It was the least she deserved.'

'That's . . . that's the "girlfriend" you told us you had? No-Kate-Moss girl?'

'It was easier to tell you that, to explain where I was. And . . . and to give me the chance to talk about her. She was my person.' He slurs a little, and it comes out like 'pershon'. 'And I was her guardian angel. I loved her.'

Aaron's hand goes instinctively to his mouth. 'Oh God, Dave. She was terrified! Call it what you like, but you were her stalker. How could you do that to her?'

'How could I do that to her? *You fucking killed her!*'

Bits of spittle hit Aaron's face, and he wipes them away. The smell of whiskey feels overpowering now and his stomach churns, but he doesn't want to keep stepping backwards.

'I did not,' he says tightly, holding his ground. *Jesus Christ,* they need to move on from this. Faye is missing, and that's all that matters now.

But Dave doesn't let up.

'You did. What did you think would happen when you decided to blackmail someone like Pemberton?'

Aaron opens his mouth to reply.

'No, don't answer that.' Dave's voice is sad and furious all at once. 'This is my time to talk. You've been pulling the strings, telling me what to think, manipulating me all these years. Now I . . . I have the upper hand.'

Aaron leans in, pushing his face close. 'You have the upper hand? *Really?* Remember, if you tell anyone about Pemberton or the rest of it, you go down with me. I can end you and your precious career.'

'Be . . . be careful who you're threatening, Aaron.' Dave is slurring again, and Aaron can't decide if this is to his advantage or not. If Dave is drunk, is he more or less of a threat?

'Dave . . .'

'You should know something, Aaron. There's a certain key piece of information I have, and I'm the only one who knows it. And I'm not telling you what it is or what it's about, but you . . . you'd better be careful who you're threatening. Or you'll be sorry.' A small stumble as Dave tries to get in Aaron's face with his last words.

Aaron's had enough. '*Shut the fuck up!* You're not telling anyone about the background checks! I'm fucking sick of this. My daughter is missing, and all you can do is go on about bloody Pemberton.'

He shoves Dave. Shoves him hard. And Dave's stupid mouth opens in surprise. And his eyes widen, processing what Aaron's just done. And he stumbles back a step, and another. It's all in slow motion or, at least, to Aaron, it seems that way. And then

Dave goes down like a sack of potatoes. A sack of stupid, thick, moronic potatoes. The crack sounds out through the still night air as Dave's head connects with something Aaron can't quite see in the dark. He bends to check on his friend. Dave is out cold. Slapping his face – gently at first, then harder – gets no response. Then Aaron sees the pool of liquid on the ground. It's blood. He knows this. Even in the dark, even when everything, including this liquid, is black, he knows it's blood. *Fuck.*

Dave's phone is on the ground beside him. Backlight on. Screen cracked. Battery at 57 per cent. Why did he lie? What had he been planning to do? Aaron snatches it and dials emergency services, then sends a location pin to Sive.

When Aaron hears the sound of an engine, he turns to find that it's not an ambulance – it's a car, making its way along the narrow lane between the warehouses. The car comes to a stop, its headlights momentarily blinding him, and the door opens and his wife is rushing towards him.

'Is she here? Aaron – where's Faye?' Sive is out of breath, tears streaming down her face.

He shakes his head. 'No, I'm so sorry. She's not.'

'Dave sent me a pin. Where's Dave?'

'That was me, on Dave's phone.' Aaron nods towards the ground. 'I . . . I think he might be dead.'

'*What?* What are you saying? Where's Faye? I thought that's why Dave sent the pin?'

'Faye's not here. I'm sorry, I don't mean to sound so negative, but—'

'I don't understand – what happened to Dave?'

Aaron lowers his voice. 'He pushed me. I pushed back. Not hard, but he tripped over a plank of wood or something. And hit his head.' He puts his hand on her arm. Reassuring. 'It'll be fine. Don't worry. It was self-defence. And not my fault he hit his head. I'll be all right. But let me do the talking when the emergency services get here, OK?'

'Aaron, Dave took Faye!'

'*What?*' Aaron stares at her, then down at the body. He shakes his head. Sive has lost the plot. Dave is his friend. *Was* his friend. Dave was lots of things – irritating, boring, well intentioned, foolish – but not a kidnapper.

'It was Dave,' Sive says. 'Bea recognized— It's a long story, but it was Dave who took her. I have no idea why, but it was Dave.'

Aaron knows why.

'Oh God.'

'Did he tell you? Did he say where she is before he fell? Because she's not in his flat. The police went there and it's empty, and all we know is Dave took Faye but not where she is. I thought when I saw the location pin that . . . Oh God, please tell me he said something before you pushed him.'

'I . . . He was saying something about a "key piece of information", but I thought he meant . . . something else. I—' He throws up his hands, helplessly.

'Aaron, he's the only one who knows where Faye is!' Sive is shouting now. 'He took our daughter and he put her somewhere and now he's dead. You just killed our only link to Faye.'

67

JUDE STANDS BESIDE THE cab, a little way away, watching the paramedics cluster around the prone body. He's dead. There's no doubt. Aaron and Sive are watching too, clinging to one another, and to the faint hope that Dave is still alive. They have to, Jude supposes. For all sorts of reasons. But she can tell from the body language of the paramedics: Dave is gone. One of them is speaking to Aaron now, gathering information on what happened, presumably. There'll be an investigation, of course, and no doubt the police are on their way, but with Dave dead, none of that helps them find Faye. As the paramedic turns away again, Jude clears her throat and walks towards Aaron and Sive.

'Guys, I have an idea. No one's heard from Maggie, right? And she said she was going to "check into a few things". Is it possible she found Faye, and Dave did something to her?'

'Oh God.' Sive looks shell-shocked.

'No, I don't mean hurt her,' Jude says, although she does in fact mean exactly that. 'Just maybe locked her up too, wherever they are. It's worth a shot, right?'

Sive and Aaron nod dumbly.

'I'm thinking about what Maggie said to me earlier. "Everyone lies." She said it was about your group of friends this weekend, but she didn't elaborate. What were the lies? Do you know?'

Sive nods. 'Maggie knew that Aaron lied about being Faye's father and why Joost went to jail.'

Aaron's hand slips off his wife's shoulder. 'Sive.'

'Stop. Not now, Aaron. Scott lied about being a pilot. Nita lied about being pregnant. And Dave lied about his mother – he didn't tell anyone she'd died.'

'Dave's mum's dead?' Aaron looks over at Dave's body, as though trying to process how this matters, or if it matters at all now that Dave is dead too. Sive nods at her husband but doesn't elaborate.

Jude thinks for a moment. 'OK, so since we know Dave took Faye, we can rule out Nita and Scott now, and focus on Dave's lie. If Maggie knew Dave lied about his mother, where would that lead her?'

'Something to do with where she's buried, maybe?' Sive asks. 'A cemetery?'

'A cemetery?' Aaron sounds baffled. 'I'm lost. What the hell's Dave's mum got to do with any of this?'

'I'm just trying to understand why Maggie has disappeared, and where she might have been going when she left Jude in the Tube station.' Sive turns to Jude. 'You said she was looking up a phone number just before she left – someone called Carol?'

Jude nods.

Aaron straightens up. 'Carol is Dave's mother's name. But why would Maggie have been calling Carol if she's dead?'

'Maybe Dave still has his mother's mobile?' Sive hazards. 'If Maggie couldn't get him on his own phone, she might have tried him on his mother's?'

'It was a landline, not a mobile,' Jude clarifies.

'Wait, so Maggie was phoning the landline in Carol's old house – the house in Stratford?' Sive says. 'But it's been sold. That makes no sense.' She stops, her face changing. 'Unless . . . unless Dave lied about that too. If his mum's dead, then what he said about selling the house to pay for the care home can't be true . . . maybe Dave inherited the house and he still owns it?'

'Jesus Christ, you're right, that's where we need to go,' Aaron says. 'The house in Stratford.'

He begins to run.

68

One day earlier | Sunday
Clarinda Gardens

ALL DAY SUNDAY, DAVE simmered and paced. Aaron texted to ask if he wanted to join them for a cable-car ride. He was visiting his mother, he said. He'd see him after the race, in the morning. *The race*. Another chance for Aaron to prove he was best. He'd been getting away with proverbial murder all these years, and now it turned out he'd got away with literal murder. Dave pulled out the photo album from the cupboard beneath the TV. One of three albums from back then, 'Stratford, 2006 to 2008' printed on the front in Maggie's neat writing. Inside, on the very first page, his favourite photo of Yasmin. Out in the garden in their Stratford house, Dave hovering beside her, grinning from ear to ear. He'd done his best to watch her, to mind her, but it wasn't enough. And all because of Aaron.

Should he confront Aaron again, he wondered, now that he'd put the pieces together? He wouldn't see him during the race – they were all competing from different locations. He'd see him after, at the brunch in the Rooftop Bar. See his smug face with his arm around his perfect wife and his three perfect children by his side. While Dave mourned Yasmin all over again and plodded through another week in his mediocre job. Aaron didn't deserve any of this. The money, the wife, the children. He should have all of it taken away. That was when Dave began to plan in earnest.

His brother picked up after one ring. Dave could hear a football match in the background. Jerry was probably in the pub with some of the lads from the rowing club, thinking about his next pint. Dave, on the other hand, was thinking about Pete Brosnan and the trip to Spain, and Scott's hypothesis that Brosnan could have faked an alibi, with the help of his brother and his digital devices. That's not what Dave said to Jerry, of course. To Jerry, he just asked for a favour. A chance to finally beat Aaron at something, he said. Jerry was the better rower. Could Jerry do the race on Dave's machine, under Dave's name? Could he beat Aaron for Dave's sake, to give him this one win? Jerry laughed and agreed. No skin off his nose, he said, and returned to the match.

Dave sat back on his couch to think. So he had an alibi. Now to decide how best to use it.

In the afternoon, he drove to the house in Stratford. It had been a while. He hadn't realized quite how long until he saw the pile of post inside the front door. A niggle of guilt unfurled in his stomach at the dust on the hall table, at the musty smell. His mother wouldn't be happy. It was probably good she was dead. Of course, if she wasn't, the house wouldn't be his at all, and wouldn't be covered in dust. He stuck his head inside the living room. Like the hall, it was dim, with heavy curtains closed against the sun and dust sheets covering the furniture. He closed the door.

Upstairs, he passed his mother's bedroom – the one she had slept in until her knees weren't able for steps – and pushed the door into Aaron's old room. How ironic that this was the room he'd chosen, he thought, feeling sick now. Yasmin's killer.

He sat on the bed and looked around and, just as it always did in here, a calm balminess settled over him. From all four walls, Yasmin smiled. Yasmin as a child, in a photo he'd borrowed from Nita and copied over and over. Yasmin as a teen, arm around Nita. Yasmin as a student, arm around Maggie. Yasmin as a housemate, arm around Aaron. Dave felt the anger surge again. His eyes roamed the walls, taking it all in once more. Yasmin with her schoolfriends. Yasmin with her co-workers. Yasmin on her own. And Yasmin with Dave.

Just that one image. His favourite photo, copied from the original in the album. Yasmin and Dave in the garden. A rare day when everyone else was out. Sun beaming, flowers in multi-coloured bloom. Yasmin on a picnic rug, a book splayed on her lap. Dave hunkered beside her, waiting for the camera timer to do its thing. He'd copied that one over and over and over. Had it blown up and papered the room. This was his happy place, his sanctuary. But now the spell was broken. Aaron had ruined it. And Aaron had murdered Yasmin.

He woke, hours later, confused at first about where he was. Then he saw her face and, for a moment, everything was OK. Until he remembered again what Aaron had done.

His phone buzzed – Jerry confirming the race start time for the morning. Dave hesitated then replied. If he was going to do something, this was the chance. On Tuesday, Aaron would fly back to Dublin.

Tomorrow morning. *Focus.*

He looked to his Yasmin photos for help. She smiled down at him, her beautiful smile, encouraging him.

Tomorrow morning is your time.

Aaron would be busy on a rowing machine, while his wife and kids made their way to meet Maggie at the Rooftop Bar.

Dave thought about that for a moment. That was where Aaron had pretended to be that night, in a bid to catch the stalker. Only Aaron wasn't there at all – he was with Nita, he'd told Dave later. He should have been with Yasmin. He should have protected her, kept her safe from Pemberton and Rosco, like Dave had tried to.

Yes. He would do something in the Rooftop Bar, Dave decided. A nice irony, all things considered. Quite what he would do, he wasn't sure yet. He wouldn't hurt anyone, but maybe there was a way to make it *seem* that way. To make Aaron worry. And Aaron would know how it felt – at least temporarily – to lose someone you love. Something legally wrong to put something morally right, as Aaron would say himself.

Dave would need to get there before Sive and Maggie, and stay out of sight. He keyed the destination into his phone and checked the travel times. If he was at Bond Street station for eight thirty tomorrow morning, he'd make it before them. He kissed Yasmin goodbye, walked downstairs, poured a whiskey, and simmered and paced.

69

THE CAB DROPS THEM at the house in Stratford, and Jude asks the driver to wait. If he's confused about what's going on or why his passengers are so tense, he says nothing. He just picks up his phone and nods. As Jude slips out of the car, Aaron is already running up the path to the front door, with Sive just behind. Now he's hammering on it, shouting for Faye. The noise is jarring in the otherwise night-time silence.

Jude scans the garden. It's overgrown, unkempt. Long, ragged grass, black in the thin moonlight. Tall weeds frame the front door, straggling up towards a broken bulb above the porch. Aaron is still banging on the door, still shouting Faye's name, but nothing stirs inside the house. The windows are inky black – except for one downstairs that's boarded up with plywood, Jude realizes, and sprayed with graffiti.

Next door, a bedroom light goes on and a curtain twitches. Two doors down, a dog begins to bark. No sound of sirens. Hawthorn is rallying the troops, but they're not here yet. Should they wait for the police? Jude wonders, as Aaron bangs on the door. There's no danger now . . . Dave is dead. There's only fear. Fear of what they might find inside. Then she remembers Scott's call from the hotel room and the man who tried to break in. Could he be here, inside the Stratford house? She opens her mouth to warn the Sullivans, then closes it. Nothing is going to stop them trying to get inside.

Aaron is still pounding on the door, and still there's no answer. Of course there isn't. Dave is dead. And Maggie? And Faye? Jude bites her lip. She's not afraid of anything, but in spite of herself, right now, she's dreading what they might find inside.

Aaron bangs on the living-room window now, while Sive steps back from the doorstep, looking around. Frantic searching. For what? Something to use to break in, Jude realizes, as Sive picks up a large stone from what might once have been a flowerbed border. With a flicker of awe, Jude watches Sive raise her hand and smash the glass panel in the front door. Protecting her hand with her sleeve, she reaches in to turn the lock and, in seconds, she's inside. Aaron follows, stumbling slightly on the doorstep, then Jude steps inside too.

The hall is dark and narrow and Sive doesn't wait to find the light switch. She's calling Faye's name, rushing into the first room on the right. Aaron is just behind her, also shouting. Jude moves more slowly, taking in her surroundings, swallowing against the tightness in her throat. On the hall floor over by the wall sits a pile of post, as though swept aside by the door. Just now, she wonders, or earlier, by someone else? She stoops and picks up a handful. A bill of some kind, addressed to Carol Taylor. A fast-food menu. An estate-agent flyer. A letter, another bill, this time addressed to Dave Taylor. Sive is right, Jude reckons: Dave hasn't sold the house. Dave lied. Maggie guessed.

This is the place.

She swallows.

*

Aaron is rushing out of the first room, still calling Faye's name, heading further down the hall towards what looks like a kitchen. Sive follows, and Jude moves into the room they've just left. It's a living room. Small, musty, silent. Dust sheets cover the furniture, giving the room an eerie, ghostly feel, and Jude shivers. Stepping forward, she touches the sheet on what must be a sofa. Is there something there? Someone? Someone little? A huddle that might be nothing or might be a small child. Jude lifts the corner of the sheet. Just the corner. Just to check. There won't be anyone here. Surely there won't be anyone here. But still. It's worth making certain. She sucks in a breath and makes herself lift the sheet. Then, as unfamiliar fear trickles down her spine, she whips it off entirely.

Cushions. Two plump cushions and nothing else.

No Faye.

She lets out a breath.

She moves out to the hall and on to the kitchen, where she can hear Aaron clattering from a room beyond, through a doorway at the far end – a garage, she thinks. Sive is trying to unlock a rickety-looking back door, but the key clatters to the flagstone floor, lost now in the dark. Sive lets out a cry of frustration and drops to her knees. Jude flicks on the light and joins her, their hands skittering across the floor in search of the key. It's Jude who finds it first, and it's Jude who carefully inserts it in the lock. Within seconds, they're in the garden, scanning a black expanse of grass and weeds. As Jude's eyes adjust, a building takes shape. A shed, at the end of the garden. She starts to run, with Sive following close at her heels. The shed looms larger now as they draw near. Planks of wood, nailed together, haphazard and falling apart. A sliding bolt. A padlock. Locked.

Shit. Jude examines it. The padlock is new, but the shed is very, very old. She grabs the padlock and yanks. A creak as the rotting wood stretches but doesn't give. Jude yanks it again. The wood yields now with a splintered whine, as the entire lock detaches and falls to the ground. The door swings open. Jude fumbles for her phone, lighting up the inside with her torch. Sive pushes past, calling Faye's name, pulling at deckchairs and parasols and a small stepladder, pushing her way into the dark, shadowy corners. But Jude can already see. There's nobody here.

They don't stop, they don't speak. Together, they run back across the garden and inside the house. Aaron is still in the garage, pulling and clattering its contents, shouting Faye's name. Sive stops in the hall, glances back, then up at the ceiling.

And now she's running upstairs, and Jude goes after her, taking the creaky steps two at a time. The landing is shadowy. Empty. Still. Worryingly still. If Faye is here, anywhere in this house, wouldn't she cry out by now? Jude, who prides herself on never, ever getting emotionally invested in her stories, pushes down an unexpected surge of panic. This is so much more than a story now, and she desperately wants the little girl she's never met to be OK.

While she watches, holding her breath, Sive opens the first door at the top of the stairs. Moonlight spills through frosted glass. A bathroom. Empty. Sive moves quickly into the next room, and Jude follows. A bedroom that smells musty and old. Dave's mother's bedroom, Jude thinks, switching on the light. A muted, pinkish glow illuminates the room. The bed is made, floral bedspread pulled taut, with no sign of recent occupation.

Together, in frantic silence, she and Sive look beneath the bed, inside the free-standing wardrobe, behind the curtains.

Nothing.

As Jude does one more check under the bed, Sive is already on her way to the room next door.

And then Jude hears the scream.

70

Three hours earlier
The Stratford house

MAGGIE STARED AT THE house, home of so many memories, now tarnished and chipped and worn. The garden was overgrown, something Dave's mother would have hated. She was always very into gardening. The house looked faded, with paint peeling off the front door. Was it always like that, or was Maggie only noticing now? The bell chimed inside, but there was no answer. She pressed it again. Outside, the street was quiet. Cars lined both sides of the road, but nothing stirred. Maggie cast her eyes across the cars. The navy Volkswagen a few doors down – was that Dave's? She'd thought so as she'd walked past, but maybe not. Lots of people drove navy Volkswagens. She tried the bell one more time then stepped to the side to peer through the living-room window. She waited, holding her breath, watching and listening for signs of life, but there was nothing, no sound. Maggie moved around to the side entrance and on to the back garden. She squinted through the kitchen window. At the back door, she tried the handle. Locked. But the key was just where it always had been, beneath the watering can by the garden wall. Hesitating for just a second, Maggie picked up the key, and let herself in.

The kitchen was cool and dim and somehow eerie. On the draining board sat two glasses, heavy bottle-green tumblers Maggie recognized from Carol's 'good' set. Rinsed and left upside down to air dry. Carol wouldn't have liked that – she always dried everything as soon as she washed it. There was no other sign of habitation. Maggie moved quickly through to the living room. Empty too. She retraced her steps and stood at the bottom of the stairs.

The first step creaked beneath her weight and she moved quickly to the next. Up, two at a time to minimize noise, out of habit more than anything else. On the landing, she paused to take in her surroundings. Straight ahead was the bathroom. Small. Dim. Empty. Then Dave's mother's room. Nobody there. Next along the landing was the room once occupied by Aaron. She stepped quietly forward, moving towards the closed door. She stopped at a sudden sound. A creak from inside, like someone moving in a bed. She stepped forward again and pushed the door ever so gently. Now she could see the bedroom wall. Her hand flew to her mouth. Every inch covered. Small passport photos. Large, blown-up photos. Polaroids. Snapshots. Photocopies. Every size, every medium. One face. Yasmin. Everywhere, Yasmin. Maggie pushed the door just enough to peer around. And there she was. Faye. Lying on the bed. Asleep. Or more than asleep.

Then, from downstairs, Maggie heard a creak.

71

10.01 p.m.

Two FIGURES LIE ON the bed. Poker straight. Laid out like bodies in a morgue. Maggie and Faye. Jude clamps her hand over her mouth as Sive, still screaming, rushes to the smaller of the two figures, pulling her into her arms.

'Aaron!' Jude screams. 'Call an ambulance. Now!'

He thunders into the room and runs to Sive and Faye.

'Is she OK? My phone's dead, I can't call—'

But Jude is already on it, passing the address to emergency services.

Sive is sobbing. 'There's a pulse. I think there's a pulse. I don't know. Check. Please check, Aaron. Please tell me she's alive. Please.'

His hand is at her neck now, and he's not saying anything, and then he's nodding. 'I don't know, but I think . . . I think so. I think she's breathing?'

Jude approaches the bed. 'I have some first-aid training. Let me have a look.' And she does. And to her great relief, far greater than she ever thought possible, the little girl is alive. A lump forms in her throat. And suddenly Jude, who never gets involved, never gets emotional, is crying too.

'She's alive. She's OK. I don't know why she's unconscious, but there's an ambulance on the way. She's going to be OK.'

Sive nods thanks through her own tears and hugs Faye to her, as Aaron circles his arms around both of them. Jude turns towards the other figure on the bed. Maggie, like Faye, is out cold, but she too has a pulse. *Oh, thank God*, Jude thinks, holding Maggie's hand as they wait for the ambulance.

72

Midnight
St Catherine's Hospital

FAYE IS SITTING UP sipping water through a straw, and Sive is by her side, holding her hand. She's going to be fine, the doctors say. They'll know for sure what was in her system once the blood results come back, but everything points to temazepam. That's what the police found on the kitchen counter, and it was consistent, the doctor said, with Faye's response. If she'd been given a higher dose, they'd have been too late, but Dave had miscalculated. You could always rely on Dave's stupidity, Aaron had said, before his face crumpled in relieved tears.

Sive had said nothing. She didn't have it in her to joke about Dave's stupidity or even to feel relief, and she still doesn't. Her daughter almost died. She's here and alive, but she almost died. Sive can't get it out of her head. And she can't let go of Faye's hand. Not now, not ever.

Maggie's in a curtained cubicle beside them, also awake, and she pulls the curtain now to peer over at Faye.

'Is she OK?' she asks in a hoarse whisper.

Sive nods. 'God, Maggie. I can't believe . . . Are you OK?'

'I'm strong as an ox. He'd have needed to give me a lot more than he did for it to . . .' She shrugs but her eyes glisten with tears.

Sive squeezes her hand. 'I'm so glad you're still here. If anything had happened to you while trying to find Faye . . .'

'Much good it did, since I didn't manage to actually do anything about it when I found her,' Maggie says with a frustrated sigh. 'God, I'm an idiot. But I had a feeling he'd got the dosage wrong. That was the only thing I could hold on to. That and believing Dave when he said he'd let Faye go.'

'What?'

'He told me it was me or Faye.' Maggie's voice shakes. 'That if I was so keen to save her, I could take her place. He didn't think I'd do it.' A hiccuppy laugh is swallowed in a sob. 'Dave getting it wrong to the end.'

'Oh my God. Maggie.' Sive doesn't know what to say.

'I couldn't let him do it to her. First I tried pouring the drugged water into his whiskey and filling Faye's with fresh water, but it was too small an amount to do anything to a fully grown adult. Then he picked up a kitchen carving knife.' She falters. Gathers herself. 'Said one of us had to swallow the drink with the drugs. And I had an inkling, though I wasn't sure, that he hadn't put enough in. I'm not a doctor, obviously, but from managing the clinic and the kind of dosages I see on paperwork, I have some idea. Not enough of it for me, anyway, though more than enough for—' Her voice cracks and fails.

'Oh God. I don't know what to say. I don't know how I can ever repay you.' Sive thinks of all her silly, stupid wishing for Maggie to be her friend; to bond with her over gin and chats and shared secrets. This – what Maggie's done for Faye – this is what really matters. This is real friendship.

'Stop. She's six. She has her whole life ahead. And as I say, I was hoping he'd misjudged and I'd be OK. And look!' A bright smile. 'I am!' Her face changes then, and she nods towards Faye. 'And after all that, he lied. He gave her the drink anyway.'

'Everybody lies,' Sive says, only half consciously mimicking what Maggie had said to Jude.

'They sure do. I just didn't realize to what extent,' Maggie says grimly.

'That's how Jude found you. When you said, "Everyone lies," it stuck. She told me, and we worked out where you were. So you did save her – you led us to the house in Stratford, even if you didn't know it at the time. Without that, Faye might have . . .' Fresh tears now.

Maggie reaches across, touching Sive's arm. 'Don't think about that. Just focus on now. Faye is safe, it's over.'

It's only later that Sive remembers the second person – the man who tried to break into the hotel suite when she and Jude were on their way to find Aaron. When Dave was lying dead on the ground in a pool of his own blood. Had Dave been working with someone else? Was Faye really safe? Sive pushes it out of her mind. Hawthorn is looking into it. And she and Faye and the rest of the Sullivans are going home.

73

Six months later
Dublin

SIVE TRIES SO HARD, but it's impossible to get past what Aaron's done. The blackmail, Yasmin's death, the dubious circumstances of Dave's demise, but mostly, what he did to Joost. There's no coming back from that. He deliberately withheld evidence that could have seen Joost given a much lighter sentence or perhaps no jail time at all. Sive still can't decide how she feels about that – whether or not Joost should have faced jail for taking a life. But, she realizes, it isn't down to her to decide, or even to have an opinion. It was down to a judge and jury, in a fair trial with ethical and competent representation. And that's something Joost wasn't given.

Joost, to his credit, doesn't dwell on what Aaron did. He seems to accept that he deserved the sentence he was given. What he is interested in is getting to know his daughter. And so, bit by bit, starting with one supervised visit a week, he and Faye have been doing just that.

Aaron has moved out. He's busy firefighting – daily newspaper columns, four different investigations, impending charges – and hasn't had time to come see the kids for the last three weeks.

Horrified though she is about what he did to Joost, Sive doesn't want to keep Aaron from his children and hopes he'll see them regularly once things die down. Though if the grapevine is correct, gardaí are now aware that his 'deep-fake' video is not, in fact, fake at all, and he'll be spending time in prison. Oh, the irony. It gives Sive no satisfaction whatsoever. In the meantime, he's heading to London for a few days, to tie up loose ends with Scott, Nita and Maggie. To grieve together for Yasmin. To talk about what Dave did. To get some closure.

The results of Dave's autopsy have come through, showing temazepam in his system, thanks to Maggie's efforts. Not enough to kill him, but it will help Aaron, who is still potentially on the hook for Dave's death. If Dave had drugs in his system, maybe that contributed to his demise. Maybe it wasn't all down to Aaron's push. From Sive's perspective, it's a distraction and nothing more. She's not convinced Aaron's story is true. Had Dave really come at him, or had Aaron pushed first? There's no way for anyone to know, and maybe it's a moot point, in the bigger scheme of what Dave has done. And what Aaron has done.

'Is Daddy coming to see us soon?' Faye asks now, as she does every few days.

'Not this weekend,' Sive says, glad to have a real excuse. 'He's going to London to see Maggie and Nita and Scott.' She opens the fridge, hoping for dinner inspiration.

'I like them,' Faye says simply, and Sive wonders how her daughter can separate any of it – separate their London friends from what happened to her there. Then again, Faye hadn't been treated badly. She didn't really know anything awful had happened at all. Dave had held her hand, taken her off the Tube and on to a bus, back to his car in Clarinda Gardens and on to

Stratford. He'd given her sweets and crisps and juice. He'd told her she was a good girl. And then she'd gone to sleep.

'They're nice people, yes,' Sive says now, smoothing down her daughter's hair, kissing her forehead and turning back to the fridge.

'Can I have a drink?'

'Just water, though, no juice.'

Faye sighs. 'Maggie gave me juice.'

'That's nice. When we went for brunch?'

'No, in Dave's house. When I was staying with Dave after we went on the train. Maggie was with us too in Dave's house and we had a party together and Maggie gave me a drink because she said I was a good girl and that my wishes would come true if I drank it.'

Sive's blood runs cold.

'Faye,' she whispers. 'Why . . . What was the drink?'

Faye shrugs. 'Funny water juice that made me fall asleep.'

74

Six months earlier | Sunday
Silchester Road

MAGGIE WATCHED SIVE GET into the taxi late that Sunday night, then closed the door. Tomorrow morning would be tough going for Sive after all that cava and all that Baileys and three kids in the mix. Maggie didn't know how people did it. She liked kids, but she was always happy to hand them back.

Before she had time to go up and check on Nita, there was a knock on the door. Only one person ever called this late. Dave.

'Why didn't you answer your phone?' he said as soon as she opened the door.

'Sorry, Sive was here. Look, I'm wrecked – we were out tonight, Nita fell, Sive's only just gone . . . '

'I need to talk to you.'

'Is it about your mother?' she asked gently.

'What? No.' He shook his head impatiently. 'I need a drink.'

In the living room, she passed him a double Jameson, and he knocked back half of it before he spoke.

'You're the only one who'll understand, Maggie, the only person in the world I can really talk to. It's been driving me *fucking mad* all day. I feel like I'm going to explode.'

'Wait – what?'

'It's Aaron. I found out this morning he's responsible for Yasmin's death, and I can't stop thinking about his smug fucking face, about him getting away with it all this time.'

'Slow down. What on earth are you talking about?'

And he told her. All of it. Pemberton. The newspaper piece. The blackmailing. Rosco. The fire. Yasmin.

Maggie tried to take it in. Aaron had done all this? All these lies. Using Dave. Blackmailing to win cases. Blackmailing for profit. Maybe – though she didn't know for sure yet – getting Sive's ex sent to jail. But all of it paled in comparison to what he had done to Yasmin.

'She was my best friend,' she said to Dave, in what sounded to her own ears like a whimper.

'I know,' he said, putting his hand on hers. 'I loved her.'

There was something in the way he said it. 'You loved her? You two . . .'

'No. She . . . she never knew.'

'Wait. That's the "ex" you were hung up on when we were together?'

His shoulders dropped. 'Yeah . . . I know, not really an ex. But I loved her more than anyone I've ever loved in my life. And Aaron fucking killed her. And he got away with it. Just like he gets away with everything.'

They'd go to the police, Maggie said. Simple. But Dave said no way. He'd go down too. He'd accepted thank-you payments from Aaron in the early years and there was no easy means to talk his way out of it. 'Doing something legally wrong to put something morally right' sounded foolish now. They needed to take matters into their own hands, as Dave's mother had always said. To play Aaron at his own game. Skirt around the law a little. They should do something to make Aaron sit up. To wipe the smug look off his face. An eye for an eye.

Maggie told him then about Joost – about her suspicion that Aaron had withheld evidence. She'd tell Sive about it, she said. Do a little bit of digging, for credibility, tell her tomorrow, and potentially destroy Aaron's marriage.

Good, but not enough, Dave said. Another idea was forming. What if he turned up at the Rooftop Bar in the morning, a little before Sive and Maggie, and led Bea away somewhere? Just for a while, just enough to make Aaron panic. Maggie wasn't sure. Sive would suffer as much as Aaron. And Sive hadn't done anything. But Dave was adamant. Sive would have to be collateral damage and, anyway, it would be fine in the end. It wasn't like he was going to throw Bea over the side of the building. Aaron deserved this. He'd been treating them all as fools for years, taking what he wanted, doing as he pleased. A narcissist who thought the rules didn't apply to him. They'd take her, and then they'd give her back.

Still Maggie hesitated. Think of Yasmin, Dave said. Think of beautiful, kind, funny Yasmin. Dead at twenty-six. Her whole life ahead of her, but instead she burned to death in a fire. A fire set to warn off Aaron.

Still she wavered.

And the worst thing? Dave said. The worst thing is, he kept going. Even after Yasmin died, even though he knew it was down to him, he carried on making money from blackmail. Putting Sive and his children and everyone around him at risk.

That was when Maggie nodded. All she had to do was keep Sive chatting. Dave would do the rest. He'd walk Bea away for a bit, let Aaron panic, then bring her back without being seen. It wasn't the worst idea.

It wasn't the worst idea until Dave changed the plan.

75

The Stratford house

THE CREAK FROM THE stairs grew louder. Maggie turned her head. Dave, presumably. Why had he changed the plan? Why had he taken Faye, and why hadn't he given her back yet?

Faye stirred on the bed, and Maggie moved to check on her. Was she asleep? Or something else? She sat beside her and felt for a pulse, looking up as Dave came into the room. He stopped when he saw her, startled at first. Then he smiled.

'So you found me. Clever Maggie.'

'Dave, what the hell were you thinking? You were supposed to take Bea, and only for a short time. They're *frantic*.'

'Good. And this is far better anyway. Really give him something to worry about. I did phone you to tell you, but you never picked up.'

'I'd lost my bloody phone again. And then I found it and called you back, but you didn't answer. I was trying for ages this afternoon – you surely saw the missed calls?'

Dave stepped further into the room and walked to the other side of the bed.

'Yeah. I just wasn't sure at that point if it made sense for you to be here. To be involved with the next stage.'

Maggie frowned. *The next stage?*

Dave was still talking. 'How did you work out where I'd taken her?'

'The lie you told. It made no sense.'

'What lie?'

'When Nita asked if we could visit, you said you'd had to sell the house and that your mother's in a nursing home. Which is most peculiar, since your mother, God rest her soul, is very much dead.' Maggie waved her hand around the room, gesturing at the photos on the wall. 'I take it this is why you didn't want us visiting?'

'Might have been just a *little* hard to explain.'

Maggie cast her eye around the room again. A kaleidoscope of Yasmin. The tie that binds. Their linchpin. And now it had come to this. Now it had gone too far.

Dave interrupted her thoughts. 'So you were at the Tube station? With Aaron and Sive? Were they terrified?' He said it with such hopeful glee it turned her stomach.

'Yes, I was there, and yes, they were terrified. I waited with them, thinking you'd give her back any minute. Then, after my marathon attempt to phone you, I found out they'd had a call from the person who'd taken Faye, and I assumed it was you who had called. So I thought everything was fine.' Faye stirred, and Maggie stroked her hair. 'I sat waiting with a journalist friend of Sive's, thinking it was all sorted and you were giving her back. Bloody hell.'

Dave looked bewildered. 'What? I never made any call.'

'I know that now. Jude – the journalist – said it was a woman, and I nearly got sick there and then, realizing it wasn't you. That it was some kind of hoax and Faye wasn't on her way back at all.'

Dave whistled. 'Holy shit.' A grin then. 'They're having a right day of it, aren't they?'

'You can take it from me, Aaron is utterly broken. Not that he doesn't deserve it, but what happened? Why did you change the plan and take Faye instead of Bea?'

Dave sat down on the other side of the bed, settling against the headboard, for all the world as though he was about to tell a bedtime story, not relate an account of a kidnap.

'I was trying to get to the Rooftop Bar before you, like we planned, but of course you'd given Sive the directions, with a ridiculous amount of extra time.' He shook his head in what looked like admonishment.

For goodness' sake, he surely wasn't going to make this her fault? Maggie said nothing and nodded for him to continue.

'When I got on the Tube in Bond Street, I looked up, and suddenly there they were. Like an apparition. The two kids, and Sive a little bit behind. At first I was fuming – the whole plan was ruined. Then the Tube doors closed and it hit me.' He smiled. 'It was like Yasmin dropped them into my hands.'

'Oh, Dave.'

'It was so easy. I just said, "Hi, Faye," and took her by the hand. She didn't think twice. Daddy's friend Dave, nice but dim, nothing to fear here, eh?' A sly smile. 'I told her I was bringing her to the restaurant and her mummy was just a bit behind. We got off at Holborn and took a bus back to Clarinda Gardens. And then we drove here.'

'Well, you've achieved your aim. Aaron is bloody terrified. Sive too, which I feel awful about.'

'Not quite awful enough to tell her the truth, though? Worried about how it might look for you, I imagine.'

Maggie didn't answer.

'Listen, stop worrying about Sive. Aaron didn't care about collateral damage when he did what he did,' Dave said, sitting up straighter, folding his arms.

She couldn't argue with that. But poor Sive. The sooner they could get Faye back to her, the better. How to do it with her photo everywhere was going to be problematic.

'How did nobody notice you?' Maggie asked, brushing Faye's hair off her forehead.

'That was easy. I put my baseball cap on her head, to hide her hair. I switched her backpack with another kid's, and put her jacket and the other child's bag in a bin outside Holborn Tube station. Nobody paid any attention to us at all. Just a dad and his daughter getting on a bus.'

Maggie found she wasn't surprised. Dave, with his slightly hangdog look and his deep brown eyes and soft features, wasn't who you'd conjure up if asked to imagine a kidnapper.

'So what's the plan for getting her back to them? It won't be so easy now her photo's everywhere. And—' Maggie stiffened. 'Dave, wait, she'll tell people. The whole point was that Bea was too small to say what happened. Who took her. But Faye will tell.'

'Yeah,' was all Dave said, and he didn't look worried at all.

When Faye woke, they moved downstairs and sat around the table. Together in the kitchen of the Stratford house, where Maggie had once chopped peppers and fried chicken and opened wine. Laughing and joking with Yasmin, planning their futures. All gone, because of Aaron. He didn't deserve peace of mind. But keeping Faye any longer was going to do damage to Faye. And Sive. And Maggie still didn't know how they were going to get around Faye telling it was Dave. She'd seen Maggie now too, of course, and a sick feeling had taken hold in the pit of Maggie's stomach. She should never have agreed to any of it.

'Would you like something to eat while we wait for your mummy?' Maggie asked Faye now. 'An apple or a banana?'

'I'm not really hungry for apples . . .' Faye said. 'I'm kind of hungry for more treats, though?'

Maggie smiled. 'I know that feeling.' She looked across at Dave. 'I could pop out to pick up some biscuits? Or do you have anything here?'

'We'll have some drinks,' Dave said, and there was something disconcerting about the way he announced it. He poured himself a triple Jameson into one of his mother's good green tumblers and held up the bottle to offer the same to Maggie.

'God, no, thanks. Do you have any bottled water or juice?'

Dave nodded and opened the fridge to take out a bottle of water. He poured some into a glass for Maggie, and asked Faye if she'd like some.

'Can I have juice?' she asked.

'I have special juice that starts out like water but then magically changes into something else,' Dave said and, with a flourish, he filled a tumbler half full of water and placed it in front of Faye. 'Now,' he declared, 'here comes the special magic potion.'

Maggie froze.

Dave reached up to a cupboard above the oven and took out a bottle Maggie recognized. Liquid temazepam.

'Dave,' she whispered. 'What are you doing?'

'Making sure Aaron knows how it feels.' He pulled out his phone and clicked through to something.

'But you've had your revenge. Aaron is going through every parent's worst nightmare. He'll never recover from this. *And* I've told Sive what he did to Joost.'

Dave handed his phone to Faye, open on a YouTube video. She took it in both hands, and watched, transfixed, as two puppies did tricks for treats.

'Of course he'll recover.' Dave switched to a whisper. 'Yasmin literally died and he was right back on his feet. Same as ever. And it'll be the same again. He'll be back to being Aaron Sullivan, super-barrister. Using people and tossing them aside to get whatever he wants. Lying.' He was hissing now. 'He's a liar and a betrayer and he's not a friend. And he doesn't deserve to go back to normal.' He poured a measure of the drug into Faye's water. 'And now he's going to see what it's like to lose someone. Like I lost Yasmin.'

'It's too much, Dave. She's a child. She's innocent.'

'*Yasmin* was innocent. Aaron didn't care.'

'Yes, but he never meant for her to die. He didn't actually kill her . . .'

'His actions caused her death. And you know something? If he'd owned that and changed his ways, shown some remorse, I wouldn't be doing any of this. But he just kept going.' He paused and looked her in the eye. 'Maggie, you're either with me or against me.'

'Oh God . . . OK. Grab me that bottle of whiskey and a fresh glass.'

76

Monday
The Stratford house

DAVE SMILED AT MAGGIE. 'I knew I could count on you.'

He pushed back his chair and reached for the bottle of Jameson, then for a tumbler from the cupboard.

As quickly as she could, Maggie tipped the contents of Faye's glass into Dave's whiskey, putting her finger to her lips when Faye looked up from Dave's phone and appeared to be about to say something.

Dave turned back with the glass and the whiskey.

Shit, now he'd see that Faye's glass was suddenly empty. Would he think she drank it all? Would he ask her?

'Do you have ice, Dave?'

'Seriously? Fine, I'll check.' He turned and ducked down to the large fridge freezer, pulling out drawers one at a time. He turned back, holding up a lump of ice cubes meshed into one awkward block. 'They're all fused together. Not much use.'

Maggie pointed at the knife block. 'Grab one of those and whack it into the ice. It'll break it down enough to use. I just hate whiskey without ice.'

Dave shrugged and turned to lay the ice on the counter.

'On a clean tea towel, please!' Maggie called. 'I have some standards!'

Dave pulled a tea towel from a drawer and put it underneath the ice, then smashed the blade of the knife into it, over and over.

Maggie, putting her finger to her lips again, tipped half of her water into Faye's glass. Then she picked up the temazepam and tipped a good glug of it into Dave's whiskey.

Faye looked confused. Dave turned around.

'That's a very special drink,' Maggie said to Faye, silently begging her not to say anything. 'It has magic in it to make a wish come true. Do you have a wish?'

Faye scrunched her eyes tightly. 'I wish for a tree that grows sweets and chocolate bars and to keep it in my room where my mummy can't see how many I have.'

'That's a great wish!' Dave said. He put the smashed-up pieces of ice into a bowl and carried them to the table. 'That OK, your ladyship?'

Maggie nodded and popped two pieces of ice in her glass of whiskey.

Dave smiled at Faye. 'Now, drink the magic potion to make the wish come true.'

Maggie watched Faye drain the glass. Even knowing it was harmless water now, she felt sick. Would Dave notice anything about his drink? She watched and waited as he took a deep swallow, then another, then another. He nodded at her expectantly, and at first she didn't know what he meant.

'Your whiskey,' he said, and she took a sip.

He looked at the clock on the wall, but it had stopped at some quarter-past-two time in the past. He nodded towards Maggie's wrist. 'What time is it?'

'Just after half seven.'

'That's the watch with GPS on it, yeah? Just thinking, maybe we don't want police using it to find you. Give it here, and I'll get rid of it.'

Maggie undid the buckle and passed it over. 'You don't need to get rid of a perfectly good watch. If it's out of range of my phone, the GPS won't work.'

Dave strapped it on to his wrist and held it up to inspect it. 'I quite like this – maybe Nita can get me one . . . Anyway, I texted Aaron to say I'd meet him to help with the search. I want to make the most of seeing his face as he suffers through this.' He nodded at Faye. 'And at what's ahead.'

'I'll stay here,' Maggie said. 'I'll be with her when she passes.' Her voice cracked, and her eyes filled as she said it, even knowing it wasn't true. 'But have another drink with me first.'

When Dave left, Maggie sat for a moment at the table, thinking.

Faye would tell, of course, that Maggie had been there. She'd been there about two hours by then. Even if Faye couldn't tell the precise timing, there was no way this was going to sound like a quick discovery and rescue. And if Dave survived – she didn't think she'd put enough of the drug into his drink to do anything significant – he'd tell that she had been part of it.

It would be his word against hers, of course, and she could say she had pretended to go along with it, which was exactly what she'd done. Just many, many hours later than when it had all started. There was one way she could make her word against Dave's win out, she thought, eying up the bottle of temazepam. As long as she got the doses just right. She reached for the bottle and got up to find a shot glass.

*

She waited until Faye slipped into a drug-induced sleep before taking her own drink and lying down beside her, holding her hand. Even if nobody found them, they'd be OK. They'd wake up in a few hours and phone the police. Blood tests would show the drug in their systems and Maggie would tell her story – how Dave had offered her the chance to take Faye's place, but then drugged Faye anyway. Faye might remember that Maggie was there for a while before she fell asleep, but Maggie could explain that – she'd been playing for time, hoping to find a way to save Faye. With a dry cloth, she picked up the kitchen knife Dave had used to break the ice. She laid it on the night-stand. Now they'd know why she hadn't just run with Faye. How Dave had managed to keep her there for so long. She swallowed her drink and closed her eyes. Faye would be safe. Faye didn't deserve any of this. Aaron, however, would yet again escape justice.

77

Six months later
Dublin

SIVE TRIES AARON'S NUMBER a third time. Still no answer.

'Mummy, can we go to the park?' Faye asks.

'Yes. Later. I need to ring Daddy now.' *Fuck*. What's going on? She tries Scott now, and he picks up. *Thank God*.

'Scott, it's Sive Quinn. Sorry to call out of the blue like this, but are you with Aaron?'

'Oh, hey, Sive. Good to hear from you. Sorry to hear about the, eh . . . split. I hope you two can work it out . . .'

'Thanks, but right now I need to speak with him urgently. I know he was meeting up with you guys to go over things. Is he there?'

'No. I'm at a job interview this afternoon so not meeting them till tonight. And Nita's at work. So it's just Aaron and Maggie.'

'Where are they?'

'They were due to go to the Rooftop Bar for a liquid lunch, I believe. They're probably on the way home now.'

'I'll try him again.' She hangs up and dials Aaron's number immediately, but he still doesn't answer. Then a text comes through.

Sorry, saw missed call. Coverage patchy. I answered but you didn't hear me. All OK? Just in Tube station. With Maggie, on way back from Rooftop Bar.

78

Two hours earlier
The Rooftop Bar

MAGGIE STIFFENS WHEN AARON pulls her into a hug. He must sense it. He leans back, still holding her arms.

'You OK?'

She nods. Of course she's not OK. But there's only so much she can say. She needs to be careful. They sit, taking a booth at the back, and Aaron opens the wine list. She doesn't want wine. She doesn't trust herself to keep her words inside if she has wine. But Aaron orders a bottle of Rioja and two glasses and she doesn't object.

'So,' he says.

'So.'

'It's good to see you, Maggie. I know the last few months have been hell for all of us, but I figured it would be good to reconnect before . . . well, just because I value your friendship.'

Before you get charged, she thinks. *Before anyone starts investigating what happened to Yasmin. Before the skeletons come out of the closet.*

She doesn't say any of it, though. She just nods and waits to see where this will go.

'Who knew Dave was such a psychopath,' he goes on. 'What he did to Faye . . . it's just . . .' He takes a sip of wine, buying

364

himself a moment, she thinks. He clears his throat. 'Anyway, I haven't told the authorities yet, but the night he died, as well as admitting he was Yasmin's stalker, he told me he set the fire.'

Maggie stares at him. *Oh, you absolute fucker.*

'Pretty obvious now, looking back, isn't it?' he continues. 'I know the police might need more than my word on it, in lieu of any evidence, but you were there. You saw what Dave was like – obsessed with Yasmin back then, the photos on the wall in the room where he kept Faye . . .'

'What are you asking me, Aaron?'

'Did Dave ever say anything to you? Maybe he admitted it before he made you drink the temazepam? Told you he set the fire?' His tone is wheedling. Cajoling. She wants to reach across the table and slap him.

'No. He didn't say anything like that.'

'Are you sure? We know he was her stalker. It's not a huge leap to assume he set the fire. And, obviously, as I said,' he adds hurriedly, 'he confessed it to me the night he died.' He sits back and folds his arms. 'Fairly cut and dried.'

Maggie bites down hard on the inside of her cheek to stop herself from speaking out. There's nothing to gain from going up against Aaron. And nobody ever wins, except Aaron. Drink the wine and go home.

But, of course, Aaron can't stop there.

'Imagine, if Dave hadn't set that fire, Yasmin could be alive today. She might be sitting here with us, sharing this bottle of wine. Talking about her kids. Or her job. Or how Nita's driving her mad.' He points at Maggie's tattoo. 'Talking about getting another one.'

Stop, Aaron, she warns him, from inside her head.

'If Dave hadn't set that fire, you'd still have your best friend, alive and well. Dave may be dead, but he shouldn't get away with it. People should know. I think if you could mention to the police that he confessed to setting the fire, it would bring justice for Yasmin.'

Justice for Yasmin. Anger bubbles up and bursts through the dam of common sense.

'Dave didn't confess *anything*, Aaron.' It comes out in a rush. 'I know. I know what caused the fire. I know about Pemberton and Rosco and the blackmail. And you.'

His eyes widen and she feels a tiny frisson of satisfaction at his shock.

'If the police come to me with questions about what Dave said that day,' she continues, 'it will be a very different story from the one you're asking me to tell. You're the reason Yasmin's dead.'

Aaron's eyes narrow. Without warning, he reaches out and grabs her wrist. Maggie freezes.

'I see you got your watch back. It must feel odd knowing it was taken off Dave's dead body.'

'I . . . yes, the police returned it to me a few weeks ago.'

'Why did Dave have it?'

'I loaned it to him.'

'That day? The day Faye disappeared?'

'No, obviously not. It was before.'

'Sive told me about you two. About him calling round.'

Maggie feels her cheeks heat up. 'Yes, well. I didn't know what kind of person he really was, clearly.'

'Only the thing is, I saw the watch on your wrist when you arrived in Oxford Circus on the day Faye disappeared. When you were talking about your missing phone. So you couldn't have loaned it to him before that day.'

Shit. 'He took it off my wrist after he drugged me.'

'Now, now, you can't do that. You can't tell me one thing then change your story when it doesn't fit.'

'It's true. He took it when I was unconscious.'

'So why did you say you loaned it to him before the day Faye disappeared?'

'I got confused.'

'Hmm. As a wise and very annoying woman once said, "Why lie?"'

'I . . . I didn't—'

'You see, I thought about it afterwards. The watch. About why Dave might have it, about why he might have seen you that afternoon. And I wondered. And then Sive told me about you two still seeing each other from time to time. And I wondered some more. And then I asked Faye a few questions about Auntie Maggie and Uncle Dave and that day in the house in Stratford. And look, she's six. She's only six. And her recollection of what happened is fairly blurry. But she told me a bit about drinks and YouTube and sitting around the kitchen table. And then I put two and two together.'

Maggie waits, frozen.

'So, I really think that you might want to reconsider Dave's confession about the fire. Or I might have to point the police towards you. And another chat with Faye. And what exactly went on that day.'

'I . . .' But Maggie can't find the right words. Admit what happened? Explain it was only ever meant to be a scare? Deny it and hope he's bluffing? She looks Aaron in the eye. He's not bluffing.

'I know you saved Faye. I'm grateful, believe me. And I don't think you intended to hurt her. But it won't look good to the police if they find out. This way – you telling the police that Dave set the fire – everyone wins.'

Everyone wins? Aaron wins. Just like he always does.

As if reading her thoughts, Aaron raises his glass. 'You know I'm right. And you know I'll come out smelling of roses, because I always do.'

79

After
Dublin

Aaron never made it back to his hotel after the Rooftop Bar that day. Maggie couldn't say what had happened, how he'd fallen. He didn't seem the careless type, the kind of person who'd stand too close to the edge of the platform. But he'd had a lot of wine – almost a full bottle – and a few whiskeys too. The platform was very crowded. And Aaron wasn't from London, hadn't lived there in a long time. Perhaps he'd forgotten how dangerous it is to step so close to the edge.

Could it be, people whispered, that it all got too much – the impending charges, the rumours, the blacklisting, the distancing. Knowing he was facing jail? No smoke without fire, after all, as they say.

Joost has been getting to know Faye and Faye's siblings, and although he's certain he and Sive will never get back together, they seem to be making it work as a kind of family. Joost has been introduced to Sive's friend Jude. She's a journalist and she wants to ghostwrite his story. They have a meeting with a publisher next week.

*

Garvin also has a meeting with a publisher. The advance, if the meeting goes well and contracts are signed, will help pay for his mother's nursing home. The publisher's not sure how much of what Garvin says they can print, but he's pushing hard, eager for the truth to come out. And anyway, he says, dead men can't sue.

Jerry, Dave's brother, is coming to terms with mixed emotions – he's grieving for Dave but horrified too that he kidnapped Faye. The police questioned him about why he did the race under Dave's name that morning, and it is this as much as anything – Dave using him for an alibi – that bothers Jerry. Making him complicit, albeit unwittingly, to his crime. How could Dave kidnap a child? Taking matters into your own hands is the kind of thing their mother always advocated, and Dave, Jerry acknowledges, probably spent too much time with their mother. He'd been happy to keep a little bit of distance when their father died, when Dave was playing landlord, when he and Carol agreed their house swap. Now, to Jerry's surprise, he owns both homes.

Scott's father knew someone who knew someone who got around his criminal conviction problem, and now he flies helicopters for wealthy customers who pay handsomely to avoid traffic on short-hop trips. He makes enough to spend a month at a time in Florida with his kids, and he might be wrong, but his wife seems to be getting just a little tired of the music producer. In the game of life, Scott has beaten Aaron after all.

Nita still feels guilty. Not about the pregnancy announcement – anyone could make that mistake, and her followers understood, especially when they saw her teary Insta Live explanation. And anyway, it was almost true, now that she's actually pregnant with twins. No, she feels guilty about the night in the hotel, when they were minding Bea and Toby. The lamp she threw at the hotel door, the shaky footage and her panicked screams. Scott was never supposed to tell Sive. The last thing Nita intended was to worry Sive. That little bit of staging and the shaky footage was only ever meant for her 50,000 Instagram followers.

Sive has a new best friend. Jude is there for her when Aaron dies, there for her when reporters flock, there for her when it all goes quiet and is somehow even harder to bear. She'll stay in Dublin for a few more weeks, she says, until Sive is back on her feet. Jude is no-nonsense and matter-of-fact. She props Sive up and refuses to let her fall apart. She drops everything to collect the kids when Sive just can't, and is surprised to discover that school-gate politics is nothing like she's been led to believe, and that, actually, the parents are very nice. Jude does all of this for Sive, but slowly realizes she quite likes having a best friend. And that, actually, she can do her job just as easily from Dublin. Jude wonders if she's going soft. Sive wonders what she'd do without her. Luckily, Jude is a true best friend, and Sive never has to find out.

Sive's career is flourishing. With the life insurance payout, she can afford childcare and has more time to write. She's sticking to parenting and lifestyle features, though; she's had enough of crime and courts to last a lifetime.

Sive reported Faye's story to the police, but when they interviewed Faye things became muddy again. Faye remembered Maggie pouring the funny drink into Dave's glass and putting water into hers. Maggie's original statement corroborated this:

she'd tried to save Faye by sneaking the doctored drink into Dave's whiskey. Sive pushed it to the back of her mind. Faye was fine, and that was all that mattered.

Sive never asked Maggie how Aaron fell or how drunk he was or what they'd talked about that afternoon in the Rooftop Bar. She never asked what his final words were before he toppled on to the tracks. She didn't want to know. She needed to remove herself now from all that had happened in London fifteen years earlier and all that her husband had done since. Maggie and Scott and Nita still send Christmas cards and the occasional text, but Sive never replies. It's time to move on from her husband's former housemates.

Every now and then a little thought surfaces. The kind of thought that belongs in the what-if world of worst-case scenarios. Did Maggie do something? Did she push Aaron? But no. Maggie was a nice woman. Practically best-friend material at one point. Plus, Sive knows that that kind of thing – nice women committing murder – only ever happens in books. And, after all, no one saw a thing.

Acknowledgements

No One Saw a Thing is based on something that happened when I was twelve and on holiday in London: my six-year-old sister and I got on a Tube, then the doors closed before my parents and my other sisters could get on too. They were left standing on the platform, watching in horror as the train took off. It all ended happily when some other passengers realized what my dad had been shouting through the closed doors and told us to get off at Tower Bridge. Of course, in the fictional version, it takes the parents a little longer to figure out what's happened to their daughter. So, first and foremost, thank you to my dad for reminding me two years ago of the story, and for bringing us on such exciting and dangerous book-inspiring holidays!

Thank you to my fantastic editor, Finn Cotton, who is unfailingly wise and kind and easy to work with, and very good at spotting all the things I don't see.

Thank you to all at Transworld, Penguin Random House, and Penguin Ireland who worked on *No One Saw a Thing* – Becky Short, Louis Patel, Emma Fairey, Beci Kelly, Rich Shailer, Tom Chicken, Laura Garrod, Laura Ricchetti (and for the laugh with the misread tweet!), Emily Harvey, Natasha Photiou, Ruth Richardson, Hana Sparks, Hayley Barnes, Laura Dermody, Sophie Dwyer, Nadine Cosgrave, Sorcha Judge, Sarah Day,

Vivien Thompson and, of course, Frankie Gray, Larry Finlay and Bill Scott-Kerr – it was so good to finally meet you in real life (and then more than once) in 2022.

Thank you to my incredible agent, Diana Beaumont: you changed my life, and you are still the BEST.

Thank you, Sinéad Fox, for reading an early copy to check for my legal inaccuracies and for never saying, 'Why do you keep making your characters work in law when you know nothing about it?' Thank you for suggesting alternative solutions for all my mistakes. Sinéad (@bumblesofrice on Instagram) is a solicitor and a blogger, and Nita could learn a thing or two from her.

Thank you, Sarah Harper (@Sarah_Harper_Writing), for all your help with my police questions – I couldn't have done it without you. Wishing you the very best on your own writing journey. It was such a pleasure to chat on email.

Thanks, too, to John Morgan of the British Transport Police, who answered my endless questions. At the beginning of all this, I didn't even know there's a separate police force for transport but, luckily, John, who's a cousin of an old school pal, happens to be with the BTP and set me straight on that and many other details. Thanks, too, to Rhian J, Sean B and James S for additional police help, and to Elaine, Jennie, Kate, Niamh and Sinéad for connecting me to them.

Thank you, Rosemarie Hayden, for help with (yet more) legal questions, and Chrissie Russell on the journalism side – it was lovely to meet in real life this year!

Huge thanks to Claudia Borgatti for all the London Underground help – I've been on Tubes dozens and dozens of times in my life, but it was only when I found myself setting a book in the Underground that I realized how little I knew. So, thank you for filling in the blanks.

My sisters are always my first readers and, as avid crime fans, they're the perfect focus group for testing twists and reveals. With *No One Saw a Thing*, they were tasked with some extra work, too – thank you, Nicola, for the rowing info, Elaine for the London info, and Dee for the medical info. I owe you each a glass of pink champagne.

Thanks to my lovely school-gate author pals, Amanda Cassidy and Linda O'Sullivan, for the WhatsApp chats and the coffees and the nights out and the brainstorming and the common sense!

Thank you to the Irish writing community – it's been lovely to meet up again in real life over the last year. I'm resisting the urge to name names because the list is very long and I'll forget people, but there was a LOT of craic with lots of brilliant writer pals at Harrogate, Murder One, Rolling Sun, Spike Island and a slew of book launches. Almost everything I know about the crime-writing world comes from conversations after events like these, mostly over wine, and mostly from Catherine Ryan Howard, Sam Blake, Liz Nugent and Sinéad Crowley. But I'm still resisting naming names.

Thank you to the absolutely gorgeous community of readers and bookstagrammers on Instagram; thank you for your incredible support and your beautiful book photos. Big thanks to my pal Sinéad Cuddihy, tireless leader of the Tired Mammy Book Club (no pun intended). I had the pleasure of meeting lots of lovely Booksta people last year and I'm looking forward to more excuses to meet up this year. And, of course, thanks to BooK-PunK, too, for all your support!

Thank you, as always, to OfficeMum readers on Facebook for your company and for the laughs. It's been ten years!

Thanks to my Sion Hill besties for your unending support and friendship. This book is dedicated to wonderful, brave Alice Hayes, who has brought us together more than ever over the last year.

ACKNOWLEDGEMENTS

Thank you, Dad and Eithne, for all the cheerleading and for continuing to keep local booksellers in business!

So much love to Elissa, Nia and Matthew – thank you for being you, and for keeping me in the real world. One of these days I'll get a whole eight hours to write and I probably won't like it at all. Thank you, Damien, for EVERYTHING, and especially for coffee and pastries and for putting my jacket on the radiator on cold winter mornings. Thanks, Lola-the-dog, for keeping me company in my office.

And thank you, dear reader, for reading this book.

If you loved **NO ONE SAW A THING**, look out for
Andrea Mara's unputdownable new thriller . . .

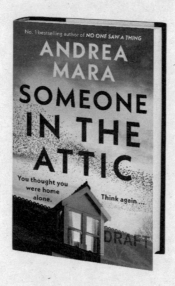

Coming soon and available to pre-order now.

Keep reading for an exclusive early extract . . .

1

THREE MINUTES BEFORE IT HAPPENS, Anya takes a deep swallow of white wine, sets the glass on the shelf, and slides further down in the bath. The water is at her chin, tepid now and cooling fast. Too fast. She should have closed the bathroom door. Chris is always moaning about steam and mildew and he *always* leaves the door open. Now, she does so too, on autopilot. And to stop him nagging. But Chris isn't here tonight. He's thousands of miles away in LA and Anya is blissfully alone. He won't know if she closes the bathroom door. She's just not sure she has the energy to get out and do it. Three large glasses of wine and a long day at the office will do that.

That's the other nice thing about Chris being away. Nobody judging her for opening a bottle of wine on a Wednesday night. Or finishing a bottle of wine on a Wednesday night. The bottle sits on the tiled surface at the end of the bath, coated in condensation. Just half a glass left, she notices now. She's had more than she thought.

Beside the wine, her mobile phone buzzes to life, startling her. She leans forward to see who it is but doesn't pick up. Chris. It's nine in Dublin, so lunchtime in LA. He'll be slipping away from his colleagues, saying he'll follow them to the restaurant. Calling to say how much he misses her. That he's got a big surprise when he comes home. It's a ring. She knows this because she saw his browsing history. She shakes her head, wet strands grazing her shoulders. The buzzing stops and she picks up the phone to text.

Sorry, can't talk. Up to my eyes, working late. Going to be same right the way through week so no point trying to get me on phone, but see you Friday when you're back x

Chris is going to have to go.

He is very good-looking and very nice. He's also bland and boring and far too particular about the mind-numbing minutiae of everyday life. Like bathroom condensation.

And sooner or later, he'll figure out who she's really seeing when she says she's working late or going for a run. His sister, not as innocent as Chris, is definitely starting to smell a rat. Though she couldn't know who it is, Anya reckons. She smiles when she thinks about him; Chris's opposite in every way. Yeah, Chris is going to have to go. Although, technically, since it's his house, *she* is going to have to go.

A faint rustle from above draws her attention to the ceiling. The mice are still there. *Dammit.* So much for Chris and his humane but 'never-fail' traps. They should have got a cat. Chris said they couldn't because of the dog. *Get rid of the dog then*, she wanted to say. Dogs are no use with mice. Downstairs, as though reading her thoughts, Ziggy barks. He's been barking all evening, and Anya has a sneaking suspicion the dog-walker didn't come today while she was at work. Anyway, that's Chris's problem. If he wants to pay someone fifteen euro an hour to walk his dog – or not walk his dog – so be it.

Two minutes before it happens, Anya slides up and takes another sip of her drink, then one more before slipping back under the water. Her eyelids droop and she decides against finishing the wine. She has an early start tomorrow, then drinks with Eleanor on Friday night. God, why had she agreed to that? Eleanor will talk non-stop about her kids and her nanny, just as she always does. There is literally no reason to stay in touch, but Eleanor is like a tenacious puppy. Sweet but irritating. It's like she sees Anya as a project. Or perhaps it's the duty of time. Thirty years of friendship isn't easy to shake. Anya knows. She's tried. Good God, she has tried.

And now Julia is back in Ireland too. Saint Julia. Although – Anya smiles to herself – she's also Divorcée Julia. Eleanor is so excited to have the three of them reunited. As though they're some kind of friend group. As though it hasn't been five years since Anya last saw Julia in person. As though they didn't have the mother of all arguments when they last spoke by phone, two years ago. As though Anya has forgiven Julia for almost destroying her business. Why did she say yes to this? Because Eleanor is like glue, really annoying glue, and doesn't take no for an answer.

Julia will be insufferable, of course. And she'll somehow drop it into conversation that she sold her business for a seven-figure sum. Anya will nod and murmur congratulations and she will not admit she already read this in the *Sunday Independent*. Julia's never been the same since the night—

Anya stops the thought before it takes off. She doesn't like to think about the night Donna died. It's not guilt, because why would it be guilt when it wasn't her fault? But Julia – though she's never said as much – thinks it's Anya's fault.

One minute before it happens, Anya takes a final sip of wine, and slips further down in the bath. A moth flits around the light. Steam melts from the mirror as the room temperature cools. Her towel, thick and pristine, hangs waiting from the hook at the end of the bath. Through the open door, the landing is in darkness, as night draws in. The only sound is the whirr of the inadequate fan. And the rustle of mice in the attic.

Louder, she thinks, half asleep, than the kind of noise you'd expect from tiny mice.

Now a creak, one she barely registers.

Another creak.

And a scratch. But her ears are below the water and the sound is muffled.

Another creak. One she hears in her mind retrospectively, when the attic hatch begins to move.

The attic hatch is opening. Swinging loose now, like a slow pendulum.

Opening all by itself.

Not all by itself.

There is someone in the attic. Chris is thousands of miles away in LA and there is nobody else in the house.

Except there is.

There is someone in the attic.

Her breath is stuck inside her throat and her body is immobile under water as a dark shape emerges through the opening and drops to the landing floor. A figure all in black. A man in a mask. There is a man in the attic. And he's—

Thirty seconds later, Anya is dead.

2

THE VIDEO IS SHORT and noisy and easy to ignore, because really, it's just another video – like all the other short and noisy videos on her daughter's phone. Which is why, at first, Julia pays no attention at all. Julia is busy. Julia, if she's honest, is also quite stressed. And while she's very used to admitting the former, she never admits the latter. People don't hire people like Julia to do the job she does if she's likely to get stressed over something as ordinary as ordering pizza and moving continent. But right now she's at home with her kids, where no one can see her, and she lets out a tiny sigh as Isla asks her once again to look at the video. This Friday night, the video is the least of her worries.

Her worries, in order of priority, are as follows:
1. Settle the kids in their new schools
2. Settle the kids in their new home
3. Encourage the kids to accept the new babysitter
4. Figure out why the garbage disposal isn't working
5. Let the pizza guy in through the outer gate
6. Find cash to tip the pizza guy
7. Make the incessant buzzing stop (see 5 and 6 above)
8. Stay calm when Isla shouts and Luca cries, and hope the eggshells she's treading on eventually become more solid.

'Isla, have you seen my purse?'

'No, but, Mom, you seriously need to look at this video.' Isla is sitting at the island, holding up her phone.

'What I *need* is to let the pizza guy in, but first I have to find cash for a tip.'

'How will you tip him?' Luca asks, without lifting his eyes from his Nintendo Switch. 'They don't even have dollar bills here.' Contempt drips from every word. *What kind of dumbass country doesn't have dollar bills?*

He has a point though. Do people tip with coins? It's twenty years since Julia last ordered takeout in Ireland, and back then she was a broke junior admin. Does she *have* any coins? In the four weeks since they moved here, she's been paying by tapping with her phone in what feels like an almost cashless society. A long way from her days fumbling for change to take the 46A to college.

'Can't you use the money you left for the babysitter?' Luca nods towards a drawer in the island. 'It's in there.'

'That's for Pauline, in case she needs cash when I'm at work. And she's not a babysitter, she's a housekeeper.' This is for Isla's benefit. Isla, who at thirteen is disgusted that Julia would hire someone to keep an eye on them while she's at work. Isla is, of course, disgusted at everything right now – the move from San Diego, the new house, her new life here, the life she left behind, life in general, her dad, and mostly, Julia. Evil witch Julia who ruined her life. *If only she knew the truth.*

'Isn't she babysitting tonight when you go to your friend's house?' Luca asks.

Touché.

'That's just for this evening because your dad has plans too. Ordinarily, she's the housekeeper.'

Luca shrugs and goes back to his game.

'Whose house are you going to?' Isla asks.

'Eleanor's. My old school pal.'

'Oh. I didn't know you were still friends with her. Is she the one you had that big fight with?'

'Nope, that was Anya, she's joining us too.' *Unfortunately.* 'Eleanor and I are good.' Are they though, Julia wonders? They've seen one another a handful of times in the last ten years and they seem to have less and less in common. The sooner she can get tonight over with, the better. She takes a five-euro note from the drawer and picks up the receiver to buzz the pizza guy through the main gate to the complex.

'OK, Mom, as soon as you get the pizza, you *have* to look at this video.' Isla holds up her phone again. 'It's so weird. I can't figure out how they did it, but it looks like it was filmed inside our house.'

'What is it – the letting agent's website?'

'No, I told you already!' Impatient. Snappy. 'It's TikTok.'

Julia bites her lip. *Hello, eggshells.* 'Right, I'll look in a sec.'

'Just because it's TikTok doesn't mean you shouldn't take it seriously. It's a video filmed *inside* our house with all our stuff. It's creepy.'

'OK, let me grab the pizza, then I'm all yours.'

Julia sighs again, louder now, as she walks through the long hallway towards the front door, her heels echoing on the white and gold marble floor. Low evening light filters through the glass panels either side of the door but she reaches for the Louis Poulsen standing lamp anyway, switching it on with a touch. Light fills the hall and she glances at her reflection in the mirror above the narrow table – the sunburst mirror she'd had shipped all the way from San Diego in a bid to make this mausoleum of a house feel like home. She smooths down her hair. Still in the suit she'd worn to work that day, she looks distinctly overdressed for takeout pizza. She doesn't even like takeout pizza. But going for drinks with Eleanor and Anya on an empty stomach is a bad idea. Especially Anya. Still Queen Bee, all these years later.

Eleanor means well, but why she invited Anya is beyond Julia. Eleanor says it would be weird to meet up when Anya's so close by, and not include her. *She's just down the road from you!* she'd said excitedly, when she heard where Julia would be living. Oh great, Julia thought. Anya Hase on my doorstep again. ('It's German actually, pronounced Ha-za,' says Anya's nasal, grating voice in Julia's head, just as it has done since they first met in secondary school.)

Of course, maybe she's mellowed since they last spoke. Or maybe she's the same narcissist she always was. Julia knows where she'd lay her money.

Now, she stands in the doorway, looking at the orange and purple sky. The longer, brighter evenings are just one of the many things about which her kids complain – *why can't it be dark already like it is at home?* They'll get used to it, and eventually they'll love that August evenings are longer and brighter. But for now, everything is other and different and strange, and they still can't understand why she uprooted them, and she still can't tell them the truth. So she's bribing them (again) with pizza. Pizza that is, of course, at least according to her kids, inferior to pizza back home. There are a lot of things Julia misses about San Diego, but the pizza that tastes the same here as it does there is not one of them. She misses her yoga sessions with Milena, the instructor who became her friend. She misses the moms from the school; never true confidantes – and she couldn't tell them the truth about Isla – but good company all the same. She misses the smell of the ocean. Brentwood, she realizes as she sniffs the air now, smells of nothing, not even cut grass. She misses the San Diego weather. *God*, she misses the weather. She shakes herself. No time for wallowing.

The delivery guy is making his way past the townhouses, and on to the wider, greener part of Brentwood, the luxury gated community in which she and Isla and Luca live in a spacious, double-fronted house with a sweeping gravel driveway and somewhat pretentious white columns holding up the porch. Having grown up in a mid-century, slightly faded home with tricky electrics and creaky floors, adult Julia has always favoured new-build houses. But there's something about Brentwood, for all its high-end newness. Something soulless, empty. And at this time of the evening, something almost eerie.

The delivery driver pulls in outside their gate and hops out with the pizzas. Feeling guilty about how long the driveway is, Julia walks down to meet him.

'Number 26 Brentwood? Two margheritas?'

'That's me. Now if only they were drinks instead of pizzas,' Julia says, reaching to take the boxes and passing the man the tip.

'Cheers.' He pockets the money without responding to her quip. Her kids are right, she's not funny. 'Never been in here before,' he says, 'it's bigger than I thought. You wouldn't think we were in the middle of Foxrock.'

'Yes. Deceptively big once you get inside the gates. It used to be a convent but they razed the whole thing to the ground about ten years ago to build houses.'

'So, from one gated community to another, eh,' he says, as he turns to walk away.

And nodding quiet agreement, Julia goes back up the drive-way with her two margheritas-not-margaritas.

'OK, now can I please have your attention?' Isla says, on Julia's return. The kitchen is shadowy now, losing light more quickly than the rest of the house, despite the huge glass wall that looks out on the back garden. As Julia moves towards the island, something brushes against her ankle and she jumps, forgetting yet again about Basil, Luca's new pet rabbit. (More bribes.) Basil is cute and fluffy and exactly what you'd want from a rabbit, except for the whole unexpected-encounters-with-small-live-animal moments that Julia is still getting used to.

Isla holds up her phone. On screen, Julia can see what looks like a plain white ceiling and an attic hatch. As she watches, the hatch drops open, and suddenly, a black clad figure lowers himself through the opening, and drops the last few feet to the floor. The person's face is covered in a balaclava, with two barely visible slits for eyes and Julia finds herself instinctively stepping back as the masked face looms close. The figure reaches forward and seems to remove the camera, because the next thing she can see is the stairs carpet, as the man – or woman? – descends.

'See – that's *our* stairs!'

'Isla, it's a beige carpet. We viewed four houses here in Brentwood before choosing this one, all with the exact same carpet. Every other house in Ireland has beige carpet.'

'Wait, you'll see.'

What she can see on screen is no longer carpeted stairs. Now it's a white and gold marble floor. As she watches, the camera sweeps across the hallway, taking in a front door with glass panels, a Louis Poulsen lamp, and a narrow side table beneath a sunburst mirror. *Her* sunburst mirror, shipped all the way from San Diego.

'What is this, Isla?'

'That's what I'm trying to tell you, someone's made a video inside our house. It looks like it's part of this viral video thing for *The Loft*.'

'*The Loft*?'

An exasperated sigh at Julia's lack of cultural knowledge. 'The new TV series. They have this like, PR campaign? Where they put up a creepy video of a guy hiding in an attic in someone's house. He lets himself out when the people aren't there, and creeps around their home. At first people thought it was real and it went totally viral.'

'Right . . .' Julia is still staring at the phone, where the video is playing on a loop.

'And then they revealed that it was all staged to promote this TV show, *The Loft*. And they put up more videos, and other people started to copy, and somehow, we've ended up here too. I'm guessing you didn't let someone in to film?'

'No, of course not . . . how odd.'

They turn towards Luca, who's eating a slice of pizza, his face lit by his Nintendo Switch. He looks up.

'What?'

'Do you know anything about this video?'

'I'm not even allowed on TikTok, how would I know anything?'

A fair point, Julia acknowledges. Luca is also only nine and never in the house without an adult. Even at thirteen, Isla is rarely home alone. So how on earth did someone get into their house?

Luca puts on his headset, cutting his mother and sister out of his world. Julia wants to ask him to take it off while he's eating, but finds she doesn't have the energy. Instead, she watches the video again.

'Could we ask the people who look after the account? *The Loft* TV people?'

'This one isn't on their account. It's a repost.'

'Wait, so it has nothing to do with the TV show?'

Isla sighs, clearly struggling with Julia's inability to follow current social media trends.

'I just *said*, people started to make their own videos. Letting themselves out of hiding spaces; pretending there's a stranger living in their attics. The TV people had to put up a disclaimer saying that they weren't responsible for copycats, don't try this at home kind of thing. But people keep doing it.'

'So this is a copycat?'

'Yes.'

'Only we didn't film it.'

'Exactly.'

Julia tilts her head, looking at the ceiling. The kitchen is silent, her children wholly absorbed in their screens. With timing that would have been comical in other circumstances, there's a sudden creak from above, as though someone has stepped on a floorboard. As though there's someone up there. And of course there's nobody there, she knows that, it's just the noise the house makes when it's quiet, but in spite of herself, a cold chill settles across her skin.

**Want more from Andrea Mara,
the Queen of the unexpected twist?**

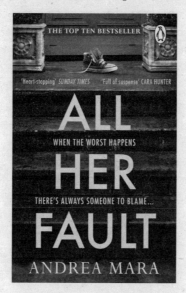

ONE MISSING BOY.
Marissa Irvine arrives at 14 Tudor Grove, expecting to pick
up her young son Milo from his first playdate with a boy at
his new school. But the woman who answers the door isn't a
mother she recognizes. She isn't the nanny. She doesn't have
Milo. And so begins every parent's worst nightmare.

FOUR GUILTY WOMEN.
As news of the disappearance filters through the quiet
Dublin suburb and an unexpected suspect is named,
whispers start to spread about the women most
closely connected to the shocking event. Because
only one of them may have taken Milo – but they
could all be blamed . . .

**IN A COMMUNITY FULL OF SECRETS,
WHO IS REALLY AT FAULT?**

OUT NOW

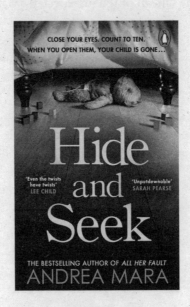

CLOSE YOUR EYES. COUNT TO TEN.
WHEN YOU OPEN THEM, YOUR CHILD IS GONE...

'Even the twists
have twists'
LEE CHILD

'Unputdownable'
SARAH PEARSE

Hide
and
Seek

THE BESTSELLING AUTHOR OF *ALL HER FAULT*
ANDREA MARA

CLOSE YOUR EYES.
The game of hide and seek is over, but little Lily Murphy
hasn't been found. Her parents try to stay positive,
but they know this peaceful Dublin suburb will
never be the same again.

COUNT TO TEN.
Years later, Joanna moves into a new house.
It seems perfect in every way, until she learns
that Lily Murphy used to live here.

AND WHEN YOU OPEN THEM, YOUR CHILD IS GONE.
Because Joanna thinks she knows what really happened
to Lily – and if the truth gets out, it might be her undoing . . .

OUT NOW